Friendship, Love and Apple Tea

Penny Canvin

CANVIN PUBLISHING PAPERBACK

ISBN-978-0-9930820-0-9

First published in 2014-09-22
Canvin Publishing
Milton Keynes, UK

Printed and Bound in Great Britain

Dedication

To my husband, daughter and parents for their love and support. And to Pam and Auntie Vi, who I wish could have read this book...

CHAPTER ONE

Come on, Libby. I've only got a few more minutes and then I'll have to log off.

It's the same every time we chat online. Libby disappears every couple of minutes to sort out a 'situation' and I sit there waiting for the beep to tell me she's finally sent a response and, to be honest, it's really stressful. Particularly when I'm clock-watching, knowing Grant will return home any minute and catch me chatting to Libby, something that is highly likely to set him off into one of his tantrums. And, on top of this, whilst I sit here waiting for her to chat, the apartment still needs tidying as I've spent all afternoon packing my case and stressing over my journey tomorrow.

LouG100136: Come on Libby, I'll have arrived at your apartment by the time you reply to this!!!!!

Another minute passes and I tap my feet together and plump up the cushions next to me, and then she's back. And about time too.

TurkishDelightLibby101: Stop with the exclamation marks!!!!!!!!!!!!!!!!!! LOL

LouG100136: And, stop with the text talk. LOL? We're in our 30's, just... Hey, can't believe it's been fourteen

1

months since I saw you.   Are you sure I'll have enough clothes?   I've packed really light but I'm with you for a month.

TurkishDelightLibby101:   Plenty!   I've told you, all you need are bikinis, a few shorts and vest tops.   It's 39 degrees here every day.

LouG100136: It's the same here in sunny Abingdon.   In Fahrenheit!   Bikinis?   Not sure about that.   I don't want to frighten the locals.

TurkishDelightLibby101: And you'll need a couple of 'knock 'em dead' dresses for our nights out, of which there'll be many.   As I keep telling you, we do have washing machines and irons in Turkey, so you don't need to bring much.   And, you and me are the same clothes size, you can borrow mine, like the old days.

LouG100136:   It's been a while since I've been on a night out like the old days.   I've forgotten how to party.

TurkishDelightLibby101:   Don't I know it?   I'm going to introduce you to the old you and take you for a night out that doesn't include canapés and a conversation about the benefits of long-term investment.   Do you think you'll manage?

LouG100136:   Grant and I do have other conversations!

TurkishDelightLibby101:   Grant and I?   How posh is that...

LouG100136:   Not posh, just proper English.   Not like wot you speak...I think I'll bring a couple of fleeces, just in case it's chilly in the evenings.

TurkishDelightLibby101:   Yes, because as a pensioner it's best to play safe...Don't be daft!   It's just as hot at night as it is in the day so no cardi, or I'll send you straight back home.   Hey, It's great they've given you a whole month off from work.

LouG100136: I haven't taken any leave for ages and they told me to use it or lose it. It's so quiet in the office. It's probably a relief for them so they won't have to find me even more irrelevant things to do each day. This morning, Mr Simpson wanted me to search on the Internet if the road works are still on the M6 as he's going on holiday to Birmingham in a year's time.

TurkishDelightLibby101: <Snort> Very exotic…It's your own fault you've so much leave to take. I've been asking you to come here since I arrived. Besides, why haven't you been away with Grant somewhere?

LouG100136: All these weekends away with Grant and his humungous social circle – I haven't wanted any other time off. I go to work for a rest. Besides, he's always too busy with work to take any more than a day off at a time.

TurkishDelightLibby101: Humungous, eh? Have you scoffed a dictionary for lunch? Lou, a whole month away from him... How's BCF going to cope?

LouG100136: BCF?

TurkishDelightLibby101: Big Control Freak – Grant - the man in your life who controls your every move. The one who's stopped you coming over since I moved here?

LouG100136: He hasn't stopped me. Well, not really. He's just been a bit grumpy about it whenever I've raised the topic.

TurkishDelightLibby101: Hang on, there's a bloke here asking for directions, back in a mo.

What? Libby, don't do this to me! I look at the clock. He'll be here any minute. Now, things have definitely been worse between us since I told him I'd booked my trip to visit Libby. In fact, he hasn't spoken to me since, and the atmosphere is unbearable. It's been so bad I almost went to stay at mum's for the last couple of days, but she informed me she has a craft fair she's preparing for and the spare room is covered in sequins and stamps and things I really don't understand.

TurkishDelightLibby101:   You shouldn't have told him. You should have just left a note. 'Dear Big Control Freak, I'm off to have some fun for a change...' then send him a text from Dalaman airport to let him know you've already arrived.

LouG100136: I couldn't do that. In his defence maybe it's because I'm coming for a whole month. He might have accepted a week.

TurkishDelightLibby101:   He'd be upset if it was a minute, let alone a month. Make sure he doesn't stop you at the last moment. You know, cling on to your leg as you go through passport control.

LouG100136: Stop it! Anyway, it's all *your* fault.

TurkishDelightLibby101:   Mine?   How come I'm getting the blame? You're the one who moved in with him within a week of me telling you I'd be moving abroad.

LouG100136: Exactly, you should have stayed with me. In our apartment. Where life was perfect.   I had no other place to go. I was virtually being made homeless (sniff...)

TurkishDelightLibby101:   Maybe life was perfect for *you*. You were totally loved up with BCF, happy in your job, content with life in general.   I'd had one too many dodgy relationships and a job I hated in that weird, virtual office. Anyway, you didn't have to move in with Grant, you could have gone to live with your mum.

LouG100136: What?   In her craft room?   One lie-in past 9am and I'd have woken up to find myself covered in sequins and felt.

TurkishDelightLibby101:   Bless her...I do miss Rita. Now remember, my place isn't plush like yours. I don't have lifts, or a Jacuzzi, or private parking in an underground garage. Will you cope, slumming it?

LouG100136: Hey, it's Grant's place, not mine. Remember the flat we used to share together before you ran off to Turkey and left me? That wasn't plush...

TurkishDelightLibby101: Very true. But you're a posh bird now. Not sure I'm going to recognise you tomorrow. Will you be wearing a twin set and pearls? Anyway, I've got to go. I've a group of 18-year-old lads that need a sensible, mature lady to show them the sights of Marmaris.

LouG100136: No-one else is available, obviously...

TurkishDelightLibby101: It's a hard job, but someone's got to do it.

LouG100136: Are you sure you'll have time for me when I get there? Sounds like I might slow you down, I don't think I'll keep up with the pace.

TurkishDelightLibby101: Probably not, but never mind. See you tomorrow! And don't let BCF talk you out of it. If you're not on that plane, I'm coming to get you...

TurkishDelightLibby101 is offline and may not respond

To say I'm excited is, well, an understatement. I feel sick with the butterflies doing somersaults in my stomach and I've no idea how I'll sleep tonight. But I don't actually care if I do or don't, I've waited fourteen months to see my best friend, exhaustion won't make the blindest bit of difference. And, to think I've planned the journey a few times but haven't quite gone through with it, I must have been mad. Yes, I guess Libby's right, Grant has stopped me to some degree, but I can't just blame him. He's hardly locked me in the apartment and thrown away my passport, it's been just as much my fault.   I mean, for a start, there's my job to

5

consider, there just hasn't been a quiet time. Well, not quite true, every day is quiet, with basically nothing to do. But, there's always been someone else off, or a new process or something to manage. It wouldn't have been right, would it? I am the office manager after all and with that comes responsibility. And boredom, a great deal of boredom. Well, whatever the reason for not going before, I'm going now. But, it would be better if Grant could be ok with it. Somehow I don't think that's going to happen.

I can't quite believe it's been fourteen months since Libby left for Turkey and I've been living with Grant. It's gone pretty quick in some ways, but dragged in others. I'm not quite sure how I live without her here, relying only on our online chats to feel close and pretend she's just around the corner. Except she's not just around the corner, she's in a country far, far away and living her dream.

Saying goodbye to Libby was the hardest thing I've ever had to do. Not even the excitement of moving in with Grant helped with that. Yes, it was sort of exciting I guess, with a new beginning for me, and he did help during those first few months when I pined for her, supporting me at the start of my new life, the one without Libby in it, a life with new friends, his friends. So, this makes me feel a little guilty when I feel the way I do about him right now, after he's been so kind and generous. After all, how many thirty-two year old women get to live in a penthouse apartment with its own lift, and balcony and under ground parking and not have to pay a penny towards it? Not many women I know of. Well, except for the partners of Grant's friends I suppose. They all seem to live like that.

I've offered to pay my way, several times, but Grant says it's not right, he's the 'provider' and all that sort of stuff. My mother thinks I'm the luckiest woman on earth, and I guess

6

she's right, but I know deep down that I wouldn't have moved in if Libby hadn't gone away. And I'm not sure I want to stay with him, underground parking or not.

Talk of the devil, he's here. The lift's just been called and is on its way down to pick him up from the car park, which gives me precisely a minute to enjoy the last few moments before the storm cloud bursts through the door. I know it takes exactly a minute as I've timed it. I close the lid of the laptop quickly as I know how the sight of me chatting to Libby online will be enough to start a fight. Or, restart the one we've been having for the last few days and paused for us to go to work today. We've had so many 'paused fights' over the last few months that I wish there was a remote control I could use to fast-forward them quickly to get the end of each over and done with. Hey, maybe I could invent one? And then I'd be really famous. I'll add that to my list of *'things to make me famous'*. There are a few ideas on there already.

I feel shattered even though I only worked the morning today, so I could get back and pack. Mr Simpson, my boss at the accountancy firm, didn't mind at all. He finds it quite exciting that I'm off to somewhere so *exotic* and I've lost count of the times he's told me how Turkey is in two continents and that a famous golfer hit a golf ball across a stretch of water and it went from one continent to the other. I made a lot of interested noises each time he repeated the story and he's promised to post me a newspaper cutting about it. Bless him. No, I'm shattered because a) I didn't sleep much again last night and b) I had to walk to and from work today. Grant normally gives me a lift into town but he left early without offering due to his mega sulk. I wish I still had my old car, I miss it, but, I can't blame Grant for making me sell it, it was a sensible thing to do I guess, as I agree it wasn't really in keeping with this apartment and the rest of the block. Thinking of my old car reminds me of my cat. Grant made me part with that too when I moved in. Well, in his defence, he's allergic to them, apparently, and it is *his* flat after all.

The lift arrives and I can hear his footsteps approach the apartment door from the corridor outside. Even his walk sounds moody. He was never this bad when we were first together, not in the slightest. In fact, he used to make me laugh, smile and feel on top of the world. How things can change in just a short time.

Maybe Libby is right, I shouldn't have told him I'd bought the ticket until I'd landed in Dalaman and was safely out of his way. But, I'd have felt mean doing that. That's why I chose to announce it three days ago whilst out to dinner in our favourite restaurant. Well, my favourite restaurant. Grant's never been keen but I'd booked it in the hope the venue might offer less opportunity for him to freak out and totally lose it. Wrong. Hey ho... I'm pretty sure we'll never eat at that place again.

Grant bursts through the frosted glass front door at such a pace that I feel a gust of wind blast past with him as he legs it towards the bedroom. I recognise this as what I call his *'serious sulking.'* I've seen it a lot over the last six months and can spot it within seconds. He throws his briefcase onto the cream sofa and carries on towards the main bedroom without giving me as much as a glance. The 'stomping' has knocked two of the plump cushions to the floor, which Grant insists on calling pillows, even though they're most definitely cushions. I bought them, and it's even what the label quite clearly states, 'cushions.' They're the only things of mine that I've been allowed to put in the place, nothing else suited the 'minimalist' style that Grant likes.

I scowl as I pick the cushions up and place them back on

the sofa, and then remind myself that it's in my interest, and Grant's, to keep cheerful as it might help to ease him out of his mood. I've got to stop complaining about him, not just to other people but to myself too. He's really not all bad, as I wouldn't have stayed with him this long, would I? So, I put a smile on my face and hope it doesn't look like wind, and lovingly stroke the soft cushions to try and improve my mood and inner calmness. This lasts for only a few seconds as I ask myself again who on earth calls cushions 'pillows'? Apparently quite a lot of people, I've found out. Well, all of Grant's friends and his parents, Marina and Joseph, entrepreneurs in the world of Interior Design. We had a half hour discussion on cushions vs. pillows once where I was well and truly put in my place. And, their argument appears to be backed up by the expensive home and lifestyle magazines that Grant buys me and places on the hall cabinet, hoping that I read them. Except I never do, as it's just not me.

I find myself checking that the cushions are back in the right place and at the right angle on the sofa and groan as I realise that this is yet another rule that Grant has made, relating to my tidiness (or lack of) around the flat. I've purposefully been trying to keep a mental note of all these rules over the last few weeks, to back-up the decisions I'm currently making about us, and I've go to say that there have been a lot of them. I should write them down in some sort of rulebook. I could call it 'The Handbook for Harmonious Life with Grant Harrison.' Hey, that's actually quite a good idea. Imagine how much easier it will be for any future girlfriends, he won't have to train any potential partners at all. Not that the training has worked on me.

'Hi,' I call out and grimace at the lack of response, then sit back down again on the edge of the sofa. I grab one of the misplaced cushions and hug it to me, then hit it against my head before throwing it on the floor. I then throw the other one to join it and feel a little better. They look good being out of their normal place, I bet they feel free and outrageous. Maybe I should throw all the other cushions around the room too, liberate them so they feel like I will once I've escaped to Turkey tomorrow.

I stand up and hover in the lounge, then walk around kicking the cushions as I go, listening to him move around the bedroom, opening and closing drawers, then to the en-suite before slamming the door behind him. I sigh and roll my eyes to the ceiling before walking towards the gloom that is my live-in boyfriend and I hear him turn on the shower. After a moment's hesitation, where I wish I was somewhere completely different than here, I tap on the door.

'Grant?' I repeat it before trying the handle. Locked. Grant only locks the door when he's angry with me, which is pretty often if truth be told.

'Grant?' I repeat, this time a little louder. 'We need to talk.'

'I'm showering,' he replies.

I stand with my back leaning against the door and look down at my feet, moving them in circles against the plush, thick pile cream carpet, making a pattern as I do so. He'll be annoyed that I'm not wearing slippers but it's the least of my worries.

'I'm leaving in the morning and I don't want to go with us like this,' I say.

'Don't go then,' he replies.

I sigh and go to sit on the enormous bed that we have, with its clean, white, cotton sheets, like a bedroom out of one of those posh magazines that we have in the hall. Next to me on the floor are my bag and travel documents, and I pick up the airline ticket to look at it for the umpteenth time today. I just love reading it, seeing my name and flight details, my journey that I'll be starting in just a few hours time. It's years since I've flown anywhere. In fact, it was Ibiza, four years ago with Libby. Now, that was an adventure. Yes, we'd shown those youngsters a thing or two, even if it did mean sleeping by the pool all day to recuperate before doing it all over again. I'd had to take another week off work when we'd got back to recover and told Mr Simpson I'd picked up some sort of virus from the swimming pools. I felt really guilty as he made his wife then cancel their trip abroad later in the year and swap to the Forest of Dean to avoid a similar fate, and he'd thanked me over and over, even buying me flowers. I doubt I'd be able to do an 'Ibiza' again, times have definitely changed and age has caught up with me. I now go to bed at the same time I used to go out and I just hope I can keep up with Libby for the next month. She used to be the party animal out of the two of us and I can't imagine she's calmed down much.

I tuck the ticket into my skirt pocket, just in case Grant has the urge to rip it up into confetti and throw it out of the Penthouse window, and then I study my passport to have the obligatory laugh at the photo. But I don't laugh, I groan. It's not so much because it's awful, but because I've changed so much. It's not just the fact my hairstyle is different. It's longer now with a fringe, not that I really like fringes on me as they stick up first thing in the morning and part like a pair of curtains by afternoon, but Grant recommended this fancy hairdresser who assured me it would really help to frame my face. For the same cost of a weekend away. No, it's not my hair, or even my clothes, which no longer have the 'bohemian' look that I'd favoured back then. It's my expression, the way I looked...comfortable. Now, I just look permanently stressed and anxious, and I suddenly realise how much I miss myself. The person in the photo looks like someone I once used to know. Maybe Libby won't recognise me after all.

Libby. My thoughts return to my best friend and I wonder again why Grant's so jealous of her? It just doesn't make sense. After all, Libby and I have been friends for what, over 20 years? He's seen the photos of us both as twelve year olds exploring in the woods behind our street, going off to the first school disco, celebrating our 18th birthdays, so he knows our history. And I've known Grant for just eighteen months. He can't expect me to wipe out all years before we met from my life just because he wasn't part of it. I wouldn't ask the same of him, I've gone out of my way to try and get on with his friends, those he'd met at university or through work. It's not my fault he doesn't seem to have any from his childhood.

The shower stops and a few minutes later Grant emerges, dressed in casual jeans but with no top. Why's he got dressed in the bathroom? We never do that, we're generally pretty liberal about walking around naked or in underwear. He moves awkwardly around me sat on the bed, as though I'm some sort of gigantic obstruction, and goes to the wardrobe to retrieve a few clothes before placing them in a neat pile on top of the duvet.

'Are we going out tonight?' I ask.

Grant looks at me for a few seconds before replying, 'I am', and he looks away again.

'But, it's my last night, I thought we'd be spending it together.'

Grant huffs and takes a bag out from the bottom of his wardrobe and carefully lays the clothing in. I nervously look towards my own case by the door and am grateful that I've closed it so he can't see the chaos inside. Normally when we go away, he gives me this lesson on how you must 'roll' your clothes, not throw them in. Something he learnt whilst backpacking somewhere in the middle of a place I've totally forgotten about, where he went with his Uni-cricket-team buddies. Or was it his rugby team? I really should pay more attention.

'Well,' he says. 'I thought my girlfriend was going to say yes to my proposal last week, rather than saying no and flying off to the other side of the world for a month.'

'It's Turkey, not Australia,' I snap back. 'And, I didn't say no. I said I needed time to think.' I can't believe he's brought this proposal thing up again. We've talked endlessly about it and it really hasn't helped.

'No,' he replies, staring hard at me. 'Your words were 'don't you think we're a bit young?' And I said, 'We're in our 30's.' To which you replied, and correct me if I'm wrong, 'Yes, but people live longer nowadays and 32 is the old 17.' Do you remember that conversation?'

'That fact is true!' I reply adamantly. Well, it is. I read it in a magazine and they gave lots of examples, so I've no reason to doubt the accuracy. He could learn a lot from the magazines that I read. All I learn from his are how cushions are called pillows and need to be placed correctly to produce the correct ambiance. What use is that?

Grant goes back to his packing, shaking his head. He hates those magazines I read. He probably worries that there will be an article in one of them which analyses men like him, and that I'll discover all his secrets and know how to handle him and work him out. Maybe I could write it? Another idea to add to my list. I should so be a writer.

As for the proposal, well, I've tried to put that out of my mind and haven't told a soul about it. Not even Libby. I will do tomorrow, though. She'll be the first and only person I tell.

I watch as he goes to the en-suite, grateful that the proposal isn't mentioned again, and wait until he returns with a toiletries bag, placing it carefully in with his clothes.

It's at this point that it suddenly hits me he's packing. 'Are you not coming home tonight?' Grant shakes his head and starts to put a top on. It's an expensive, designer brand top, one his ex-girlfriend bought him before we'd met, that cost a fortune but just looks like, well, any old top that I'd buy in a shop that Grant can barely walk past, let alone go into. Apparently, he can't bare to part with it as it reminds him of this 'super' art exhibition they went to together, and only wears it when he's sulking, just to annoy me. Which works.

'But, you were going to take me to the airport!' I exclaim. Grant pauses what he's doing and glares at me. Obviously not, I realise. I guess it's a bit too much to ask, under the circumstances. I'll book a taxi.

'Where are you staying?' I fold my arms and stare at him, trying to look as annoyed as possible. I'm not very good at it, probably because I don't actually care where he's staying, but I think he needs to know I'm not happy he hasn't even discussed it with me. Although, in his defence, I didn't run the fact I'm off to Turkey past him either. I'm secretly rather grateful that I won't have to deal with his mood all evening. Or in the morning. It's a win:win I guess.

'Well?' I repeat.

Grant shrugs his shoulders, turns and says, 'Depends on how the night goes.'

This comment should hurt me but it really doesn't. I've gone past the stage of caring possibly because, deep down, I've considered our relationship has come to an end and Grant is free to do as he wishes. Mind you, I hadn't realised

14

Grant had reached this decision too and so I do feel a little annoyed that he's considering staying out all night with someone whilst we're still technically together. This is all too stressful and mixed-up so I do the most sensible thing I can – I turn around to leave before it gets out of hand. It's a fight I'm not going to win. And, in fairness, I do feel for him and can understand why he's so angry, I've hurt him and he's every right to be cross and want to hurt me back. I didn't mean for any of this to happen.

I walk out of the bedroom to the hall, grab my handbag and keys and head to the front door. As I open it he shouts, 'Who knows who you'll be spending your nights with, once you're with *her*."

He literally spits out the word 'her' and it sounds so vehement that I can't stop myself from turning round and walking quickly back towards him. 'What's that supposed to mean? What sort of woman do you think Libby is? I'm going to spend a month with my best friend, to relax and try to work out everything that's going on in my head.'

I know he dislikes Libby, but the way he speaks about her still surprises me. Whenever I think back to those last few months before Libby left for Turkey, and how she tried to distance herself from me to give Grant and I time on our own, even though I wanted to spend every last possible minute with her whilst I could, I get so angry. I just can't help myself. She did it for me, for us, yet he's still so spiteful about her. And to think I defended him every time Libby said how she felt he doesn't like her, reassuring her it was all in her imagination, even though I knew inside that it was true. He really was, and still is, so anti-Libby. Convincing her to spend her last night at our flat, before leaving for her new life, took a lot of persuasion and it had gone really well to start with. But, when I'd woken early to take my friend to

15

the airport, I found she had already gone, leaving a note telling me she couldn't bear goodbyes. Grant convinced me it was for the best and that it was 'typical Libby' and, if I'm honest, I still feel a grudge towards Grant for that, him taking a last opportunity to slate her rather than just let things go.

He's now trying to stare me out and says cockily 'If you decide to stay there, let me know as soon as possible. There's plenty of women who wouldn't mind moving in here.'

I turn and close the door behind me. He's right. There's always been other girls on the side lines, women that would do anything for the luxury home, social life and treats galore with, it has to be said, a gorgeous looking man. When you put it like that, I have to ask myself why I hadn't said yes to his proposal? But, as I hear the vase smash against the inside of the front door, I know why. And, all I can say aloud is 'Arse'!

CHAPTER TWO

I'm melting, literally melting. I'm sitting with my eyes closed and my head and shoulders against the white wall, rubbing the back of my hand across my forehead to stop the sweat from running into my eyes. It's not supposed to be like this, I should be looking glam and all touristy, smiling and flouncing around with my friend, not sitting here hugging my bent legs in front of me alone, and with makeup sliding down my face. The combination of the intense heat and a severe lack of sleep is really starting to take its toll and I don't know how much longer I can stand it before my body gives in and frizzles to a little pile of embers on the path, only to be mopped away by the enthusiastic cleaners that have passed me several times since I sat here, fervently keeping the area outside 'Dalaman Airport Arrivals' spotless.

I've the mother of all headaches too, mainly because I'm so dehydrated and probably moments from falling unconscious. I've sipped at my bottled water, not knowing if and when I'll get anymore. I'm not going back into that building, I might miss Libby arriving and then she'll be looking for me, and will give up and leave, and I'll be left here forever. Ok, I know I have a tendency towards being slightly over-dramatic at times, but I'm seriously worried that I'm hurtling towards a state of severe sunstroke. Or something even worse, although I can't think of what that could be. I guess it's death. Yes, that's probably where I'm heading.

I'm wondering whether to pour the contents of the water bottle over my head like I've seen them do in films where they wander aimlessly across the desert, praying for a miracle to save them from this hell... Yes, I'm so like one of those wanderer thirsty desert type souls, someone whom people back home will probably read about in tomorrow's newspaper: M*ysterious exhausted, yet elegant, wanderer perishes outside Dalaman airport waiting for the best friend who never arrived.*

I just can't believe that Libby isn't here. We've talked about this for so many weeks. Why has left me here this long, unprotected and vulnerable to the elements, minutes away from fading into some form of delirium? It will soon be turning dark and I'll face other threats, like predators, such as... umm, well... big cats. Yes, they probably have huge, big cats in Turkey who will pounce on and kill a tourist in seconds. Or lizards. Big, long, vicious lizards. I glance around quickly, wondering if they're lurking in the shadows, ready to pounce but I can't see any. Yet.

How much time has passed since I got out here and sat down? It must be an hour or maybe even two, surely. I can barely lift my limp arm towards me to check my watch but, I need to know, and so I pull it slowly up towards my face. Right, I've now been sat here for... six minutes? No, it's way longer than that. I shake my watch and tap it, again I've no idea why I do this but it seems, well, the right thing to do as it has obviously stopped, hasn't it? It still says six minutes. I'll check my mobile phone instead. That will be right. What? It says the same time as the watch. Oh, it is actually

18

only 6 minutes. Well, six minutes is still long enough to get sunstroke, or be eaten by large cats, and it's 6 minutes longer than it should have been for my friend to meet me.

I suddenly feel tearful. I'd imagined the reunion so many times since planning the trip. I'd pictured me running out of the building, across the concourse to my friend who would be waiting with arms outstretched, crying tears of joy, mascara streaming down her cheeks. And my large but attractive and sophisticated hat would be flopping from side to side whilst my red, wavy and shiny hair flowed behind me. And, little girls would watch me in awe, pointing and wishing they were me, the mysterious and elegant woman they'd spotted on the plane... but instead of that, I'd come stomping out of the arrivals building after having stood in the Visa queue for forty minutes, and baggage reclaim for twenty, to be met with a heat similar to that of my oven when cooking a Sunday lunch. My 'large but attractive' hat squashed and in need of reshaping, thanks to the devil child who'd sat next to me on the plane thinking he could fit it under his seat whilst I wasn't looking. My hair, dull, flattened and stuck to my back in a hot and sticky mess. And, instead of my friend, I was greeted by a group of tour reps and taxi drivers who all rushed forwards to try and claim me. I'd literally had to fight them off, none of them willing to accept that I had alternative transfer arrangements.

I've honestly no idea how Libby does her job, greeting hot, sweaty and tired passengers as they arrive. She does it several times a week, too. But maybe other passengers are a little more cheerful than I'm feeling right now. I feel slightly remorseful, maybe I did shout a little loudly at the reps to leave me alone, watching them scatter and run back to re-form their little group where they've stayed for the last few minutes, glaring at me from just a few meters away. Oh well,

I'm sure they've had worse tourists than me to deal with. From what Libby has told me, some can be a nightmare, and I've a very good reason for being so moody. My friend has forgotten me and left me here to perish. How much worse could it be?

Thinking on the positive side, as I always strive to do but generally fail miserably, I'm quite grateful, at least, for finding the one small piece of shade outside arrivals. I'm tucked into the white brick alcove just enough to keep out of the way of the continuous stampede of tourists oozing out of the doors, whilst still in a position where I should be able to see Libby when she arrives to collect me. That's if she does arrive and hasn't decided that I'm not worth the trip and can find my own way to Marmaris. I gulp at the thought. What if Libby has been distracted by one of her new friends, and decided not to bother collecting me because she'll have so much more fun with them and I'll be in the way? I close my eyes and drop my chin back down to my chest and take a couple of deep breaths to calm myself.

'Hello lady, you would like my taxi, yes?'

I look up and see a taxi driver stood in front of me, grinning, a little insanely in my opinion, and I sigh very loudly before giving him one of my *looks*, the one that Libby says would send people running for cover and begging for mercy within 5 seconds. It works. His grin fades immediately and he backs away, then turns and scurries towards the group of drivers and reps. I can see him pointing to me, waving his arms around like a windmill, and the reps shaking their heads sympathetically at him, then pursing their lips and folding their arms before glaring at me. Wow, they're in a real clique over there, all standing and staring at me as if I'm some sort of monster. I'm just tired, hungry and immensely disappointed, can't they see that? I groan aloud. This is perhaps the tenth offer of a taxi I've declined in as many minutes, and my patience has well and truly gone back into the departure lounge, boarded a plane and flown out of this stiflingly hot oven of a place and back to Blighty.

In fairness, my patience ran out by the time I'd reached the Departures lounge at Luton Airport after having received a dozen texts from Grant since midnight begging me not to get on the plane. I ignored each and every one, it was best that way and as soon as I got to Dalaman, I turned my phone back on and expected to see another load of messages sitting there waiting for me, but there's been none. Fingers crossed it stays that way, although I know it will be eating away at him, knowing I'm here now with Libby. Well, I *should* be here with Libby, but there's still no sign of her.

I close my eyes again and sigh. What if Libby really doesn't turn up? What if I have to eat a humungous slice of humble pie and ask one of the scared taxi drivers for a ride, or plea with a tour rep for a seat on a coach? I bet they'll draw straws to see who gets lumbered with the 'crazy English woman.' What's worse is that I don't even know the address I need to go to. Well, I didn't think I'd need it, did I? Libby is supposed to be here, and she knows where she lives, obviously. There's always the chance that one of the tour reps knows Libby, it's probably a small world over here in the land of Tour Reps, I bet they're one big happy family. Not that they look very happy over there in their pack, all still glaring at me. But, if they do know her, maybe they'll change their minds about me and totally forget their first impressions and see the real me, not this tired, crazy lady and they'll all want to become my best friend. OK, I realise that this is fairly unlikely to happen and I prepare myself to walk to Marmaris and battle the predators and dehydration.

'Excuse me,' a male voice says.

I sigh loudly, hug my knees tighter towards me, pushing my face into my legs in the hope that, if I can't see whoever it is that's come to harass me, maybe he won't be able to see me either. Unlikely, but possible.

There's a few seconds of silence and I think he may have given up already and walked away. But then he taps me on the head. Actually taps me, like a little woodpecker.

'Do you mind?' I snap, looking up at him. 'Jeez, you taxi guys are persistent.' The sun is slightly blinding me, even with my sunglasses on which, by the way, really don't suit me at all but they were the only ones I could afford at the airport which don't make me look like Elton John.

'I've come to pick you up,' he replies.

Is he kidding me? 'Look,' I say very loudly and in my best assertive voice, the one I reserve for the difficult conversations at work that I occasionally have to have with Mr Simpson when he's in one of those moods. 'I know they've sent you over to check me out and report back how mad and grumpy I am, and that you'll all have a good laugh. So, let's not waste each other's time. Just get back over there and leave me alone.' I gesture to the gang of reps and taxi drivers but they've all rushed off to greet another wave of arrivals.

He follows my gaze then looks back to me grinning. The smirk really winds me up. 'I don't know what it is with you guys around here, but I'm not interested. My friend's coming to collect me and I won't need any of you. Not one.' His grin breaks out into a big smile and he laughs gently. My blood, which was already at boiling point in this heat, is creeping up to an un-recordable level. He obviously doesn't believe I have a friend coming at all. 'I do have one, you know. A friend.'

'Well done you,' he replies, 'and I've come to collect you on her behalf.' He holds out a hand, to help me up, but I flick it away angrily.

'Look, I'm very tired and virtually dehydrated,' I say, 'after being left out in this heat for hours.' He doesn't need to know it's for, let me look at my phone, ten minutes. Ten minutes? Time seems to stand still in this place. 'And, I'm not interested in going off with a strange man, thank you very much. I have a fiancé!'

I glance back over to the pack, who have reformed now that the crowds are starting to thin again, and they're watching us, whispering and slowly moving in a little nearer, in the hope of hearing the conversation a bit more clearly.

The man puts his head on one side and looks at me quite seriously. 'Well,' he says calmly, 'that's very nice for you. But I'm here to take you to your friend Libby. You are Lou, right?'

I'm thrown for a second. I have no idea who this guy is or how he knows my name. I look him up and down; he doesn't exactly look like the other taxi drivers, I'll give him that. He looks and sounds, well, British. 'How do I know you're not just someone trying to drive me off somewhere? You could take me hostage.' Wow, I hadn't even thought of this as a possible scenario, I've been so busy thinking of the dehydration, then the predators, and I'd never seen this one coming.

'Now, that would be very brave of me indeed,' he replies, and then he laughs again, which is the wrong thing to do if he has any hope of me not losing it completely. I let out an exasperated breath and shoot up from my sitting position, not in a particularly lady-like manner as my legs have gone to sleep having been bent under me for so long, and my flip flops have got tangled up, and I get a head rush. I have to grab his arm to stop myself from falling and I hear the gang of reps gasp. I glance over his shoulder again to see them make gestures as though swigging from a bottle. 'I stood up too quick!' I yell at them, 'I'm not drunk. I've only had one G&T on the plane, thank you very much.' This just makes me sound overly defensive and a little drunk although I'm sure they've seen worse than me on these airport runs. So, I've no idea why they're so shocked. As soon as I'm steady again, I let go of the guy and fold my arms and glare at him.

He looks at me for a few seconds and then folds his own arms. I'm not sure if he's mimicking me or if I'm making him feel a little defensive. It's what you do, isn't it? Fold your arms when feeling defensive? I watched a guy talk about it on a daytime show once, so it must be true as the hosts were all over him and thought he was fantastic. He frowns at me and then says 'How would I know your name if I was a strange man wanting to drive off with you?' He waits for an answer.

'Well,' I eventually reply, 'you could have... read my luggage label.' I turn to point at my small case, which is propped up against the wall, noticing that the label is nowhere to be seen.

Several seconds pass as we stand there, both looking at the case and then at each other. Whilst his eyes stay locked on my face, my eyes move involuntarily from his head to toe, and back again. He's dressed in a white linen shirt and cut-off jeans with trainers. Is this what kidnappers wear nowadays? I have no idea and try to think of films or TV shows I might have seen which feature kidnapper types. The only one I can think of is *Home Alone*, with those guys trying to catch that pesky kid and he looks nothing like them, although they weren't real kidnappers I guess. My gaze is now back on his face, and his curly fair hair and piercing blue eyes. I actually let out a small gasp, I've never seen eyes quite that blue before. I cough hoping that, if he heard the gasp, he'll think I've a sore throat or something and I feel grateful I've my sunglasses on so that he can't see that my eyes are literally locked onto his and have just quickly roamed all over his body.

'Are those lenses?' I ask, pointing at his eyes. Why did I just do that? I didn't need to even mention his eyes, now he'll know that I've noticed them.

'Umm, no. They're all my own, both of them. Do you want me to poke them to prove it?' he asks.

I can't help but smile a little and realise that, if I want to leave this boiling cauldron of an airport, I'll need to admit defeat.

'I guess I'll have to trust you,' I announce, 'that is, trust you're not a kidnapper. I'm not too sure on the lens situation.' I wiggle my finger accusingly at his eyes and then turn to pick up my case and ask, 'Where's Libby?'

'She's had to work, short notice I'm afraid, and she's very sorry. So I offered to collect you for her. My name's Seth, by the way, Seth Daniels.' He holds out his hand, which I shake weakly. Seth Daniels doesn't sound much like a kidnappers name. I wished he'd opened with that one, it would have saved me from the last few cringy minutes.

'Lou, Lou Granger,' I reply, although I've no idea why as he knows who I am. 'Do I look dehydrated and close to collapse?' I ask.

'Umm, not really,' he says, 'although you do look a bit hot and bothered.' He goes to take the case from me but I snatch it away. I may be weak, but there's no way I'm letting him carry it, he might run off with it, although why I have no idea. I keep my eyes firmly on the ground as we walk through the pack of reps and taxi drivers, ignoring the whispers and giggles and then we go past the coaches which are already full of excited holidaymakers and just waiting for the final few before they can pull away. After passing a multitude of white minibuses, all with their doors open ready for their passengers who are being bundled in by locals with cigarettes hanging out of their mouths, we stop in front of a blue convertible sports car.

'Flash car,' I say, with a not-so-discreet hint of disapproval. I really don't like flash cars, although I've no idea why. 'It's British.'

'So am I,' he replies. 'I drove it over here, from the UK.' He opens the boot and gestures to the case.

'No thanks, I'll have that on my lap please,' I snap, again not knowing at all why as I struggle with it into the passenger seat. Having it balanced on my lap reminds me of my mother who always insisted on letting the Labrador we had, when I was a child, sit on her lap when on the sofa. She could barely see the TV over the top of it. Seth frowns at me as he gets in but makes no comment.

Feeling a need to justify my ridiculous decision I say, 'It contains important things, like my...umm...like my purse.' I look directly ahead of me, avoiding his eyes, those blue, piercing... stop it, I tell myself. They're just eyes, and they've been 'smirking' at me for the entire time I've known the guy.

'And your engagement ring?' he asks. I frown. What's he talking about now? He picks up on my confusion and says, 'you told me back up there that you have a fiancé. But, you're not wearing a ring. I was wondering if you have it in your case.'

I glare at him and sigh. What is with this man? Is he a detective? 'I haven't got it yet, if you really must know,' I snap back.

'Oh,' he replies, as he starts the car, putting it in reverse to leave the very small space that was sandwiched between two minibuses. 'What about the fiancé? Have you got him yet?'

'Of course I have,' I answer through gritted teeth. How can someone I've only just met make me cross this quickly? Ok, I haven't technically got a fiancé, or a ring, but what's that got to do with him? The fact is, I could have a ring and a fiancé. In fact, I could have lots! Maybe it's the combination of tiredness, dehydration and near-sunstroke and the fact my best friend hasn't turned up for our long-awaited reunion. Whatever it is, the drive to Marmaris is going to be a very long journey. Particularly with an annoying man sat next to me, and a bag the size of a fridge on my lap.

CHAPTER THREE

I watch Seth out the corner of my eye as he drives us away and can't help but notice the size of his hands as they rest on the steering wheel. Wow, they're huge and make me think of builders' hands, not that I've ever looked at builders' hands, but I'm sure this is what they'd look like. He must sense my stare as he turns and looks at me, and my eyes dart forward, hopefully concealed by my shades.

'Hoşgeldiniz,' he suddenly says.

'Bless you,' I reply, and he laughs. This guy is so rude.

'It means welcome,' he replies, 'to Turkey, I mean. Your home for the next few weeks.' I do a strange little laugh, pretending I knew what he meant, then smile awkwardly and look away. The butterflies return to my stomach and it hits me that I'm about to see my friend very soon. The sensation could also be due to me being very hungry and I regret not wanting to pay for the snacks offered during the flight. I scoffed all my emergency sweets on the plane, actually before we'd taken off, and my eyes scan the pocket in the passenger door, just in case there are any goodies there, but it's empty. It's a clean car, that's for sure, and it makes me think of Grant and his immaculately kept vehicle where he flips out if

I spill a single crumb. I wonder what he's doing, if he's back at the flat yet after his night out, and if he's alone.

We drive slowly towards a security guy in a hut, pull to a stop and I raise my eyebrows as I hear Seth speak in fluent Turkish to the guard. Well, I presume it's fluent Turkish, but it could be anything at all. The only words I've learnt in preparation for the trip is 'beyaz   şarap' just so that I can order a white wine in a bar if I find no one speaks English. As, that would be a complete disaster. The unsmiling security guard waves us on and within minutes we're on a dual carriageway, the sides separated by a grass area lined with trees and small bushes. The sky's a perfect blue, not a cloud in sight.

'Ooh, Zebra crossings!' I exclaim. I've no idea why as I'm sure they're not exactly mentioned as a 'must see' in the *Lonely Planet Guide to Turkey*.

Seth glances at me and says 'Yes, we have them here too. Fancy that.'

I'm not going to bite. I'm too tired and I'm not sure whether he's being sarcastic or playful. I decide to try and make some pleasant conversation. 'Why is the road lined with yellow and white stripes on the kerbside?' I ask. 'Looks like a long snake.' Seth laughs and shrugs his shoulders. With the risk of being guffawed at again, I stop myself asking about the huge signs in the central reservation. They remind me of how signs would be on the roads in America, although I've no idea why. I haven't ever been there, although it's one of my dream destinations, a road trip to visit as many places as possible. One day.

The next few miles are in silence. After hardly having any sleep due to the upset after the fight with Grant, and followed by a flight from hell, I'm feeling more and more tired as the heat beats down onto and through the car. Even though the roof is down, it's like being in a fan assisted oven with hot air entering the car and then blowing around my face and hair. How is Seth not melting? I've seen at least three locals walking along the side of the road, not in small vests, but long sleeved shirts, and they hardly look like they've noticed the heat either. Maybe I'm not well. What if I've some type of fever, or I've caught something from the air conditioning in the plane. I've read about that. I could be in hospital by nightfall and in the newspapers back home by the weekend. I decide to break the silence to take my mind off my pending slump into ill health.

'So, how did you know it was me? At the airport,' I ask. There's no reply and I look at him, and realise he hasn't heard me as I'd spoken with my head pointing towards the roadside with my voice lost in the breeze. So, I repeat the question, rather too loudly and right in his ear. He jumps, stares at me and then composes himself.

'Well, I won't lie to you. It was difficult,' he says. 'There were so many women sitting on the floor, outside in the heat with their chins dragging on the ground, scowling at everyone going past. I wasn't quite sure which one would be you.'

I glare at him and am pleased when he looks at me and averts his eyes immediately. My stare hasn't lost its impact. I turn my back to him and hear him laugh, so I spin my head back towards him.

'Look,' he says, apologetically, 'Libby has photos of you all over her apartment and she showed me one again this morning. I recognised you, even in the very large hat. You've a distinctive face, ok?'

Distinctive? What's that mean? Is it the same as calling a woman 'handsome'? I've always been confused by that, being called handsome when you're female. Not sure if distinctive or handsome is a compliment or not. I pause for a moment and then ask, 'Are you her boyfriend?' I've actually no idea why I've asked this, as he's introduced himself as Seth and I know Libby's boyfriend is called Jude, and I've seen lots of photos of the love of her life and he's definitely not this guy. Jude has dark hair, a stark contrast to Seth's golden locks.

'No, I most definitely am not,' he replies. 'I'm a friend of hers.'

'Good,' I say, almost in a school-ma'am way. 'Because, her boyfriend sounds a bit of a jerk.'

Seth laughs again. 'What makes you say that?' he asks.

I shake my head, too tired to explain fully. So, I just say, 'It's his name.'

'What's wrong with the name?' Seth asks, raising an eyebrow.

His eyebrow is starting to annoy me, it moves around a hell of a lot. 'His name's Jude. What parents would call their son Jude?'

'Mine,' he replies. 'I'm Jude's brother.'

I wince, quite loudly. This is not going particularly well. I suddenly recall Libby mentioning Jude's brother and wish I'd paid attention more to the name she quoted. A few more minutes pass, again in silence, before we pull up at a junction with traffic lights and my mind is taken off the awkwardness in the car by a display on the side of the lights, at car window height, which seems to be counting down from 20. 'What on earth is that?' I ask.

'It's showing how many times you've insulted me or my family members since being here,' he replies. He looks straight at me and I turn my face away towards the door and ignore him. 'It's counting down until it changes for us to go,' he says, and I can tell just by his voice that he's smirking.

'Neat,' I say. Neat? Why did I say that? How old am I? 15? I'll be saying *groovy* next.

We shortly pull away and Seth suddenly states 'I must say, your fiancé is very trusting, letting you come here for a month. He might not get you back home again.'

'Grant has every reason to trust me. I'm a very honest and loyal girlfriend. What gives you the right to think I'll find someone here and leave him?" This guy is unbelievable.

'I meant, you'll fall in love with the country and might not want to go back to England". Oh well, I'm still going to huff at him. 'What happened to the fiancé?' he asks, glancing at me quickly. 'You just referred to yourself as his girlfriend.'

What? Is this guy a police officer or something? He's picking up on every single word I utter. I tut so loudly that it's not even covered up by the wind whistling through the open roof. 'Girlfriend, fiancée, what's it to you? Does it really matter?'

'Obviously not, as you're not wearing his ring,' Seth replies.

I glare at him, mouth open and lost for words, and he laughs loudly. I clutch my case closer to me and bang my head against it a couple of times. No one has ever wound me up this much before. I'm hoping it's the tiredness, the heat or jet lag. Can you have jet lag after a four-hour flight? And, why didn't I put this damn case in the boot? It's crushing my legs and I'm actually starting to worry about removing it from my lap once we reach Libby's. I learnt about that on my First Aid at Work course, that removing a heavy object that's crushing a person could kill them. I try to wriggle my toes and am relieved to feel them move. After a deep breath I ask, 'Can we change the subject?' through gritted teeth.

Seth's expression has now changed to one of seriousness

and he looks quite remorseful. Maybe I'm being a little over sensitive and should just shrug off his teasing. I'm a bit out of practice with being teased, it's not something Grant would do, or any of our friends and it reminds me of my brother Robert and how he winds me up within the first minute of us seeing each other. I miss my brother as I haven't visited in the last year, and he hasn't been able to come and stay as he has three children and the flat isn't exactly child-friendly.

'You and Libby have been friends for a long time, huh?'

Seth's question brings me out of my daze. I sense he's trying to make peace with me. 'Since school,' I reply and, for the umpteenth time that day, feel tearful. There's no way I'm going to cry, and so I take a deep breath to calm myself. Seth is going to think I'm crazy. In the short time knowing me, he's seen me cry, laugh, shout and head-butt my suitcase.

'Yes, she said that too. You must miss her.'

Oh great, my plan to not cry lasted all but two seconds. A tear is now rolling down my face. It's not even a small one. It's huge. I brush it away with my hand as inconspicuously as possible, but Seth's spotted it and holds out a hanky. I take it, dabbing at my face as though I'm a delicate lady, and then blowing my nose like a trumpet. He surprisingly makes no comment.

I quickly compose myself and turn to him, smiling. 'It's the wind in my eyes. From this silly, soft-top thing of yours,' I say.

'Of course,' Seth replies. He turns on the stereo, setting it at a low-ish volume, and the sound of exotic music drifts softly through the car, unhindered by the wind whistling past as we drive along.

I like the sound and it brings me back to reality, the fact that I'm here, on holiday! My mood instantly lightens. 'Who's this?'

'Tarkan,' he replies. 'He's Turkish. Have you not heard him before?' I shake my head, stopping myself from asking 'why would I have?' He's just making conversation. Seth takes one hand off the wheel and rustles around in the glove box before passing me a CD case. I look at the photo of the singer.

'He doesn't look Turkish,' I say, frowning.

'What exactly does Turkish look like?' he asks. I go to answer and then realise I have absolutely no idea. 'Were you expecting him to be wearing a Fez?'

I tut again, I don't think I've ever tutted so much in such a short space of time. 'Of course not!' But, inside my head, I had totally been picturing the singer in a Fez. I realise how incredibly ignorant I am about different cultures. Seth looks the type of guy who has travelled the world, compared to me who has barely been out of the UK other than day trips to France and the Ibiza holiday. I decide the trip will be more pleasant if I at least try and make conversation. 'Have you travelled very much?'

Seth nods and replies, 'I guess so. Have you?'

I shake my head. 'Not very much at all,' I reply. 'Would love to though.' I really would love to see the world, but I've no idea when or who with. There's no way I'd do it alone and, apart from Libby, I haven't got many close friends. In fact, those I do now have are all connected with Grant and so won't probably want to know me once they find out about the rejected proposal. Not that they're the sort of people I would want to stay in touch with anyway, if I'm honest. My only other friends are the girls in the accountancy firm I work in and most of them are married or in serious relationships. So, unless I brave it alone, I may not get to explore Planet Earth.

'Where would you love to go the most?' Seth asks.

'America, on a road trip,' I say instantly. I didn't need any time to think about it, it's always been on my wish list. I've this romantic notion of me sat in a car with the man of my dreams, and us driving into the sunset from state to state. I have no idea why I've just told him something so personal, so I add, 'I doubt it will happen, but I'm not giving up on the dream.'

'Me too,' Seth replies.

'Really? I'd have thought you'd already have done it.'

'Nope,' he answers. 'Never been to the States at all, but always wanted to. Not on my own though. Like you, I've always pictured it being with someone I really care for. And, that hasn't happened yet.'

I can't think of anything to say back to that, other than to acknowledge I get what he means as it's how I feel, and so I just nod. I must admit I'm surprised by the fact that he's single and hasn't found someone special yet. He's actually very attractive and seems a decent guy, even though he's annoyed the hell out of me.

I sit and watch him for a few minutes, my eyes hiding behind my sunglasses still, and I start to wonder how well he knows Libby. She has a new life here, and Seth is part of it whilst I'm not, and I can't help but feel a little isolated, like the odd one out.

After a few minutes, I can't keep it in any longer. 'Does Libby ever tell you that she misses me?'

Seth looks at me, and for a moment I think he's going to mock me, or raise an eyebrow again. I instantly regret asking until he says, 'Very much, she talks about you all the time.'

I smile and look back out towards the opposite carriageway. Two guys drive past on scooters in vests and T-shirts and I'm horrified to see that, not only are they without crash helmets, the one in front is driving one handed whilst holding a tray containing coffee take-outs. 'What is going on over there?' I squeal, pointing at them.

I wave my hands at the riders and look at Seth for a reaction. But, there's none, not even one of his eyebrow movements, so I shrug and accept that maybe this is quite commonplace and I pray silently that they don't come off their bikes. I immerse myself in the scenery which keeps changing, one minute completely flat and full of lines of small trees and crops, the next outlined in the distance by large hills. I love this variation, and how different it is to home. Or maybe it's like this back there, but I just don't notice it. Every now and then I can see a small white house in the middle of a field, with a terracotta roof, and wonder if this is like the house that Libby lives in. I realise that I haven't even seen a photo, but also that I haven't asked to. Have I taken enough interest in her new life here? I really don't think that I have. I could at least have asked for more photos. In fairness, she doesn't have regular access to a computer, or emails, so it would have been hard for her to send them. She can only chat online with me when she works at the welcome evening once a week at the largest hotel she covers. But this doesn't excuse the fact that I haven't even asked her for any.

After a few miles of little to see, buildings gradually come into view and I see my first mosque, with the blue tipped minaret on the top. Gradually, I see more and more of them, all equally as beautiful and bright.

As we pull up at a roundabout and wait for the traffic lights to change so that we can turn left, Seth says 'we'll soon be there. Tired?'

I nod. I'm straining to keep my eyes open if I'm honest, but I don't want to miss anything. They're probably just buildings and roads to Seth, but to me it's all so different to home and, although I've only just arrived, I'm already beginning to dread leaving here in a few weeks. We're getting closer and closer to Libby and there's no way I'm going to sleep and miss this last part of the journey. Absolutely no chance. Zero.

Twenty minutes later, I'm snoozing and having a great dream. I'm lying in the sun, hair flowing in glamorous, shiny locks onto the bright white towel, me wearing a golden swimsuit, and locals walking past admiring me, the mysterious stranger from distant shores. As they pass, I smile at them, feeling the sun on my face, and splashes of water on my cheeks. Big splashes of water. Splashes of water? Is it raining? This doesn't fit with my dream at all! I don't like rain at the best of times so why has it dared to come into my dream, my lovely dream where I look mysterious and gorgeous in gold, and with perfect hair? The splashes become heavier and I can hear someone laugh. I open my eyes and slowly come back to reality, realising the car isn't moving. And there, right in front of me, with her head at the wound down window is Libby, flicking water from a bottle onto my face.

'Wake up, you dribbling, sleepy idiot!' she laughs. I am so happy that I grab her, almost pulling her into the car. Libby shrieks and kisses me, cupping my face in her hands. 'It's so good to see you!' she says, 'you look so...'

'...hot and dehydrated and visibly shaken from my brush with death after melting at the airport where I'd been abandoned? It's about 100 degrees in this car even without a roof on.'

Libby laughs and looks at Seth. 'Wow, you must have had a fun drive here. See, I told you she exaggerates.' Seth smiles and Libby turns back to me. 'Yes, dear friend, it's at least 100 degrees, nearer 200 probably. I'm surprised you've survived the journey, you're a medical marvel.'

'Yes, I am actually,' I reply, a little stroppy, hurt by the lack of compassion or remorse about leaving me there, alone and facing the elements. I look at Seth for some support and then instantly wonder why I bothered, as he's just smirking again. I give him a disapproving look, which just makes the two of them laugh. 'How long have we been here, in the car?' I ask them, stretching out in the seat.

'Just a couple of minutes,' Seth replies, walking towards the door which Libby has removed herself from, and he opens it so I throw my case on the ground, forgetting about the possible fatal side effects of removing a heavy object from my squashed legs, get out of the car and stretch again, then throw myself at Libby for a hug that I've waited for so long. Wow, I've missed her. I yawn loudly.

'Classy...' says Libby and I laugh. 'I'm so sorry I couldn't meet you. Forgive me?'

Now that she's acknowledged the fact she wasn't there, and has apologised, I'm a little happier. 'Of course,' I reply. Within just these few minutes of seeing her, I feel like we've never been apart. I ruffle her hair with my hand. 'It's so short,' I say and she nods. She looks absolutely stunning, with her dark hair in a cropped, pixie style and a beautifully tanned face.

'Well, thank goodness for Seth, rescuing you from danger and bringing you safely to me. I'm sure he's looked after you.'

I do my normal thing when I don't actually agree with something but not want to get into a discussion about it. I nod and make a strange noise. Libby, though, knows me too well, frowns and puts her head on one side. I sigh as I realise that, although I feel irked, he *has* driven carefully here and delivered me safely to my friend. And, I guess he did sort of rescue me as who knows how long I'd have survived the heat and impending danger of the airport. I turn to Seth and give him a nod and smile, and he grins back.

'That was Lou's way of saying *thank you Seth*,' Libby says and then she links arms with me and guides me along the residential road we're in. I look around and wonder which one is her home. 'Did you see the beautiful view at the top of the hill as you got near?' Libby asks. 'The one I'd told you about?'

I frown and look at Seth. 'Did I?'

'Umm, no,' Seth replies, as he follows us carrying my suitcase. I go to get it from him and then stop, not wanting to start that battle off again. 'You fell asleep about 10 minutes before we got there.'

'Did she snore?' Libby asks. 'She always snores.'

'I do not!' I so do...I've even woken myself up on a number of occasions. Grant makes me wear these strip things over my nose, which I remove as soon as he's fallen asleep as they make me look like *Adam Ant*.

'She did,' Seth says. 'I had to turn the music up. Snored. Dribbled and talked loudly. Very entertaining.' I go to protest but don't have the energy and I just watch the two giggle together at my expense. I feel the odd one out. Libby and Seth stop walking and I guess we've reached the apartment.

'Right, I've got to dash,' Seth says and puts the suitcase down. 'Are you ok carrying this up?' he asks.

'No problem,' Libby says, grabbing hold of it before I can.

'Be careful with it,' Seth says, 'It contains some very, very important things apparently.'

Libby looks at me and frowns, and I pretend I haven't heard him. She turns back round to Seth and asks, 'You not coming in for a drink?'

Seth shakes his head. 'Sorry, someone I've got to go and see.'

Libby hugs him, kissing him on either cheek. 'Well, thank you for delivering my precious cargo,' she says. 'I owe you one.'

'It was a pleasure,' he replies, with a tone that actually says *never again*. 'Good to meet you, Lou, and I'll see you around real soon.'

I nod politely and catch Libby's warning look. So, I say 'Thank you. I'm sorry if I was a little...'

'...cranky?' Seth continues for me. 'Short-tempered, hot and bothered? Understandable. Long plane journey, minutes from death and away from that fiancé of yours.'

'Fiancé?' exclaims Libby loudly, almost falling over. I can't believe he's just announced it like that, when I haven't even got a fiancé. Not that he knows that, obviously, but it's the principle. Seth, I decide, is a troublemaker and I scowl at him.

'I'll explain later,' I say to Libby, giving Seth a wave of my hand as I turn away from him. I catch his eye before I turn, and he's grinning at me again.

'I think we'd better get inside,' Libby says, frowning at me. 'It appears there's a lot for me to catch up on.'

As she walks ahead of me, I stand and look at the building. I'm in front of a white archway, with a stone swan perched on the top with its wings outstretched. To each side is a block of apartments, probably five floors tall, each with a small balcony. Some have colourful mats hanging over them, and a couple have cages containing small, yellow, chirping birds. Bougainvillea hangs from the front of each floor and the deep pink is beautifully vibrant. Libby has walked through a metal black gate under the arch and has turned to wait for me.

'What do you think?' she asks.

'It's perfect,' I reply, grinning from ear to ear. 'Absolutely beautiful.' And I really mean it, I think it's one of the most beautiful apartment blocks I've ever seen. How different to the one I live in right now. Well, did live in. I've a feeling I may have already been evicted.

'Let's hope you still feel that way when you get inside. It's the third floor and there's no lift.'

But, I really don't care. It could be at the top of a mountain and I'd climb without a complaint because I'm here, and that's all that matters.

CHAPTER FOUR

The masculine apartment door is so out of context with the more feminine exterior of the building, and I can't help but stand back and look it up and down. It's huge, in fact massive, and made of dark, thick wood, with metal curved bars winding up and down it from top to bottom, and is in stark contrast to the lightness of the brick finish surround. I watch Libby open it, expecting her to have to ram it with her shoulder, and to hear bolts clanging loudly just like in a scene from a prison-break film, but it swings open easily. I'm almost disappointed. Inside is bright, light and incredibly warm. 'I'll give you a few minutes to get your bearings, and then you're telling me all about this 'fiancé' of yours', Libby says as she kicks off her shoes, placing them on a colourful mat by the door, and points at my dusty plimsolls. I look down and wonder what's wrong with them. 'Sorry, dusty' I say, 'from all that standing around in the middle of nowhere for hours waiting for my friend that didn't arrive.'

She ignores this dig. 'No, it's not that. You need to take your shoes off too,' she says, 'we don't wear them inside over here.'

'Oh,' I say, 'ok.' I struggle to remove them from my hot,

swollen feet and would really feel much more comfortable with them on, but I'll do as she asks. I huff and puff as I do so though, to prove the point that it's a bit annoying for my stinky feet that now look like two large baps. I should be used to having to remove my shoes inside a house, as I'm not allowed to wear footwear at all at Grant's, due to our plush, expensive carpets, but I was so looking forward to a month of no rules. And, this floor is marble throughout, so it's not as though I'm going to ruin a carpet. On top of this, Libby was the most 'un-house' proud person I knew and would have thought nothing of walking into our apartment, when we lived together, in a pair of muddy trainers, traipsing dirt all over the place. What's happened to her?

I hold up my shoes and she smiles at me and says 'It's what we do here, you'll get used to it.' I'm not too sure who 'we' are and presume she means Turkish people rather than the two of us. I place my tired looking shoes onto the small rug, which is full of pretty sandals and trainers, and step onto the marble floor. 'Wow,' I gasp as it feels like heaven for my hot little feet. For a few seconds, I just stand there, looking down at them, willing my feet to shrink back to their normal size, and then I start wandering, looking around me as I go. The apartment is so clean and clutter-free, it's hard to believe it belongs to Libby. The one we'd shared was full of stuff and clutter, quirky ornaments and posters, boxes and bags, which were strewn everywhere. Here, other than a few magazines strewn across a coffee table, it's quite bare and there's a great feel about the place. I walk to some doors and feel the long, chintz curtains, loving the simple cream colour, which blends with the dark wooded furniture in the room.

The doors, which come off the lounge next to the small kitchen, lead to a compact balcony, and I walk out onto it and stand to admire the view of the opposing block and the bougainvillea spilling over from most, if not all, of the other apartments, climbing up and down to the surrounding balconies. Libby has a couple of pots of flowers next to the small table and chairs, and I notice fairy lights wound in and out of the iron grills. I look forward to seeing them lit up later, once the sun has gone down. In fact, I'm just looking forward to the sun going down, the heat is just as intense as at the airport and I'm grateful for the glass of ice-cold water that Libby passes me.

I carry it with me as I walk slowly back into the lounge and then to the bathroom, which is small and compact, but incredibly neat and tidy. I realise that there is a washing machine in here and point to it, frowning at Libby who's followed me in. She shrugs and says 'What? It's a washing machine. In a bathroom where things get clean. What's wrong with that?' Actually, there's nothing wrong with it whatsoever and if the bathroom we'd shared back in the UK had been big enough, the washing machine could have gone in there if we'd have thought about it. But, it was hardly big enough to fit us in, let alone an appliance. Libby walks back into the lounge and closes the shutters on the windows facing the sun, then switches on the ceiling fan. The breeze is pleasant to start with but, after a while, just feels that it's spinning warm air around. She leads me to a bedroom and tells me it's mine. 'Two bedrooms?' I ask. Libby nods and walks back out. The bedroom is simple yet perfect, like the rest of the apartment, and I sit on the bed for a minute, touching the silky sheets realising there's no duvet, but I guess there's no need for one with this temperature. I look up and sigh with relief when I see there's a ceiling fan. Hopefully, if the air cools later, it will help to make the room temperature a little more comfortable.

I wander back into the lounge and towards the kitchen

where Libby is standing, touching the colourful, soft throws on the sofa as I pass. 'These are pretty,' I say.

Libby looks over to me. 'Stops the sweat soaking the sofas.'

'Umm, good to know,' I reply, quickly pulling my hand away. 'When's the air con come on?'

Libby laughs. 'Wow, you're going to find it hard after your luxury pad you've been used to. Here,' she says, passing me a magazine. 'This is your air con. You fan yourself with it.'

I smile sheepishly. 'Sorry.' I hope I haven't offended her. I wasn't criticising the apartment, it's just that I feel I am slowly melting and have no idea how anyone can survive this temperature.

I watch Libby preparing food and feel instantly relieved. With the excitement of my arrival, I'd forgotten how hungry I am. 'You cook now?' I ask.

'You know I do, I've told you often enough when we've chatted, and you always make sarcastic comments, remember?' I do remember, and I wonder if my sarcastic retorts ever made her feel I didn't care, or wasn't interested in the small detail. But, selfishly, I've spent months just hoping Libby would suddenly turn up, back in Abingdon, saying 'Nah, it's not for me, I'm coming home.' It hasn't happened yet and, now that I'm here, I don't think it ever will. Who'd swap this, when they've nothing to come home for other than a mopey friend?

I watch her, busy with the plates and food, which never happened when we lived together. That was always my domain, not that I'm very good at cooking. Well, definitely not now, as I'm so out of practice. Grant prefers to eat out and hasn't been too keen on my meals. Apparently, I lack attention to the *nutritional value*...Libby used to love my cooking though.

I wonder how else she's changed and hope we still have

things in common. Have we grown so far apart that this month will be awkward? I hope that my visit's not too late, and that her life hasn't moved on so much that we're different to the friends we once used to be. Or, that *my* life has moved on and changed me too much. I tell myself off in my head; of course we're still the best of friends, we just need to catch up with our lives again. Just because Libby's made me take my shoes off and is now cooking a meal, it's no big deal.

'What are all these spices?' I ask, as I pick up the pots on the breakfast bar, trying to read the labels, but realising they're obviously in Turkish. 'Are they the same types of spices we have at home?'

'Some of them,' Libby replies, 'but some are Turkish, although Stella said she saw them in the supermarket back home when she visited her mum. In the International section.'

'Who's Stella?' I haven't heard Libby mention her before. Is she her best friend over here? Has she replaced me? I bet she has. I suddenly don't like Stella very much.

'She's one of the reps on my team. She's been here ages. You'll probably meet her, I'm sure.'

'Umm,' I reply, a little under-enthusiastically, 'can't wait.' Libby turns and gives me one of those looks and I sip my water and try to think of something to say, to change the subject. There's no way I'm going to ask if Stella is her *top* best friend. What am I, ten years old? No, Libby is quite free to have as many friends as she wants. Quizzing her about Stella would just make me sound desperate and there's no way I'd stoop that low. No way whatsoever.

'Is Stella your best friend?' I suddenly blurt. Why do I do that? I give myself a telling off in my head.

Libby doesn't turn round but I can tell even by the back of

her head that she's smiling. 'No,' she replies, 'because you know full well that you are, and will always be. And you're also still as needy as always and need constant reassurance, ok?'

I go to disagree but actually Libby is right. I've always been like this, jealous of anyone that tries to muscle in on our relationship. I've worried myself sick that she'd move on, find another friend, and not want to be with me. Umm, I'm going to keep an eye on that Stella.

I top my glass up with more water and am starting to feel like my hydration levels are returning to normal.

'There,' Libby says, turning and holding out a plate to me. 'Chicken salad and some rice. Ok?'

Ok? It's better than OK. I'm starving and, seriously, a packet of crisps would have done. This looks fantastic. I take it from her and she grabs her own plate then we walk out to the balcony and I sit down whilst Libby goes back to the kitchen and returns with two glasses of chilled white wine.

'Fancy one of these?' she asks, smiling.

I nod as I most definitely do. I restricted alcohol on the plane, only because it never looks right with breakfast. The sun is still quite strong but is moving round to the other side of the building now and is starting to feel almost manageable. I hope that my bedroom is cooling down and wonder what will happen if it's too hot for me to sleep, for the entire month. Is that possible? I'll ask Libby later.

We clink our glasses together. 'Here's to a fantastic month with my best friend,' says Libby.

'Absolutely,' I reply. 'Wow, this salad's good.' I honestly can't believe the strong flavour from the tomatoes and salad leaves, so different to the tasteless ones from the supermarket at home.

'I guessed you're probably still avoiding carbs,' Libby says.

'I'm on holiday, so I don't care,' I reply. To be honest, I'm literally grieving carbs and I have been ever since I've had them 'removed' from my daily diet. Not that the removal was particularly my decision, but more from taking advice from Grant and his circle of friends. They all raved about low carb diets and, I've got to be honest, all the girls in that group look fantastic. I'm not denying that it's done me good, and kept me in better shape, but I've sometimes found myself watching others eating a baguette and planning how I can swipe it off them when they're not looking. Oh, bread. I could so polish off a huge, great big plate of it.

As if reading my mind, Libby gets up, goes to the kitchen and returns with a big basket of chunky bread. My eyes light up. Oh, how I've missed it.

'Eat!' Libby says, and I don't need to be told twice. I grab at the crusty delight and quickly shove it in my mouth. Wow, I've missed it. My glass of wine disappears a little quicker than it perhaps should and I smile as Libby tops it up. 'This is like the old days,' she says.

'What? Like all those times when we'd sit eating salad on our balcony at the flat in beautiful weather?'

Libby laughs. 'I meant stuffing our faces and drinking a bottle of wine. It's a good job we didn't have a balcony, Big Beer Man would have been shouting down to us, and Neurotic Nina would have been singing up to us, asking us if we could hear her cat calling out her name. Remember her? And, all of that whilst the rain poured down and the smell of the chippy wafted across the road to us.'

I giggle. 'Yes, I guess a balcony wouldn't have had quite the same attraction as it does here. Mind you, I did actually hear Nina's cat speak once. It said hi.' Libby raises her eyebrows at me. 'I did! I swear to you!'

'Like how you heard that dog say 'bless you' when you sneezed at the bus stop that day? Hey, I wonder if Big Beer Man is still at our old block. I kind of miss him.'

'Me too. I miss the stomping around. And the belching.'

'And, the scratching,' Libby replies. 'Do you remember the scratching? It used to shake the walls.'

We sit for a few seconds grinning in silence, reminiscing. Then Libby asks, 'Anyway, enough about Big Beer man, what's this about an engagement?'

I sigh. I'm grateful to Libby for holding out until I'd eaten, and I realise I've actually forgotten Grant for the last half hour.

'I'm just starting to relax, and I don't want to get wound up again. So, is it ok if I give you the short version?'

Libby puts her head on one side and touches my hand, and her finger moves to where a ring should be. She frowns and asks, 'Are you engaged?'

I shake my head. 'No, most definitely not. I turned him down.'

Libby sighs with relief. 'Well, that's all I need to know for now. Stay chilled and relaxed for a bit longer. I'm sure you'll tell me more as soon as you're ready. But, I've got to say I'm so happy you didn't say yes.'

I'm not surprised she's happy I turned him down, and am grateful to Libby for not pushing it further. That's what a true friendship is all about, knowing when to step back and give each other breathing space. I will talk about it, but just not yet.

'So,' I ask 'as we're not going to talk about my love life, can we talk about yours? When do I get to meet Jude?'

Libby smiles, her eyes lighting up at the sound of his name. 'Tonight if you're up to a walk out to the bar. He's...' Libby looks up wistfully and her smile grows broader…'fun', she finishes.

'Fun? Just fun?'

'Not just fun,' Libby answers. 'He's ambitious and intelligent and very good-looking. You saw the photos right?'

I nod. I can only think of one photo and remember he did look good in it. He's tanned and dark, and looks a lot different to his brother with his golden hair and blue eyes. Umm, those eyes. I picture Seth and realise there's a smile on my face.

'Earth to Lou,' Libby says and I come to. 'Who are you thinking about? I recognise that look.'

'I am so not thinking of a man,' I exclaim, a little over dramatically as half the bread in my mouth flies out.

'As long as it's not Jude, I don't care,' she laughs.

'Of course not!' I answer, shaking my head and tutting. Actually, although very nice on the eye, Jude doesn't look or sound my type, and I wouldn't have ever thought he'd be Libby's either. But, seeing as she now cooks and keeps a tidy flat, maybe her taste in men has changed too. 'I'm just happy to be here, that's why I'm smiling.' I can feel myself blush and hope she hasn't noticed. 'So, tell me more about Jude and you, is it serious?'

Libby hesitates before answering. 'Not sure, although I do really like him. He's a bit cross with me about something at the moment.'

'Something?'

'Yes, it's what I wanted to talk to you about actually. When I told you I had some news.' Libby puts down her knife and fork and looks poised to make an announcement of some sort. Her news, I'd forgotten all about it in the excitement of coming over here. A thought suddenly hits me and I take a sharp intake of breath. They're going to get married, that's what it must be. How exciting, I'll be the bridesmaid, stylish and floaty in a beautiful dress and gliding down the aisle, which is bound to be on one of the gorgeous beaches here, and everyone will be looking and wondering who I am. Well, they'll be looking at Libby more, obviously, as she'll be the bride. And, when I say everyone, I'm leaving out Stella, whose invite will have mysteriously been lost in the post. But still, how exciting is that! I've no idea why Jude would be cross with her about a wedding.

Ah, maybe it's not a wedding at all. Maybe she's thinking of coming home. Yes! I punch the air with delight and Libby jumps back a little. Libby coming home would be even better than me being a stylish bridesmaid.

'Tell me, tell me,' I say excitedly as I jump up and down a little in my chair.

'Calm down,' Libby says, 'It's about work.'

'Oh...' I hadn't thought it would be about something boring like work. I feel guilty as I know that my 'oh' sounded a little, well, lame and disappointed. But, that's because all happy thoughts of weddings or a return home have just gone flying over the side of the balcony and landed with a hefty thud on the path below.

Libby tops up our glasses. I go to stop her but change my mind. I'm on holiday, and it's so long since I shared a drink with my friend. There's a lot of catching up to do.

'I'm going to start a business,' Libby announces excitedly.

I raise my eyebrows. 'Really?'

Libby has done nothing but surprise me with the whole career change thing since leaving Abingdon, she's so resourceful. After numerous jobs since leaving school, including a brief stint at the accountancy firm with me, she'd never really settled, being too fickle to stay in one role for long particularly in an office, doing the same thing every day. She needs to be around people, chopping and changing, organising herself and others. But even so, giving up the last job she had, which was in a virtual office, and moving to another country as a tour rep was something that I'd never envisaged her doing. At 30, she'd been a little older than most of the other reps at the resort but fitted in quickly and was soon promoted. And, with the increase in salary, along with the savings she'd brought from home, she moved out of the shared rep accommodation and into this apartment on her own. But, starting her own business? That's a massive leap.

'Can you do that over here? Start a business?' I ask.

She ignores the question and my negativity. 'You know how I've told you that some of the customers from last season have come back again this year and remembered me?' she asks.

I nod. This hadn't surprised me as, once met, Libby is never forgotten. It's not just her looks, it's her personality and presence, she just seems to ooze energy and charisma. Not like me. I quite often zap it. It's been a bit difficult sometimes hearing how some of the customers have seen Libby twice or more over here, whereas I haven't seen her at all since she moved, until now.

'Well,' Libby continues, 'they remembered me on some of the day trips from last year, which I don't really do this season. I tend to do the evening tours instead and the airport runs and hotel visits. But, on my days off, they asked if I'd go with them to places by taxi or hire car, and show them some of the less touristy sights and interesting places, off the beaten track. So, I became a bit of an *unofficial* tour guide. I've even had complete strangers approach me, friends of past guests who have had me recommended to them. It's got me out on my days off, meeting new people, and I had lunch bought for me. I've loved it. But, I've been thinking about making it a bit more official.'

'How will you transport people around, by taxi?' I'm a bit confused, how is she going to make a living doing this?

'Nope, I've bought a jeep with some of my savings and had it all painted up. You'll love it, it's pink,' Libby explains enthusiastically.

Ooh, my mind drifts off with the mention of pink. We've always both loved the colour. Our hall and bedrooms were both painted in strawberry milkshake pink back in our old place. I pull myself back to the conversation. 'I can't believe how much money you brought out here with you, you must have been really rich and I never knew!'

'Cost of living is less here,' she says, 'and I have my wages too. Anyway, the jeep was really cheap. A Turkish boyfriend of one of the reps wanted to get rid of it, they're moving back to the UK.'

I want to say 'why doesn't he keep the jeep and you move back to the UK,' but I don't. 'But, are you allowed to have a business here?' I ask again. 'Haven't you got to be Turkish or something? Have you looked into it?' I'm worried that she hasn't. I start to picture me visiting her in a jail, where she's been thrown into a cell with no light, and only bread and water. And I'll be leading a campaign to fight for her release, and I'll go to London to plead with the Prime Minister. Then, British people all over the world that have been incarcerated will all ask me to help them with their plight. I'll be so busy.

'Stop fretting,' says Libby, bringing me back to the present predicament. 'I've got a lawyer guy sorting it all out. It would be easier if I went into business with a local here but I want to do it on my own. It'll be tough, but I'll get there.'

I sip my wine whilst I take all of this in. 'So, why's Jude cross with you?' I suddenly say as I remember why we got onto this subject. 'You said it was to do with work.'

Libby shrugs. 'Jude thinks I should do it in partnership with him, as he knows a lot about business over here and thinks I'm not strong enough.'

'Well, why don't you?'

'Because, I don't think it will work out, the two of us,' she replies. 'You know what happened with my parents when they ran their business together. It tore them apart, and totally stressed them out. I don't want that happening to Jude and me. I want us to stand a chance.'

Libby lost her Dad to a heart attack when we were at school together, which she's always put down to being caused by the stress of the business he ran with her mother Ruth before they separated. It was a terrible time for all of them. 'It might not be like that for you two,' I say, stroking her arm.

'Well, we won't find out, because I'm not doing it with him,' she says, 'and he can be as angry as he likes. This is *my* business idea, not his or anyone else's.' We carry on eating the last of our meal, and then she says, 'I've got a uniform too. Wait there...'

She runs off to her bedroom. Her enthusiasm is infectious and I can already picture her in the jeep, chatting to customers, telling them all about the country, culture and traditions. This is so Libby. It's a shame she can't come home to do the same thing but it's obvious that it wouldn't really work out in Abingdon. You know, picking up people in her Vauxhall Corsa, taking them to the sights such as the, well, the newly paved town centre. Ooh, there's a Michaelmas Fair in October, that would work. Sort of. I won't mention it, not yet.

'Here I am!' Libby shrieks as she runs back in. She's out of her tour rep uniform and now wearing a pink pencil skirt, black short sleeved fitted shirt and a pink chiffon scarf tied elegantly around her neck. She looks a cross between an air stewardess and a Pink Lady from Grease.

'Do you like it?' she asks.

'Go Greased Lightening!' I half sing. 'You look fantastic, it's so...you!' I beam.

Libby throws another chiffon scarf over to me. 'Try it on' she orders.

I tie it loosely round my neck, not wanting to tighten it due to the amount of heat radiating off me. I fear it will stick to me and not be able to be removed, other than by the local A&E department.

'Perfect! Now,' says Libby. 'The rest of your uniform is in your wardrobe.'

'Eh? What do you mean, *my* uniform.' I'm a bit confused.

'Well, that's the other bit of my news,' says Libby. 'I thought you could join me over the next few weeks. I can be the driver and you could be the guide. Or, vice versa. It will be our unique selling point, you know, two lovely ladies for the price of one, and we'll be together, all the time you're here... are you ok? Say something.'

I realise that I'm just staring at her, my mouth slightly open. She's being serious, she actually means this. I scratch my head and stand up, and then pace around for a few seconds whilst trying to run the idea through my head. As is my usual style, a load of questions all flow out of my mouth in one long stream. 'Am I allowed to? Won't I get into trouble? It's not even easy to stay here as a visitor for a long time, let alone work. I've looked into it! Will I get thrown out of Turkey and not be allowed to come back? What if the Embassy spies on me and then I'll be in the newspapers at home, and journalists will all go round to my parent's house? Work with you?'

Libby just looks at me, and then pats the seat for me to sit back down, which I do. 'Stop panicking. Come on, it'll be fun,' Libby answers, laughing. 'You won't officially be working with me. You'll be coming with me to keep me company. I won't be paying you or anything, you're coming as my guest, my friend. So, there are no laws being broken. I'm not that silly, I wouldn't risk it all, would I? Everything I've built up over here in the last year? I've checked it all out.'

I start to calm down. She's obviously very excited and I've put a damper on things. Libby leans over, straightens my scarf and then sits back. 'And, what do you mean? You've looked into it?'

'What?' I ask.

'You said, in the middle of all that babble, that you've looked into being able to stay here.' She suddenly beams. 'Have you been thinking of coming here too? To stay?'

I shrug my shoulders. 'Not really.' But, I have. Quite a few times, actually.

Libby gets up and hugs me. 'Come on, join me with this over the next few weeks and then, who knows? You might want to stay? But, even if you don't, it will stop you twiddling your thumbs and avoiding Grant'

She has a point. I knew there'd be some days she would be working whilst I'm here, she can't take the whole month off. She's done her best, by swapping shifts around though. And, if we do the jeep work instead, we'll have fewer days apart.

'I just wasn't expecting to be working,' I reply at last. 'I was coming here to relax and to spend time with you.'

'It's not going to be hard work for you. We'll be out, driving around, taking people to lovely places and telling them about this wonderful country. We'll be eating good food, seeing great scenery. It's hardly going to feel like a day in the office with boring old Simpson.'

I start to warm to the idea. It's not really work, is it? Not when I compare it to my usual, mundane, office job back home. I begin to picture myself in the passenger seat, telling tales of romance and mystery to an eager audience, them enthralled by my natural storytelling skills. My hair flowing in the breeze as we zip along. The customers will clap at the end of the trip and tell all their friends, and I'll become a character that everyone will know and point at in the street. This could work.

'Lou, focus!' Libby shouts. 'I'm still talking.'

'Sorry, I'm just getting used to the idea. When do we start though? What about your rep work? Have you handed in your notice?'

'Nope, not yet. We'll test the water and, if it looks like it's working, I'll hand it in straight away or at least go part-time. And it'll mean that next season is sorted and I won't have to worry about whether the holiday company will keep me on.'

Although excited for her, it suddenly hits me that she's obviously decided she won't be coming home, not now that she's planning her business and talking about next season. She has everything she wants here – a home, a job, a wonderful climate and a boyfriend. There's nothing to attract her back home, not even me. So, it's best that I make these next few weeks the absolute best, for both of us. Like she says, I might even think about staying. I nod and say 'I'm in.'

Libby grabs me and shrieks, 'You'll love it! Now, go and freshen up. You're stinky and look a state, and we need to get ourselves out for the night!'

Rude. Although, totally true. And so off I go. I'm about to have my first night out with my best friend in 14 months.

CHAPTER FIVE

We leave the apartment a couple of hours later to head into town. I can't believe how quickly it's turned dark compared to home. But, the heat is still here and I'm starting to realise that it may stay this way permanently. Still, it'll be fine, absolutely no problem at all I tell myself, even though I don't have the first idea how I'm going to survive for the month like this. I'll need plenty of cool showers, like the one I just had. Although, a cold one wasn't intentional but due to how the water is a little cool by this time of the evening, as it's solar heated and has reached its 'peak' by early afternoon as Libby explained to me through the bathroom door as I shrieked whilst showering. And, it apparently depends as well on who else is taking a shower at the same time in the apartment block. I'm not sure if she made this bit up, but it could be true and I just hope that there are a lot of neighbours who aren't too keen on keeping clean.

We giggle and chat as we make our way into town, arms linked like schoolgirls as we go past a small garden centre, which seems to be in the middle of the residential street, and then over a small bridge. We pass quite a few people and Libby greets most of them by name. Is there anyone here she doesn't know? I can hear music in the distance, which is the bar area we're heading towards, and a strange noise from under the bridge we pass, which apparently are frogs shouting to each other. Again, I thought that Libby made this up but I overheard another couple talking about the noisy frogs.

We're both dressed in almost identical maxi dresses, and I can't stop touching Libby's new pixie cut hairstyle. Each time I do, she pulls away and tells me off. She says I remind her of when her mum used to spit on a tissue and dab at 'invisible' dirty marks on her face.

There's so many hotels on the way, most of them fairly small and family run, but they all seem so alive, towels hanging from each balcony and murmurs of conversation from guests sat around the poolside bar. I feel a lot better than I did earlier but, although the meal helped top up my energy, the several glasses of wine zapped it, leaving me with a slight deficit. Maybe it's best I don't drink any more tonight, although I think abstinence is unlikely.

We've talked non-stop, about nothing in particular. I've caught Libby up on boring news from home – how the pub on the corner of our old street has changed its name three times since she left, but still has the same staff working there. How I often bump into her mother Ruth, and get quizzed as to what Libby is up to even though they speak to each other every Friday. It makes me think of my own mother Rita, and I vow to text her when I reach the bar so she knows I made it here safely. I've had my phone switched off only because of the continuous texts and calls from Grant. I just can't deal with them right now. Surely he must be getting bored of me not answering? It's not that I won't ever reply, I just can't face it tonight. I want to enjoy this special evening without him ruining it.

Talking about Libby's relationship with Jude, I've offered to stay in a hotel a few nights whilst I'm here, so they can have some privacy at the apartment but she laughed and said he rarely stays there. If they want a night together, she'll go to his apartment instead. He lives a short distance away in a place called Akyaka with Seth. I'm looking forward to meeting this man of hers and wonder how different he'll be from his brother, other than in looks. A lot, according to Libby, as Seth is much quieter and the most serious out of the two whilst Jude is a little loud and can come across as 'arrogant.' Whenever someone is described as 'coming across as arrogant,' I normally find that they are very arrogant indeed. Again, I'm surprised, as Libby has always disliked arrogant men and it makes me really keen to find out what it is in him that she's fallen for.

We turn onto a promenade, with the sea now on our left, and I feel a slight breeze in my hair and am immediately a little cooler. I've tied my hair away from my face, mainly to stop it sticking to my cheeks, but also just because Grant hates it tied back and I've missed wearing it like this. He says it makes me look 'lazy.' What exactly he means, I'm not sure, because you use up more energy tying hair up then leaving it down, but I'm a peace-keeper and it hasn't been something worth arguing over. I think of him and wonder what he's doing right now. Although I still have some feelings for him, I know I'm no longer in love with him and I'm not quite sure I ever was. The last eighteen months since we met haven't been totally awful, as he can be the best company and it's not as though we argue all the time. Just more often than not. He's probably sat in a bar somewhere with this colleagues talking stocks and shares over a cocktail and Bellini. Or, chatting to a pretty blonde who looks the same as all the other girls in his group of friends on a night out. Clones.

That's what I often thought when looking at the cliques, the group I wasn't really allowed into because I was so different. All dressed the same, hair and make-up identical, and names all following a similar phonetic pattern, like Poppy and Tiggy and Fifi. Unless they started to call me Louie, I would never have qualified for entrance into their gang.

'Oi, come back.'

I realise Libby is shouting to me. She's stopped outside a bar whilst I've wandered on daydreaming. I turn and hurry back.

'Sorry, didn't hear you. Things on my mind.' I screw my nose up and she knows what I mean. Or, *who* I mean to be more accurate.

'Well, put him out of your head. We're going in here, my favourite bar, and it's unlikely well be back out before midnight. And I don't want to see a mopey face. Understand?' I nod obediently and she smiles, grabs my arm and pulls me towards the entrance.

'I'm blooming starving,' I say, the smell of a neighbouring steak bar drifting up to reach my nostrils which are grateful for not being singed at this particular moment by heat for the first time since I arrived here.

Libby laughs and drags me though the door. 'Still hungry? After my lovely salad? In that case, meze, darling,' she says. 'Lots of little dishes you can munch on all evening. We need to fatten you up a bit. Look at you'

'I thought Meze is Greek?'

She ignores me as she manoeuvres us through the bar. Inside, it's already quite full, mainly with couples and families, most of whom seem like holidaymakers. There are several waiters walking amongst them, all dressed in short sleeved white shirts and blue denim jeans. I wonder out loud how they can wear jeans in this heat and Libby tells me it's quite normal to see them wearing jeans in the day time too, and that at the start and end of the season they often wear warm jumpers whilst the foreigners are still in vests and shorts. I observe how they're all so smart, clean-shaven and with short, well cropped jet black hair, and each of them smile and say hello as we pass. As we sit down, one of them approaches the table and kisses Libby on both cheeks.

'Hamil, I want you to meet my best friend in the world. This is Lou,' she says to him. He turns and looks at me, takes my hand and kisses it gently. When he smiles, my heart melts, he is so incredibly cute. It's getting easier by the second to see why Libby doesn't want to come back home. She's surrounded by beauty, both landscape and human.

'Very pleased to meet you, Miss Lou,' he says and walks away, glancing over his shoulder and winking at me as he goes. I realise that I'm still sitting with my hand half in the air from where he's kissed it, and with a big grin on my face.

'Lou, you can put your tongue back in now.'

'Wow, he's very nice. In fact, they're all very nice,' I say as I glance around at all the other waiters. There's not one 'un-cute' guy amongst them.

'Go steady, it's only your first night here,' she says. I should heed her warning. I think it's because I haven't seen any men outside of our circle of friends back home. It's as though there's been a drought and I'm suddenly in a rainstorm.

I can just see the front of the restaurant from our table and quickly admire the view of the beach. It's completely clear of anything, and I see how the sun loungers are stacked up neatly in a pile on the edge. I'm looking forward to seeing what it's like during the daytime and can imagine that the beaches are full of sun-worshippers, all striving for the perfect tan. The promenade itself is spotless, despite the amount of people walking past, and the energy and atmosphere is vivacious. It's so different to a night out back home. Here, everyone seems carefree and happy, but then again, they are on holiday. They're not worried about work, or bills to pay. They're here to have fun, pure and simple.

Libby nips quickly to the bar and speaks to Hamil and then returns to tell me she's ordered a few dishes to try. 'And I don't mean him!' she snaps at me. I pretend to look offended that she could even think I'd want to, but we both know I would most definitely like him as a dish to try and smile as he arrives with a couple of cocktails, plants them on the table, winks at me and leaves. I look at Libby who shakes her head at me.

'I can't help it,' I say. 'I've serious withdrawal symptoms from fun and frolics.'

'Frolics?' she asks. 'You sound like someone from an historical drama. Maybe it's not a bad idea to have a bit of fun with someone whilst you're here. It will get the control freak out of your system.'

I don't even respond, as I think that she's right. But I'm totally out of practice where flirting and frolicking are concerned. I wouldn't honestly even know where to start. It's something I'd never been very good at anyway, Libby would always be the one to start chatting to a couple of men on a night out as she knew I'd ruin our chances within the first sentence. My opening line would be about the weather or how scandalous the house prices are. I once opened a conversation with a line about a nit epidemic at the local schools. We never saw those guys again.

Half an hour later I'm full of food and feeling a little tipsy from the cocktails. Meze, I decide, is even better than tapas which, up till now, has been my favourite food. Well, that and Chinese. And Indian. In fact, let's just say I love all food. My particular favourite dish tonight has been the flat bread, which actually started off as quite a big, ball-like loaf but, when I stuck my knife in, deflated into a delicious round treat. I spread loads of garlic style butter on each piece and it was delicious. Long, green peppers shared a plate with large, half tomatoes with a spicy tomato paste dish alongside which, Hamil tells me, is called Cemen, the spelling I know because he writes it on a serviette so I don't forget it. Apparently it contains tomato paste, walnuts, garlic and a variation of spices. I am already determined to make this dish one day, whether it's here or at home and he tells me he'll help me if I'd like him to. When he's gone, I read the serviette again and see he's put his phone number and name on there, plus a couple of kisses. I smile and show Libby.

'Get used to that,' she says, 'they're going to love you over here.' It's a long time since I think any other man has noticed me. Mainly because I've hardly ever left the apartment back home without Grant next to me.

'You can talk,' I reply, 'the amount of men that seem to know you in here.' Honestly, Libby is permanently either speaking to, winking at or kissing a guy.

'It's my job!' she exclaims, holding her hands up and shrugging. 'Look, I know the guys in the bar here as I bring them lots of customers, and there's a load of holidaymakers in here that I've seen either on the airport run or when visiting the hotels. Hey, it's a perk of the job.' I've got to admit, I'm jealous. I have no perks to my job, other than a free mince pie at Christmas which Mr Simpson hands out to each of us whilst singing 'Deck the Halls' and wearing a Santa hat. Oh, and the pencil with the firm name stamped on, which I was awarded for working a year with no sick leave. I went sick the next day in protest.

'When are we meeting your man?' I ask, changing the

subject. I'm getting impatient, I've been in the country for several hours now and still haven't seen the guy.

'He'll be here in...', Libby looks at her watch, '...10 minutes. Hopefully. He's probably got held up at the bar.' Jude, I've found out, owns two bars in partnership with Seth. One is here in Marmaris and the other is in Akyaka. He spends his time between the two whilst Seth, it appears, takes responsibility for the administration and management of both, plus a small property rental company where they hire out holiday homes on behalf of clients during the summer season. It sounds like Jude has the more enjoyable role.

'Why didn't we go to Jude's bar instead?'

'The food here is gorgeous, whereas Jude's bar only does snacks, plus it's karaoke there tonight, which is mega loud. And, he hates being disturbed when he's working.'

I see Hamil gesture to Libby and she grabs my arm. 'Come on, there's a table free on the roof terrace. We can go for the last ten minutes or so now that you've finished scoffing. The View is... well, come see.'

We go up the steps, me holding onto the bannister so it's not as obvious the alcohol has made me a little unsteady.

'Thank goodness you didn't bring Grant, what a storm cloud that would have been hovering over Marmaris!' Libby says as we reach the top. I can't help but laugh. Grant would so not like it here, it's just not his *thing*. It's not that he doesn't like having fun, it's just that he prefers places that are a little more serious, full of culture and historical places. Although, I know that Turkey has some wonderful cultural sights, including here in Marmaris. He just wouldn't be able to see past the fun.

On the rooftop, we see a load of large, terracotta coloured cushions laid over the floor and several people relaxing on them, strewn around. I grab Libby by the arm as she goes to some spare cushions against the wall. 'Look, I'm not into this type of thing,' I say to her, concerned. She looks to where I'm pointing and frowns.

'What do you think they're actually doing?' she asks.

'They're smoking... well... you know? Stuff,' I reply and gesture to the huge pipes and devices they're holding. There's drug paraphernalia everywhere and I go to walk down the stairs. It's not that I'm a prude, but it's just that I'm, ok, a prude and I'm surprised Libby is even ok with this, she wouldn't have condoned it back home. I give her a very judgemental look.

'Don't be daft,' she says. 'It's a hookah, shisha, a flavoured tobacco, that's vaporized and then smoked. Look, they're sharing them. When you've finished, you put it back on the table and someone else has a go.'

I'm not entirely convinced but I try to pretend I'm just playing, even though she can see straight through me. We continue over to the wall and look down below. There's a huge amount of people walking up and down the promenade, and I look towards the sea where I spot a double-decker boat sailing away from us, full of people standing on the upper deck, some of them swaying and dancing to music I can just about hear. Libby explains it's a night time cruise, full of people who go to dance, drink and have a good time before returning to shore a couple of hours later. How it's not rocking with the dancing, I've no idea. The breeze here is refreshing and I stand for quite a while whilst Libby sprawls out on a cushion next to me and checks her phone. When I sit down, Libby asks what I think.

"That wall's so low. Anyone could fall over it,' I reply.

'The view,' Libby responds, raising her voice. 'I meant, what do you think of the lovely view. Wow, you've got so serious. You'll be doing a risk assessment in a minute, interviewing staff and customers and compiling a report for the Health and Safety Executive.'

Actually, she's right. What's happened to me? I wasn't like this years ago. Or, more accurately, eighteen months ago. I sit next to her and straighten out my legs, noticing how swollen my ankles and feet still appear. We sit quietly for some time, until Libby breaks the silence by asking suddenly, 'Do you love him?'

I spin my head round to face her. 'Who?' I ask.

'Hamil, the waiter downstairs. Who do you think? Grant!' Libby sits forward, looking intently at me.

I hug my knees to me and shake my head. 'No, well yes,' I start. And then, 'No, I don't think so.'

I then find myself tearfully explaining how Grant is so different to me, and how everyday is a struggle to try to get him to accept me for who I really am, and that I just can't do it anymore. Saying this out loud makes me realise that it must be difficult for someone else to understand why I've stayed with him, if things are so bad. But, it hasn't all been bad, and he does have a lovely side. But, I just haven't seen it as much lately because I just seem to disappoint him so much and make him cross. I've let him, well, mould me into this... stranger. I've forgotten who I am, that's the hardest thing, and I miss me and I'm not sure if I'll ever find myself again.

'I'll help you,' says Libby, hugging me tight. 'I remember you. And I'm going to go and find you and bring you right back. I promise.'

I know she's right, and I'm so grateful that I'm here, and that I finally made it. If I'd have left my visit any longer, who knows what would have happened to me. I dab my eyes and, after a minute of silence, I say, 'your turn now. Do you love Jude?'

Libby wrinkles her nose up, then gently smiles. 'Not sure. I think I could, if he lets me, but I don't think he will. He's very closed off. And free.'

Free? I wonder what she means by this. It sounds like her dreams of a future with Jude differ to his, maybe. She wasn't long ago saying how she didn't want to jeopardise their future relationship by going into business with him yet, if he's free, he maybe doesn't see a future at all. I tell Libby how I saw her mother a couple of weeks back, at a garden centre, and that Ruth said how much she looked forward to Libby settling down and, if that's in Turkey, then so be it, as long as Libby is happy.

Libby tuts. 'I'll translate that. What my mother is really saying is that she hopes I can make her a grandmother. She's desperate for me to bring her babies, and mentions it every time we speak on the phone. But we all know that it's not likely to happen, not any time soon, if at all.'

I must agree, Libby and children just don't mix. She has a sister who is Mother Earth, four children all under the age of 10, with Libby as God-Mother to the eldest and we used to have her come to stay with us every now and then at the flat. I'm not being over-critical but we had some really close calls with the youngster, sometimes ending up in A&E. Libby just seemed to have no understanding of what a safe environment is for a child, and how they can get themselves into very dangerous situations. One time, the poor child ended up with a rubber glove stuck to her scalp with nail varnish. It's too much of a long story to go into.

I decide to be daring and we try some of the hookah but I decide within two tries that it really isn't me, although I can't help but feel that I must look quite cool smoking it. I ask a young guy to take a photo of me with my camera. As well as not particularly liking the taste, I'm really quite concerned about the amount of lips that have been around the hose, and check my bag for my hand sanitizer, wondering if Libby would notice me putting it on my hands and then casually brushing my fingers against my lips. I get my chance when her phone beeps and she checks it to read a text message. 'Come on,' she says, 'change of plan. Jude needs to meet us at his own bar. He can't get away.'

We go down the stairs and I follow Libby to the bar, pulling my purse out of my bag ready to pay. I'm looking forward to spending these Turkish lira, they look pretty cool compared to my own currency, but Libby leans over the counter, kisses Hamil on the cheek, then turns and walks away, telling me to follow. I'm confused. Have we just legged it without paying? I hesitantly look back to Hamil who blows me a kiss and looks away. 'Aren't we paying?' I ask, as I catch her up at the door.

'Don't panic,' replies Libby. 'This is the first stop of the weekly pub-crawl I lead around town. Twenty young people I take in there, who spend a huge amount of money to have a good time, so they gave us tonight on the house.' This makes me feel better, I thought I'd just been an accomplice in a crime, my first ever.

Most of the bars we pass have guys standing outside, encouraging passers-by to come in, and each one of them greet Libby and kiss her on both cheeks. At this rate, it will take us hours to get much further than a hundred yards. She says a few words in Turkish to them and I'm impressed. It's the first time I've heard her speak the language and she sounds so good, as good as Seth did earlier. I'm pleased that she knows so many of the staff and we're not being hassled to enter each bar, it all looks a bit much for the group in front of us and they're literally running past the bars, waving the waiters and door staff away. It doesn't seem to upset or offend the staff, they're still smiling.

We reach Jude's bar and it's fairly quiet outside but, when I follow Libby in through a sliding patio door, we're hit by the sound of someone singing very loudly. I say singing, that's a bit kind. Inside it's decorated as a beach hut and waiters are walking around in very small clothes, most of them female wearing bikini tops and shorts, which I think is a wise idea considering the heat in here is like 100 degrees plus. It's not quite what I expected, I thought it might be, well, a little more 'classy,' although why I don't know. I've never even met Jude but I guess I was basing it on Seth's style. At the tables, customers are drinking a large bowl of liquid through a straw. I see the signs on the walls, 'fish bowls', and guess that's what they are. I'm so thirsty, I fancy one straight away but am a bit worried about what it contains as the colour is so bright and screaming out E numbers.

We stand at the bar whilst Libby talks to a waiter and I'm fascinated by how he's making a cocktail, shaking a container around in all directions and tossing it in the air, not even watching as he catches it. I wonder to myself how many he's dropped. He turns and points to the corner and I follow his gaze to see a guy sat at a table with two young women. Libby grabs my arm and walks towards them and, as we approach, the guy looks up and smiles, and Libby leans in to kiss him on the cheek. She smiles awkwardly at the girls, who both get up to leave, and he stands to hug them then watches them walk away.

'Jude, this is Lou,' Libby says. He takes my hand, kisses it and smiles. His stubble feels really rough and I have the urge to wipe my hand on my maxi dress, but stop myself. Although I recognise him from the photo I've seen, his smile is what gives him away as it's identical to Seth's. As is the eye shape and thick hair, but I can already sense that's where the similarities end. We sit down, with Jude in between us and a fish bowl arrives on the table exactly at the same time. I hurriedly grab the straw and take a sip.

'Thirsty?' he asks.

I nod. 'It's been a long day,' I say and I go on to start telling him about the plane journey from hell but notice he's already switched off and is looking at his phone. He puts up a hand to stop me, and places the phone to his ear, soon speaking in Turkish.

I trail off, mid sentence and look at Libby. 'He's busy, always busy,' she says but looks a little embarrassed. I watch him as he stands, pushes past me and walks around talking. He is good looking, I'll give him that, with obvious charisma too and I watch him run his hand through ruffled long dark hair, tied back loosely in a short pony tail, which looks a whole load better than it probably sounds. He's dressed in an open top, 3/4-length trousers and flip-flops. He appears so laid back, he may as well be horizontal.

He finally finishes his call and stands next to us again. 'Lou, you have got to get out in the sun. Seriously, your shoulders and arms are transparent!' Then, he walks off to the bar. I rub my arms subconsciously and I'm pleased he can't see my legs in this maxi dress, they're like milk bottles. I guess he's just being honest, but he was a bit direct.

'Hey, don't worry about it,' Libby says. 'He's just joking, although they do look a little pale. They'll soon get tanned.' I nod, this time next week I'll be bronzed and probably passing as a local. Except for my red hair and freckles, which might give away the fact I'm not Turkish. 'How's the fishbowl?'

'Fantastic,' I reply and she looks pleased. Over the next 30 minutes, we both sit and watch Jude flounce around the bar, joking with clients and staff, whilst listening to the endless queue of willing Karaoke volunteers. We laugh at an elderly couple who sing 'I've got you Babe,' him swinging his hips wildly side to side and her slapping him to stop, pointing at his hip suggesting she may be concerned it could break at any time. Another couple that we presume to be their friends are cheering them on and get up to dance followed quickly by most of the customers in here. I look at Libby who is still watching Jude and I wonder how she feels about him ignoring the fact she's here. But, she doesn't look bothered. Perhaps it's how it has to be when you run a business like this, being friendly with the customers, male *and* female, and showing them a good time on holiday.

I'm not sure I could be like Libby, I'm quite insecure and massively jealous, although I haven't been with Grant. But maybe he hasn't ever put me in that position. When we're out, he's always attentive and only has eyes for me. I feel a small pang of guilt as I think of him, at home on his own, and wish I'd at least returned his calls. Maybe I should try him now. But, it's too loud in here and I really can't be bothered to get up and walk outside. Besides, if we move from this table, we'll never get it back as the place is full with more and more people coming through the door and I really don't think I can stand. I'll sort it tomorrow. But until then, I've this second fishbowl to get through.

CHAPTER SIX

An hour later, the day is finally catching up with me, helped by rather a large consumption of alcohol, and I desperately yearn for my bed. Just like old times, Libby and I have been singing. We started with '*Take a Chance on Me*,' standing back to back doing all the Abba actions, and were joined by two guys with beards who were on their way to the bathrooms at the back of the bar. A group of young women thought we were an Abba tribute act. We followed this with '*Wonderwall*' and then '*Wannabe*' by the Spice Girls. We have a little fan club going, with the two pensioner couples being our main groupies, clapping and cheering and egging us on. We sit with them at their table for a while and chat. One of the women reminds me of my Nan who died when I was small, and I find myself telling her all about Grant. She's very sympathetic and suggests that I list all of his good and bad qualities, which I do on a serviette using her favourite bingo pen that, for some reason, she's brought out for the evening and we find that there are more negatives than positives. In fact, there's only one positive and that's regarding his love of purple, and we conclude that, although he does seem to love me very much, I don't feel the same way and that if it's not right, I shouldn't try and force it. She looks over to her husband who's fallen asleep and is snoring, and she looks back to me and smiles. I really do hope that when I'm her age, I'm sat there with my love of many years.

Jude has somehow recruited Libby to help him behind the bar as he's a member of staff down and needs to talk with a new rep who has come in with a friend. The rep is unsurprisingly stunning with a skirt so short my new friend tells me she can see what the *young lady has had for breakfast*. Occasionally, he goes back to the bar to get more drinks for his new acquaintances, but other than that, there's not much contact between him and Libby. Perhaps I've got more of a problem with this than she does, although her energy has dropped in the last half hour but this could be down to the fishbowl cocktails we've consumed and the fact she's had a long day. My new friend and her group stand up to leave and we say goodbye. I laugh as I watch them make their way to the door, doing the conga and waving to the customers as they go. I miss them instantly and snuggle into my chair, rest my head against the back, close my eyes and listen to a strangled rendition of '*My Way*' being belted out by a Geordie woman who keeps adding 'Pet' onto each line, much to the amusement of her audience.

'Sleeping Beauty, we meet again,' a voice says very close to my ear, which makes me jump.

I open my eyes to see Seth smiling at me. 'Oh, it's you,' I say, without a smile.

'Ah, just the response a man wants to hear,' he answers with a very straight face and I can't help but smile.

'Sorry,' I reply. 'It's just that I'm so tired. I wasn't asleep.'

'I know,' he replies. 'There was no dribbling or snoring. Unlike earlier. How's your first few hours in Turkey been?'

'Wonderful,' I reply, and decide I will smile at him after

all. It really has been great and it's hard to believe I'm actually here, I've dreamt about it for so long. 'What about your day?'

He rolls his eyes. 'I had a nightmare passenger to collect from the airport but, other than that, great.' He's clearly aching for me to retaliate, but I'm too tired.

'Can you take me home to bed?' I suddenly ask.

'Wow, you're forward,' he replies. 'We've only just met.'

I put my head to one side and squint suspiciously at him, and he smiles back at me. 'I'm exhausted, and I want to go to bed. And Libby seems like she's set to stay for the night, working while your brother entertains the ladies.'

'Sounds about right,' he replies. He looks at Jude, and I see his mouth harden and a frown appear. Then, he turns his gaze to Libby and his eyes and mouth soften. He watches her for a moment and then looks back to me. 'Come on. I'll get you home.'

I stand up to follow him and I can't help but think about how he just looked at Libby. Maybe I misread his expression but I swear there was something there. But, I'm tired and a little tipsy, so it was probably nothing.

Libby's stacking a huge pile of glasses and looks as tired as I feel. I remember that she worked on the 'night flight' transfers last night, plus did a hotel visit earlier today before I arrived. She must be shattered.

'And where are you taking my best friend?' she asks Seth with an accusatory glance.

Seth smiles. 'Don't worry, I'm not stealing her. She needs sleep so I'm taking her to yours. You look like you could do with bed yourself.'

'Give me 5 minutes, and I'll come with you. Jude can get behind the bar instead of wafting around. I'll go and let him know.' She walks quickly towards Jude, where he's still sitting with the two female reps, and I can see him staring at us, then realise it's actually Seth he's looking at. The two brothers' eyes meet and I look from one to the other and decide that there's some sort of conflict there, possibly just a case of brother rivalry, and I make a mental note to ask Libby about them later. Although, why I'm interested, I don't really know.

I follow Seth outside and we sit on some comfy seats just on the edge of the beach. It's cooled down quite a bit now, unless I've just got used to it, and when the patio doors are pulled together it's reasonably quiet although there are still hoards of people walking past, and other bars pumping out music adjacent to this one. But, it's a dull thud rather than a nightclub style boom. I take a deep breath, relishing the smell of the sea and air, and exhale slowly. We sit in silence a while until Seth points out some of the landmarks, both on the shore and at sea. He tells me about the castle near to the marina, and I look towards where he's pointing, noticing the boats, so pretty, lit up and bobbing around. Near to the marina is busy Bar Street which, by this time of night, will be full of young groups and couples, out to dance and drink, Seth tells me. In the very distance I can make out a cruise ship and I point it out to Seth. It looks huge compared to everything else over there. 'You're lucky to see it,' he tells me, 'it's only here generally on a Monday and only for a few hours. It will be gone soon, off to its first port of call.' And, as he says it, we can see it's already left port and is turning, and the foghorn sounds in the distance three times. We can only just hear it. I wonder what it's like on there as a passenger, and try to guess where they're going. I can see the passengers standing on the deck and I decide that a cruise is definitely something on my list to do. I could meet lots of people, visit mysterious lands, and make friends with the

Captain who would invite me to sit at his table when dining, and all the other passengers would wonder who I am. Yes, I really must do that. And, it's probably something I can do on my own too, I bet lots of single people go on cruises.

'I so wish I was on that ship' I say out loud. 'I wonder where it's going?'

'Next stop is Egypt, I think,' Seth replies, 'although they change itinerary every few weeks. I thought a USA road trip was your dream?'

'It is,' I reply, 'but a cruise looks fun too.' I'd forgotten I'd told him about my USA road trip. We sit in silence again and I look at him as he watches the ship continue on its journey away from the port. He's still smiling and I can see the small creases at the sides of his eyes, and how they glisten in the moonlight. His wavy blonde hair appears less unruly than his brother's and looks soft and well cut. Suddenly I find myself touching it and it makes him jump.

'Sorry,' I say, blushing. 'I thought I saw something in it, a spider or insect. But there's nothing. Nothing at all. Not a sausage.'

Seth laughs. 'Well, I'm pleased about that. Especially the lack of sausage in it, that would be...weird.'

I nod and look away whilst he brushes his hands through his hair. I have no idea what just gave me the urge to touch him like that. After all, I've known him for, what? A few hours? And, why did I bring a sausage into the conversation? 'How long have you been here?' I ask him, to hastily change the subject.

He puts his head on one side as he thinks about it. 'Five years, almost to the day,' he says. 'I'd been working in Spain for a while and Jude wanted me to bring the car over for some reason or other, so I drove it over here and ended up staying to help him set up his business. And I've never left.'

Wow, the furthest I'd ever driven a car was for a hiking trip to Wales with the girls from the office. How did he drive it from Spain to Turkey? I can't help but feel a little in awe of Seth and his travelling adventures, and I realise how boring my life must seem in comparison. I feel a little ashamed about what I've done with my life so far, or not done to be more accurate, and how different it's been compared to the dreams I had as a young girl. If he asks me to talk about myself I'm going to have to make something up, like how I travelled across Russia to find the birthplace of a literary hero, even though I don't know any. I need to get my story straight just in case, and make a mental note to research the topic at the next available opportunity.

'What help did Jude need?' I ask. He doesn't seem the kind of guy to need any help, if you ask me. Confident, a touch arrogant, and very much in control. He reminds me a little of Grant, except for the three-quarter length trousers. Grant wouldn't wear those if you paid him, he spends his whole time during the summer months tutting at people that do.

'Jude's good at the front facing stuff, and knowing what customers enjoy and want, but he struggles with the serious side of business, like the finances. He has lots of plans, and will succeed whether I help him or not, but won't necessarily achieve his goals in the most moral or financially viable way. He acts first and thinks later.'

'Libby is a little like that,' I say. 'She gets so excited about things and jumps straight in with no plan in place, whereas I'm a little more cautious.' I can't help but worry about her being with Jude if they're both so spontaneous. She needs someone to keep her feet on the ground and it sounds like he does too.

'Really?' Seth replies. 'I haven't seen that side to her at all.

Has she told you about her business idea?'

'Yes,' I answer quite simply. I wouldn't be surprised if Seth knows more about it than I do. 'I hope she's thought it through properly, and that it's all legal and above board.'

Seth nods. 'She seems to have done her homework, but she's going to find it tough. She could do with a business partner, for support and to watch her back. It's a very competitive industry around here.' I don't like the sound of that but, then again, what right do I have to worry about her when she's done well so far, with her new life here, and with no help at all from anyone. She's more switched on than I'll ever be.

'Like Jude?' I ask. Seth looks confused. 'As her business partner,' I add, 'do you think they could work together?'

'No, definitely not,' he replies, a little more aggressively than I'd expected. He sits and shakes his head. 'Jude wants to but it wouldn't be the best move for Libby. She needs someone sensible.' Talking about Jude has changed Seth's mood again so I change the subject.

'What about your parents? Are they in the UK still?'

'Nope,' he replies, 'Spain. Although, they travel between the two quite a bit and occasionally visit us here.'

I think of my own parents and their lack of travelling, the furthest being a quick trip to Istanbul once and to Fort William in Scotland for one of their wedding anniversaries. It's no wonder I'm not the adventurous sort. Mind you, they seldom spend more than a few days in each other's company, and can barely make their way around a supermarket without getting lost.

'What's your first impression of this place,' Seth suddenly asks.

I think carefully and then say 'Beautiful, hot, alluring and vibrant.'

'Yes, but enough about me. What do you think of Marmaris?'

I narrow my eyes at him again but, when he smiles, I have to smile back. I can't help but admit he's growing on me. 'I can see why Libby doesn't want to come home. I really hoped she would, but that's never going to happen. Not when she has all of this.'

Seth doesn't answer, but he gently nods his head in agreement. There's nothing back at home that can beat what she has here, not even me. I suddenly realise that there's actually nothing back at home for me either. A few days ago, I may have said Grant, but not anymore. It's over between us, I've just the formalities to sort.

'So, why don't you stay and give this a go?' he asks me, as if reading my mind.

I shake my head and say, 'Can't.'

'Why?'

I look down at the floor. 'Its complicated, I can't just leave home. I've things to do and sort, a job. Commitments.' Only one of these things is actually true, my job. But, it's not as though I'm indispensable, or that anyone would particularly notice if I wasn't there.

'Commitments,' Seth repeats, 'of course, I forgot. The fiancé. Or boyfriend. Whatever he is, he's someone to go home for I'm sure.'

I sigh. 'I'm not so sure about that. But, I've things to sort out where he's concerned. Anyway, Libby is settled here, she wouldn't want me cramping her style.'

We both look up and watch her in the bar, chatting to Jude who has finally moved away from the young women he was entertaining. Seth and I realise at the same time that they seem to be having some sort of row as Jude slams his hand on the bar surface.

Seth jumps up as though he's going to dive back into the bar, but stands still and watches. I stand too and watch Libby who's now walking towards us with just a quick look back towards Jude who's already making his way back to the women.

'What was all that about?' I ask Seth.

He shrugs his shoulders. 'Get used to it, they squabble all the time.' I raise my eyebrows in surprise. I know Libby can be a little feisty when she's passionate about something but I have never seen her as the squabbling type, she's just too laid back for an argument, unless she's fighting her corner.

Libby reaches us and smiles with not even a hint of any upset. 'Let's go,' she says.

Seth turns and starts to lead the way. I link my arm in Libby's and we follow him. 'You ok?' I ask.

'I'm fine,' she says. We both glance back at Jude as we leave the bar, but he's not looking. He's too busy deep in conversation with his female entourage. 'Just a business disagreement. Jude's still not keen on my jeep idea and wants me to hold off on the launch for a week or so. But I said no, we start in a couple of days and told him to butt out.'

'A couple of days?' I knew it would be at some time during my visit, but I hadn't realised it would be that quick. 'I need sleep for about a week before I can do any type of work.' Libby laughs and I realise that she doesn't think I'm being serious. But the thought of any work within the next fortnight makes me shudder. I'll talk to her about this in the morning, now is not the right time.

We walk towards Seth's car and I'm incredibly grateful that he has it parked close by. The walk to the beach was lovely, but I don't think I could do the return trip, not tonight. For the first time since I arrived, it feels chilly but, as everyone else is walking around in minimal clothing still, I think it's probably tiredness rather than the temperature having dropped. I make a loud and exaggerated 'brrrr' sound as we reach the car, as though it's started snowing and I'm wearing a bikini, and Seth opens the boot and takes out a jacket, which he places around my shoulders. I thank him and climb into the back of the car, which isn't easy seeing as it's really a two seater, and I expect Libby to climb in with me but she puts the passenger seat down and climbs in the front. It's understandable when there's hardly any space back here, but I'm still a bit miffed. Trust Seth to have a sporty little car without proper seats in it. I fidget around and get into a semi-comfortable position where I can rest my head against the back of the seats and we set off, the three of us in silence. I watch as Seth turns to Libby and puts his hand on her arm. She turns to look at him, gives his hand a squeeze and lets go, then looks straight ahead. Seth watches her for a few more seconds and then turns his gaze back to the road. I feel a little uncomfortable, as though I'm intruding and shouldn't be here, and I'm jealous of their friendship and, for some reason, want him to look at me like that. But, that's a ridiculous thought, I've only just met him and it's not as though I like him much, is it? Actually, yes, I do, but that's beside the point. I can't help but feel there's something going on between them, or possibly has been in the past. Libby's never mentioned it, but then again, why would she?

It's only a few minutes before we reach the apartment, having been passed by a couple of minibuses, full of people who seem to get off at random stop points, only to be replaced by hoards of others waiting to get in. It feels so late, but when I look at my watch, it's only just gone 11pm. And, it looks as though a night out in Marmaris has only just started for many, the paths are full of tourists, all dressed up and off to party.

I peel myself out of the car, indelicately as it's such a squash to get through the small gap between the door and front seat, and Libby pulls me out. I go to give the jacket back to Seth but he tells me to keep it and he'll pick it up tomorrow. The thought of seeing him the next day pleases me, despite how much he annoyed me when he came to collect me from the airport, and I say a polite goodnight, let him kiss me on each cheek and walk away to leave them both to say goodbye to each other. I go through the archway, smiling up at the swan glistening in the moonlight, and I can smell the subtle scent of the flowers and plants from the balconies. I look back as I hear the car engine start and wave as Seth drives away.

I have all intentions of sitting with Libby and chatting on the sofa, like the old days, but as soon as I get in the apartment and kick off my shoes, remembering to put them on the mat, and plonk my bottom down on the comfy cushions, I can feel my eyes instantly become heavy. Libby looks at me and smiles.

'Get to bed and have a good night's sleep,' she says. As I go to refuse, she puts her hand up at me. 'I've been up since the early hours too and really need my sleep. Go and get ready and I'll put a glass of water next to the bed. You'll be gasping by the morning, after all that wine and fish bowls and the heat. And remember, don't drink from the tap!'

Oh yes, I almost forgot that. It apparently can wreck havoc with the tummy and it's not a pleasant thought. Particularly as you're not allowed to put toilet paper down the toilets here, you have to put it in a little bin next to it. I thought Libby was joking, but it's true. I've witnessed it in the bar toilets tonight. I've forgotten twice already and hope

I haven't caused a sewer emergency. Can toilet paper be traced back to an owner?

I kiss her on the cheek, pause and then kiss her on the other one. Well, that's what everyone seems to do here, and I make my way to the bathroom. By the time I get to my bed, the water is there on the bedside cabinet, the ceiling fan is twirling and the lights are all off in the rest of the apartment. So, I get undressed, take off what little make-up I had on, fall into bed and close my eyes ready for a peaceful night's sleep.

CHAPTER SEVEN

What the hell is that noise? I wake with a start, taking a few seconds to realise where I am, and am instantly terrified by the wailing I can hear from outside. At least, I hope it's outside and not in the apartment. It's barely light, if at all, and I scramble to find my watch next to the bed. I then have to find my phone, to shine on my watch, and realise I could just use the phone to tell me what the hour is. Just gone 6am?

There must be some sort of emergency happening, there's no other explanation, and I'm scared. How am I supposed to deal with an emergency in a foreign country? I can barely get outside to the assembly point at work when we have a fire alarm test, I just seem to turn into a headless chicken. But, I suddenly realise that I've got Libby here and she'll know what to do. I'll go and find her, and I just hope she hasn't already dashed outside and left me here.

I rush out of my room, expecting to find Libby floundering around in a similar state, but she's nowhere to be seen. Yet, it's as loud in the kitchen and lounge as it was in the bedroom and I step out onto the balcony where I'm hit with the noise at an even higher volume. Yet, there's absolutely no one moving around when I look down to the street. I listen for a minute, and then step back inside, closing the balcony doors and sitting on the sofa for a little longer just in case Libby comes to join me. I wonder if I should go and wake her but decide not to, if the noise hasn't woken her, there's little chance that I will. How can she be sleeping through this? Still, if she's not bothered by it, it can't be something that's life threatening, or could be declared a national emergency.

As suddenly as it started, the noise stops and peace is restored. I stay still for a few more seconds, just in case it starts again, and then wander slowly back to bed. I decide to change into my slightly more modest pyjamas, just in case it happens again and we end up outside, congregating in the street waiting for the emergency services to come and rescue us. I glance at my phone and see more missed calls from Grant which must have come in last night after I'd gone to bed. I keep forgetting about the two hour time difference but would have been too tired to have dealt with him last night plus, having had a drink or two, it would have ended in a row, or with me doubting my decision and promising something I wouldn't be able, or be willing, to honour upon waking. We can re-start the argument later today. I throw my phone on the floor, refusing to read the texts, or listen to the voicemails, and I close my eyes, soon drifting back off to sleep.

When I wake again, I feel surprisingly refreshed and see, when I look at my watch, that I've had another two hours sleep since the disturbance. I lie still for a moment and watch the ceiling fan going slowly around but soon feel dizzy and so climb out of bed. I can hear the clinking of mugs and spoons coming from the kitchen so I pull on a light dressing gown and walk through to find Libby there. We hug each other, delighted to be saying good morning face to face after all these months, and she grabs my hand and leads me to the balcony where she's set it up ready for breakfast. My eyes widen at the sight of naughty food that I've had to avoid for the last year or so. Bread, jam and pastries. My stomach rumbles in anticipation of being reunited with its long, lost love – carbs - and I sit down and dive straight in.

'I could get used to this, having my breakfast ready for me each morning,' I say.

'Don't get too comfy,' Libby replies, 'I'm just being nice to you as it's your first day here, but you can get your own from tomorrow.' I laugh and then realise she's being serious.

'Charming,' I say and she smiles. I point at one of the plates. 'Pancake roll for breakfast?'

'Borek.'

'I only asked,' I reply and we giggle. I bite the cigar shaped pastry. 'Yum, this is gorgeous,' even if I have no idea what it is I'm eating.

'I made the borek first thing,' Libby says. 'It's just filo pastry, with goats cheese and spinach inside. Glad you like it.'

'You made it?' I ask, and realise that I'm pulling a face that is actually saying 'you're kidding me?' I know I sound and look really rude, but honestly, I still can't believe that Libby cooks, and does a brilliant job of it too. Filo pastry? That's something I've only ever seen done on the 'Great British Bake Off.' Can my friend be turning into Mary Berry? Within seconds, I've eaten it and am grabbing another. Libby sits watching me, and I realise I look like a pig, but I honestly don't care.

I suddenly remember the noise I heard in the night. 'I can't believe you missed the incident,' I say, learning forward, eyes open wide. I stand and look out over the balcony to see if I can spot anything that I may have missed in my sleep-induced confused state a few hours ago.

'What incident?'

'That noise!' Libby frowns and then shrugs her shoulders. Is she kidding me? 'How could you have slept through it?' I ask. Maybe it's all those nightclubs she's been to since working here, they've broken her ears. 'It shook the walls,' I say, my voice getting louder, eyes emphasising each word to help her try to recollect what I'm talking about. She still doesn't get it and goes back to eating her bread and jam. 'All that wailing,' I shout, and do an impression.

Libby still doesn't look up but sighs. 'It's Ezan, you numpty,' she replies.

I frown. 'Who's he?' I ask.

'Not he, it's the call to prayer. Have you not seen how close we are to a mosque just here?'

She points in the direction of the back of the flat and I look around the side of the balcony, quickly seeing the minaret of a mosque literally a stone's throw away. 'They call to prayer 6 times a day. We don't generally hear the first one, it's at about 4-ish at this time of year. But, the dawn one is loud. It's beautiful, isn't it? I loved it when I was first here and it used to wake me, but I sleep through it now. Luckily, I catch the others through the day if I'm around.'

'Luckily?' Wow, it confirms my concerns about her hearing. 'What's the plans for today?' I ask, changing the subject.

'We need to go to the supermarket, to get some food in. We'll catch a dolmuş.' She sees me raise my eyebrows and smiles. 'A minibus.'

'Where's the bus stop?' I have images of it being miles away up a dirt track and of us standing in the blazing sun. After all, it's hot already and the day has only just begun. I was kind of hoping that yesterday's weather was a one-off.

'There's not a bus stop as such,' she says as she gets up and takes her plate through to the kitchen. The apartment is small enough for us to continue chatting whilst she's inside and I remain on the balcony. Back home, I'd have to follow her, as Grant's apartment is enormous. 'You just flag them down wherever you are when they pass you,' Libby calls out. Ah, that explains what I saw last night, along the main road on our way back home

Although it's only a trip to a supermarket, I'm quite excited. I haven't been grocery shopping for what feels like months, as Grant insists on doing it online and takes full charge, probably so I'm not tempted to put any refined products or carb-laden goodies into the trolley. I think he has a list of favourites stored, titled 'tasteless and bland,' which he sets to automatically re-order each week. I've been so tempted to slip the driver a bit of cash to sneak in some tasty goodies. I wonder if they're allowed to do that? I would, if someone asked me to. I'd be known as 'the woman who will get you what you need and not let anyone else know'. Could I be arrested for that? If so, I might pass.

I'm also keen to use the trip to find my bearings as I slept during the drive into town yesterday, and I didn't see anything until I reached Libby's, so I'm bursting to see the place in daylight. My thoughts turn to Seth. We didn't exactly get off to a great start, and I accept I insulted him numerous times, although I was provoked. I hope that he's forgotten the worst of my behaviour and that the time I spent with him yesterday evening made up for my earlier rudeness. For some reason, I'm keen for us to be friends.

My phone buzzes in my pocket and I retrieve it, glancing quickly at the screen and see that I've now 17 text messages from Grant. I should be thinking about ending one relationship before even thinking about starting a friendship with another guy. On top of this, a waiter has already given me his number. I can't help but say 'I'm such a slut' out loud, which is a slight exaggeration.

'About time,' Libby says, and picks up the phone to see the missed messages, and looks at me sympathetically.

'I guess I should ring him,' I say.

'Have you read any of the texts?'

I shake my head, and take the phone back to start the dreaded job. I read the top two and shrug. 'They start a bit nasty, then nice, then desperate, and end on a nasty. He probably thinks I'm ignoring him, which I am.'

'Yes, and add to that the fact you turned down his proposal and have gone off for a month to be with a friend he doesn't like very much,' Libby adds. 'That's probably made the control freak even worse than normal. Well, we'll go in 40 minutes which should give you time to get showered and ready. So, if you want to talk with the BCF, do it quick before we go. I don't want a grumpy face on the ride into town. You'll scare the tourists.' Libby stands and walks to the kitchen, patting my shoulder affectionately as she goes.

I sigh. The phone call needs to be made so I might as well get it over with. I press the number listed in my favourites and wait for it to connect then suddenly remember the time difference and cut off quickly. It will be really early back home and, although he's sent a text within the last half hour, he might have since gone back to sleep. I try to think what he'd be doing right now. Is it one of the mornings where he gets up early and goes to the gym? I just can't think straight, I've only been away 24 hours but it feels a lifetime has passed by, and I've lost track of what was, up until a short time ago, normality. Is this 'phone call procrastination'? Probably. But it means I may have an argument-free morning if I avoid a conversation with him.

I decide I'd better send a text to at least show willing. This may appease him although I doubt it. 'Bit early to call. Speak later?' I press send, and watch it go, then feel guilty I didn't put a kiss on the end. So I quickly type 'x' and send again, which I regret instantly. I often send kisses to people by accident, out of habit. I've sent several texts to Mr Simpson at work with an accidental kiss at the end of it. I also once sent a dodgy photo which was meant for Grant, and Mr Simpson couldn't look at me for a week without blushing. I made up some story about it being a photo of a risqué burlesque dancer I'd seen in Covent Garden but even Mr Simpson knows that burlesque ladies don't do those type of poses...

I quickly send another text to try and balance things out. 'Off out for day. Bye,' with no kiss. I put the phone away, before I'm tempted to text again and make things even worse.

I finish up my breakfast, stuffing the last of those little filo pastry things in my mouth, and take my plate and cup through to the kitchen. Then I go off to shower and get ready for the day, including make-up which I'd rather not be putting on at all as I know it will melt away within a couple of hours, but I feel so white and frumpy compared to my glamorous and sun-kissed friend. And, you never know who you might bump into, do you? Not that I'm expecting to meet anyone at all, but I could see someone like Hamil from the bar, or someone famous. Or Seth. Not that I'm interested in seeing Seth, but well, you need to look your best, don't you?

As I pass through the lounge I can hear Libby in her bedroom on the telephone. I catch her saying Seth's name, and I'm not sure if she's speaking to him, or about him, as she's whispering and it makes me feel disappointed that she finds it necessary to do this as she never had secrets from me when we lived together. What is it that she's keeping me out of? And what's it got to do with Seth? I'm not sure why it even bothers me, but it does. I just have to accept that she has her own life here, and I'm just a visitor sharing it with her for a short while. Anyway, she could have been speaking to Seth about work, or about Jude, and that's if she was speaking to Seth at all. There's nothing to say it's anything secret and, after all, I'm just over the moon that I'm here, with her.

CHAPTER EIGHT

Well, travelling in a dolmuş is definitely an experience that cannot be compared to anything I've encountered before. I've been in some packed mini-buses, normally to do with hen weekends, or work outings, where it's all become a little squashed and raucous, but I've never been crammed into one quite like this. Libby tells me that dolmuş actually means 'stuffed,' and I can see why. There are loads of these little buses driving around, all full to the brim. Libby let me sit in a seat near the front and the driver gestured to her to sit on a cushion balanced on the wheel arch next to me. She doesn't seem to find this unusual, whereas I 'm sitting wide eyed, staring at her hunched up, looking like a little gnome fishing. She rests her head back on the window and closes her eyes. Wow, she looks tired. I can only imagine how demanding her job must be physically, what with the hours and the heat. I think of my job back home and there's no comparison. The most tiring day there is when we have to do an audit of all the office equipment, so that Mr Simpson can update his database that his son-in-law designed for him, for what reason, no one knows. I wonder what they're doing right now, back in the office. I bet Tina has been sent to the post office for yet another book of stamps as the boss insists on posting everything rather than using email as he doesn't trust anything electronic other than the infamous database. He said he read something about Trojan Horses and that it will cause a huge problem if we get a 'herd' of them on our network.

As we get near to a roundabout, a guy flags down the dolmuş and gets on, placing a goat on my lap as he pays the driver. An actual goat, with huge horns and long, brown matted hair. It eyes me suspiciously and bleats in my face, making me jump violently. An old lady next to me laughs and shakes her head and Libby is literally wetting herself whilst the goat continues to stare me out. The guy waits for his change, which the driver is sorting whilst driving at the same time – I'm freaked out so much that I don't know if I'll ever get on one of these dolmuş things again. Then, the man turns round, takes the goat from my lap and shuffles through the gap between the two front seats to sit next to the driver in the passenger seat. The driver shows no sign that he cares about the four-legged passenger, it's obviously quite normal dolmuş etiquette. But I swear I'm permanently scarred for life. The goat continues to stare at me, peeping round the seats, and gives the occasional bleat which just sets Libby and the old lady off again.

Although an animal lover, I'm cross with this wiry haired, smelly creature as I realise I've hardly taken in my surroundings so far on the journey as I've been watching the daft animal in case it butts me or something. This is too weird. I realise how the bars and shops that we're passing are dwindling in numbers. We drive for another half a minute or so, then Libby stands up, says something to the driver which I presume is stop, and grabs my arm to pull me up to follow her. As the dolmuş comes to a halt, I jump out and the goat gives a loud bleat and everyone in the vehicle laughs, including Libby. I force an embarrassed smile, which suggests I find it funny too, but I really don't and awkwardly brush my skirt down, wondering how many bugs and fleas I have jumping all over me. I can still smell the animal and a guy walks past and I'm sure he wrinkles up his nose, so I say loudly to him 'It was a goat,' causing him to speed up quickly to get away from me, and Libby to squeal with laughter. I'm so pleased that I've caused so much entertainment for everyone. Not.

The sun is intense, feeling as though it's increased by 10 degrees since boarding the dolmuş, and we pass several families walking, obviously off to the beach, the adults carrying all manner of equipment such as balls and lilos, and the children running around, with sun hats on and hopefully layers of sun cream. I can't imagine they can stay on the beach too many hours because, if they did, they'd frazzle. We soon find ourselves turning into the car park outside a supermarket and the good news is that people coming out look considerably cooler than us going in, and so I am pretty sure there's air conditioning in there.

I'd really thought that supermarkets are the same the world over, selling the same types of foods and goods, but it's so different. It's the colours of the fresh food, vibrant and varied, with a rich smell. I try to explain this to Libby but I know she doesn't get it. She's been here too long now and takes it all for granted, it's her new '*normal.*' She walks up and down the aisles, popping things into her basket, which I instantly take out, look at, turn around in my hands and then place back. This appears to annoy her a bit, but I need to know what each item is and the packaging doesn't always make it obvious.

I notice that the customers are a mixture of locals and

tourists, the latter walking around in shorts and strappy vest tops. Some of the females are even in bikini tops, which I think is pretty disrespectful, and the men with no shirts on at all. It's revolting. I'm sure they wouldn't do this in their own local store back home and I find the close proximity of their flesh with fresh produce a little distasteful. Boobies on the bananas is just not right and I tell Libby, who agrees with me, and we watch the locals scowl at the scantily clad shoppers and I quickly join them to show my distaste. After all, I'm virtually a local, I'm here for a month. I might try and design a leaflet of some sort, to suggest appropriate apparel whilst food shopping, and Libby could hand them out on the coach transfers from the airport. And, I'll be really popular as a crusader for decency and will be in all the local newspapers. The supermarkets will adore me, *the mysterious traveller who cares*. I so wish I carried around a notepad and pen to record these bursts of inspiration as I know I'll have forgotten it by the time I get back to Libby's.

At the till, it's obvious the cashier and Libby know each other quite well as they chat away in Turkish. I obviously have no idea what they're talking about but Libby gestures to me and the cashier smiles and waves, and I wave back then turn and look outside at the car park which is quite full, but with cars parked higgledy piggledy and not quite in the marked spaces. No one appears to mind. If this were home, there'd be an officious parking space enforcement person, walking around and pointing to cars, measuring the distance of the tyres from the lines and issuing tickets which demand a ridiculous amount of money.

I quickly catch Libby up as I realise she's walking towards the exit and we carry a bag or two each. 'You up for a walk back?' Libby asks.

At first, I think of how far it was by bus, and have a slight wobble as my body contemplates the feat ahead. Can I walk that far? But then I think of the goat, and how my legs are itching, and my skirt smells of goat fleas and goodness knows what else, and a walk seems the best option. 'We can stop on the way for a drink,' she says, and I nod. I guess I can make it. Crossing over the road is a feat in itself. Wow, these drivers are crazy. I fear we'll need to stand at the side, waiting for a break in the traffic, for ages, it's so busy. But Libby grabs my arm and pulls me right into the road, and I close my eyes preparing to die together. A car pulls up sharp, which is just as well as Libby keeps going, and all he does is toot his horn and she puts her hand up to acknowledge the fact he's there, but keeps her eyes forward and marches on to the opposite kerb. I just decide to keep my eyes forward too, although I'm tempted to close them again until we reach the other side. I look round to see locals crossing confidently too and it's only the tourists who are standing on the paths, clinging on to each other and looking desperately for any opportunity to cross this crazy road.

We chat as we walk, just about *stuff*, like what's changed in the Abingdon High Street since Libby left. Which, in fact, is absolutely nothing. And what films are in the cinema at the moment, which actually I have no idea about as Grant doesn't like the cinema and I don't like going on my own. The only time I tried it, a strange man sat behind me and made funny noises every time a mild racy scene came on. I dread to think what he was doing. I'll have to go out to places on my own now, and thoughts of my impending separation from Grant make me check my phone and I spot a couple of missed calls from him. I decide it's best I ring, I owe him that at least, and it will mean the texts may then stop. It's a bit later now and I hopefully won't wake him.

After a couple of rings he answers. And it goes something

like this:

'Yep?'

'Hi Grant, it's me.'

'Yes, I know.'

'You ok?'

'Yep.'

<Awkward silence>

'Sorry I missed your calls and texts.'

'Well, you're obviously busy. I've got to go, in the middle of something. With someone'

<Line goes dead>

I grimace and Libby asks 'Good phone call?' with a teasing twinkle in her eye.

I sigh and we continue walking. I see that I've missed a couple of texts too from Grant and they give an indication as to why he sounded so pissed off with me. 'Any chance of you ringing to say you're ok? Don't you care about us at all?' And... 'If you don't ring me in the next ten minutes, I'll presume you don't give a shit and have already moved on.' That came in an hour ago, probably whilst I was playing with the food in the vegetable aisle. He'll either decide that I haven't bothered to read his texts, or, that I've already given up on us. I feel a mild pang of guilt as I realise both of these options are actually true.

After passing several clothes stores, we end up back at the first bar we visited last night and take a seat outside under the shelter of a parasol. It's barely 10:30am and there's already a scattering of sunbathers spread out along the beach. They'll be frazzled by midday.

'I'm not sure I want alcohol,' I say to Libby.

She laughs. 'I'm having a coffee, actually, so that's fine.'

'Oh, me too,' I add, although I actually did fancy some alcohol if I'm honest, just a refreshing cocktail, but I guess it is still early. The waiter arrives and I look up to be met by a dazzling smile and huge dark eyes twinkling at me. 'Hamil,' I say, and he nods, then reaches for my hand, kisses it and holds it tight. I've impressed myself that I've remembered his name, as that's really not a strength of mine although, in fairness, I stared at the serviette he wrote his name and phone number on several times before I went to bed last night and then again this morning. I realise he's still holding my hand and feel Libby's stare from across the table, so I pull it carefully away. He turns and kisses Libby on the cheeks and says, 'Two coffees?', acknowledges her response, looks at me for a few seconds then turns and goes back inside.

'Put your tongue away,' Libby says.

'He's gorgeous. All dark and mysterious and smells all… Turkish.'

Libby laughs. 'What does 'Turkish' smell like exactly?'

I actually don't know and have no idea why I said that and so I just shrug. I continue to watch him walk around inside the bar and can't help but notice how tight his black trousers are at the back.

'Stop ogling,' Libby says and kicks my leg gently.

'I was admiring the tailoring of his trousers,' I reply quite seriously. I know she doesn't believe me and so I turn my attention to the beach. In the distance, to the left, I spot another cruise ship moored in the port and wonder how many of the people walking past us have come from it to explore what's on land. I don't see anyone that looks like a cruise passenger. I'd definitely look like one. I'd dress stylish yet nautical, and everyone would know straight away that I'm an exotic traveller on an adventure at sea. I'm a little disappointed that, if any of the passers by are passengers, they haven't really got into the spirit of things.

I think back to my conversation with Seth last night about

the cruise ships and wonder what he's up to today. I find myself picturing him in a tight pair of trousers like Hamil's and smile, and then I shake my head to remove the thought. What is wrong with me? I blame it on the sun.

Hamil brings our coffees and, after walking away, we laugh at how he's put a small biscuit on my plate but not on Libby's.

'Favouritism,' she says.

'He's just making me feel welcome,' I reply. 'I'm a new girl in town and I need looking after.'

'Maybe I do too,' she replies.

'As if,' I laugh. She laughs too. I've never known Libby need looking after by anyone.

'Hamil's a nice guy,' she says, 'but don't tell Jude I said that. He can't stand him.'

'Why?' I can't imagine anyone not liking Hamil, although I think females may form a more favourable opinion of him than males.

'Long story,' she says. 'Hamil worked for Jude for a while, was his headwaiter. But, he left quite suddenly after they had a row over something. Or, as Jude says, a difference of opinion. And that was that. Jude hasn't spoken to him since.'

'Bit harsh,' I reply. 'Must have been something important for Jude to have reacted like that.' Sounds a bit more serious than a difference of opinion.

Libby shakes her head. 'Once Jude makes up his mind, that's it. There's no going back. I wouldn't want to get on the wrong side of him, that's for sure.'

I can totally see how Jude could be like that, even from the short time I've spent with him. He's got that look, a demeanour that's hard to explain, that you can feel rather than see. He reminds me a little of Grant and I find that ironic, considering how Libby and Grant clash, yet she's fallen for a man with similar attributes. I wonder if Seth shares any of his brother's characteristics and I really hope he doesn't.

We sit and chat for about half an hour until I volunteer to go inside and pay for the coffees, just so I can see Hamil, but am disappointed to be served by another waiter. Although, I perk up a little when I notice his trousers have similar tailoring. I suddenly feel a little ashamed of my lecherous behaviour, it really isn't like me and maybe it's just the thing with Grant, and the heat and sun. We leave and buy an ice cream from a neighbouring kiosk and I carry it in one hand whilst holding two of the grocery bags in another. As we come to the road that we need to turn at, Libby points ahead of us. 'This is the path you follow if you want to go to the bazaar and marina. You can't miss it.'

Bazaar! 'Ooh, we could go this afternoon.' I've read up about the bazaars, they sound fab, full of hidden treasures, an Aladdin's cave.

'No can do,' she replies 'I've got to go and cover an airport run. Text came in this morning. So, you could go and explore on your own and tell me all about it when I get back?'

What? On my own? Is she crazy? Libby knows I can barely find my way around Abingdon, a town I've lived in for years. What hope is there for me in a place I've known for less than 24 hours? I'll end up lost or kidnapped. Yes, I'll be kidnapped and no one will ever see me again because, even if I escape my captors, I won't know where to go and then Libby will feel guilty and will wish she hadn't let me out of her sight, and my mother will hold her responsible forever.

'Don't panic,' she says, knowing that I'm concocting some type of drama in my head. 'It'll be good for you, an adventure. And, it's a straight road there and back. Even *you* can't get lost.'

I sigh as I accept it's only for a few hours and I guess it will give me a chance to buy Libby a little something. I didn't get the opportunity to shop for her before coming over, not even in the duty-free shop at the airport, and so I accept my fate and hope that I not only find my way there, I find my way back too.

CHAPTER NINE

A couple of hours later, after a light lunch and twenty minutes nap on the balcony, I'm walking along the promenade heading towards what I hope is the bazaar and marina. There's a lot of people milling around, again a mixture of tourists and locals, and I can feel the intense heat beating down on me as I follow the light coloured path. I can see the pathway stretches a long way ahead, almost dead straight, and I pretend in my head that I'm Dorothy following the yellow brick road. I even have a little sing to myself, which attracts the attention of a few people walking past me in the opposite direction.

I'm pleased I've worn my floppy hat as well as my sunglasses, as the reflection from the path is blinding. I feel like a bit of an adventurer, navigating my way around this foreign land alone. Well, a slight exaggeration, I'm just making my way along a path to a bazaar with a hundred other tourists but there's still a multitude of potential hazards, I'm sure.

I soon find myself at the foot of a statue of a man and stop to read a plaque at his feet that informs me I'm looking at Ataturk. As I stand there, squinting in the sunlight trying to concentrate, a guy approaches me. 'Boat taxi?' he asks.

I look up at him, shake my head, but smile as he seems quite friendly and nice. 'No, not right now, another day maybe. I'm off for a walk.'

I turn back to carry on reading the sign, feeling it's a little too rude to walk off straight away, but he continues to stand there so I feel obliged to make conversation. And, he's definitely up for chatting. Before long, I've found out quite a bit about Ataturk, how he was the founder of the Republic of Turkey, and the first president, and I must say I think he sounds like a really decent guy, transforming the country by building schools and making primary education free and compulsory. And, he even brought in a new alphabet, which increased the literacy in Turkey to over 70% within a few years. I find this quite impressive and want to know more, but my new tour guide keeps asking questions about the UK, which I've no clue about; politics and history are really not my strong points. And, he asks me if I've met a) the Queen b) any of the Spice Girls and c) either of the Hairy Bikers (he's apparently seen their cooking show on YouTube). He's disappointed I haven't met any of them and so I thank him for our chat and politely decline his 8th offer of a boat taxi to a place nearby which I can't pronounce but will ask Libby about later. He doesn't seem offended and points me in the direction of the bazaar, waving goodbye enthusiastically and jumping back on his boat which now has a couple of tourists waiting next to it. After walking another hundred yards past more boat taxi guys, all asking me to join them, I find myself going through the main entrance to the bazaar. I silently congratulate myself for finding my way here, and for staying safe from potential risks and hazards. I guess I'm a better explorer than I'd thought.

The sun is no longer beating down on me due to a

covering over the bazaar, which is a see-through plastic type of roof, but it's still pretty warm and I feel as though I'm in a very large greenhouse. There are several pathways criss-crossing each other with shops either side and I'm taken aback by the variety of goods for sale. Clothes, shoes, spices, suitcases, leather – it's incredible. For a moment, I just wander really slowly, taking in the sights and smells which engulf me. Occasionally, I get jostled by the crowds, quite often where worried parents are trying to keep their children with them, which seems to me to be virtually impossible. You could easily lose yourself in here, within seconds, let alone a small child. I can't help but wish that someone was here looking after me, I can't be certain I'll make it out of here before nightfall.

It's hard to get a close look at the goods outside each shop as, the moment you stop to take a peek, you're pounced on and virtually dragged inside. I've no real intention of buying much today, other than a gift for Libby, and I'd really relish the chance to window shop but it's not looking hopeful. I politely say no each time I'm grabbed, and I feel reassured by the fact I'm not alone. Many tourists are in the same boat as I. We should maybe all group together, link arms and storm our way through, gawping confidently at windows. Mind you, some of my fellow wannabe-browsers do seem to ignore the invites, putting their hand up to signify *back off*. So, I start to do the same, but with a smile so I don't appear too rude.

I slowly burrow deeper and deeper into the maze and regularly spin round to keep track of which direction I've come from, but one path starts to merge into another and I soon give up, hoping that I'll find a way back out when the time comes. I guess I can ask someone to point me in the direction of Ataturk.

I notice that one of the stalls has a beautiful collection of carpets hanging down and the colours and weaves draw me towards them. For a moment, I wonder how on earth anyone could transport something so big home until I see a sign which says 'We Send to your House.' Now, I know I can be a bit cynical at times, but is it unreasonable for me to have a teeny bit of doubt that the carpet may not turn up at your door one day in the near future? I'm going to ask Libby about it later. Hey, maybe I could become a carpet delivery specialist, transporting rugs and mats around the world, hand delivering them with a smile. I'll add that to my list of jobs, it's growing everyday.

Whilst staring at the mats, I'm pounced on by a guy selling Turkish teas and spices and, as I'm caught off-guard, I find myself being guided somehow into his shop. I've finally lost the strength to say no.

Inside, I'm sat down quickly on a wooden chair and given a brew to try. I hesitate. This could be a kidnapper's ploy. It could be spiked, and the shop owner could wait patiently for me to collapse and then will cart me off to a waiting car which will whisk me away to goodness knows where. But, I'm also hot, bothered and thirsty and, before I've fully thought this through, I've taken a sip and it's spicy, but pleasant, and the good news is that I haven't passed out. Although I only sipped it seconds ago.

'What is it?' I ask suspiciously.

The man grins, widens his eyes and whispers, 'Sex Tea,' enthusiastically.

I jump up out of my seat. Sex tea? What does he mean? I go to bolt through the door as quickly as I can but stop as I see him laughing. 'Don't worry,' he says, 'it's not bad tea. Not what you say is *dodgy*.' He grins and points at the shelves all around the store and I see boxes of the stuff, all marked as sex tea, with smiley faces and exclamation marks galore on the signs. It can't be bad if it's so publicly advertised, can it? There's all other types of tea too. I sit back down and frown at him.

'It's good, yes?' he asks.

Actually it is, although I'm still not entirely sure that I won't suddenly become amorous and frisky. I nod and then smile at him, which appears to cause huge delight and he pours another drink. 'This time, apple tea,' he announces and gives it to me. 'No sexy lady with this one.' I can't help but smile at him, he's grinning from ear to ear and it's infectious. Plus, this is a tea I've heard of. I have a sip and find it very refreshing.

'You buy, yes?' he asks.

I shake my head. 'I want to buy my friend a present, but she lives here and so would drink this quite often. I need something different.'

'Ah yes,' he says, holding up his finger then dashing off to the back of the store. Within seconds, he's back. He holds up a small pack of glasses. 'For your apple tea with your friend,' he says. I must admit, they are quite sweet, tiny, shaped like a miniature carafe and delicately engraved. Would Libby use them? He takes one out of the packaging and asks me to hold it. I do so and he sits next to me watching me turn it around in my fingers. 'It's good, yes?' he asks, and I nod. I tell him I'll buy them and he claps his hands and blows me a kiss. I'm not entirely convinced Libby will want them but, if not, I'll take them home with me. It's not as though I'll have to run it past Grant to see whether they'll meet the strict entry requirements to join his expensive crystal glasses in the drinks cabinet. They'll be fitting into whatever kitchen I find myself in upon my return to the UK. Probably a dilapidated bedsit somewhere with a communal kitchen area I'll share with a gaggle of students who won't care about my apple tea glasses at all.

He jumps up and starts to wrap them. 'Hold on,' I say, 'how much?' He gives me the price in pounds, which confuses me. 'What is it in Turkish Lira?' I ask. He frowns, as though I've just asked something totally ridiculous, and he gets a calculator to work it out. Why does he need a calculator? It's his own currency. But then I remember Libby saying that you can buy with pounds or euros and that most tourists do. But I'm not a tourist. Well, technically I am, but I'm almost a local, staying here for a month. I have no intention of behaving like a tourist. I tell him about why I'm here, and for how long, and this has no effect whatsoever as he just continues grinning then gives me the price which doesn't sound too bad, and so I accept and they're straight in a plastic bag, on my arm. He insists I drink the rest of my apple tea and asks if I'd like the sex tea too, which I decline hastily. Another customer comes in and I take this as an opportunity to jump up and leave, waving at him as I go.

I'm now exhausted and the shops start to confuse me. In fact, it seems like it's the same five or six shops I've walked past numerous times. Am I going round in circles? Clothes, bags, leather, carpets, spices and belly dancing outfits. How on earth do they all make a living, with so many shopkeepers competing against each other? No wonder they're so aggressive with their selling techniques, they have a lot riding on it.

I decide to try and head towards the centre of the bazaar, for no other reason than presuming it may be a bit of a hub with coffee shops or something, but have no idea how to get to it. So, I follow the direction that the majority of customers are going in and eventually find a small bar with a couple of spare seats outside. I literally fall into the chair and put my head in my hands. I feel, and probably look, a real state and I'd actually do anything to be instantly transported to Libby's apartment in some way, maybe by a time machine. Yes, a time machine. That would work well. But, as this is unlikely to happen, it's best I order a drink before I fully dehydrate and shrivel up. So, when the waiter approaches I point like a typical tourist at the bottle of water on the huge poster next to the kiosk and she smiles and says 'water, of course' in perfect English and walks off, and I feel a little silly. I look around to see if anyone witnessed my awkward tourist moment and see two faces at the neighbouring table smirking at me.

'Come and join us.'

I wasn't expecting to see anyone I know, only having been in the country a day, and I smile uncomfortably at Jude and Seth then move over to their table. I'm kissed on the cheek by both of them and am quite pleased that my floppy hat is hopefully covering the worst of my dishevelled face until Jude announces, 'You look like a beetroot.' I put my hand self-consciously to my face and can feel the heat radiating from it. It's boiling in this bazaar, what does he expect?

The waitress brushes past and puts the water on the table and I thank her, in English. Had I not have bumped into these two, I'd have tried to express my gratitude in Turkish, having learnt 'thank you' last night, but I know I'll make a fool of myself and would rather it not be witnessed.

'Been shopping?' I look up at Seth who is pointing at the plastic bag I've put on the table in front of me.

'Oh, just some glasses, for apple tea. Thought Libby might like them.' I take them out of the bag and show him.

'Doubt it,' sniffs Jude. 'She's not really into glasses. Or apple tea.'

'Oh,' I reply, feeling a little embarrassed. I thought she

might like them, but obviously not. Maybe I'm being a tad sensitive but I'm sure Jude is smirking.

'Pretty though,' Seth says. 'If she doesn't like them, you can keep them and take them back to the UK with you.'

'That's what I thought,' I say. I'm glad he didn't say 'take them back home.' I wonder if he purposefully said the UK. If he did, it was pretty thoughtful of him.

'How much did you pay for them?' asks Jude.

I tell him and he laughs. 'What on earth was the price you started at if that's what you paid?' he asks.

'That was the price the guy said when I asked,' I reply, looking confused.

'You didn't barter?' asks Seth, raising his eyebrows.

Barter? Oh no, I grimace. Libby told me about bartering in one of our online conversations. You're not to pay the starting price, she said, knock them down and haggle. I didn't do any knocking at all, not even a tap.

'They saw you coming,' says Jude and laughs. Seth smiles too, not quite in the same way.

'I wasn't to know,' I say and put the glasses away and tuck the bag down by my feet.

Seth looks at me sympathetically. 'Offer a third of the asking price and go from there,' he says.

I nod and make a mumbled sound that is my way of saying 'thank you' when I'm not actually that thankful at all. I have no plans on going shopping alone again. It's too dangerous, I decide, and touristy. And I'm not a tourist…

I gulp at my water, and it's empty within a minute, but I find another one placed in front of me, courtesy of Seth, within seconds of finishing it. Jude takes a phone call and turns away from us, so Seth and I make small talk, me telling him about the boat trip man, and the statue and he tells me a little more about Ataturk. It's difficult to hear him as Jude's voice gets louder and louder until he suddenly slams the phone down on the table, making me jump.

'Guess who that was?' he asks Seth. His face has darkened and his eyes are wide. Whoever it was has wound him up, that much I know.

I look to Seth who just shrugs his shoulders and turns back to me, but Jude pulls at his arm and makes him turn back to face him.

'Any idea why I got that call?' he asks.

'Why would I?' Seth replies and then repeats it more strongly when Jude snorts at him.

'Well, it's nothing to do with you,' says Jude, 'and don't forget that.' He stands, grabs his phone and turns to leave. Then, spins back and awkwardly kisses me on the cheeks. 'Watch that brother of mine,' he says, 'he's a dark horse, especially with the ladies,' and leaves. Seth watches him go, frowning.

'Brothers,' I say, with a smile and awkward laugh.

Seth nods. 'Do you have any brothers or sisters?' He's clearly trying to change the subject and ease the atmosphere.

'One brother,' I reply, 'Robert, fifteen years older than me, married with three children. We're very different, but fairly close. We don't get to see each other as much as I'd like.' I think of Robert and miss him. I'm very fond of my big brother, even though I don't tell him often enough.

'I'm very different to Jude too. We're nothing alike.'

'I noticed,' I say and sip at my water. They really are so different, both in looks and temperament. 'Must be hard to work together, then.'

Seth nods. 'Totally,' he says, 'but it works most of the time. A vast difference of opinion but we agree to disagree.'

A group of women bustle past and all stop to say hello to Seth. He stands and kisses each on the cheek, which seems to take forever, and asks how they are, and when they answer I can hear that they're British. After a quick chat, they leave, with one of them looking round and smiling at Seth in a 'cutesie' way completely ignoring me, and I watch him looking at her until she's turned the corner out of sight.

'Friends of yours?' I ask, which is quite a ridiculous question as they obviously are.

'Acquaintances, really. Worked in the Akyaka bar a couple of seasons ago, now they've moved on to other things. The one walking at the back of the group is a friend of Libby's, she works as a rep. Her name's Stella.'

'Oh,' I reply. So that's Stella, the one Libby mentioned yesterday. I give the back of her head one of my looks, and will her to look round so she gets the full effect, but she doesn't. I feel a tad jealous and for a moment can't work out which friendship I'm jealous of, whether it's Stella and Libby, or Stella and Seth, although I've no idea why either should bother me.

'I've had a couple of awkward meals at Libby's where I think she's tried to fix us up. You know, I've turned up and Stella's been there, just by coincidence. Took her out a couple of times, but we didn't hit it off.'

'She's pretty,' I say.

'Yes, she is. And fun. But she's not for me.'

I wonder who would be for him, who his ideal woman would be. He's not exactly your average type, with a traditional background and lifestyle. I think it would have to be someone pretty special.

I've downed my second bottle of water but still feel over-heated and put my hand to my nose, feeling the heat bouncing off my hand. Seth is watching me.

'Have you any sun cream?' he asks.

'Yes, thank you,' I snap. 'I just need a bit of time to get

used to the heat. It's alright for you, you're used to it.' I feel extremely self-conscious, knowing I now look like an oompah loompa from *Charlie and the Chocolate Factory*.

I've had enough now and want to leave. 'I need to go,' I say, and stand up, grab my bag of glasses, and turn to walk away from the table, accidentally banging Seth on the head with the bag as I go. 'Sorry,' I say, although not entirely meaning it. That'll teach him for pointing out my Rudolph nose.

Seth stands too. 'I'll walk you out of here, it can be a devil to navigate.'

I scowl at him. 'I'm quite capable of *navigating* my way out of a shopping centre,' I snap. He makes it sound like a military manoeuvre. 'I know exactly where I am, thank you very much, and I don't need a man to help me.' I go to give him some money for the drinks as he sits back down, but he refuses to take it.

'My treat,' he says, 'it's just water.'

I put down some coins anyway. 'I'd rather pay,' I say, and turn to leave.

'Can I at least point you in the right direction?' he asks.

I ignore him. 'Bye,' I say and I spin round and leave.

I've no idea how he can make me smile one minute, then blow a fuse the next. He's so smug and sure of himself, and good looking. Very good looking, with that floppy, curly blonde hair and blue eyes. And large hands, which I couldn't take my eyes off again as they cradled his glass. And good thighs, which I noticed when I bent down to pick up my bag, all tight in those trousers. I'm confused as to why I took any notice of his physical attributes, not when his personality gets me in so much of a tizz. Maybe that sip of sex tea did something after all.

Right, I need to walk out of here. It's only a bazaar for

goodness sake, just shops and lanes and... I totally need help to get out of here. I've no idea which way to go and it all looks the same. I gulp as I realise I'm lost already, so I take a guess and walk down an aisle which I think I remember coming through on the way to the bar. Or did I? It seems to go quickly round in a circle as, within minutes, I'm back where I started and look up to see Seth watching me from the café. He raises his glass of water to me and smiles. I so wish I could tip it straight over his head but I keep walking, pretending that I meant to come back here, stopping and looking at a shop window before scuttling away to avoid the shopkeeper who comes to beckon me in. I take another lane and go to the end of it, but it's a dead end and I have to turn back. Maybe he's gone now, he was ready to go when I left the table. But no, he's still sat there, this time leaning back in the seat, arms folded, still grinning at me. I'm now getting very hot and bothered and can feel a mild panic rising. What if I can't ever get out of here? What if I go round in circles for hours, or even days, and I'll end up living in here forever? The mysterious bazaar woman. And Libby will think I've left already and gone back home. Maybe I should text her, just in case. A last message, telling her how much I love her and to remember me...

Libby thinking I've already gone home... I suddenly burst into tears, right there in the middle of the bazaar. I don't have a home! I put my bag down on the floor whilst I search for a hankie in my bag, and ignore the people that have stopped as they pass and are looking at me. They can look all they like, I'm having a bit of a meltdown here and I've more important things to worry about than looking silly in the middle of a bazaar. Suddenly, I feel someone hold onto my arm and pick my bag up, and it's Seth.

'Come on,' he says, 'let's get out of here,' and I nod

weakly and walk with him. Within a minute, we're out in the sun and I look back to the bazaar, vowing to never go in there again. It should have a safety warning or something. I bet that hundreds of tourists have disappeared in there and never been found. It's brutal.

My phone is vibrating in my bag and I grab at it, see it's Grant ringing and cut if off. That's all I need.

'You ok?' Seth asks.

I nod gently and sniff. 'Fine now thank you, it must have been the heat. And the jet lag.'

'Yes,' he agrees, giving no indication of finding the idea of jet lag from a four-hour flight incredulous. 'I've the car here, let me drive you home.'

'I'm fine, really,' I say, but in a tone that says 'yes please, carry me to the car and get me straight home.' He holds my hand and I don't pull it away, but just follow him the short distance to where he's parked. I honestly don't think I could walk back all the way to the apartment, not feeling like this, in the bright sun and blistering heat.

I keep my eyes closed all the way back in the car and, when we arrive at the flat, he gets out and opens the door for me and I thank him and walk slowly away. 'Your bag,' he shouts and I turn to see him holding up the apple tea glasses. As I walk back to get them, I hear Libby call out and see that she's run out to the car. She takes one look at me, then looks to Seth, then back to me and wraps her arms around me. 'You ok?' she asks.

I just shake my head and can feel myself start to cry again.

'Jet lag,' Seth says. 'That's all.'

I'm grateful that he doesn't tell her how I made a fool of myself in the bazaar and got lost, and I smile at him and he smiles back, causing his eyes to crinkle at the edges and we stare at each other for what seems like minutes but is probably just seconds.　Libby starts to lead me to the apartment, and I look away from Seth, hearing his car start up a few seconds later before driving away.　I just want to get inside the apartment and flop onto the sofa and not think of anything or anyone else, and am grateful that Libby is back already from the quick job she had to do.　The next time she has to work whilst I'm here, I vow to not go anywhere, but just lock myself away in the apartment until she's back.　It'll be far safer.

A couple of hours later, the temperature has dropped in the flat and, having had a quick nap, I'm feeling tonnes better.　In front of me is a glass of water, next to a glass of wine, and a plate of the most gorgeous looking pasta.　Carbs.　Oh, how I'm enjoying being friends with them again.

'I warn my tourists all the time,' Libby says, after I've explained about my nightmare when navigating the bazaar.　'But, they just don't believe me how hard it is in that place to find your way out.　Remember that, if you go to Istanbul. It's supposed to be ten times worse.'

'Do you like the glasses?' I ask Libby, seeing them on the worktop.　'Be honest.'

'Lovely,' she says, with bright eyes, and I can tell she means it.　'Have always wanted some for the flat, but never bought any.'

'Jude didn't think it was _you_,' I reply.

'Bah,' she says, 'how would he know?　It's not as though we've discussed our preferences for glassware.　Ignore him.'

We talk about what to do for my second night here and decide we'll have a quiet night in, which suits me just fine. 'Chatting and planning,' Libby calls from the kitchen.

"Planning what?' I ask.

'Our first job tomorrow.'

'Tomorrow?'　I really don't feel up to it.　I'm traumatised,

116

from my second 'near death' experience since being here.

'I haven't had a chance to fetch the jeep today from the paint shop, so we'll pick it up in the morning,' she continues, oblivious to my distressed expression. 'I've got everything ready so there's not much to do when we get up. They don't want a picnic tomorrow, just the tour.'

I guess this could be fun. It will be good to get out and about and see the wonderful sights that, so far, I've only seen on the Internet when looking longingly at the place she now calls home.

So, we stay in and have a great evening chatting whilst Libby shows me the delights of Turkish TV although she has some British channels too that seem fixated on our old quiz shows and '*Only Fools and Horses*.' Actually, seeing Del Boy cheers me up, how could it not? By bedtime I'm feeling almost back to normal and ready for the next day. And, my nose is only a slight shade brighter than the rest of my face, which is a bonus....

CHAPTER TEN

Right, I'm off to work for the day. Well, work is perhaps a strong word as I'm actually going to be sitting down, feeling the sun on my face and having fun. I've got to say that, after questioning Libby multiple times about the legalities of the business last night, and having seen the official documents she waved in my face, I'm still a little concerned that we may end up getting arrested. And, as I told her, I'll probably appear in one of those documentaries shown during the daytime back home, where viewers will yell at the screen, and wrinkle up their noses, and be glad to see the Turkish police throw me in a cell and fling the key into a forgotten cabinet where it will never be found.

Libby walks into the lounge, applying pink lipstick. 'What on earth's the matter?' she asks. 'You're looking all flustered. You're not still imagining that arrest scene, are you, on that UK documentary you seem obsessed with?'

'Of course not, don't be silly.' I am so imagining that scene.

Libby throws me the lipstick. 'Come on, you need to look the part.'

I've had a stressful morning already, despite only being up

an hour or so. Ten text messages from Grant, all before breakfast which, considering the time difference, he'd sent very early. Ranging from 'oh woe is me' to 'I hate you', some of which he'd written during the night. I'll speak to him later, when we're back from the trip, as it's not going to do either of us any good to speak right now.

Libby grabs the large bag from the kitchen which she showed me earlier when checking we have everything we need for the trip. There's a map, sunscreen, blankets and water bottles. Apparently, she is driving and I'm navigating. I barely know how to get from the apartment to the supermarket, so I don't fancy our chances today, but she doesn't seem concerned. And I'm not going to worry her by bringing it up as plenty of others have already expressed doubts about the whole business idea, including Jude and Seth. I can't help thinking about how they've both had quite a bit of experience setting up a business and working over here, and I hope that Libby's not just being stubborn, refusing to listen to their advice. She is a bit like that. In fact, a lot like that. I might try and talk to her about it later, when the time's right.

'All I need now are the jeep keys,' she says. The home phone starts to ring. 'Can you look for them?' she asks, as she runs to the phone in her bedroom.

I have no idea where I'm supposed to look, seeing as I've never seen them before and it's not my flat. A clue would be good but she's chatting away on the phone in Turkish, much to my disappointment as I've no idea what she's talking about and I'm fairly nosy, so I make a start with the mountain of magazines on the coffee table next to the sofa. Libby has always loved reading magazines, which is why I brought a few over for her, and I pick them up to check the keys aren't underneath and then tidy them back into a neat pile. Wow, Grant has done this to me, he's made me a domestic goddess when it comes to cleaning. I stop myself from putting them into alphabetical order. Then, I continue looking, searching under the sofa, behind the sofa, around the sofa but no sign of any keys.

Libby walks back in. 'It was one of the bars, confirming I'm not doing karaoke tonight. Have you found them?'

I shake my head. 'I've checked the sofa and coffee table.'

She rolls her eyes. 'Have you *tidied* my magazines?'

'No! Well, yes, a bit. Look, where did you last see them?'

'Well, they were hanging on the key hook near the door, but they're gone. Have you moved them?' she asks.

I shake my head. 'Of course not, why would I move your keys?' I can see that Libby is starting to look a tad stressed.

'You've done nothing but try and tidy the place since you got here,' she says. 'Maybe they looked messy hanging there and you've moved them somewhere more suitable, as in, hidden.'

'What?' Now, that is so unfair. Am I really that bad? I never used to be bothered about clutter or mess at all. Grant has a lot to answer for.

Ten minutes later we are still looking for the blasted keys and, by this time, we're both hot and bothered and starting to really panic. Plus, we've got a bit snappy with each other.

'Great!' Libby says. 'Our first clients and we're already late. Fourteen months without losing a thing and as soon as we're 'flat sharing' things mysteriously go missing!'

I feel hurt. 'Don't blame me, I haven't touched the stupid keys. Maybe it would have been a good idea to look for them a day or so before the trip, rather than a few minutes before we're due to leave?'

'I've been busy, not that you've noticed. I've a friend come to stay, I'm juggling a couple of jobs and trying to start a business. It's not easy, you know.'

We stare at each other, both with our hands on hips and chins jutting out, then we both spin round and start looking again, although there's nowhere left to try.

'Maybe he has a spare set?' I suddenly say, 'you know, the guy that's painted the jeep?

'Nope,' says Libby, 'There's only one set. I've got to try and get a spare cut. I definitely put them on the hook, by the door, just before you arrived. I know I did.' We both go to inspect the hook, for the fourth time.

'Jude and Seth will love this,' says Libby, storming over to the sofa, where she sits and puts her head in her arms.

I perch beside her and rub her back. 'Tell me why they're so against it again?'

Libby shrugs. 'I don't know about Seth, I would think he's just looking out for me and considering the logistics and business revenue.' I nod, giving the impression I understand what she's talking about but I'm not entirely sure what the logistics could be, but this is not the time to ask. 'And as for Jude, well, he wanted me to set it up as his business, under his name. He doesn't think I'm up to it. He says I don't know enough about business here and that I need advice, and guidance and a mentor. Believe me, I've had a lot of advice and really looked into this. I know what I'm doing and I don't want any business partner, particularly him. But, seeing as I can't even find the keys for our first booking, maybe he's right.'

I frown and bite my lip. It's my method of stopping myself saying something I might regret as I'm pretty hopeless at being tactful and I shouldn't ever give advice to anyone. Not trusting myself to keep quiet, I stand and walk around, checking places already searched. Then, I go into my bedroom, the only place we haven't searched, not that they'd be in here as I've never touched them and would have no need to. I check the top of the dressing table and the drawers, then underneath the bed. I go to the chair in the corner of my room and feel around the cushions, then lift Seth's jacket which has been hanging on the back of the chair since he lent it to me that first night. I realise that it feels heavier than I'd expected and give it a shake. Something jingles and I put my hands in the pocket.

'I've found some keys!' I shout out, pulling them from the pocket and dropping the jacket to the floor. I run from the bedroom and literally bump into Libby who's on her way from the lounge. She grabs them from me and checks them over. With a beaming smile she hugs me tight and spins round to grab the bag and her shoes.

'Where were they?' she asks, as we both fly through the door.

'Seth's jacket,' I reply.

Libby stops walking abruptly and I bump into her. 'Why were they in there?' she asks. 'Did he give them to you?'

'No,' I reply. 'He just lent me his jacket the other night when he bought us home, and I hung it on the chair in my room.'

'Are you sure they were in his jacket?' she asks a little, in my opinion, accusingly.

'Of course they were!' I snap. 'Where did you think they were, under my pillow?' Why's it feel like I'm getting the blame for this? We walk to the jeep, Libby frowning the whole way and there's an awkward silence. Yet again, it appears to Libby that Seth can do no wrong whilst I, on the other hand, appear to be a key thief.

As we reach the jeep Libby eventually asks, 'what possible use would Seth have for those keys?'

I give a little sigh of relief, pleased that I'm now not

considered the prime suspect and shake my head whilst contemplating her question. Why would he have had them? Had he taken them on purpose? And, if so, he must have had them in that pocket all evening as I was wearing it when we returned to the apartment and I'd have surely felt him slide them into the pocket.

Although I'm sure he's guilty of something, I can see how worried Libby's starting to look, which she doesn't need on what should be a great first day in business. So, I put my own feelings to one side and try to ease her tension. 'Maybe he picked them up by mistake, sometime before he'd come to the airport to collect me that first day, brought them to the bar that night to give to you, but forgot.

'I guess so,' says Libby and I'm relieved to see her relax a little. Actually, what I just said does sound plausible although I still have this tiny bit of doubt, a gut instinct that I'll have to try and work through later. Now is not the time.

Libby pulls open the garage door and I immediately forget all about the key conundrum as the bright pink paintwork blinds me.

'Wow,' I say, staring at the jeep.

'Well?' Libby asks, jumping in the driver seat and starting the engine.

'It's...... very pink,' I say, stepping out of the way as she drives out. I close the garage door, avert my eyes as I walk towards the highly visible vehicle and jump into the passenger seat. The paintwork is easier on the eye when inside.

Libby pulls quickly away and we're off to pick up our first clients. We must look like we're floating along in a humungous pink marshmallow and I'm slightly embarrassed by how other drivers are staring at us. Being twenty minutes late, we whizz through back streets, all narrow and dusty,

123

swerving around a few stray cats that seem to have a death wish, and I put on my sunglasses to stop the grit getting into my eyes. I can't believe how quickly Libby is driving and I hold onto the seat and hope for the best.

Luckily, my phone buzzes and distracts me from the threat of a collision. When I pull it from my pocket there's a short text on screen. 'Don't bother ringing. I'm busy,' it says. I sigh and tuck it back in my pocket. Then, I take it back out and switch it off. Grant will have to wait until later, I'm really not in the mood now, there are more important things to do. But I then spend the next few minutes thinking 'what if mum rings and it's an emergency, and she can't get hold of me, and…and…' so, I turn it back on again. There's immediately another text. 'Just tried to ring you and your phone's not even on. Thanks a lot!' I growl loudly and throw my phone into the footwell and put my head back on the headrest.

Libby looks at me, which I'd rather her not do as her eyes leave the road that she's careering down, and pats my leg. She understands and words are not needed. After only a few minutes, and several near misses with various vehicles and/or animals, we're pulling up beside a hotel. Apparently, normal practice for day trips is that the clients wait outside their hotel at a set time, ready for collection. But there's no one here and so Libby tells me to wait in the jeep while she goes in to see if they are waiting inside for us. Whilst she's gone, I grab the bag off the back seat and tuck it under my feet, then I dust down the seats as they're covered in dust from the road. I reapply my lipstick as it's all gone, probably by me nervously biting my lip for the last few minutes. I look up to see Libby walking down the steps, alone.

'Where are they?' I ask, seeing there's no one following her. Libby gets into the jeep, starts it up and drives away.

'They're gone!' she replies, looking close to tears.

'But, we're only 20 minutes late,' I say.

Libby nods in agreement. 'Someone else beat us to it. Another firm pulled up and offered them a good deal and they took it.'

'What? Whilst they were waiting for us?' I ask, in a rather high-pitched voice.

'No, the second they came to wait outside. The reception guy said a jeep pulled up and they were off.'

'Bloody cheeky gits!' How could they nick our clients? It's outrageous.

'You can't blame the customers,' says Libby. 'They're on holiday and wanted a safari and someone else has come along and offered it to them. It was totally our fault, we were late.'

'But even if we'd have been on time, it sounds like the other jeep would have got to them,' I exclaim.

'Yes, but we'd have been early if we hadn't lost the stupid keys, and would have been parked up at the foot of the reception steps. I just don't get how another jeep just happened to be driving past and saw them, just like that,' Libby ponders.

'What do you mean?' I ask.

'Well, it's not as though this hotel is on a main road with passing traffic, it's tucked out of the way. So, I can't see how a jeep would be pulling in here by accident. It's as though they knew the clients would be here, waiting for a day trip, don't you think?'

Could this be true? Could someone else have known we were coming other than the tourist that had booked us? And, how would they have known we wouldn't be on time? After all, we were late only because someone had taken the keys. Before I can stop myself I ask, 'Do you think Seth took those keys on purpose?'

Libby shakes her head and frowns. 'No, never. Why would he?'

I glance out of the window. She may trust him, but I don't. I need to look into this further and get all my facts together so I can prove to Libby that he had something to do with it.

'There'll be more customers,' Libby quietly murmurs, 'besides, we now get the day together. Shopping?'

I get an instant lift in my mood and nod. 'Most definitely.' So, we drive back, get changed and do what every woman should do when they've had a bad day. Get a large dose of retail therapy!

CHAPTER ELEVEN

I can't believe that I've already been here five days, it's whizzed past so quickly. Libby and I have shopped, relaxed, sunbathed, eaten good food and had a fair amount of wine and cocktails, and, I'm starting to unwind and feel like I'm actually on holiday.

There have been a lot of awkward exchanges of text messages with Grant but luckily only a few voice calls. Well, maybe more than a few as he persists in ringing me every hour but I ignore most of them. Well, not exactly 'ignore,' I just keep the phone on silent so I don't know when he's calling. When we do talk, it's difficult. It starts with him begging me to come back and apologising for anything and everything, but ends with him calling me all the names under the sun and blaming me for anything and everything. I've tried to have a rational conversation, and explain how I feel it's best we part, and how it's just not working out, but it always ends in a fight. After most of our heated discussions I put the phone down but within five minutes he rings back and tells me he's going to come over here to get me and take me home. The thought of that scares me although I don't think he will. He doesn't do hot weather, or holidays, or

Turkey. Not that he's ever been here, but I just know it's not him. Plus, he wouldn't see what I see. He's no idea where Libby lives and I made sure I hid any trace of her address from his apartment, just in case. Libby suggests I should send him a post card saying it's over. If he doesn't stop hassling me, I think I might have to.

I'll have to see him again, obviously, and I do need to. I have to tell him that I don't dislike him, or hate him, I just don't love him anymore and I'm not entirely sure I ever did. The truth is, he came along at a time when my life was tumultuous after Libby had announced she'd be leaving, and I knew I couldn't afford to keep the place on my own. Grant was just there, like a Knight in shining armour, stepping straight in to save me. I feel embarrassed about it now, about why I've stayed with him at all, but I remind myself it wasn't all bad, particularly at the start. We had some fun, and he introduced me to a lifestyle I'd never known before. But, it's over now and it's time to stop the pretence, for both our sakes. It's only fair.

I'll go back to the UK, talk it through and pack my belongings to take to my new home, not that there will be much. He'll have probably thrown everything out by the time I'm back, my clothes and possessions strewn across the landscaped gardens for all and sundry to see. I might see if Mum can go and collect everything whilst I'm still over here. He's unlikely to throw a tantrum and shout at her, they like each other. Yes, I think that's what I'll do even if I am shirking a bit of responsibility.

I do have moments here in Marmaris where I question myself as to whether I'm doing the right thing. Libby's moved on and, despite me telling myself I'm virtually a local, this is just a holiday for me, and when I'm back home in a few weeks I'll be alone and back to my old job whilst trying to find a home or flat share. Maybe I *could* settle with Grant. He won't have to worry about me coming over here anymore as I'd have done it, and will be unlikely to be able to afford to do it again for a while. So, he could go back to being the old Grant, attentive and sweet, and I'll have a home and won't have to share a flat with a complete stranger who could, let's face it, turn out to be a lunatic.

But then I suddenly swing to the opposite end of the emotional scale, remembering how unhappy I was even before I turned down the proposal and told Grant I'd be visiting Libby. In fact, I know deep down I've never been totally happy whilst being with him. I'd be going back to him just because there's no other options open for me. Which, whilst convenient, would be totally wrong.

So far, I've dodged the direct questions from Libby about my plans, and what I'm going to do about Grant. I haven't spoken to him on the phone when she's been in the room, I've taken it outside, but, I can't avoid the questions forever. And, I'm going to get it over and done with today when we stop for a drink. It'll be good to get her opinion, and support, and she'll know exactly what I should say to him to finalise everything as quickly as possible. I'm pretty hopeless at anything confrontational.

We're laden down with shopping bags after visiting the local market and are en route to Jude's bar. The goodies bought today are T-shirts, a couple of handbags and a nice selection of fresh fruit and veg. The colours and smells of the fresh goods on those stalls were indescribable, and I loved every minute in that market place. Plus, I had a go at haggling and I've got to admit I'm pretty good at it. I'm adding it to my list of new jobs to explore. I could mentor tourists and they'd make a documentary which follows me all around markets of the world. Even dangerous ones! I could be like that bloke from *Eastenders* who's turned into a sort of vigilante. My haggling was so good, I bought T-shirts for a price so cheap I can't even work out how they could have been made. As the home made cardboard posters next to the stalls said, 'Cheaper than Tesco,' 'Cheaper than Asda,' and then... 'Cheaper than Shoplifting.' Hilarious. The one thing I definitely did avoid buying was underwear, due to seeing a sign about crotch-less knickers described as 'Air Conditioned Pants.' It sort of put me off underwear buying after that.

I'm keen to get to Jude's bar, not because I'm thirsty as we haven't long stopped for water, but because I'm bursting to confront Seth about the jeep keys. He's been away for the last couple of days and is due back this morning to work at the bar as Jude is off to Muğla to see a wholesaler, or something like that. To be honest, I wasn't really listening when Libby told me, as I was too fixated on what I'm going to say to Seth. As Libby knows, I don't let go of something until I've found out the truth.

We're not sure exactly where Seth's been, Jude only said he had a 'damsel in distress' to rescue somewhere. Libby thinks that's nonsense as she's never seen Seth with any damsels since knowing him. But Libby is, at the end of the day, just a friend of his, nothing more, so she wouldn't necessarily know everything about his personal life. I'd rather believe he hasn't got any woman on the sidelines, damsel or not, although I'm not sure why I care. It's not as though I'm interested in him. Well, not much.

We both get the impression that Jude isn't happy with Seth at the moment, and Libby presumes it's something to do with the business. I wouldn't be surprised if it's because Jude's been left with all the work to do whilst Seth has flounced off. And, I stress the word 'flounce' as I imagine this is something Seth would do. Libby, I've realised, is overly protective of Seth, even though it's his brother she's in love with and I can't shake off the feeling there's something she's not telling me about the two of them. But, it's really none of my business and probably not a big deal at all. I do have a tendency to read into things too much. Anyway, I've more important things to sort with Seth, like, why did he have the keys in his jacket.

We reach the bar and sit at the front under parasols, tucking the bags under our seats so we can stretch out our legs. Without even asking, one of the waiters, a lady, brings 2 bottles of water and glasses and puts them on the table.

'Thanks Fi,' Libby says and the woman responds in the most beautiful Scottish accent, all soft and lilting.

'Haven't seen her here before,' I say, taking the top off the bottle and pouring it in the tall glass. I'm pleased to see there's no ice in it, that's one thing I definitely don't do here. It can apparently have a dodgy effect on the stomach, which is all I need. I read that in a blog before I travelled out here and Libby confirmed it's the first thing she warns tourists about when they board the airport transfer bus to get to the resort.

'Fi's worked here ages,' answers Libby, 'but she's been away for the last three weeks. Her father's poorly. Jude gave her time off to go home.'

'That's nice,' I say, 'As in, nice that Jude gave her the time. Not nice because her father's poorly, obviously.'

'They used to go out together, Jude and Fi, for two years. Ended a couple of months after I arrived here.'

'Ooh, did he leave her for you?'

'No,' she replies a little abruptly, 'not at all. I met him fairly early on but didn't date him for months. I dated a few other guys first.'

131

'Floozy,' I say, and she laughs. 'Don't you mind her working with Jude, if they were once an item?'

'Why would I?' Libby asks, 'I'm with Jude now and they split up ages ago. She's lovely.'

Libby is so different to me, so laid back, about everything. I would love to think I could be a friend with any of Grant's ex-girlfriends, but the truth is I can't bear their name being mentioned. I have to accept the fact that, as most of them are brokers, he still works with them. But, I don't socialise with them or go to any of his work do's if it means I have to sit next to them. Libby really doesn't feel threatened by anyone, she's so confident in her own skin.

'She's at least fifteen years younger than us,' I point out. I've no idea why I said this, I'm sure Libby can see that for herself. Still, it provokes no response in her at all.

After a few seconds she says, 'Talking of younger, have you any idea how old Hamil is? Seeing as you're flirting with him on a daily basis?'

'I am so not,' I snap back, although it's possibly a little bit true. We've just had a drink in his bar and I was slobbering over the table every time he came near us. There's just something about him, he oozes sex appeal and I can't stop myself imagining things I'd like to do with him. Mind you, most of the men I've met so far here have had that effect on me, even Seth. In fact, particularly Seth, even if he is a sneaky key thief.

There's a few moments of silence and then Libby says, completely out of the blue, 'It must have sometimes been fun'

I look at her frowning, not sure what she's referring to.

'You and Grant,' she says. Phew, I thought she meant Fi and Jude, which would have been an awkward conversation. Even more awkward than this one that I've been trying to avoid.

I sigh and think long and hard about this before answering. 'There were moments of fun,' I finally say. 'But I'm damned if I can think of any now.' Each time something comes to mind, I know it's just my own 'fake memory,' not how it really was, but how I wanted it to be. 'Have you ever wondered why he was with me?' I ask. 'I'm a...a...,' I struggle to find the word, '...pauper.'

Libby laughs. 'Who says 'pauper' nowadays? You sound like you're a character from Oliver Twist. Look, he obviously just likes a bit of rough,' and I have to laugh. 'Hey,' she continues, 'you're totally good enough for him. In fact, you're too good. Stop putting yourself down. How do you think your mother will take it, this break up of yours?'

I roll my eyes. 'She'll find it incredulous I said no. And Dad will go on and on about all the holidays I'll miss out on.'

'Like your road trip to the States,' she says. I can't believe she's remembered my road trip dream. 'Do you remember how you made a scrapbook when we were at school all about the trip, the car you'd be in, the man you'd be driving with, the fun and romance you'd have. You used to cut out photos from the holiday brochures and magazines. Don't tell me you've given up on that dream too? You've given up everything else.'

'Not everything,' I say, feeling a bit defensive. 'Grant would never have wanted to do the road trip with me. He's more of a luxury hotel type of guy, and he'd want to choose the car. He'd go for something sensible and efficient. But, for me, it's got to be in a Cadillac, or else there's no point.'

She laughs. 'That's right, you and your guy in a caddy.'

There's silence again as I think of the road trip, and then thoughts come back to mum and dad. 'Do you know, mum actually said 'Try a little harder. You can learn to love

133

someone.' How sad is that, if you have to force it?'

Libby nods in agreement and we sit quietly and sip our drinks. There's no way that Libby would settle for being with anyone that she doesn't love, or that she knows doesn't love her. And, I'm the same, it just takes me a little longer to realise when things aren't right, that's all. I may not be as much of a 'go getter' as Libby, or the most assertive or determined of people, but, I don't do anything I don't want to do. It hits me again that, although I'm here with Libby now, in a few weeks time it will be back to me being on my own and I wonder how I'll manage to say goodbye to her again. As though Libby has read my mind, she reaches for my hand and gives it a squeeze.

'I thought it was you two,' a voice says, 'I could just see you over the top of the shopping bags!' I look around to see Seth standing behind us. He leans in and kisses Libby on both cheeks, then awkwardly does the same to me. I'm conscious that my cheeks are damp with sweat and am a tad impressed he doesn't quickly wipe his lips to remove my germs.

Libby pulls the neighbouring chair towards our table for him but he says, 'Can't stay, delivering some bottles for Jude. Just wanted to catch up and see how you are, and how your first jeep trip went.'

Whilst I do a very dramatic tut, Libby groans and shakes her head. 'It didn't,' she says, 'they went with someone else before we got there.'

'You're kidding me' Seth replies and sits down after all, right next to me. His leg pushes up against mine and I feel a bit of a jolt go through me, and I quickly pull my leg away. Then, I let it flop against his again. He's wearing knee length shorts and I can feel the hairs on his lower leg brush against my own skin. Jeez, this guy's a sexy, key-stealing fibber.

Libby shakes her head. 'Nope, definitely not joking.' Libby has begged me not to mention the keys being in his jacket and I've promised her I won't, begrudgingly. If that's how she wants to play it, then so be it. I won't go against her wishes, ever.

'We were late because we couldn't find the keys to the jeep, and that's because you'd taken them and hid them.' Sometimes, I hear myself speak and could slap myself immediately.

'Lou!' Libby exclaims, and I look at her disappointed face. Yes, I'd promised not to say anything but I can't resist when he's sitting here looking all innocent, staring at me bewildered, and gorgeous, although the gorgeous has nothing to do with this obviously.

I continue, in my best *Poirot* style. 'We looked everywhere for them and eventually found them in your jacket pocket.' I remove my sunglasses, lean forward, tilt my head on one side and stare at him, waiting for a reaction.

'What were they doing in my jacket?' Seth asks, then 'and why are you looking at me like that? Is there something wrong with your neck?'

I put my head back up straight and say, 'Nothing wrong with my neck, thank you very much. And don't change the subject. Let's get back to the jacket. And the keys.'

'Look,' he says, 'the last time I saw my jacket it was around the shoulders of a tired and grumpy woman.'

'Yes, it was!' I say, pointing my finger at him. Did he just call me grumpy? Seth looks at my finger and then at my face.

'Then why did you put the keys in my pocket?'

'Aha! ' I say, still pointing at him, but this time wriggling my finger aggressively. 'Who said anything about a pocket?

I just said that they were in your jacket.'

Seth and Libby look at each other and frown.

'Lou,' Libby says, 'Where else would they be, other than in a pocket?'

I think about that for a second and then shake my head. I'm not going to be distracted so I ignore her. 'What were the keys doing in there?'

'Hey,' Seth answers, looking at me, then Libby, then back to me. 'I haven't worn that jacket in ages, I just keep it in the boot of the car in case I need it. They could have been in that pocket for weeks.'

'I only picked them up a couple of days ago,' says Libby. I can see how she's struggling with the idea that Seth could have had something to do with this. As far as she's concerned, he's an angel, a blond, curly haired, strapping angel whose leg is so tight against mine I can feel the pulse in it.

I pull my leg away and move my chair to distance us. Seth touches my arm and stares at me. 'Look, I don't know how they got there but, whatever happened, it would have been a mistake.'

Libby smiles at him reassuringly. 'Well,' she says, 'no point worrying now. We lost our first clients but tomorrow's another day.'

'Tomorrow?' I ask, looking quickly at her.

'Well, not exactly tomorrow, the day after. We have still got that one, haven't we Seth?' she asks.

'Well,' he replies, 'there's good news and bad news.'

'Typical,' I mutter under my breath, but not quiet enough as they both look at me.

After a few seconds, Libby looks back to Seth and says 'Good news first.'

'Ok, well, I've two clients for you. They just rang to check times and to make sure it's definitely the two gorgeous girls they've heard about, and they want you to take them for a picnic over to Liar's Throat Island.'

'Hear that, Lou?' Libby says. 'Two guys on a picnic!'

'One each,' I reply and we laugh.

'I'm sure Jude will be delighted about that,' Seth says, with a hint of a smile.

'He can trust me, it's business,' says Libby, and raises her eyebrows at me as I giggle. 'And the bad news?' she asks.

Seth makes a sad face that even I have to laugh at. 'It's nothing to do with the booking. It's about tonight. I've just seen your old boss, and they need you to work, just a few hours. He asked me to tell you. Well, ask you.'

'Tell me,' Libby says. She sighs and puts her head back, then looks at me.

I smile back. 'That's fine. Besides, I've had you to myself the last few days, we knew you'd have to work sometimes whilst I'm here, and you've already had shifts covered so you could be with me. You working tonight will make up for the money we lost from today's jeep trip disaster,' I say, turning my head to glare at Seth and then dramatically turning back to Libby, 'and I can relax and put my feet up. And do, well, stuff.'

Libby doesn't look convinced but I'm really ok about it. To be honest, it'll actually be nice to have a night in and relax. Maybe I can phone Grant and have a really good talk, so that everything is sorted and it's not hanging over me.

'Wait!' exclaims Libby suddenly. 'I've a great idea. Seth, what are you up to tonight?'

'No, no...' I stammer. I can see where this is going. 'I'm fine really, I've things to do.'

'Yes,' Libby says, 'stuff. Well, you can do 'stuff' with Seth instead. Seth?' she asks, looking pleadingly at him.

He looks apprehensive, and I can't blame him. I've literally just sat and accused him of sabotaging Libby's business, and for being a key thief, and I can't say we've a brilliant history of being nice to each other since I arrived. Yet, he does still have a hint of a smile there. 'I'm good at stuff. And, I know how time consuming 'stuff' can be. So, let me help you with it. Unless,' Seth continues, 'you're going to get *MI5* in to continue quizzing me about my jacket, shine a bright light in my face or torture me. I swear I've told you all I know.'

Libby laughs and I scowl at her. This is not a laughing matter as far as I'm concerned. 'Fine,' I finally say, fake-smiling at both of them, the smile I reserve for times like when Grant buys me a new blouse he's chosen that I don't particularly like, or advised me on a word choice I've just made that obviously isn't grammatically correct or appropriate for a particular situation.

Hey, I tell myself, it'll be fine. I mean to say, how awful can it be, to spend an evening with a guy who, I have to admit, is pretty good to look at and makes me laugh, in a strange way. I only have to smile and make polite conversation and stare into those blue eyes, so blue and... stop it, I tell myself. They may be gorgeous eyes but they're hiding something, and I won't fall for any of his schmoozing. I need to look at tonight as being an opportunity to interrogate him further and find out the truth about the keys, and any other secret he's hiding. Wow, I am going to be the new Miss Marple, elegant and analytical and sly, ready to solve any mystery I come across.

Looking at his watch he says, 'I'll take you to dinner, if that's ok with you?' I nod. 'I'll pick you up at 7, which gives you precisely 3 hours and 17 minutes to do some of that important *stuff*.' He kisses us both on the cheek, lingering a little longer on mine compared to Libby's. Moments after he's gone, I sit there smiling as I can still smell his aftershave and, when I look at Libby, she's giving me one of her satisfied grins.

'What?' I ask her.

'You've got a date!' she says.

'I so have not! I'm going to have a meal out with someone who just happens to be a guy. A guy who, for all I know, could have a whole collection of women on the side-lines, and a multitude of keys he's pinched. And, if you remember, I already have a boyfriend, even if I'm not technically with him anymore. So, how could this be a date?'

'Seth definitely does *not* have a collection of women, I doubt he even has one. The mystery woman we tease him about has never been seen by anyone'

I give a sarcastic laugh. 'That figures, an invented girlfriend.'

'And I doubt if he has any key collection either,' Libby continues. 'You're single, albeit with a small issue to sort. You should be making the most of your new single life.'

'I am doing exactly that,' I announce, a little mysteriously.

'How?' Libby asks.

'I've a date with Hamil in a few days.' I hadn't told Libby about this yet, I haven't really found the right time and I can't say I'm 100% sure about it myself. With what's happened with Grant, I could quite happily never go out with a man again. But Hamil keeps asking, and he's fun and flirtatious and, I'm not going to lie, makes me feel attractive and sexy. And it's a long time since I felt that way. So, I've convinced myself that a date will be fun.

'What?' Libby asks. 'Wow, two dates in a week, which one will be your favourite, I wonder.' I flick my hand at her and she laughs. 'Look, just be careful. Hamil is a nice guy but he's a flirt and takes out a different girl each week. He's only probably after one thing.'

'That's what I'm hoping,' I say, smiling mischievously, and she gasps in mock shock. To be honest, if he makes a move sexually, I wouldn't know what to do. It's been a long time... But, the thought of it excites me.

'You could do a lot worse than Seth,' Libby continues, 'he's very cute.'

I have to admit that she is right about that. He is cute and, despite really wanting a night in, I'm not exactly dreading going out to dinner with him.

'C'mon, let's go. It seems Jude isn't coming here any time soon.' We gather our bags and say goodbye to the Fi. I need to get home and get ready for tonight, not that I'm going to make lots of effort, obviously, as it's not a date, it's just dinner. With a man that I have no feelings for at all. Nothing. Absolutely none. Although, it would be rude to not use my new body lotion I bought at the airport to match my perfume, and carefully apply my makeup, and wear the short dress I haven't yet dared to put on yet, as it's a little tight around my chest and leaves little to the imagination in terms of its length, especially with the killer heels I've brought with me. Yes, I'm not making any extra effort for Seth whatsoever.

CHAPTER TWELVE

Well?'

Although I have my eyes closed as I'm savouring the flavour of some of the best food I think I have ever eaten, I'm still aware that Seth is looking straight at me, chin balanced on his hand, waiting for a verdict. I refuse to be rushed, this gastronomic experience is truly too spectacular to be cut short. I'm going to finish this mouthful in my own time.

'Truly fantastic,' I finally answer, opening my eyes only long enough to grab another forkful before closing them again to lose myself in the taste. Seth laughs and, when I open my eyes a few seconds later, he's picked up his knife and fork which he'd laid down, purely to watch me eat, and is now tucking into his plate.

I knew as soon as I walked in that Seth hadn't been exaggerating when he said it's the best local eatery for miles. It's absolutely packed, and mostly by locals, which I also use as a measuring stick for how good an eating-place is. Seth drove us to the restaurant near to Akyaka, which is where he has his apartment with Jude, and gave me a quick tour of his hometown before parking up. I've got to say, Akyaka looks gorgeous, much quieter and smaller than the hustle and bustle of near-by Marmaris. He's promised to show me where he lives when we leave and, depending on the time, we might go to his for a coffee, which I'm quite looking forward to as I'm very nosy when it comes to other people's homes. I'm the sort that can't resist staring through a window that doesn't have the curtains pulled when you walk past on a dark night.

When we got to the restaurant, we were quickly shown to our seats at a table against the far edge of the dining room, with the local Azmak River right next to us, separated only by some plants placed along the edging. I'm mesmerized by the white geese and ducks that keep swimming up to spy on us, obviously checking to see what food they might get later. Well, birdies, don't hold your breath, with a meal this gorgeous, the chances of having any left overs are pretty remote.

Although it's still hot outside, it's pretty cool and breezy in here as the front and sides are open, and I take in the surroundings as I eat; the wood supports leading up to the wooden ceiling which has those medieval type circular metal lights hanging down with candle type bulbs around them, vines winding down the supports and into pots. Although the restaurant is technically indoors, it feels like we're eating Al Fresco.

So far, we've had a pretty nice time considering how I felt about it all before he arrived to collect me. I admit I spent a long time getting ready and have scrubbed up well, if I do say so myself. But, like I explained to Libby, it's not in any way for Seth's benefit. Nope, not at all. I don't really care if he's noticed what I'm wearing or not, although he did look impressed when I opened the door to him, and he told me I looked gorgeous, which had no effect on me at all. No, I just let it go over my head because, in my opinion, this man is a fibber and I'm not going to believe a word he says. It doesn't matter how much his eyes twinkle, or he runs his fingers through that very thick, blonde, curly hair. Or, occasionally, touches my arm. It may indeed make my heart flutter a little, but it's not because he has any effect on me, well, not a voluntary one. I am a woman, after all, and he does happen to be very attractive, so I can't stop these natural responses that I have no control over. Plus, I'll blame it on the heat, it's what I blame everything on over here.

I politely told him he looked good too, because he does and I'm actually a nice, polite person. He's wearing a suit, light coloured with a Neru collar, proper shoes, which are the first ones I've seen him in since getting here, not that I've been looking or paying too much attention, obviously. And, although I don't trust him, I have to admit he's made a lot of effort for me tonight and it's only fair to reciprocate any compliments.

I look up to see him watching me again. 'Better than Abingdon food?' he asks.

I giggle. 'Not sure about that. The ambience let's it down a bit here compared to my local. I mean to say, what's with the beautiful music, aromatic smells, and the ducks on the pond outside. I get to see drunk youths and stray dogs from my favourite restaurant back home.' Actually, this isn't strictly true, there are some lovely restaurants where I live, but it's made Seth smile.

'Now, that is hard to beat,' he replies, laughing.

A waiter comes to the table, dressed quite formally with a black tie, and speaks to Seth in Turkish. I take a sip of wine whilst I listen to Seth respond. Wow, he sounds good and I'm surprised at myself for finding it a bit of a turn on.

'You speak Turkish really well,' I say, after the waiter has walked away. I need to slow down on these compliments. He might start to think that I like him. Which I do, and I'm liking him more and more as the evening goes on.

He shrugs. 'I had to learn quickly, it's impossible to run a business without being able to communicate. Besides, it's my home, so I like to speak the local language. Libby's getting really good, have you heard her?'

I nod. Libby speaks beautiful Turkish. 'I'm hopeless at languages,' I say. 'I still have nightmares about the language lab at school, where each one of us in the class would sit in a cubicle with headphones and a microphone, and the French teacher would randomly pick one of us and listen in and then speak, and I'd jump a mile. I was terrible. I think I'd have to live in a country where English is the first language. That makes me sound very selfish, I guess.'

'Not selfish, more a case of you not having confidence in the fact that you could pick up the language relatively easily if you had to.' I nod, if I made the effort, I'm sure I'd get there. 'Is that why your dream holiday is an American road trip, so there's no language barrier?' he asks, smiling.

Wow, he remembered. 'Probably.' The conversation so far has been surprisingly easy and fun, and I have to admit I'm enjoying his company. But, despite the urge to tell him every little detail about my road trip dream, I need to focus and interrogate him to find out more about him, the jeep keys and any mystery women he might have.

'So,' I say. 'Tell me more about you. Are you single?'

'Wow, that's a direct question. Are you interested?' he asks with a cheeky smile.

I feel myself blush. 'I'm just nosy,' I reply, which is actually true, my inquisitiveness regularly gets me into a lot of trouble. 'I just can't imagine a guy like you would be on his own out here.' I silently tut at myself, as this is the equivalent of saying 'how can a guy as gorgeous as you be single?' which is very cheesy and openly flirtatious.

He puts his head on one side and leans towards me. 'And, what exactly is a guy like me?'

'Well...' I stammer, literally drowning in those blue eyes. 'Own business, young...'

He laughs. 'Young? Not sure about that one.' He swirls his drink around in the glass, looking at the last of the wine in it. 'I guess I'm just too busy with the business to have time to meet anyone, or take them out to dinner on a school night, like we're doing now.'

'A school night?' I laugh, 'then I feel honoured you found time for me.' I pause and then say, 'what about before you came here? You must have had someone then? I mean, at home.' I realise I don't even know where his home is, so add 'which is where, exactly?'

'You're being a detective again,' he says. 'Should I ask for a lawyer to be present before I answer?'

'What?' I ask, opening my eyes really wide and pretending I don't know what he's talking about. It's not that obvious, is it?

'The questions. You've lots of them and I feel like I'm being investigated. I haven't recovered from the 'Jeep Key' interrogation yet.' I should apologise but can't think of what to say, as I'm not entirely sorry. He saves me by adding, 'I'm kidding,' and I relax a little. 'Now, home. That's a difficult one. I've been travelling virtually all of my adult life, and even before that. My parents couldn't settle and wanted to see the world and so they took Jude and me with them all over the globe when we were small, and home schooled us for $3/4$ of every school year. Now, they live in Spain for half the year, and the UK for the rest, and they still travel whenever finances and health allow. I guess that's why I

145

found it hard to settle myself once I left school. I've ended up living in various places, but rarely the UK. In fact, I only return there when necessary.'

'To see your folks?' I ask.

He shakes his head. 'I tend to visit them when they're in Spain if I can. I don't like to be without the sunshine for very long, and I find the rain hard to live with. Plus, I've nothing left in the UK for me to go back to really, most of my friends visit me here.'

'And girlfriends?' I ask, trying to not look that interested, as though it's just a random question.

He smiles. 'If you're asking if I have one, the answers no.'

'Why would you think I'm interested? I was being polite and making conversation'. I scowl and look away, even though I had totally wanted to find out if he has one.

He leans forwards to me, as though about to whisper, but when I lean nearer to him so I can hear, he only says 'I've had a few, but nothing serious.'

Umm. A few. What exactly is a few. I mean, is he talking single figures? And, is it a question that is appropriate to ask or will he think I'm interested in him. Which, obviously, I'm not. I'm just curious. And, whilst I think about it, I'm not quite sure I like the phrase 'but nothing serious' and I wonder if the girls he's talking about know that that's how he sees his relationships, that they were *nothing special*. It might have been to them. He's probably one of those men with a girlfriend in every country across the world. I feel myself prickle a little, although I've no idea why. It makes no difference to me what romantic ties he has, I've no interest in him. Nothing at all.

'So, no girlfriend at the moment?' I ask and instantly give myself an internal kick. What made me ask that? I've no idea where it came from. I continue staring at my food so that our eyes don't meet.

'Nope,' he replies simply, and I force myself to look up at him and see that he's smiling at me in a way that's saying 'are you interested?' I look back to my plate and keep my eyes on the food. I'm not going to look at him again for at least ten minutes, just in case his eyes draw me in and I ask another ridiculous question.

I decide to change the subject. 'Sounds like you've fun parents.'

'I guess so.'

He guesses so? I raise my eyebrows, as I think of how I'd have loved a childhood like the one he's had, living around the world, being home schooled. Although, I don't know what my chances would have been like, having mum or dad teaching me. Neither was too keen at helping me with homework once I'd left Primary school. 'Jude's the favourite, always has been and always will be. He's the one that's *achieved*. I'm the one in the background, the quiet one. So, I always went pretty much unnoticed and that hasn't particularly changed for my parents now we're older.'

'Aw,' I say, before I can stop myself. That makes me sad. I much prefer Seth to Jude and can't understand why his parents wouldn't. I find myself touching his arm, and then stop, pulling my hand quickly away. I'm not too sure what Seth thinks about touchy feely demonstrative gestures. 'But you're in business with Jude as an equal partner, aren't you?'

Seth nods. 'Yes, but he's the one people notice. The loud and charismatic one. I do the planning, and he takes to the stage.'

'Like Wham,' I say, in all seriousness. Seth frowns.

'You know. Like, you're Andrew Ridgeley and he's George Michael. And, no matter what you do, he'll always be the one that everyone talks about forever.'

'Ah, of course,' Seth replies, smiling again. 'Then you and Libby must be Pepsi and Shirley.'

I laugh and splutter my wine a little. I like that idea and have an instant picture in my mind of the four of us singing, like in that *'Last Christmas'* video, playing in the snow and staying together in a log cabin. I think I'd definitely be Shirley, particularly as she married that guy from Spandau Ballet. That's just the sort of thing I'd do.

'What did you ask the waiter for?' I ask, remembering how Seth spoke Turkish so well a few minutes ago.

'The Menu,' he replies.

'Dessert already?' I ask, feeling it's a bit rude as I'm still eating.

'Dessert?' he says. 'We haven't chosen the mains yet.'

It turns out that what we've been eating is only the Meze starter, and I'm full up already. How am I supposed to fit any more food in? I'm still chomping away on the last bits on my plate and, to be truthful, I'd find it hard to let any of this gorgeous food go back out to the kitchen unfinished.

'Full?' he asks, obviously noticing the panic in my face.

I nod. 'Me too,' he replies. 'Let's leave the mains and wait to see how we feel about dessert in a minute. '

I find out from Seth that this is apparently very normal. A lot of people do this, they make their way through the meze and then see how they feel, most of them ending up full and satisfied, and just asking for the bill. I can't imagine being able to do that in the UK. You'd probably be forced to eat the main or be banned from attending the restaurant again.

I put down my knife and fork and take a sip of wine. Wow, this meal has been incredible and has distracted me from interrogating him about the jeep keys. But, somehow the mystery is beginning to feel less important than it did before.

'So, who do your parents favour out of you and *your* brother?' he asks.

Umm. I haven't really thought of that before. I picture Robert and wonder what he's up to right now, and I think of his very sweet three children, my two nephews and lovely niece. I haven't seen them for ages. 'I think it's Robert,' I reply. 'He's provided them with grandchildren, and I haven't.'

'And why haven't you?' asks Seth. 'Have you put it on hold? Been a career girl?'

'You *are* joking' I say. 'I've been in the same job since school, am badly paid, disgruntled and bored, and entertain myself at my desk by seeing how many paperclips I can try to clip onto my little finger. Which, by the way, are 8. And it hurts.'

'8? Is that it?' he replies. 'No wonder they prefer your brother.' I laugh. 'You don't sound particularly fulfilled.' He fixes his blue-eyed gaze on me and I have a mini panic as I feel I should answer and defend myself, but I stop as I know that he's actually right. Realising I'm not going to answer, he asks, 'So why stay in the UK, in that area? Why not travel and have an adventure, like your American road trip?'

'I've a plan as to how the road trip must be,' I reply, 'and so far it just hasn't worked out. I'm not doing it unless it's absolutely to the plan.'

He puts his head on one side. 'So, what's the plan exactly?'

'Well,' I say, looking down at the table and fiddling with my wine glass. I fear I'm going to make myself sound stupid, but I guess I'm probably beyond that point now with Seth, I've done nothing but embarrass myself in front of him since I arrived. 'It has to be with the right companion, Mr Right in fact. Someone that's whisked me off my feet and wants to

149

travel round the States with me as his wife. In fact, we'd get married in Vegas whilst we're there.'

'With Elvis conducting the ceremony?' he asks.

'How else could it be?' I reply, and we laugh again.

'But, what if you don't meet Mr Right, and you never get to see the States? Wouldn't you rather go alone than not go at all?'

I shake my head. 'Nope, it has to be that way, or else I don't want to go. And, I really believe it will happen one day, even if my parents and everyone else I know thinks it won't.' I'm actually not 100% sure myself it will happen anymore, but I'm not going to tell Seth that.

'But, I thought you have a boyfriend, or fiancé...' his voice trails off and I look up at him expecting him to be grinning, but he actually looks quite serious.

I shake my head. 'He's my past. I just haven't 'finalised' everything yet,' I say. 'And my parents don't know and it will take a long time for them to get over it. They'll grieve for the life they could see me having with him, where I'd marry into money and provide them with grandchildren dressed perfectly and able to play piano at ten months. It will be a shock to them.'

I take a big glug of wine. Grant. I've barely thought of him all evening, and haven't even felt my phone vibrate with a text or call.

'I'm sorry it hasn't worked out,' he says.

'Don't be. Besides, I'll be fine once there's no loose ends...' my voice trails off.

Luckily, the silence is broken by the sound of ducks squabbling and we peer over the edge to see them down at the water's edge. 'See,' Seth says, 'even ducks have relationship issues.'

I smile, the evening has returned to its earlier state of ease.

I find myself telling Seth how different this meal out has been for me as I'm not used to being able to choose the food I want, the wine, have my hair pulled back, wear the dress Grant dislikes, talk about my friendship with Libby without hearing a tut or worse. Just saying these things out loud makes me see how trapped I've been, yet I never seemed to know that at the time. And, how would I ever go back to that life now that I've seen how bad it's been for my well being, having had a peak at how life could really be.

Although it surprises me to say it, Seth has been great company, and I no longer either want, or need, to mention the Jeep key situation. I somehow trust he had nothing to do with it, and bringing the subject up would just ruin the evening. And, I'm pretty sure there's no mystery woman either. And, even if there was, what's it to do with me anyway? I look away from the ducks and back to Seth, and find him watching me. Then, after several seconds of staring into one another's eyes, he reaches out and holds my hand. I literally feel my heart kick into action, pumping blood around to parts of the body I haven't felt tingle for a long time. We stay like this for a while until we're both suddenly aware of the waiter standing next to us and the moment is gone. We both smile.

The dessert menu is in Turkish and Seth reads it to me, first in Turkish and then English, which is definitely a form of foreplay in my book as his accent makes me melt. There's really so much choice I don't know what to have although, if I'm honest, I shouldn't have anything as I'm completely full and my dress is not exactly forgiving. I ask Seth what he'd suggest. 'Well,' he answers, 'I was going to order us the chocolate pastry but I changed my mind after what you'd told me about Grant ordering for you.'

I smile and squeeze his hand. 'You're not Grant,' I say,

151

'nowhere near. Couldn't be any more different.' He lifts my hand and kisses it, very slowly and seductively. His eyes lift and he stares at me as he carries on, and I just wish that we were somewhere private, as all sorts of thoughts fill my mind of how I'd like to respond.

Seth puts my hand down. 'Let's get this dessert ordered so we can get out of here,' he says, smiling a little mischievously. He tries to call the waiter over but he can't seem to catch his eye and we both start to get restless, suddenly anxious to leave the restaurant.

'Let's forget dessert', I say, and he nods and smiles. I'm pretty certain we'll quickly be heading to his Akyaka apartment and I'm tingling all over. How has the evening ended up like this, when I was so set on interrogating him and exposing him as a liar and a betrayer. Yet, here I am now getting excited about going back to his place and continuing with the hand kissing and whatever else we might end up doing. Seth stands up. 'Ill go over and pay', he says, 'I need to have a quick chat with Deniz anyway, and it means we can make a quick getaway. Wait here for me, I won't be long.'

I smile as he leaves the table and watch him walk across the restaurant. Even his walk is sexy. I watch him speak to the waiter, who then directs him to the bar, presumably to speak with Deniz, and I look back over the edge of the table to see if the ducks have made up and are friends again, but they're nowhere to be seen. Maybe they've gone somewhere private too. I reflect on my adventure so far, how almost a week ago, I was in Abingdon, fighting with my boyfriend/ fiancé, and now I'm having dinner with another man who I have feelings for already. How did this happen so quickly? And, is it sensible? Hey, I've spent the last eighteen months being sensible and look where it's got me. Maybe I need to throw caution to the wind and enjoy myself with a man I've known for just five days. Just the thought of being so reckless, compared to steady and sensible, excites me.

I jump suddenly at the sound of a buzz and look at the table to see that it's Seth's phone. It's lit up with a text message. I go to look away, feeling I'm intruding, but my curiosity gets the better of me. Well, he wouldn't have left it on there if he wanted things to not be seen, would he? And it's hard to not read it, it's literally calling out to me, facing me and right in front of my eyes. Well, if I turn the phone slightly round, which I find myself doing.

<< Can't wait to see you soon, what would I do without you in my life? Xx>>

He's got one of those fancy phones that displays a picture of the sender next to it and I feel my heart sink when I see it's a very attractive woman with dark long hair and the hugest eyes I've ever seen, smiling.

I shouldn't be upset or disappointed. After all, I get a ton of texts each day from Grant, and his are worded not far different. And, they're completely unsolicited. Maybe this text is too. Perhaps Seth is being stalked, or maybe it's a wrong number. Yes, bound to be. He doesn't have a girlfriend, he told me. It's just a beautiful woman, texting the wrong number and looking all gorgeous.

I gaze over at Seth who is still talking, and he catches my eye and smiles at me. I smile back and turn back to see the ducks have returned. If they had swum away to have a quick, passionate moment, it's over very quickly.

The phone buzzes again. I try to keep staring at the ducks but eventually give in and look back at the phone and it's another message.

<<Seth, he's out of my life for good. It's just us now.>>

What does that mean? I actually feel my heart jump into

life, beating quickly and racing, but I feel cold and hot at the same time and my eyes fill up.   Well, it's definitely not a wrong number. And, I get the feeling that it's not a stalker either.   *'He's out of my life?'*   Who is she talking about, and what's it got to do with Seth?   And, *'it's just us now'*?   This is obviously why he hasn't got a girlfriend, because the woman he's been with had someone else but now it's over and it's going to be just them.   How could I have been so stupid, to think he'd be interested in me.   I was just a stand-in, until the woman he wants is available, which is now, or so it appears.

One of the ducks quacks and I turn to look at it, and it's looking back at me as if to say *'well, you've been here 5 days and started to like a guy and was about to go off with him to his house and do who knows what.   What did you expect?'*   The duck's right.   It's a good job the text came in now and not an hour later.

'I've paid up.   Let's go.'   I look up to see Seth standing next to me.   He smiles, then frowns as he sees my face. 'What's up?' he asks.

I gulp and then pull the hardest face I can manage and fling his phone at him.   'You've had some messages,' I say. 'From... from....'   I can't finish the sentence.   One, because I don't know what to call her.   And two, because he's reading the messages and is frowning even harder than I am.   He breathes out through his nose, making it flare, and he looks really angry.   He shakes his head, puts the phone in his pocket and looks back to me.

'It's no good just standing there and looking at me,' I snap at him.   'You left the phone on the table, I couldn't help but read it, so don't even start to think about having a go at me. And it's a good job I did read it!'

'I'm not going to have a go at you,' he says, 'and why's it a good job you read it?'

'I was about to make a fool of myself', I reply, standing

and pushing my chair back very loudly, with it scraping across the floor. I grab my bag and storm past him towards the exit. The waiter smiles and goes to shake my hand and then steps back, obviously thinking better of it as he catches the look on my face. I get outside and Seth soon catches up with me.

'Lou...' he begins to say and touches my arm, but I flick it away.

'Why didn't you say?' I ask. 'You said you didn't have anyone.'

He runs his fingers through his hair, looking really frustrated. 'I said I didn't have a girlfriend, and I don't. But, I've other people in my life and I hadn't realised I had to list them all for you. Jeez, Lou, not everything is all about you. There's other things going on other than the dramas with your boyfriend, fiancé, lover, whatever he is.'

This stings me. I told him all about Grant because he'd asked me, he was interested, wasn't he? Or did I get that wrong too?

'I was going to go home with you!' I shout at him.

'I hadn't invited you,' he replies and I feel humiliated. He looks like he regrets saying that immediately. 'Look, I didn't mean it like that. Tonight's been good, it's been...'

'...fun?' I finish for him. He nods. 'Yes, just a bit of fun,' I continue. 'I don't know why I thought it would be anything else.' Mind you, why should I have thought it would be more than that, I've known him 5 days and seen him a handful of times.

He frowns and looks confused. After a few seconds he says, 'It's complicated, but not what you think.'

I sigh. 'Maybe it's complicated for you. But, for me, it's very simple indeed. You took me out for the evening whilst Libby worked. And, I had a good meal, and now I want to go home. Alone.'

'Come on, let's get in the car,' he says and starts to walk away. Just as he does so, a taxi pulls up and a couple get out.

I run up to the driver's window. 'Can you take me into Marmaris?' I ask. I pray he speaks English. The driver nods and I breathe a sigh of relief as I pull the rear door open.

'Lou,' Seth calls out and walks back.

'I'm getting a cab,' I say and get in. The window is down and he puts his head in.

'Come on Lou,' he says, 'At least let me take you back to Libby's.'

I shake my head. 'Thanks for the meal,' I say, and I stuff a handful of notes into his shirt pocket. 'There's my share of the bill.'

He stands back to retrieve the notes, presumably to give them back to me, and I take my chance, telling the driver to go. I can't help but cry on the drive home, with the driver passing me a tissue and singing along with the radio to me, smiling kindly. I only have myself to blame and should have paid attention to my gut instinct. It's rarely been wrong, and I'll be on my guard now and won't believe a word he says ever again. And, I wish his mystery woman all the luck in the world, she's very welcome to him.

CHAPTER THIRTEEN

'So, let me get this right' Libby says, pausing to take another lick of her ice cream. We're walking in what feels like 200 degrees heat, on a pathway which goes all the way from Marmaris to Içmeler which, I get the impression, is a very long way. I'm melting, my feet ache and most of the ice cream is on the path as it's dripped off the cone quicker than I can lick it. 'You're angry with Seth because he was going to take you back to his place to give you a seeing to, but that's before you found out he has a friend who just happens to be female, and you don't fancy him anyway because he's ...rank?'

I tut and give her one of my looks. 'Yes,' I snap, 'that's about it although you left out the bit about him being a liar and a rat and...'

'...a key thief' she butts in. 'Of course.' Libby continues licking her ice cream. How come half of it isn't down her top like it is mine?

I stop walking and pull her gently by her shoulder to spin her round to face me. 'You don't look very upset for me,' I say.

She removes her sunglasses to look directly at me and

replies 'Upset about which bit exactly? That you didn't get to go back to his place for a fumble, or that he has a mystery girlfriend that you have no proof of? Or, the fact that you found jeep keys in a jacket pocket. He's not a very good thief if he took something from us and hid them in our apartment. Don't you think he'd have thrown them away, or took them somewhere else? I think you're over-reacting.' She starts to walk on again.

I stand, mouth open and aghast. Then, I walk quickly to catch her up. 'Over-reacting? I don't think so.'

'Lou, I love you very much, you know I do. But, you've a history of over-reacting and dramatising. Oh, stop looking so outraged, you know it's true.'

This is scandalous. Me? Over-reacting? I'll admit I can get a little carried away with things and look into them too deeply. And, yes, I can then get a bit fixated on my suspicions. Not that this is a suspicion, I'm pretty sure it's all true. But, over-reacting? No way, never. Well, possibly a little, but not much at all. Libby is just one of those naturally laid back people that really don't look into anything too deeply at all. And, she trusts absolutely everyone, unless proved otherwise, which isn't necessarily a good thing.

'There's no proof of any lying,' she says, 'and you're just cross because you almost jumped into bed with him without thinking it through.'

I sigh and shake my head. I so do not feel cross with myself, I just feel, well, betrayed. And, who's to say I would have gone to bed with him? We might have just kissed and cuddled a bit. Yes, I admit I was imagining more happening, but we'd had wine and the atmosphere was intimate. Once out in the fresh air, we'd have probably calmed down a bit.

We carry on walking in silence and I realise we haven't seen a bar for about 20 minutes, but at least we're now under trees and the sun has stopped grilling us. We don't pass many people, probably because no one else is as daft as us walking out in this heat. *Mad Dogs and Englishman* come to mind.

After a few more seconds of ice cream licking, I ask Libby, 'Give me an example of how I'm over-reacting.'

'Ok,' she says, 'you don't know for sure that this woman who text him is his girlfriend. Maybe they're just friends.'

'No,' I snap back. 'You should have seen his face. He looked, well, really cross and confused and... and... suspicious. And she looked all gorgeous in that photo, all big eyed and dark and mysterious.'

Libby laughs. 'Mysterious? Look, if you ask me, you're just a bit miffed that you didn't get to snuggle up with him in his house. And, if you really want my honest opinion, you like him more than you're letting on.' I tut. 'And, at the end of the day, you do still have Grant. It's not over and he texts you at least ten times a day. How's it different to this woman texting Seth?'

'Because, Seth knows all about Grant and I don't know anything about this floozy.'

'Floozy?' she laughs. 'Haven't heard that phrase for years. She's probably this really nice woman who just happens to be friends with him. Did she look like a local?'

'I didn't get a brilliant look at the photo, it was a private message after all,' I protest.

'Umm, you just read the text instead.' She ignores my over-the-top tutting. 'Look, you've known Seth for, well, not quite a week. So, if you've fallen for him and feel let down, you've only yourself to blame. What happened to the, 'I just want to spend time alone and recharge my batteries?' You were quite keen to deplete your batteries last night with a guy you hardly know. And then there's Hamil too. I don't think he's expecting just a dinner and walk along the promenade.'

'Well, good.   Maybe I'll like a bit of fun with him. Perhaps it's the new me.'

She laughs at that, which I'm a little offended by, as it's not that ridiculous a notion, is it? 'You'll be needing a holiday when you get back to the UK, after all these men and sexual encounters. You'll be worn out.'

Actually, it is a bit laughable. I know that it's not really me.   I haven't had a huge amount of sexual encounters before, despite my age, and never with guys I've only just met. And, although I'm in my early thirties, I'm not really sure I'm up to the job.   It's just not me.   I mean, I'm interested in Hamil, of course I am, and it's not as though I have any commitments.   Well, yes, technically there's a boyfriend who wants to be a fiancé but other than that I'm free. But, I'm hopeless at being anything associated with the term 'sexy.' I'm a self-confessed 'up-tight' and self-conscious woman. Having wanton sex with literal strangers, without a care in the world? There's no point me even going there, as much as I might dream of it. Unless Hamil can prove me wrong which is always a possibility.

We walk on in silence for a while but, although we've had words, there's no atmosphere. That's what we're like, Libby and me. We can have a bit of an animated discussion but then it's done and dusted. We go past a strange looking bar. I say bar, but it's not a working bar, there's no drinks on it, or bottles, or customers or staff. It's completely desolate. But, there's a huge snake sculpture forming the worktop and then going up to the roof before disappearing into the trees. It looks as though it's part of the hotel grounds that we're passing. The snake's head is huge, about the size of 3 footballs, and it's staring straight at me, no matter what direction I look. Libby doesn't look interested in it at all, she's obviously seen it a million times. I take a photo and then walk on.

After what seems like hours, we finally hit a bar and I wonder where all the customers in there have come from. It can only be accessible by walking, as there's no road here from what I can see, and we haven't seen anyone go past us. So, they could only have come from the other direction, Içmeler, and this gives me hope that we're not too far away from our destination as the approaching visitors do not seem too hot and bothered.

I can see a youngish couple laughing at the propped up welcoming board at the front of the bar and can't resist having a read. 'Flat beer, watered whiskey, slow food, crap music, horrible staff, terrible service but satisfaction guaranteed!!' I smile and look at Libby who's reading it too. 'Don't you love it?' she asks as she makes her way to the counter. And, I have to say I do. I'm really starting to feel settled here, and I love this crazy sense of humour. It's refreshing and fun, and I could totally get used to this.

Although packed, we get a great seat by the water's edge and sit quietly sipping cold lemonade. We realise the bar belongs to the hotel set against the backdrop of hills on the opposite side of the path and I watch kids, presumably guests there, come down a water chute next to us straight into the sea below. After a while, a guy comes down, who isn't of the smallest build and it looks like he's got stuck. His wife has to come and help coax him along, getting him to wriggle gently until he finally is released from the plastic trap. We both frown whilst watching but cheer when we witness his release. 'I thought it was big beer man from below our old flat,' I say.

'Wouldn't that be funny if we actually saw him here?' Libby asks. We wonder how many people from Abingdon are in Marmaris or Içmeler at this very moment, or whether we're the only ones. Wouldn't it be strange if people in this very bar lived just around the corner from me, or were customers of the company I work for, or are friends of Grant. Although some of those scenarios are possible, I can't imagine any of Grant's friends ever coming here. It's just not their style, but it is mine.

'So, how come you haven't met this woman of Seth's?' I ask Libby, 'he is Jude's brother after all.'

She shrugs. 'Exactly. That's why I don't think she is his 'woman.' If she was, Jude would have mentioned her, and he hasn't, not at all. I haven't seen Seth with anyone since I've been here. I mean, he's taken women out for a drink here and there, but nothing serious. He's too busy working. I think you've read the signs wrong, honestly. He's a really nice guy.'

'So why did you pick Jude over Seth, if Seth is so good?'

Libby frowns. 'Odd question,' she says.

I shrug. 'Just curious' I reply.

'Well, he's just not really my type, I suppose. You know me, I never go for the nice guy. I always go for the one that's complicated or a screw up.'

'Is Jude complicated or a screw up?' I ask.

'Not a screw up, but he's not an easy guy to read,' she says. 'He's got a spark and he makes my heart race. Seth doesn't do that for me. He's too nice.'

I smile. 'We've never had the same taste in men, have we? Look at you and Grant, you've never got on or seen eye to eye.'

'Grant's a totally different kettle of fish,' she says and turns in her seat and looks away towards the sea.

I'm not sure if I'm over-reacting but I feel as though I've touched a nerve. I'm sure of it, but I've no idea what or how.

'I'm just saying the two of you have never got on. Believe me, I really wanted you to be friends, but it just never worked out, no matter how hard I tried.'

'No, you are definitely right there,' she says and looks back at me, her head on one side and her chin resting on her hand as she leans on the table. Her eyes have hardened and she seems almost hostile. To me, how they were together really was a big deal. I tried so hard to make it all ok, and it was more Grant than Libby that caused the problems as she can get on generally with anyone, and I saw her try. Yet, nothing worked and it was exhausting always being piggy in the middle.

'Look, he just didn't like me,' she says, 'it's as simple as that. Sometimes people just don't click.' She makes it sound that simple, but I don't believe for one moment it was, and it's always felt like there's something that neither are telling me.

'Grant was always very open about the fact he disliked you,' I say, 'but you never made a fuss, or said you felt the same way. But you did dislike him, didn't you?'

She hesitates for a while, then nods. 'Yep, I did,' she says, 'sorry. I really tried to like him Lou, but I just couldn't trust him, he just didn't seem right for you. You weren't yourself when you was with him, you were different somehow.'

'That's what he said when him and me were first together, and I'd go and stay with him for a night or so. He said I was different, until I'd been away from you for a few hours and then I'd be nice.'

She looks at me, confused. 'Different how?'

'Just that I'd act differently when I'd been with you, and that he didn't trust you and thought you were...'

'What?' she asks, sitting forward.

'Well, you were a bit *common*'

She snorts and it sounds like a half-laugh, combined with disdain. 'What else?'

'Flirtatious and *easy*. That's what he thought about you.' I feel terrible saying it, as I'd never describe Libby in that way, but she's asked for the truth and I'm giving it to her. Seeing how upset she looks I add, 'It doesn't matter any more, now that Grant and I are splitting up, he can think what he likes.'

This doesn't seem to make any difference to how she's feeling right now so I won't tell her how he also said that he felt she appeared desperate and, if she'd had a chance, she'd have come onto him without giving me a thought. It's nonsense and a lie, I know she would never hurt me in any way, or betray me.

Libby looks back at me, bites her lip and then says, 'Grant doesn't know me at all and I really hope that you don't go back to him. He's really not worth it.'

I nod. I know she's right and I don't want to go back.

'I wasn't going to get between you,' she continues, 'as it wasn't any of my business, and I was leaving anyway. And I'm sorry I left in the night, that last evening I was with you, but I just couldn't stand the atmosphere my presence was causing in your apartment and it was just best to go. I know it upset you, and I'm sorry.'

'No, don't be sorry,' I reassure her, seeing how upset she is. I hug her and she hugs me back and, by the time she pulls away, her eyes are dry and I can see the moment has passed. Her phone ringing breaks the short silence. Whilst she answers it, I pick up my bags and go and pay for the drinks then wait under the tree. After only a small amount of time, she comes to me and it's as though the last few minutes didn't happen. The old Libby is back. 'That was Seth.' I roll my eyes and she hits me with her bag. 'Tomorrow's gig is definitely on. Two men, all to ourselves, for our first jeep picnic safari.' She looks like a child, all smiles and excitement and I grin back.

She tells me we're now heading straight to the dolmuş stop down on the beach at Içmeler as we need to hurry back to Marmaris and buy goodies at the supermarket for the hamper we'll take with us. Exploring Içmeler will have to wait for another day. Seth has triumphed again in Libby's eyes by managing to arrange this jeep safari with a couple of guys who want us to take them to a secluded picnic area off the beaten track, somewhere not full of tourists, but that's quiet and isolated. And, although still angry with him, I can't help but feel a little thankful that he's somehow got us this trip. It will be fun and Libby and I will get to spend the day together, out in the sunshine, with hopefully a good couple of guys who want us to show them a good time. And, if anyone can show guys a good time, it's my bestie and me. Yep, my mind is quickly cleared of any negative thoughts of Seth, the mystery woman and Grant and Libby's conflict. Tomorrow is now our priority and it's going to be a good day.

CHAPTER FOURTEEN

Today, there's been no chance of the jeep keys going missing, we put them by the front door last night, both of us checking they were there about twenty times, and this morning it was the first thing we both went to grab. And now, the two of us are in the jeep, basking in the sunshine despite the early hour. Well, 9am is early for over here, the place hasn't woken up yet. We drive past bars and restaurants where the staff are already out hosing down the paths. This town is spotless. I can't imagine people doing that back home, hosing down the pathways. I see a road cleaner come out of hibernation about once every 5 years, but that's about it.

The hamper's packed, the blankets are under the back seats, there's a whole load of fresh water to drink plus wine and beers for our guests, all packed tightly into a couple of cool bags. And, we're both in our uniforms that Libby designed and insisted on, looking like the Pink Ladies on a day trip to the beach. I've told Libby that she's Rizzo and I'm Frenchie, but she wasn't amused.

I actually had a good night's sleep, somehow having started to get used to the heat and the call to prayer in the early hours, and realise that I've now been here for a whole week. I'm so settled, it feels more like I've been here months.

This morning, all thoughts of Seth are out of my mind. Completely. I am not going to think about him at all. Nope, not at all. Not one little bit. He's history.

'So, have you heard from Seth?' I ask Libby. I slap my forehead, having no idea where that came from and I'm really quite disappointed in myself. I need to give myself a stern talking to later. Again.

'What, since he rang me yesterday to tell me about our booking? Er, no...' She shakes her head and concentrates back on the road. There are a few taxi drivers and a couple of dolmuşes, but that's it. It's strange to see it so quiet.

I try to take my mind off Seth who, for some reason, has decided to dominate my thoughts again. 'What's the plural of dolmuş?' I ask Libby.

Libby glances at me, raises her eyebrows and shrugs.

'I was wondering if its dolmuşes or dolmi.' She laughs and shakes her head. It's a serious question. 'Don't you know?'

'No,' Libby answers. 'Haven't really ever thought about it or had to have a discussion in Turkish about it. But, if I had to choose, I'd say that it's just dolmuş whether there's one of them or a hundred. Maybe you should ask someone Turkish, like Hamil. It can be your opening line on your date. Actually, don't do that, it'll put him off and you won't see him again.'

I laugh. She's right. I do talk about some boring crap sometimes, but it takes my mind off other things. Like Seth.

'Heard from Grant today?' Libby asks.

I feel myself tense and just say, 'Nope, nothing since yesterday. Thankfully.' She nods but I can see her clench her jaw, the thought of Grant has wound her up as much as it has me. This has been the longest he's gone without either trying to ring me or text me, and I'm feeling optimistic he's starting to get the message. It's taken a week but it looks as though I'm finally getting through to him.

Changing the subject I ask, 'So, tell me again how Seth found us these two guys?'

Libby is slowing down, looking at hotels on both sides of the road, and I hold out the piece of paper I've been keeping in my hand to show her the hotel name we're looking for. She quickly glances at it and keeps driving ahead. I am the navigator, a title that I intend to use throughout the day, even if it only means I hold pieces of paper in front of Libby's face.

'They found *him*,' she replies. 'They said that someone had recommended us and that he'd know how to sort it. He bigged us up and we got the gig. We should be grateful to him.' She gives me one of those looks which is actually saying 'so, give the guy a break, you neurotic, strange friend.'

I make a loud humph sound. 'Well, I guess we should be grateful he hadn't taken the keys this time.'

Libby ignores me. 'Here we are' she says, and puts on the brakes. 'And, wow, there *they* are, our guests for the day. Today is looking good already.'

I follow her gaze and gasp aloud. There, on the steps of the hotel, are two incredibly good-looking men. They're not just good looking, they are like models. I feel like a letch, as my tongue is virtually hanging out of my mouth and I make a really creepy sound, which Libby instantly mimics, causing us both to start giggling like school girls. I'm not even ashamed, these two are gorgeous and I feel we've been well and truly blessed on this fine morning. Any thoughts I may have had of giving up on men totally have just gone flying out the back of the jeep.

Libby jumps out to go and greet them. As she leaves, she

turns round and says, 'Be careful, don't make your life even more complicated.'

'I'm just looking, nothing wrong with that,' I reply and smile. I swear I'm dribbling. 'And make sure you remember Jude, you know, the love of your life?'

Libby smiles and turns back round, and carries on over to them. I stay in the jeep and check my lipstick in the mirror and, as they come over to me, I go to say 'Morning' but instead of that I just let out a very weird sound, my voice constricted by pure lust. I cough, as though to clear my throat and try again, this time more successfully.

The taller of the two walks round to my side of the jeep, says good morning, kisses my hand and smiles. He has teeth like they do in those American shows, you know, all white and straight and, well, perfect. His friend introduces the two of them to us as Dave and Steve. They're incredibly well spoken and polite, smartly dressed in linen shorts and shirts. I instantly decide they're University students who've just finished their studies and are enjoying a well-earned break before going to their first job, probably as doctors or something equally impressive. I could high five Libby if it wouldn't look too obvious. They go to jump into the back of the jeep but Dave stops and says 'How about I sit in the back with you?'

I look at Libby who nods. 'As long as you can navigate from there,' she says as I climb into the back. Then, more quietly, 'and you keep your eye on the map.' I giggle.

As Steve climbs into the front, Libby checks with him that it is just the picnic tour they're after. The boys look at each other and grin. 'Yes please, if that's ok with you two lovely ladies. Is there really a picnic?'

'Yes,' replies Libby. She looks concerned. 'That is what you want, isn't it?'

They look at each other and then turn back to Libby and nod. 'As long as you're both going to eat with us, that's fine.' Libby nods but gives me an apprehensive look in the mirror, and I realise that we only made enough food for two, not realising that we'd be sharing with them. Plus, there's not quite as much food there as she probably thinks there is. This is due to me eating several of the borek and a few slices of the bread. And a few tomatoes. Well, quite a lot actually.

'Somewhere secluded, obviously,' says Dave, moving a little closer to me, rubbing his legs up against mine. Wow, he's friendly, a little too much but it's better than them being hostile or all quiet and serious. It would be like being with Grant.

'Of course,' answers Libby. 'I know a lovely little alcove where no one will disturb you. Are you hoping to sunbathe?'

The men smile and Dave answers, 'Why not, as long as we're careful with the sun tan lotion,' which causes Steve to look round and they both laugh, rather eccentrically.

I'm not quite sure what's caused the frivolity, and I can see by Libby's expression in the mirror that she's not sure either, and I wonder if the two of them have either been drinking already, or if they're just a couple of characters, which is my polite way of saying 'strange.' I'm hoping it's the latter, as I'm good with strange people, finding it very easy over the years to attract them to me and it means I won't have to hide the bottles of wine we've brought. We drive off and I'm feeling confident that this day is going to be a success and we'll be able to prove Jude wrong about the business not being a good idea. It suddenly dawns on me that, although Seth wasn't sure about the business either, it's him that's got us these customers, so maybe he's not as much against it as I'd thought. Or, maybe he just likes to get one over on his brother, which is more likely. Whatever, we're going to enjoy the day.

My mind goes into overdrive as I think of how these guys will tell everyone in the whole resort about us and how great the trip is, and we'll be booked up every day and will be named 'Entrepreneurs of the Year' and will feature in *Hello* magazine, or something like that. Not that entrepreneurs are commonly talked about in *Hello* magazine. Maybe there's an actual entrepreneurs magazine, I'll have to research it when we get back and send the editor an email to start the ball rolling.

Luckily, the cove is only 20 minutes away and so I don't have long to cope with Dave sitting literally on my lap, breathing in my ear. I've tried moving a bit further away but have now run out of room, trapped between him and the front passenger seat. If he carries on, I'm going to have to start taking about dolmuş and plural rules.

'So, who told you about us?' Libby asks Steve.

'We met a guy in the bar the other night. We said what we wanted, he said he knows two ladies that could cater for our needs.' He gives a sly look at Dave and they both give a little laugh again. Strange. 'He gave us a number to ring for a guy who'd arrange it with you direct. Seth, I think.' Libby nods. 'He's a good guy, didn't ask many questions, just made sure we were serious and would definitely turn up.'

'He is a good guy, isn't he Lou,' Libby says.

'Smashing,' I smile sarcastically at her in the mirror.

I've no idea what questions they thought Seth might ask them but am pleased he checked they were serious.

'How long have you lived here?' Dave asks me.

'I don't,' I reply and then suddenly panic. What if he's from the authorities and is testing me, to see if I've got visas, and permission to work and all of that type of stuff. 'Well, I do and I don't. I'm visiting, but don't worry, I'm not actually working or claiming money or anything like that.' If I didn't want to sound suspicious or draw attention to myself, I just failed miserably.

He smiles and puts a finger up to his lips and then to mine. 'Don't worry,' he says, 'we won't tell anyone. You can trust us, we just want to have a good time.' He puts his hand on my knee and I flick it away quickly. 'Sorry,' he says, 'a bit soon, or just not part of the deal?'

'Both!' I reply, frowning at him.

'It's just you're, well, very pretty.' I frown for a few more seconds and then relax a bit. Sweet-talking easily wows me.

'Thank you,' I say, 'but leg stroking isn't what's on offer here.'

'Of course not,' he says, looking truly apologetic. His friend turns round and shouts 'be cool!' at him and Libby and I laugh, which seems to set them both off again. They're behaving like two schoolboys yet are clearly all man. I wonder how old they are, it's difficult to tell.

The jeep comes to a halt as Libby pulls up at our destination and I exhale loudly at the sight in front of me. This is truly one of the most beautiful things I've ever seen, just like on a postcard, and in the middle of nowhere, a hidden gem. The clients look delighted too. We're in a tiny cove, bordered by trees and shrubbery, with white sand leading up to a clear, blue sea. It's the sort of thing I've seen on those adverts that holiday companies start to show on TV just after Christmas, when we're depressed about the winter, the amount of money we've spent on the festivities and are courted by adverts promising us a wonderful getaway.

'Wow,' I say, 'this is so private.'

Dave jumps from the back of the jeep and holds a hand out for me. 'Just what Seth promised,' he says. Umm, did he indeed, I think to myself. Once I'm out of the jeep, Steve slaps Dave on the back and they high five again, then walk off to explore.

'They're a little excitable,' I whisper to Libby, as we watch them walk away.

'Very,' she replies. 'Steve had his hand on my knee virtually the whole way here. After flicking it away ten times, it was just easier to leave it there.' I shake my head and tut, but when we look at each other we can't help but laugh. We look back to our guests and find them standing and staring at us.

'Well?' Steve asks.

We look at each other puzzled and then Libby realises what they mean and jumps into the back of the jeep. 'Sorry guys,' she calls out. I'll get the blankets, we'll be with you in a minute.'

They thank her and then turn back to look at the sea. She throws one to me and I walk towards them. 'Where would you like us to put you?' I ask.

'We're totally in your hands,' Dave says. 'This is a first for us. You put us wherever you think is most comfortable.'

'Ok,' I reply, a little hesitantly. I'm not exactly experienced at positioning blankets on sand and haven't the first idea where would be best. But, if that's what they want…

'Are you putting us right next to each other?' asks Dave suddenly. He's looking a bit uncomfortable and I wonder for a second if he has a problem with 'personal space' and 'comfort zones.'

I look at Libby who's joined me, putting the other blanket down next to mine. 'Well, that's generally how it works,' she says. 'We all go together, it's not a massive space here.'

Their eyes light up. 'Wow,' says Dave. He looks like he's won the lottery and has warmed to the idea of our 'cosy' blanket placement. They hardly give us a chance to put the blankets down at all before throwing themselves on them, one each. We smile politely at them and go to get the food.

'Do you think they're been drinking?' I ask.

We turn and look at them for a few moments. They're deep in conversation, wide eyed and giggling. 'Possibly, well, they are on holiday I guess. A bit early in my opinion but, hey, nothing to do with us. Maybe it's good that we're starting on the food early, it might calm them down a bit.'

We carry the hampers over and, in that short amount of time, see that Dave and Steve have taken their shirts off, and we both stop dead and stare. These guys are as good out of their shirts as they were when wearing them.

'Don't you get burnt,' Libby says, which brings me out of my slightly hypnotic state. 'I've got some lotion you can put on in a moment.'

'Lotion,' Steve says to Dave with a huge grin. I decide that they are obviously just very smiley guys. And slightly insane. We walk back to the jeep to get parasols and lotion.

'Your tongue was actually hanging out then,' says Libby. 'Haven't you seen a six pack before?'

'Not a real one,' I giggle, 'just in photographs. Wow, they're a couple of handsome guys.'

'They most definitely are. Pesky Jude! Why aren't I single?' she asks and we laugh.

This is when it hits me that Jude isn't just a casual fling for Libby, she really is serious about him. I knew she liked him, but I hadn't realised quite how much. Me, on the other hand, am free and single. Well, apart from Grant not getting that we're actually over. And, Hamil waiting for a date. And, Seth.

As if reading my mind, Libby says 'It was good of Seth to sort this for us. I wonder who it was that told these guys to ring him?'

I shrug. 'Probably one of his mysterious friends, lovers, whatever.'

'Oh, come on Lou, pack it in! Look, even you've got to admit he's done us a favour here. Yet, you insist in thinking he's a bad person, just because of that text message.'

'Messages,' I correct her. 'Plural. Look, we're going to have to agree to disagree about him. I don't trust him, he has too many secrets along with secret girlfriends and all sorts of skulduggery.' I have no idea where that word came from. 'Although yes, I'm grateful to him for sorting this out today. OK? '

Libby shakes her head. 'Don't judge everyone by Grant's standards!'

This takes me back. Where did that come from? The conversation has suddenly turned serious. 'What's that supposed to mean? Grant may be many things but he's always been honest and faithful.'

'Really,' asks Libby, putting her hands on her hips.

'Yes!' I state loudly.

Libby goes to reply and then stops. After a deep breath she says, 'Let's put Grant to one side for the moment and talk about Seth. At the end of the day Lou, you're judging him based on *your* standards of honesty. You, that has a guy back home who doesn't even understand you're breaking it off with him. And, here you are a long way away, angry because a guy you met a week ago didn't sleep with you because you found out he has a female friend that he hasn't told you about. Yet, you're about to go on a date with a waiter who clearly just wants to have some fun with you, but, for some reason, you can't seem to stop thinking that Seth's being secretive, deceitful and, let's not forget, a key stealer. When, all he's actually done is get us a day's work with two very nice and good-looking men who are currently waiting for us to provide them with a picnic. Can you give the guy a break?'

I go to answer back, but I can't think of what to say, so I huff and puff and try to stare her out.

"Um, ladies?'

'In a minute,' I shout out to the guys. 'Look, Libby, I agree about Seth. I've maybe misjudged him, or been a bit too judgemental. But what they hell did you mean about Grant? What's he to do with this?'

She shakes her head. 'Nothing'

'Libby?' I ask again.

Just as she looks like she's going to answer, one of the guys calls out again, this time a little more impatiently.

We turn with our best fake smiles, which fade in approximately two seconds. Because, there in front of us, lay Dave and Steve completely naked on the blankets, grinning.

CHAPTER FIFTEEN

'They're naked,' whispers Libby, looking a bit like an awkward ventriloquist talking with a fake smile still in place.

I nod and bite my lip. 'Yes, and laying on the blankets. Your blankets. The ones we sit on when in the flat. Blankets I don't think I can ever sit on again.'

We carry on staring at them. 'Do you think there's any chance that they're just after an all over tan. Ooh, maybe they're naturists,' I say.

Libby doesn't reply but just carries on staring. I, on the other hand, turn back to look at the jeep. It's one of those moments where I think that, if I can't see them, they can't see me. Maybe they'll disappear. Or, at least, cover themselves up.

'Is there a problem,' asks Dave.

'Should we have waited a bit?' asks Steve.

My resolve to not look runs out and I turn back to face them. Steve slaps Dave around the head and says 'We said we needed them to guide us and then you went and ruined it by saying we should get our kit off.'

'They were chatting!' Dave shouts and slaps him back. 'And we've only got 4 hours, one of which has already gone.

I thought I should start things off.'

I'm rooted to the spot whilst Libby walks slowly towards them. Which, in my opinion, is quite brave as she's heading towards all manner of flesh and dangly bits.

'I'm not quite sure what you think this is, but it's definitely not a nudist camp. I suggest you put your shorts back on,' Libby says. Steve looks embarrassed and moves to get his clothes.

'See, she's telling us what to do and being dominant. I said she would,' Steve says to Dave in a very loud whisper that even I can hear from where I'm standing. They start to get dressed and Libby walks back to me.

She rolls her eyes as she grabs the wine from the cool bag and pours two glasses. By the time she turns and walks back, they are both dressed, well, the bottom half anyway. And they both look a bit sheepish.

'Here,' she says, holding out the drinks.

'Sorry,' says Steve.' Its our first time doing something like this.'

'Ours too!' I say, feeling a bit sorry for the pair as I walk towards them.

'Really?' asks Dave. 'Seth said you were very experienced.'

Libby gives me a look. 'I am,' she quickly says, 'Lou's just starting out with me.' They look pretty pleased about this, for some very strange reason that only they could know. I've given up trying to work these two out.

We both sit down on the blankets with them and start taking out the food. After what I've just seen, I can barely look at the small, cigar shaped pastries. In fact, I don't think I'll be able to look at them in the same way again.

'Oh,' said Dave frowning. 'There really is food then!'

'That's generally what a picnic means,' says Libby, looking

at me and raising her eyebrows. 'Surely it's not the first time you've had a picnic?' The men laugh nervously and take a plate.

Libby grabs some lotion out of the other bag. 'As you seem keen to keep your top half clothes-free, you ought to put some lotion on. You're starting to look a little pink.'

'This is more like it,' says Dave to Steve, and they pat each other on the back and turn away from us, both moving along with their plates of food to be just in front of Libby.

We raise our eyebrows at each other and Libby puts some lotion on her hands and passes me the bottle. Oh well, there's worse jobs in the world I could be doing. This isn't exactly a chore, even if they are weird and freaking us out a bit. We take a guy each and rub the lotion into their backs with both men making contented sounds, a little over-the-top and strange in my opinion, but at least it might keep them quiet for a few minutes.

I go to squeeze some more lotion onto my hands and accidentally squirt some onto my blouse. Tutting, I go to grab a serviette. 'Lou, that'll stain,' says Libby 'let's remove it quick' and she starts to rub at my blouse whilst I continue to apply the lotion to Dave's back. I notice that Steve has turned his head to watch and he taps Dave on the arm. Dave then turns round and watches Libby as she continues to dab at my clothes.

'Maybe you need to take it off for her,' Dave says, and Steve nods in agreement.

We stare at them for a few seconds and then Libby slams down the bottle and folds her arms. 'Right,' she says, 'I've had enough of this. You're like two randy adolescents. What is wrong with you?'

'It's like we said,' Steve explains, 'we haven't done this before.'

'Done what before?' asks Libby. 'Sunbathed, eaten a picnic, acted normally?'

'No,' replies Dave. 'Been with women like you.'

Libby stands up which, I must admit, is a much more menacing stance and I stand to join her. 'What do you mean, women like us?'

Steve turns to Dave and asks nervously, 'What's the correct terminology? I don't want to offend them. Particularly that one,' pointing at Libby, 'she looks a bit moody.'

'Well?' repeats Libby, definitely looking moody. Even I'm scared.

'Hookers,' says Dave.

'Prostitutes,' says Steve.

And for a few seconds, we say absolutely nothing, then we slowly start to repeat the names they've just used and find ourselves waving our arms around like a couple of lunatics, screaming at them.

'You see,' says Dave, shielding himself. 'It's not the correct terminology. We've angered them.'

'Angered us?' I shout. 'We're not prostitutes, or hookers. We're... we're... what are we?' I ask Libby, frowning.

'Escorts!' shouts Libby

'Ah, that's the word. Escorts,' repeats Dave.

'Not that kind of Escort!' I shout, kicking sand at the pair. 'Tour guides. You know, as in escorting you around the place. Do you understand?'

The men jump up. 'That's not fair,' says Steve, brushing away the sand I've just kicked all over him. 'That'll stick to the lotion and we've got it in all sorts of places!'

'Not fair?' I say, moving angrily towards them. 'I'll show you not fair.' I go to kick more sand.

'Look,' says Dave, backing away. 'There's obviously been some confusion. That guy told us you were hookers, and...'

'What guy?' I ask. 'Seth?'

'Yes.' said Dave. 'Well, not exactly. But he didn't say you weren't. The first guy we spoke to said what you do for a living and told us to go to Seth and he'd arrange this trip, which he did. We presumed Seth was your, well...'

'Pimp,' says Steve. Dave nods in agreement.

There's silence again for a few seconds, as we all look from one to the other, until Dave says, 'So, I guess there'll be no sex then?'

Libby growls in frustration, grabs their wine glasses from them, spilling a little on the blankets before pouring the liquid away. She turns on her heels to march back to the jeep. I yank at a corner of the blanket two of us had sat on, nearly causing Dave to stumble as he's still standing on it. Steve goes to grab another corner to help, but I bark at him to back off and that I'll do it on my own.

'Are we going?' asks Dave.

'Yes,' says Libby. 'Your tour is most definitely over. There's nothing to explore, especially us!'

The men follow behind, heads down like two naughty children, until we reach the jeep where they climb into the back. We continue to pick up all our things and throw it in, narrowly avoiding their legs which they quickly move out of the way.

'Will you be dropping us back at the hotel?' asks Steve.

'We're hardly going to leave you in the middle of nowhere!' I snap, 'I doubt either of you would have the sense to find your way back,' and I climb into the front seat and yank angrily at my seat belt, slamming it into the catch.

Libby jumps in, starts the car and crunches the gears as she struggles to find the right one to pull away. The journey home is in silence. Libby's annoyed but I am seething. Is this Seth's idea of a joke? How could he humiliate us like this? What was he trying to do, trying to achieve? My cheeks grow redder and redder and I'm on the brink of crying. I feel, well, cheap and used and ... and...I can't believe I've been mistaken as a hooker. Me. I've never done anything *hooker* like in my life. I haven't even been to an *Ann Summers* party, that's how risqué I am.

Wow, this jeep moves quickly when an angry foot is slammed down to the floor. I hear the guys whisper something about them 'being about to die at the hands of a mad driver' and I spin round and give them one of my most scary looks and they quickly stop and look down at their feet. But I put my hand gently on Libby's arm and she slows down a little. I look at her face and, apart from her jaw being clenched, it's hard to tell what she's feeling right now. This is her business, her dream, and once again it's been sabotaged. And, surprise surprise, the same guy is involved.

Libby screeches to a halt by the hotel which we seem to have got to in half the time it took to get to the cove. She keeps the engine running, takes it out of gear and yanks the handbrake on. They don't move, just sit there and I realise they're waiting to be given permission to leave the vehicle. They look totally terrified. I glance round and point to the road and they jump out over the side.

Libby starts to pull away but Steve jumps in front of the jeep causing her to slam the brakes on. He looks from her to me and decides that I'm the safer option, so comes to my door and holds out a wad of money. I grab it and hand it straight to Libby, who starts to count it. Then, she hands it back to Dave who's bravely standing next to her door. 'You didn't get your tour,' she says. 'You didn't get anything you were promised.'

I look at her confused. She shrugs her shoulders and says, 'It's not their fault.'

I don't get how she can be so gracious, but I can't do anything about it. She starts to move back into gear but Dave shouts stop and leans in to kiss Libby on the cheek, then tries to give her a hug which she quickly pulls back from with a look of 'seriously?' Steve goes to kiss my cheek too but decides against it, taking my hand and awkwardly shaking it instead. 'No hard feelings?' he says. I look at Libby and we have to smile, although it's more of a hint of one than a grin. These aren't bad guys, they've been duped as much as us and were just out looking for fun.

'No hard feelings,' I reply.

'If you change your mind,' Dave shouts after us as we pull away, 'we're in room 314.'

Within a few seconds of driving, Libby suddenly starts to laugh and I have to chuckle too. Soon, we just can't stop and there's tears steaming down our cheeks, which we don't even bother to wipe away. Seriously, did all of that just happen? You couldn't have made it up, it's like we've been on a secret camera show and any moment now someone is going to pull over the jeep and tell us it was a prank. I'm laughing so much I'm having to pat myself on the chest as I almost can't catch my breath. Libby does the same and then stops, looking down at her blouse.

'What is it?' I ask her and she puts her hand in and pulls out a wad of notes.

'How the hell did he put that there without me feeling it?' she asks and laughs again.

'He's one sneaky dude! Well, at least we got paid,' I say. 'Not bad earnings for our first day as a couple of hookers? Thanks to Seth.'

Libby stops smiling. 'What do you mean, thanks to Seth? Oh no, don't tell me you think he's behind this? What is it with you?'

'Well, he's the one who booked us and spoke to them, and promised we'd give them a good time. How could he not be behind it?'

She shakes her head. 'Think about it,' I continue. 'You said yourself he'd tried to talk you out of doing the business on your own. Then, when you still go ahead, the keys went missing, before turning up in his pocket, and now this.'

'No Lou, that's unfair,' she replies, 'the keys were a mistake. And Seth would never have sold us as a pair of prostitutes. I know him, he'd never do it.'

'Look, I know you think he's great, but I think you've been conned. He's a sneak and a liar. Why can't you see any bad in that guy? Is it because he's Jude's brother, or do you have a bit of a thing for him?'

Libby looks really hurt. 'A thing for him? I'm going out with his brother, thanks very much. It wasn't that many days ago you thought he was brilliant yourself, about to go back to his place and snuggle up with him. Not everyone is a cheat and a liar. Jeez. Grant's really messed you up.'

I spin my head quickly towards her, causing it to make a loud click, but I ignore it. 'Stop blaming everything on Grant. This is nothing to do with him! Why do you keep bringing Grant into everything.'

She doesn't answer for a while and just stares ahead, but I'm not letting her off that easily. 'Well?' I yell.

'You always think everyone's out to get you. Lighten up Lou, you're so...'

'What?' I ask, realising my voice has gone up an octave and I'm crying. I can't believe how we're arguing like this.

'Stressy,' says Libby.

I gasp. 'Stressy? Give me an example!'

I wait for her to look sheepish and struggle to come up with something, but instead she instantly dives into a ton of

184

examples. Loads. 'Other than this Seth thing? Every email, phone call, messenger or Facebook chat we've had, you've said about being unhappy. It's either Grant, or work, or your mum. Lou, you've decided to stay in this position you're in, unhappy and unfulfilled. You wouldn't have done that years ago. You'd have changed it, flipped it all into a positive. Its what I loved about you. But, you've lost that zest. He's taken it, stolen it right from under your nose.'

I curse and look away, out at the roadside. I am so angry, I can't even think straight. How dare she? Libby's supposed to be my best friend and all she can do is bring up my faults, everything that's bad about me, every little thing. Yes, I have been a bit moany and down, but I thought I could talk to her. I trusted her. I agree, I'm different since she's been gone, which wasn't my fault I want to point out, and I have been happy sometimes, haven't I? I try to think of when, so that I can tell her and make her feel bad, but I soon realise that I can't think of anything. Nothing at all.

I can't even blame it all on Grant. I could have stood up for myself more, and not given in. The bottom line is, I had nothing and he offered me a great life, or what looked like a great life, and I took it. The difference between Libby and I is that she was unhappy with her life and went out to build another one. I let someone build mine for me.

I finally say, 'You just got up and run away from everything.'

'Everything?' replies Libby. 'What was there to run from? I was in a 2 bedroom rented flat, with a job I hated and a friend who'd just found the love of her life and wanted to spend every minute of her time with him. All I could see in my future was me growing older and staying single forever. So, I grabbed an opportunity and I'm living my dream. This business idea, the jeep safari, is going to work and I don't need you putting a downer on it because, in a few weeks, you'll go back home, make up with Grant and spend the rest of your days moaning about him. And I'll be here, living my dream.'

I go to retaliate but stop myself. I don't actually know what to say because she's absolutely right. My job is a bore, I'm with the wrong man and there's nowhere I can call home. When I go back, I'll probably move in with my mother and everything will stay the same, I won't have improved anything, and I won't be living any dream, because I don't even have one. I feel incredibly sad.

Libby pulls up outside the apartment. 'Oh Lou,' she says, looking at me. 'I'm so sorry. I didn't mean those things.' She hugs me.

'Yes you did,' I say, 'because you're right. I have nothing in my life I want to keep, except you and my family. And you're here, and my family have their own life back home.'

'Then stay,' Libby replies, 'with me. And build a life here. We won't let any one get between us, not Seth or Grant. We'll be fine, I promise.'

I nod, and forlornly climb from the jeep, chin on my chest like a sulky teenager, gather up the hamper and blankets and shuffle my way into the apartment behind Libby. And, despite feeling like it's the end of the world, I can't help but make a little smile as I picture the neighbours' faces when they see the pink jeep parked outside. I hope they'll be wearing their sunglasses…

CHAPTER SIXTEEN

Libby gives me one of those looks as I return to the table, where her head is on a slant, eyes slightly closed, lips almost pouting. I, on the other hand, am grinning.

'What?' I ask, faking innocence and throwing my arms out in a very exaggerated manner. She obviously just saw Hamil kiss me, a little passionately I agree seeing as he's at work and had leant across the bar, grabbed me by my shoulders, pulled me towards him and planted his mouth on mine in front of a huge group of customers. It was unexpected and lasted for seconds and I've got to say I've never been kissed like that before, or seen anyone kissed like it, other than in movies. If that's what he's like in front of customers, what's our date going to be like?

Libby is clearly concerned about me, but what's there to be worried about? I'm old enough to know what I'm doing, and I'm single. Well, Grant doesn't seem to agree with that yet, but I am. Talking of Grant, I've had several texts this evening from him and he's spouting nonsense about coming over to see me if I don't see sense and ring him. Although I think he's just trying to intimidate me, I'm pleased he hasn't got Libby's address, just in case. Yes, the date with Hamil will be fun. Nothing serious, no drama, just fun and lots of kissing by the looks of things. And, who knows what else. I'm just going to go with the flow.

I've told Libby that it's my new motto, *go with the flow*. She's sick of it already, as apparently I'm not the flowy type, whatever that means, and I've said it ten times since walking to here from the apartment. Maybe she should try not counting. Although, counting might help to take her mind off our crap day. I must admit, I'm not quite as angry as I was earlier and I can see the funny side, but I feel my heart rate increase every time I think of Seth's involvement.

Sitting here now, with a cocktail in my hand, I find that picturing the guys laying there naked earlier isn't quite as upsetting as it was at the time. In fact, it's quite a pleasant image. They were actually a couple of very good-looking men, it could have been worse.

I'm still a little upset however about our fall out, and what Libby said to me. Not that she wasn't right, she was absolutely spot on. But, the truth always hurts and it's left me feeling fragile and even more unsure about my future than I already was. What I do know is that I don't want to go back home to the life I had before, and am now surer than ever that things need to change. But how, well, that's going to take a bit of work.

I sent mum a text earlier to say hi, and to let her know I'm still alive, and her reply 'crafting like crazy and making you a tissue holder' made me almost tear up my plane ticket. I love my mum, I truly do, but I can't bear the thought of moving in with her when I go back. I say her, my Dad's there too, but not that often as he goes on walkabouts for months at a time. Mum doesn't talk about it, so I've never found out where he goes, or what he does. But, whatever, I'm not moving back in with them, as great as they are.

I'm still feeling unhappy about the whole 'Seth's secret woman' situation. Whether I've any right to be or not, I'm hurt that he has this other woman, as I honestly thought he was interested in me and, although I know I've only just met him, we had a connection. I felt it, in the restaurant, and I'm sure he felt it too, but, I obviously got that wrong and so I can't trust any feelings I have about him anymore. I don't know how he feels about me, how involved he is with his mystery woman or what involvement he's had in the Jeep business going wrong. But, I've got a gut feeling and I don't trust him, despite Libby telling me how paranoid I'm being and, when I finally find out what he's done, Libby is going to have to eat one huge piece of humble pie. Probably a whole dish full.

I'm brought back from my daydreaming by Libby squealing and I look up from my quickly diminishing drink to find Jude has crept up behind her and grabbed her from behind. They kiss, a little too passionately in my opinion seeing as I'm sat right there, although it wasn't far different to how Hamil just kissed me.

Jude leans over and kisses my cheek and then sits down on the far edge of the booth we're in.

'What are you doing in here?' Libby asks. 'You hate it in this bar. Hamil's in, by the way.'

Jude grimaces and looks at Hamil behind the bar, and pulls a face. 'Was going past and saw you. I wanted to know how it went today. Get stood up again?'

I find this a bit rude. Yes, we got stood up with our first trip but today was a success. Well, if you ignore the fact we were booked under the misconception of being prostitutes. But, they at least turned up this time and paid us which, for a pair of pretend hookers, equates to a good day.

'No, we didn't get stood up, but it wasn't quite what we

expected. Or what the clients expected,' answers Libby. She looks at me and I decide it's a good time to go to the restroom, even though I've only just been. I really don't want to hear it all again, and I have this slight urge to slap Jude, I'm not sure why. As I walk past Hamil he winks and blows a kiss, which I blow back.

I hover around in the restroom a while, running my wrists under the cool water and, when I eventually return to the table, Jude is red in the face and laughing hysterically. He looks at me and it seems to make him worse. 'That's the funniest thing I've heard in a long time,' he says and I look awkwardly at Libby who is looking a little worn. Nice to see he's so supportive, not.

'I'm pleased we've amused you,' I say, sitting down, smiling politely.

'I don't know what Seth was thinking, sending guys like that to us,' Libby says, hitting Jude with the menu to try and calm him down. It doesn't work.

After a few moments, when he's composed himself, he says, 'Look. Don't be too hard on my brother. He probably saw it as a business opportunity, blinded by the commission he'd make out of it. I've told you, he's ruthless in business.'

I look at Libby and raise my eyebrows in a *'I told you so'* way but she totally ignores me, so I huff a bit and screw my nose up. Ruthless in business, that explains a lot. We were just part of one of Seth's business deals. But, although he obviously couldn't care less about *me*, how could he do it to Libby. I mean, he likes Libby a lot and she's his brother's girlfriend. He wouldn't do that to her, would he? 'But, I'm sure he wouldn't have purposefully hired us out like, well, escorts? That's taking business a but far, no?' I ask. I can't believe I'm sticking up for him.

Jude shrugs. 'I've known him all my life and he still

surprises me. What chance do _you_ stand having known him just a few days?' he asks. I wonder if Libby's told him about our meal out. I feel myself blush as I realise she probably has.

'I know I don't know him that well,' I say, quietly, 'but I'm not convinced he'd have done this on purpose.'

Jude rolls his eyes and then smiles at me. 'Bless,' he says, unashamedly patronising me which I choose to ignore, going with the flow as I now strive to do. 'You're as bad as Libby. Neither of you can see any bad in him.'

'We just don't go falling out with everyone like you do,' Libby replies. Her eyes flash for a second and then soften and she tries to change the subject. 'Hamil's taking Lou on a date in a couple of days time.'

Jude looks me up and down and slowly shakes his head as though in pity. 'Wow, you're keeping yourself busy. First a night out with my brother, and now a date with a waiter who has ten English women a week slobbering all over him. Slow down, you'll be worn out before the trips over and will need another holiday to recover.' Libby slaps him, but his words have already stung me, and he clearly couldn't care less.

Jude smiles sarcastically and stands up to leave. 'You'll understand Seth one day,' he says to Libby, 'and you'll wish you'd have listened to me. Never trust the competition.' He kisses Libby on the cheek, nods to me and walks away.

'What's he mean, the competition?' I ask her.

Libby shrugs and closes her eyes, running her fingers through her hair. 'Seth showed an interest in the jeep business, as well as Jude. I turned them both down when they asked to go into business with me. Like I said, there's no way I'd work with Jude and I'm sure that Seth would have been acting on his brother's instructions. Jude might make it look as though they don't see eye to eye that much, but they're as thick as thieves. Believe me. Look, I've had great legal advice, I've a good relationship with the bank and have made a ton of contacts for myself since working in the holiday business. I'll be fine. Especially with you here by my side.' She smiles at me and, although she says she's fine, her eyes tell a different story.

I realise, not for the first time, how tired and worn down she looks. Today hasn't just been disappointing for her, it's presented yet another obstacle for her to overcome in her new business. I decide there and then to put my worries about Seth behind me, and concentrate on supporting my friend instead. Maybe Libby is right about Seth being a good guy. If I'm honest, he's nicer than Jude, and it's not doing her any favours, me moaning about him all the time. She has enough on her mind. I'm just going to have to let this go. And, I'll be there for her, if and when she needs me.

CHAPTER SEVENTEEN

I can't quite believe that all of this has been on my doorstep since I arrived. How come I haven't noticed it or even heard about it. Why's Libby kept this all secret? I bet she's been planning to show me all these local sites later in my holiday. Well, too late. There's a new tour guide on the block and he's sexy and gorgeous. Hamil has made my day.

Having spent all of yesterday and last night worrying about our impending date, I could have saved myself the stress. He's been quite a surprise, not at all what I'd expected as, after a week of flirting, winking and kissing, I thought Hamil would literally jump on me within minutes but he couldn't be more different. I wouldn't have put him as a guy that would be into nature and the environment, and so passionate about his country, and there's been none of the arrogance he shows when working in the bar. He's what my mum would call 'a sweetie', having gone out of his way to make sure I've had a brilliant day. Attentive, quietly spoken and entertaining.

His English is perfect, even though he's embarrassed sometimes and doesn't think he speaks properly. I asked him where he'd learnt to speak English and I find out that it was at school, but then from watching British TV shows, predominantly '*Only Fools and Horses*'. Every now and then, he cracks me up by speaking like *Del Boy*, calling someone a plonker, and telling me how one day he'll be a millionaire.

Apart from a peck on the cheek first thing, when he picked me up, he hasn't been overly demonstrative, although I've kept my distance a bit. I guess I'm not quite as ready to embrace my sexual freedom as I'd thought.

So far today we've been on a small island, called Liar's Throat, where I saw bees nesting in small white boxes, so many of them, stacked on top of each other. I didn't believe Hamil at first, quite adamant that bees live in hives, but apparently that's what these boxes are. And, as if on cue, a load came flying out and flew all around my head as we walked between them along a path. Hamil told me to keep calm and not wave my arms about, which I found hard as I normally look like a ninja warrior if anything buzzy comes near me.

We found a small cove where we paddled then sat in the sun and chilled out. Images of the dreaded jeep safari from two days ago came back to me and I forced thoughts of the naked guys out of my mind, well, after a minute or two, obviously. We ended up in a beautiful restaurant for lunch which wasn't far from the centre of Marmaris in metres, but could have been a hundred miles away. It was so secluded, full of local families and groups eating outside, soft music playing in the background and a breeze fleeting across our faces. Hamil introduced me to the owner who turned out to be his uncle, who was just as charming although I felt a tad uncomfortable with the nudging and winking going on between the two of them. Was it about me? I don't think I've been nudged or winked about before.

Anyway, that's all forgotten as we're now in a beautiful

amphitheatre, really near to Libby's apartment. She had mentioned this place but it was on my first or second day and I guess I didn't pay much attention. Well, there's just been so much to take in during the last couple of weeks and my priority was to just be with Libby and relax. But, now I'm settling, I want to see more places like this and immerse myself in the atmosphere and culture. I want to be a part of it all, not just as a visitor, but like Libby. It's starting to feel like home.

As we sit on the amphitheatre steps Hamil tells me that, in the summer, there are outdoor concerts held here and where quite a few well known names have performed. As the sun is starting to fade, I can imagine how it must be quite spectacular. I need to get Libby to check if there are any concerts due whilst I'm here. It would be fantastic, the acoustics and atmosphere, something I don't think I could ever experience in the UK despite the many outdoor music festivals. This is just so different, opera and ballets, all the things I've never witnessed. Maybe it's an age thing, I've never fancied watching those types of performances before, but now I want to.

My legs are aching from walking up and down the huge stone steps. At home, I'm the sort who normally finds a lift or escalator and I'm pretty lazy. I never used to be, maybe it's the quick and manic lifestyle that I lead with Grant. Everything has to be done yesterday, no dawdling (it drives him crazy) and I suppose I've just fitted in with him. My legs have become lazy lumps and are not happy with me for making them up their game. They already feel like jelly.

Sensing my lack of energy, Hamil puts an arm around me and I lay my head on his shoulder. I'm suddenly very tired and enjoy the last few minutes of sun on my face and, as I close my eyes, he puts a finger under my chin to turn my head towards him and kisses me, just like that. It's quite a demanding kiss, not gentle, and it goes on for longer than I'm entirely happy with, and I tell myself to enjoy it and match Hamil's passion, but I just can't. I try to relax my shoulders and put my hand on his leg, but I still can't get into this. My head is telling me to let myself go, but my heart is shouting no and wagging its finger in protest. What is wrong with me? I pull away for air and look at him. His eyes are wide with lust and pleasure and he kisses me again, and I re-close my eyes and that's when I realise what's stopping me. Because, all I can see, is a pair of blue eyes, crinkling at the edges and floppy, curly blonde hair, tickling my face. Seth. What's he doing in my head? Has he not caused enough upset?

Right, I'm determined to not let him ruin this for me, so I press against Hamil and explore his mouth with my tongue, and run my fingers through his hair. For a second, I think it's working but, as he starts to run his hands over my face, and down my neck, I pull away again. Seth's there in my head, frowning at me, questioning what I'm doing. Hamil doesn't understand why I've stopped and pulls me back to him, but I push him away, shaking my head. Not wanting to hurt his feelings, I glance over my shoulder and tell him that people are looking at us and I don't feel comfortable, even though no one is paying any attention at all. He frowns, but then smiles at me, and strokes my face. 'Of course,' he says gently, 'you'd like us to be somewhere private.' I don't, but I'm not going to argue, it's easier to let him think this, as long as he doesn't try and find us somewhere secluded, or I'll have to come up with a new excuse.

I stand up, my legs very wobbly probably after all the smooching, and Hamil holds my arm to steady me then holds my hand. I put my hat back on, deciding it's a good kissing barrier, and ask Hamil if we can walk home. His eyes light up and he puts an arm around my waist, pulling me to him. 'Very nice,' he says, 'to take you home to relax, yes?' He rubs my backside and I suddenly get what he means.

I smile but say in my most assertive voice, which if you could hear it you'd crack up, 'No, I really do want to go back. To sleep.' Then, seeing his face, I add, 'On my own. It's the sun, Hamil, I think I've been out in it too long today.'

He looks disappointed and concerned, and I feel bad. He touches my forehead, under my hat, and shakes his head. 'You must take care of yourself,' he says, 'you're not used to this heat and it can really harm you.' I nod and try to look poorly even though I feel totally ok other than wanting to distance myself from this hot guy because, every time he touches me, I see Seth in my head and I feel I'm going crazy. I want to go into a dark room and smash all thoughts of that blonde haired guy out of my head with the biggest baseball bat I can find. Which, I realise, sounds a bit violent and unnecessary, but it's the effect he has on me.

As we leave the amphitheatre I say, 'You don't need to walk me back, I can find the way.'

'Oh.' He now looks even more disappointed and stares down at his feet, and I feel so guilty. None of this is his fault. I pull away from his arm around me and hold his hand tight.

'I've had a great day today,' I say. 'Thanks for showing me such great places.'

He looks back up and smiles again, but his eyes no longer light up. I've zapped him of all energy. I'm like a big, wet blanket, wrapped around him. 'I've had a great day too. I loved spending the day with you. You'll join me again, yes?'

I nod.

'And maybe the night too?' he says and bends his head

very expertly to kiss me again under my hat. He's got to have done that before! I've got to say that I feel a flutter in my stomach which almost makes me want to invite him back, just to see what happens but, as I start to respond, a car horn blasts next to us and I jump. We both look up and, at first, my heart almost stops as I recognise the car as Seth's but then realise that it's Jude driving. It's not quite dark and I can clearly see his face and notice that he gives me such a look I instantly feel guilty and ashamed, and want to flag him down and explain everything. Like 'It's not what you think,' even though it's totally what he thinks. I'm kissing the guy, aren't I? And, rather passionately now I come to think of it. Even though I didn't really want to. Or did I? Ok, I might have wanted to at that one moment, but I didn't want to earlier. Because, I was thinking of his stupid brother.

I watch as he drives away, knowing full well he'll go gossiping back to Libby and Seth and telling them how I was virtually having sex in the street. That's maybe over exaggerating, but I may as well have been. I had the guys tongue down my throat for goodness sake, so it would be hard to convince anyone it was one-sided. I wasn't exactly pushing him away, was I?

'Ignore him,' Hamil says as I step back from him. 'He's an idiot. Please let me walk you back, it's almost dark.'

I shake my head. 'No need. I've got to go and... and... pick something up for Libby. Over there...' I say, pointing to a hotel on the corner. I'm grateful there's a hotel there, as I just held up a finger to point at whatever was on the corner. It could have been a public toilet.

He doesn't look convinced but nods and kisses me quickly on the cheek, grabs my hand and kisses that too, and then starts to walk backwards. He has a sad little face and for a second I almost change my mind again, but I need to be sensible. This will just complicate things even further and I've enough on my plate. I've got a soon-to-be-ex-boyfriend texting and calling me, who just can't seem to understand that it's over and wants to come and 'save' me from who or what I don't know. And then there's Seth, and the way I feel about him, even though I don't know why as it's unlikely he feels the same way about me. I've known him just over a week, and I've still got this ridiculous notion in my head that there's something between us, a spark, a moment. Yet, we've had more cross words than good, and he has a woman he's involved with that's now left someone else for him. And, she's vey pretty and gorgeous and probably local. What chance do I have? And, do I even want a chance?

'Catch up with you tomorrow?' he shouts and I nod. And, as he turns, I walk over into the hotel. I wander around the pool, feeling a little self-conscious in case the staff think I'm an intruder, then peer over the wall to check he's he's definitely gone, sighing with relief as I see the coast is clear. The pool side is empty, as everyone is getting ready to go out for the evening, so, I wait a few more minutes and then walk back out of the entrance and off to the apartment. I think a cold shower is a good idea.

CHAPTER EIGHTEEN

'Ok,' I say out loud, to no one in particular, looking at the worktop and bag of groceries in front of me. I've said 'ok' several times now, whilst staring at the food, but haven't moved towards it yet. It's still all staring at me, aubergines and potatoes all waxy and expecting something wonderful to happen to them. They're going to be disappointed, I just can't seem to work up any enthusiasm. It feels like it's ages since I've cooked and I've lost my culinary mojo. Somehow this food has got to turn into a meal, which depends on my involvement, but this evening ahead is not one that I'd either planned or technically agreed to. My beloved friend has thrust it upon me.

I once again turn away from the food and choose instead to go and sit back down, open my magazine and sip my third glass of cold water, hoping for some inspiration to hit me from somewhere. Libby wafts back through the lounge, looking all made up and gorgeous, stops and stares at me. Then looks at the bag of food on the worktop.

'Cooking's coming along then?' she asks.

I sigh. 'The food's confusing me. It's all different and un-English.

Libby laughs. 'Un-English? Does it not understand your instructions? Like, 'chop yourself up and throw yourself in a pan?' I scowl at her and put the magazine down. 'Get a grip. It's not going to cook itself. You've gone two weeks without cooking, it won't kill you.'

'More than that, actually,' I say, standing back up. 'Grant doesn't like me cooking as it makes the flat smell. I've only done it a handful of times since you've left and that's when mother's come to visit, as she refuses to eat out in restaurants unless it's with her crafting friends.' Libby laughs, not at all sympathetic. I sigh over dramatically. 'I wouldn't mind if I was cooking for us two. But him?'

Libby is at the mirror, which hangs on the back of the door, retouching her lipstick. '*Him* has just had 200 flyers printed for our business, without charging us,' she says, 'so, you can at least cook him dinner.'

I nod. 'I bet he's all fussy and allergic to everything.' I've no idea why I think this, I just do. 'It was you that invited him, why am I having to look after the guy?'

'Because, I've been called out to work for a shift at the karaoke bar to earn some money to keep me living here in this apartment, and will be back by the time you've got round to cooking it. In fact, at this rate, I'm not sure it will be any closer to resembling a meal. I might bring some kebabs back, just in case.'

I sigh again, even more dramatically and she tuts at me. I guess she's right. It's not much to ask me to do, seeing as she's looked after me for the first fortnight of my visit. But, couldn't we have thanked him for the flyers in some other way? Like, well, saying thank you, or getting him a cake? I bet he'd like a cake. 'He's been really mean to me, remember,' I say, shuffling over to the kitchen.

'Remind me how exactly he's been mean to you? You

haven't spoken to him, you've hidden every time he's popped by and not left the apartment for the last three days in case you see Hamil and he gets all amorous and excitable again. Honestly, you can't keep hiding from these guys forever, you'll be going home in a couple of weeks. Make the most of it whilst you're here.'

I admit I have been a bit of a recluse since the Hamil date occurred but I've enjoyed just chilling out and hanging round the apartment, sunbathing on the roof terrace. I've met the neighbours, who are all very pleasant and chat a lot, even though none of them speak English, so I've actually no idea what they're saying. And I've detoxed too, having a rest from wine drinking after two solid weeks of boozing.

I start to cut the aubergine. It's a vegetable that I've eaten more times in the last two weeks than in the rest of my entire life and I now can't get enough of it. I'm going to hunt it down in the supermarket back home and cook it everyday. As I go to wash it, my phone beeps on the worktop next to me. Libby glances at it as she goes past and pulls a face. 'It's him whose name we don't like to mention,' she says. 'Oh, hold on, I keep forgetting that there's a few guys names you don't like to hear mentioned at the mo. It's the UK one, BCF, still pining and begging you to come home.' She flounces off to the bedroom and I pull a face at her.

I put down the knife and read the text and my heart sinks. 'I'm not giving up, I'm going to come and find you, and bring you home!' This text is the result of an hour of texting back and forth this afternoon, and I feel a slight flutter of panic as I picture him actually finding me over here. Could he? Marmaris is a big place, the chances of him locating me are remote, but I am now known by quite a lot of the bar staff throughout the resort. It only takes him going in to the right bar and asking about me.

I even tried ringing him only half an hour ago, preparing myself for a very difficult conversation, but it went to voicemail and so I left a long message telling him it was no point texting, or coming over, and that we'd talk when I'm home. But, he's ignored my voicemail.

Libby comes back through, kisses me on the cheek and says she'll see me in no time at all, then asks, 'and what illness do I tell Hamil you have today if he enquires?'

I sigh, feeling a little deflated. 'Nothing,' I'll talk to him tomorrow. I can't let this go on.' He's been hounding me for the last couple of days and Libby's pretended I've been under the weather. So far I've had a stomach upset and ear ache. If I carry on avoiding him I'm going to need to think of more illnesses, although we could say I have 'women's problems,' as I've found that's always worked in the past. Men completely change the subject when you say things like that. It's not that I didn't enjoy Hamil's company the other day, but it's just all too complicated. My head, and heart, seem full of chaos and confusion. And, our visitor who is due here very soon has caused some of that chaos.

As Libby opens the door to leave I call out, 'and don't be long. I don't want to be left alone with the Pimp!'

'The who?' a voice asks. It's Seth, stood in the doorway, holding a bundle of leaflets in one hand and a bottle of wine in the other.

Libby kisses him on the cheek, turns and smiles at me. 'See you later.' I grin back, with a look that only Libby will understand.

Then, I look at Seth. 'Come in,' I say, in my nicest, pretend pleasant voice. 'Make yourself at home.'

He looks a little awkward as he walks in, hesitates for a moment and then comes towards me, kissing me on both cheeks. As we haven't really spoken for while, and the last conversation was a bit strained, there's an atmosphere. I put down the knife, realising I'm pointing it directly at him, and take the wine through to the kitchen, put it in the fridge and then return and take the box of leaflets he's holding out to me.

'Open it,' he says. Not even trying to look semi-interested, I sigh as I lift the lid to see the flyers neatly arranged in a pile, and am greeted with the smell of fresh print. I put my head on one side to read. 'Libbylou's?' I say.' What's that in English?' Seth laughs and I suddenly realise what it says. 'Ah, Libby Lou's. It's us.'

'Libby's suggestion, she wanted both your names on it. Do you like it?'

I smile and nod. The graphics are actually really good, a photo of the pink jeep set in the cove we visited the other day. Thank goodness there's no naked guys in the background. I presume the photo was taken before we went there, I don't think Libby would have chosen it as the location to go with our new marketing scheme. 'But, I'm only here for another couple of weeks. She'll have to change it when I'm gone. She should have just stuck with Libby's.'

Seth takes the box back off me, puts the lid on and stands it on the worktop. 'I think she's hoping that you'll stay,' he says.

I shrug. 'Well, I can't. Two more weeks and then I'm out of here.'

'Just when you're starting to enjoy yourself,' he says.

I roll my eyes. I knew Jude wouldn't have been able to keep his mouth shut. 'Look, it was just a quick kiss, nothing more than that. So, there's no need to mention it, or talk about it, or, or...'

'Hey, relax,' he says and puts his hands on my shoulders. 'I've no idea what you're talking about. Libby said you'd had a few days here relaxing and she was starting to see the old Lou back. That's all.'

'Oh.' I suddenly feel a bit stupid.

'Who have you been kissing anyway?' he asks.

I look at him and awkwardly swallow, the type that is almost a gulp. 'Hamil. I had a bit of a date. Sightseeing, walking, that sort to thing. Nothing more.'

'Except a kiss,' he says.

'Yes, just the one. Just an ordinary old kiss. I didn't even enjoy it.' I scrunch up my face to reinforce the fact that the kiss was quite awful, and turn back to the worktop and put the chopped aubergine and potato into a baking tray and place it in the oven. When I look back, he's thankfully turned away and has walked over to the balcony. I've no idea why it was so uncomfortable, telling him about Hamil. It's nothing to do with him after all. Particularly as he has his own woman in the background who I'm sure he's kissed plenty of times. She looked like a kisser in the photo…

'Tell me,' he asks, turning back round, 'what have you got to go back home for exactly?'

This takes me by surprise and I'm not too sure I like him even asking me. Why does he think it's any of his business? It's not as though he knows anything about me and my situation back home. Well, apart from everything I told him at the meal the other night, but that's all. Ok, so I might have given the impression I have nothing back home but, that was when I liked him, and thought he was interested in me. Now, he's just a key-stealing pimp.

'I've got lots to go back to, thank you very much,' I snap. He looks at me and raises his eyebrows, waiting for more information. 'I've got my job for a start.'

'Ah yes, the office manager role at the accountants company, which you hate.'

'Hate's a strong word. I'm bored, that's all, and I'm needed there. I'm an important...' I search for the word... cog.' Yes, cog, that sounds good.

'Ok, what else, apart from being a cog.'

I tut loudly, shove the fish into the oven, and stand back up to face him. 'My mother needs me,' I say. There. He can't turn that into a negative. That's an honourable reason, to go home for my mother. He might be happy letting his parents flit around between countries, but I'm not like that. She needs me, well, sort of. Actually, she doesn't at all and will be quite annoyed that I'm about to take over her beloved craft room.

Seth sighs and walks to the cupboard to get the glasses. I realise how he knows where they're kept and feels comfortable in helping himself. It makes me wonder how many times him and Libby have shared a glass with each other, on their own here. I tell myself to stop it, I can't keep torturing myself with thoughts like this, they're just friends and again, it's not my business. My stomach feels totally knotted up and I pick at some of the freshly cut bread to take my mind off everything.

Seth carries the glasses to the table by the sofa and sits down on the throw that I put there earlier. Ew, the throw. Images of Dave and Steve, lying there naked on that very same blanket, come into my mind and I stifle a grin as I see Seth smooth it down with his hand. I'm instantly disappointed though as I remember that Libby's washed it since the incident, she could barely carry it back into the apartment without retching.

I take the bowl of bread, along with the bottle of wine, over to the sofa, but decide to sit on the chair opposite rather than next to him. 'To keep you going,' I say, pushing the bread towards him, 'dinner won't be long.'

There's an awkward silence for a few seconds and so I break it by asking, 'Busy? Haven't seen you for a few days'

'Kind of,' he replies.' I've something I'm trying to sort. Family stuff.' He gives a wry smile.

'Oh,' I reply. 'Nothing too serious I hope.' I actually don't hope for anything to not be too serious for Seth at the moment, but it's a nice thing to say and I had promised myself to be kind to him for Libby's sake. Seth is her friend and it won't hurt me to try and get on with him. After all, a few days ago I wanted to get on him, let alone get on *with* him, and I feel my eyes drawn to his trousers that are tight again around his thighs. I look away quickly, stopping any thoughts of that nature before they get me into trouble.

Seth shakes his head. 'Just some brotherly dispute,' he replies. 'I'm sure it will turn out ok. What about you? How was your jeep safari the other day with the two guys?'

I'm surprised by the question, thinking he must have heard by now how it went, either from Libby or, more likely, Jude.

'You haven't heard?' I ask.

He shakes his head, frowning. 'Haven't seen either of you,' he replies.

'And your brother hasn't said?' I ask.

He shakes his head again. 'We're not exactly seeing eye to eye at the moment, so we haven't chatted much. What is it? What happened? Did they let you down?' He looks annoyed.

'Well,' I begin. 'I think it was us that let them down. The short version of the story is that they thought we were escorts, expected us to rub sun cream into places that really should never see sunlight and probably felt we delivered an appalling service.' I stand up quickly, totally avoiding his incredulous look, and march over to the oven to check on the veg and fish.

I'm suddenly aware that Seth is stood next to me. 'Escorts,' he asks. I nod. 'Why the hell did they think that?'

I shake my head. 'No idea. I was going to ask you the same thing. What did you say to them?' I'm trying to not look accusatory but I can tell by Seth's face that it hasn't worked.

'You think I told them you're escorts?' he asks. He slams his hand down on the counter. 'Why would you think that?' I must admit, he looks really shocked and a bit angry. 'That's why you called me a pimp when I was at the door! Of course I didn't tell them that,' Seth snaps. 'I'd have never sent them to you if I'd have known that's what they were after.'

'Then it was whoever sent them to you. Which was who, exactly?' I ask.

'I've no idea. Look, when they contacted me they said some guy had given them my details as I knew about a jeep safari with a *difference*. I presumed the difference they were referring to is the fact it was two ladies driving the jeep. It's unusual around here.'

'A unique selling point,' I state. Seth looks at me and nods. By his expression, I'm fairly confident he's innocent, as he looks mortified. 'Oh well, too late now. It's done. And, for a couple of new hookers, we got paid quite well.' I laugh nervously but when I look at Seth, he's not smiling. He's looking genuinely embarrassed and sorry.

'Besides,' I continue, 'its early days and I'm sure we'll get a proper customer soon. One that turns up and doesn't expect any extras. Like you said, we've a unique selling point.' I smile as I say this and he starts to relax a little.

'You said *we've* a USP. Does that mean you're thinking of staying and doing this with Libby?'

I hadn't realised I'd said *we*. But, I do admit that the thought of staying is becoming more alluring. 'A slip of the tongue,' I say then add, 'I really hope it all works out though, for Libby's sake.'

Seth nods. 'This is why it might have been better if she'd have gone into it with a business partner. Someone who knows the risks and issues. It would have made all the legal stuff easier too.'

'Like you?' I ask. Again, I'm almost hoping to see something register on his face to confirm my suspicions. But, there's nothing.

'No, not me,' replies Seth. 'Not my type of thing at all. I've no experience in that line of work. But Jude's keen to be involved. '

'Libby told me.' Seth moves out to the balcony and sits down. I go to join him, taking my wine with me. 'Are you competitive, you and Jude.'

'With each other?' I nod. Seth thinks carefully before answering. 'Not really,' he finally replies. 'Well, to be honest, I've never done anything that Jude has considered worth competing for. Like I said, we're so different. I'm no threat to him. And, he's not a threat to me. We both want very different things in life.'

'If you're the one who plans, and analyses and considers the risks and benefits of each business idea, and does all of the work, are you the money man too?'

Seth looks at me strangely. 'What, you mean like an investor?' I nod. 'No, I just make sure it's financially viable and worth the risk before going to the real moneymen. That's the bit I'm good at.'

'And Libby's business, do you think it's financially viable?'

Seth's considers this for a moment. 'Possibly, but I'm not sure how the earnings can cover the over-heads. The jeep needs fuel, and it's a full day's work, possibly for little reward. And she needs to make sure all the legal stuff is in place too, insurances and so on. As I said, it would be easier if she went into business with someone here, someone local with the right credentials. But, you know Libby, she wants to go it alone. Well, with you preferably.'

I think about this for a few moments. It doesn't sound like a bad idea, when he puts it like that, and Libby should consider it. But she's too independent and stubborn. This is her business idea and she doesn't want anyone taking over. Maybe I can look at her plan with her, see if I can suggest anything, and show some support. Not that I know anything about business plans, other than bits I've picked up from watching *Dragon's Den*. I struggle to organise myself generally, let alone in business. But, it will be a bit of support at least, and it sounds like she's going to need it.

CHAPTER NINETEEN

I top up our glasses and we sit in silence on the balcony, both deep in thought. I can't stop thinking back to what Jude said about his brother, how Seth looks at each opportunity to find ways to maximise the earnings, no matter what. But, nothing Seth has just said makes me believe Jude at all. Seth doesn't sound like he's after the business, in fact he can only see the risks and so I doubt he'd want any part in it. He's genuinely concerned about Libby and clearly cares for her, so I'm pretty sure he wouldn't want to send us off with a couple of guys looking for sex. And, she is his brother's girlfriend. No matter how much rivalry there is between them, I don't think he could do that to either Jude or Libby. But, what if he's pulling the wool over my eyes? There are still the jeep keys, and his secret woman. He hasn't been entirely truthful so far, so I need to be wary of trusting him. But, those eyes...

The sun is almost down yet the warmth of it is still there. I've gradually got used to these hot evenings and it's another reason why I can't bear the thought of going home. Whilst I'm here, I'm going to make the very most of it. In a couple of weeks I'll be shivering outside the airport back in the UK, waiting for my mum to come and pick me up.

I get up to go and get the dinner, putting some for Libby on a plate and wrapping it in foil, and minutes later, we're tucking into our food and the atmosphere is light, chatty and pleasant. In fact, we're almost back to how we were a few evenings ago, before I found out about the mystery woman. I'm keeping those thoughts at the back of my mind, and have accepted that maybe things will never be easy between Seth and I, which is a shame as I really do like him, and he's looking so good tonight. And smells good too. I breathe in and get a waft of his aftershave. If it's one thing that gets me, it's nice aftershave.

We talk easily about our lives, and I realise it's gone ages since I've willed Libby to come home. In fact, I've given up looking at the clock and part of me is kind of hoping she's been delayed. I'm starting to enjoy myself. Seth now knows about my parents and how they live this sort of 'together/not together' life. I don't normally talk about them and their situation, as I've never really considered it unusual, but I quickly realise how different they are to his parents who barely seem to move without the other one by their side. That said, my parents can still show affection for each other, normally if I stay the night at theirs, where they make so many awkward sounds and noises that I have to get in the shower, no matter what time of night, and squirt the shower head into my ears to try and remove any trace of the sound. Then, I have to face them in the morning when they act like young teenagers, only to fall out again the next day. Honestly, they drive me a bit crazy.

We find that we've a difference in our friendships too. Even though I've only a handful of what I'd call friends, rather than acquaintances, and one best friend, obviously Libby, Seth hasn't really got any. With his parents being so

212

free-spirited, he and his brother changed schools many times, often home schooled too, so he never got to make or keep many school friends. And, with his extensive travel ever since, he tells me how he doesn't have one friend that he's known for more than 3 years, and I can't get my head around what this must be like. Take Libby and me for example, we've known each other forever and have such history. I can't imagine a life without someone like that, someone that totally gets you and has been through so many changes in life with you, always by your side.

Seth feels very settled here in Marmaris. He says it's the only place he 'd call home. I agree with him it feels much more of a home to me than the flat I was in just a few weeks ago and my thoughts return to Grant. How different this evening would have been with him instead of Seth. We haven't really ever tried small talk, other than if it's about his work, and the world of stock brokerage, or the cost of everything, about him, him, him. Seth's humble and holds back from talking about himself unless I push him. They're like chalk and cheese.

I look up to see Seth watching me and I realise that I'd drifted off in my thoughts and I hope I haven't either missed something he's said, or talked out loud, which I have been known to do. He smiles at me in such a genuine way, and I smile back and sip my wine. I'm so relaxed that, when I hear my phone beep, and I know instantly who it'll be, I don't even move to pick it up or feel my stomach clench. Seth looks across at the phone though, where I've left it on the windowsill just inside, and then says, 'Libby tells me Grant is planning on coming over. When's he arriving?'

I'm a little annoyed that Libby has been talking about my private life with him. I know we're getting on now this evening, but up until his arrival he was in my bad books and was the enemy. There's something about Libby and Seth having secret conversations that I'm not part of. 'When did she tell you that? I ask. I didn't think she'd even been in touch with him or seen him, particularly as he didn't know about the escort palaver, but then I haven't actually asked her.

Seth can obviously sense in my tone and expression that I'm not happy about him knowing. 'Sorry, she wasn't gossiping,' he adds, in his defence, 'she told me on the phone the other day. Wished she'd have told me about the 'escort' situation too. She's worried for you, she thinks he's coming over and that he'll ruin everything. I don't like the sound of it either.'

I sigh. 'I don't know why it bothers *you*,' I say, still a little irked he's even discussing this with me, as though it's anything to do with him. But, he does look genuinely concerned. I find myself telling him about the texts and voicemail.

'Do you want him to come here?' Seth asks.

'No way,' I say, very sure in my tone. 'It'll be awkward and I'll tell him everything I've already told him, that its over, and he'll plead or argue, and it will be a blazing row and I'll get really upset and probably end up giving in for a peaceful life.'

'You can't,' he says, and holds my hand in his. 'You know he's not the right guy for you, he doesn't treat you like the real Lou.'

I laugh. 'That's the problem. When I'm with him, I don't treat me like the real Lou either. I have no idea who she is when he's around.'

'Then you mustn't give in,' he says, 'unless he's what you want. Maybe the two of you can work things through.' He looks at me kindly, although his eyes clearly give away the fact he thinks this would be the worse decision ever.

'No, absolutely not. Grant won't change, believe me.' I stand to clear the plates. 'These last few weeks have introduced me to the old Lou. And, I've missed her, plus I'm enjoying being single again.'

'Ah,' he says, 'the kiss with Hamil.' He smiles but I can't help but think he looks a tiny bit jealous. My heart skips a beat.

'Look, it was just a kiss at the end of a nice day out, nothing more than that,' I say, blushing but hoping he won't notice. As I turn with the plates to take to the kitchen, I can't help but snap, 'just because I like being single, it doesn't mean I'm after another man. Women can enjoy their own company, you know!'

I crash around with the plates in the sink and then decide I'll wash them later. If I carry on like this, they'll be all broken and I'll have to buy Libby new ones. And, although I've a lot of spending money left, seeing as I haven't really been to many places to spend it, I want to keep a load of it to use when I get home as I'll be needing somewhere to live and will be short of pennies. The thought of finding a home fills me with absolute dread and is enough to occasionally make me question my decision to break from Grant. I could just put up with our differences and enjoy our life, with a home and nice things, and I could even give up work and become a lady of leisure. Could I do that? I look at Seth as I walk back to the balcony and know that I can't. There's more to life and, somehow, Seth represents that although I'm confused as to how. How does he even raise these ideas and thoughts in me?

Seth has moved the chairs next to each other so they are both facing the wonderful sunset which is almost over as it becomes nightfall. I sit and sigh as I bid goodnight to the sun. The atmosphere between us has gone and, if I'm honest with myself, I'd like there to be more between us. But there's the other woman to consider, and the question mark over Seth's involvement in the possible sabotage attempts with Libby's business. I don't trust him 100% and it would be like jumping out of a humungous frying pan into yet another fire. A gorgeous fire, I admit, but a fire none the less. And, I already feel singed and burnt. I find myself looking again at Seth's hair, the way it curls and flops around, and that bit of stubble he has going on. And his strong thighs and...I'm suddenly aware of his hand on mine again and I look up to see he's staring straight at me. This goes on for a few seconds, me hardly breathing and I force my eyes to look away, focussing on the now familiar sound of the frogs in the nearby brook.

We both watch the small cat that lives around here with a bundle of kittens cross the gravel road across from us, into the garden centre. This garden centre, it's nothing like ours at home, which are normally huge affairs with restaurants and shops inside. This is on a tiny bit of land between the houses and flats, all underneath plastic sheeting, and it sells the most beautiful plants which I saw yesterday when I braved the outdoors for a few minutes. These kittens have walked past me almost every day since I've been here and I can't believe how big they've grown, in such a short time. Mind you, if all the neighbours have fed them with as many titbits as I have each day, it's no wonder.

I look back to Seth and see he's watching me again, and is smiling. 'What?' I ask, 'have I got dinner on my face?'

He laughs. 'Not at all, I just can't take my eyes off you sometimes. You... I don't know how to explain it.'

'Try,' I say. Yes Seth, please try, I need to know.

'You perplex me. Is that even grammatically correct?'

I laugh. 'I've no idea, but thank you anyway. You perplex me too.' Was that a compliment? If it was I realise that I've just accepted it, something I have to force myself to do after a telling off from Libby. I've always found it awkward and a little embarrassing but, according to my dear friend, it's rude and offensive to laugh at people who are being nice to me.

We look at each other again for a few seconds and then it happens, just like that. A kiss, Seth gently meeting my lips, it's so perfect. It's not like it was with Hamil days ago. This is soft, and intense and…incredible. He pulls away for a second to look into my eyes, and then puts his lips back on mine and this time it's a little harder, and passionate. And then I'm kissing him back, my arms circled around his neck, my fingers touching his curls. We kiss for a while, then stop, and when I open my eyes he's looking at me, smiling again. I playfully hit him.

'What was *that* for?' he asks, still smiling.

'I'm not sure,' I say and then I reach out, cup his face in my hands, stare into his eyes and kiss him again. It feels so right and, minutes later, I snuggle into him and we sit and look at the now black sky. Seth strokes my arm and I can feel his breath on my neck and, for this one special moment, I don't want it to end. All of the feelings I had for him the other night, at the restaurant before that text arrived, have returned and the doubts have gone. I trust him again.

'Are you sure it's over with Grant?' he suddenly asks.

'Totally,' I say, 'it was over long before I came here, if I'm honest.'

'It's just, I'm kind of falling for you and I don't want to get in the middle of anything.' I turn to face him and stroke his face.

'You're not in the middle of anything. I've told him it's over and I'll sort things when I get back there.' It's quiet for a moment and, although I'm trying not to, I can't help but feel a bit confused. He's asking me about Grant, when he's got that woman. But, I'm not going to say anything and ruin the moment. I'm not. Absolutely no way.

'Aren't *you* in the middle of something?' I suddenly blurt out. Wow, I'm useless at being diplomatic.

I feel Seth stiffen and he pulls his arm away from me and sits forward. 'It's different,' he says.

'How?' I ask. 'Her text suggested it's not that different at all.'

'I'm not romantically involved with her. It's not like that.'

I nod, as though believing him but I'm still not sure.

'Hey,' he says, touching my face, 'it's not something that is going to get between us, it's being sorted. You need to trust me.' And, despite my subconscious screaming at me not to, I put my arms back round him and lean in to kiss him, and he responds hungrily.

Just as I think we may need to move to somewhere more comfortable, the roar of an approaching car and the screech of tyres make us both jump and we sit up straight and lean over the balcony to see who it is. Through the arch and down the path comes the stomping of feet and for a moment I think that it's Libby. But, we both realise at the same time, it's Jude. He looks up and sees us, points to Seth and shouts, 'Get down here... Now!'

Rude, I think to myself. Where does Jude get off on shouting at someone like that? I hope Seth tells him where to go and we can get back to our... hang on, Seth's getting up from the seat. I look at him confused, and then follow him as he walks towards the door, but he tells me to stop and sit back down and that he'll be back in a moment. So, I do as I'm told. This looks like a yet another brotherly dispute and I really don't want to be part of it.

I sit back in my balcony seat and can just see Jude who is now standing there, glaring up at me. I politely wave, but he ignores me and turns to Seth who approaches him from the front door of the apartment. The streetlight is just bright enough to show how Jude's face is like thunder. As Seth reaches him, Jude pushes him in the chest, knocking Seth backwards a few feet. I gasp and sit closer to the front of the balcony, putting my hand to my mouth. I have no idea what I'll do if they start to fight. I think I'll be like one of those women you see in shows where they stand and shout, 'No, leave him, you brute', rather than running down there to stop it. I'm not cut out for confrontational situations.

I see Seth lean towards Jude and say something, then Jude spins his head round to look up at me. I sit back in my seat again and pretend to look away at something of interest, touching the bougainvillea and examining the petals and leaves. Whatever it is they're talking about, Seth definitely doesn't want me to hear as he keeps telling Jude to keep his voice down and looks up at me anxiously a few times. I pick out a few words and realise they are arguing about someone, a woman, and I know it's her, Seth's mysterious *friend*. For a pal, she sure is causing some problems. I try to stay calm, he promised me it was nothing that I needed to worry about, or that would come between us, didn't he? She's someone he needs to tie up loose ends with. That's all.

But, why would she be of any concern to Jude? Maybe it's someone else they're talking about. My heart literally stops as I suddenly think they might be talking about Libby. But why would Jude be angry with Seth about his own girlfriend? There could only be one reason, and Seth must have done something to break his brother's trust which means Libby is keeping something from me too.

I watch Seth trying to calm Jude, but he's having none of

it and Jude turns to walk away, spins back, points up to me on the balcony and shouts at Seth, 'Why don't you tell Lou all about her? I doubt you have the guts to be honest. It's just not your style.' Then he sneers at me and walks away back to the car. Seth stands for a few moments and watches until he's driven off then walks slowly back to the apartment, head down and as though he has the world on his shoulders.

I go to the apartment door to meet him but, when he walks in, he goes past me and picks up his jacket from the sofa.

'Sorry, I've got to go,' he says coldly, and turns to walk away.

'What? Just like that?' I ask and walk after him. 'Why not stop for a coffee, calm down a bit,' I say, smiling. But, he doesn't respond. I touch his arm but he flinches slightly and pulls away.

'Look,' I say, 'I'm confused. What the hell have I done?'

Seth stops and looks at me. 'Absolutely nothing,' he replies, 'why does this have to be anything about you?'

This doesn't make any sense. I don't understand how things can change so quickly between us. It's not the first time it's happened and I can hear my annoying inner voice already starting to whisper, 'I told you so.'

'Look, thanks for dinner,' he says 'it's been a nice evening but...'

'But?' I ask.

'But, I've really got to go. It's nothing you've done, Lou, believe me.'

He walks away from me and I follow him again. 'I guess that seeing you tomorrow is out of the question?' I ask.

Seth shakes his head. 'Not sure, I need to sort things sooner than I thought, sorry,' he replies.

'Is it about *her*?' I ask. 'The girl you were talking about with Jude?'

Seth nods.

'Is it Libby?' I ask, folding my arms.

'Of course it's not Libby,' he says angrily, and shakes his head at me.

Was I actually kissing him just a short while ago, and feeling something for him, and did he really say the nice things to me? Because now, he clearly doesn't want anything to do with me again and only has *her* on his mind, whoever it may be.

'But, what about us?' I ask.

'What about us?' he replies. 'Look, I've things to sort, do I have to run everything past you first?'

I feel embarrassed and uncomfortable. 'No, it's clearly none of my business.'

'Correct, it isn't.' Seth then closes his eyes for a second and sighs. When he looks up at me, there's a glimmer of regret. 'Look, I'm sorry, it's just a bit complicated.'

'Yes, so you said,' I reply.

Seth looks as though he's going to say something but then rubs his eyes with the back of his hand and walks out of the apartment. I stop myself from following him, knowing I'll make a fool of myself as he won't care less, and I move back to the balcony to watch him wander down the path. He doesn't even look up at me.

I feel as though I've been on an emotional roller-coaster for the last few days, with the ups and downs of the jeep safari, the threat of Grant arriving, the kiss with Hamil, and then with Seth. And now this. His *complicated* secret woman who is supposedly just a friend but has caused animosity between him and Jude, and for Seth to walk out from what was, up to then, a really good evening where he'd declared some feelings for me. And I started to feel something for him too, and moments away from showing him just how much.

Although he said it's not about Libby, it could be. I mean, it's not as though he's the most open and honest man I've met. He's a walking secret and I can't see any other reason why Jude would be so angry with him unless it's about a woman they're both involved with. Is it just a case of Jude not liking the fact that Libby and Seth are such good friends, or could there be something else going on between them? Or, if he's telling the truth and it's not about Libby but about the secret woman of his, I find it really hard to believe that Libby doesn't know about her. Does she know and is keeping it from me?

I suddenly realise someone is coming up the path, and my heart sinks a little as I see it's Libby and not Seth, coming to apologise. I wave, unenthusiastically, and wait for her to come up the stairs. As Libby walks in, she stops, looks at me and then walks straight over to hug me. She knows me so well and can see I'm a wreck.

'What's he done now?' she asks and I burst into tears and then pour out the whole story about the evening and then Jude's visit whilst she pours us both a glass of wine. After I get to the end of my sorry tale, Libby sits back, tilts her head to one side and says, 'It might not be what you think, she could just be a friend, an acquaintance.'

'But, he'd have told me if it was all innocent, he wouldn't have to lie. Or go all secretive and angry. And Jude definitely knows more about it than I do. He was furious, you should have seen him. What's it all got to do with Jude?' Libby must at least know something about Jude's involvement in all of this, surely.

She kicks off her shoes and stretches her legs out over the sofa and onto my lap.

'I'm not sure,' she replies, and then catches my expression.

'I promise you, I've no idea other than Jude has been complaining a lot about Seth these last few days. All I could tell was that there's been a fight brewing but, other than that, I'm in the dark as much as you are.'

I do one of my splendid trumpet nose blows into the rather wet tissue and Libby looks at me sympathetically. 'What's Jude been complaining about specifically?' I eventually ask her, once I've sorted my nose out.

'Well,' says Libby, 'he's just gone on about Seth winding him up, going off all the time and not answering his phone, disappearing for hours on end, that type of thing. He thinks Seth's up to something, and has said a couple of times that I should warn you off him.'

'I didn't know that I was on him.'

Libby smiles and pats my arm. There's absolutely no point in me denying my feelings for Seth anymore, she knows me almost better than I know myself. If Jude hadn't come over, I get a feeling I might have taken my friendship with Seth to a new level but probably never will do now after tonight. In a way, it's best it happened like this, before I got in too deep.

Libby looks as though she's going to speak, but then stops. 'What is it?' I ask

'I just wouldn't worry too much, Jude gets cross very easily and they always fall out. They'll be best buddies by tomorrow and I'm sure Seth will come to see you and explain everything. And you can then carry on where you left off.'

Libby puts her feet back onto the floor and carries her glass to the kitchen. 'I'm off to bed.' she says. 'Try and get some sleep,' then she blows me a kiss and goes off to her bedroom.

I sit quietly for a few minutes, not really knowing what to

think. I try to piece together everything that's happened over the last few weeks but all I end up with is a jumbled mess. The jeep keys, the 'hooker' trip, the kiss, the mystery woman. It's as clear as mud. But, I know one thing for sure, Seth is keeping something from me, and I'm determined to find out what. And I just hope that Libby isn't involved somehow. Because, if she is, I don't know if I can ever forgive her.

CHAPTER TWENTY

Yes, I know I'd decided not to see Hamil again, that it's really not me, this flirty, sexually liberated woman who *goes with the flow*. And, yes, I know I'd decided that it's not fair to lead him on if I don't feel the same way as he does, and that he's just out for a good time and I'm on the rebound and blah, blah, blah. The blah's are all the stuff that Libby has gone on about which, up until this morning, I'd agreed with. But, after last night with Seth, I don't feel the same way this morning about anything at all; Hamil, Seth or Libby. Maybe I *should* just relax a bit and have some fun, no strings attached. What's the harm? It's not as though I'm a young girl out for something serious and may end up getting hurt. I'm over thirty and am quite aware of what Hamil wants. So, I've decided I'm going to show Seth what he's missing. Libby thinks I'm crazy but I don't have to run everything past her or get her approval. After all, she doesn't tell me everything, that's for sure. Her, Seth and Jude can have a whinge about me later, when they get together and gossip and collude and, well, whatever it is they do. I've no idea, to be honest, but I actually don't even care this morning. I've decided that today marks the birth of the new me!

Hamil's taken me to his friend's hotel for the day which has the most spectacular pool that is empty, except for us being in it. In fact, the whole hotel is empty as it doesn't open until next week and so the staff, most of whom are friends with Hamil, are preparing and are delighted to have some 'pretend customers' for the day to look after. So, we've been waited on and provided with excellent service and attention, and given the whole place to explore. Well, when I say the whole place, I've managed to avoid Hamil's attempts at taking me to look at the bedrooms. It may be the new me today, but that would be going a little faster than I'd like. Maybe a bit later, who knows.

We swim, sunbathe, swim, play pool, drink, swim... it's fantastic. Oh, and there's a fair amount of kissing going on too, which is also enjoyable. It's helping me along my journey of the new, sultry, sexy me. Maybe that's how I'll be known when I get back to Abingdon, the sultry sexy one, and I'll have a whole new group of admirers and I won't ever think about Grant, or Hamil or Seth. I'm annoyed with myself that, out of those three, Seth is the one that I think will be the hardest to forget and so I'm going to have to work on my new persona pretty quickly.

I'm so relaxed, I've fallen asleep a couple of times, Hamil too. And, when we've woken, we've smiled at each other, had a quick kiss then gone back into the pool. We've cuddled in the water. When I say 'cuddled' it's been a bit more X-rated than that. It appears that my bikini top is a little easier to untie than I'd thought and, after tying it back up numerous times after each fondle, I've given up and taken it off. I'm going topless. Yes, my new sexy, sultry persona is brazen and confident with body parts getting tanned which have never seen the sun before. And, there's clear evidence from Hamil that he enjoys being pressed up against me in the water half naked. It's a long time since my nudie breasts have been pressed up against a man other than Grant and I've got to admit I'm enjoying it. Enjoying it a lot, as it turns out.

At lunchtime, the waiters brought us out freshly grilled kebab meat with gorgeous bread and salad and we ate in the sun, attended to by several of them who all seemed to be fighting over us. I replaced my bikini top for that bit, but took it straight back off once we'd eaten. It's quite empowering watching Hamil hungrily eye up my body and a couple of times I swear he goes to kiss my nipples, but I've pushed him away as there's too many staff around. He's taken a couple of chances in the pool though and I've rested my head back against the edge and let him. His mouth, slight stubble on his chin and the sun has turned me on.

One of the waiters comes to sit by us to chat and I feel a little self-conscious with my bikini top off and I roll onto my front, although I'm sure they've seen it all before with the hordes of women semi-naked on the beach. We hear that the hotel has 200 rooms and is already at 75% capacity for its opening week. The staff are understandably nervous about it and Hamil ends up doing a deal of some sort where he'll come and work here on one of his nights off, and in the daytime too between his split shifts, to give them a hand. He tells me after the waiter has walked away that the money comes in handy as he sends it home to his family and he's also saving to travel in the next few years. He hasn't long finished his National Service, which they still do over here, and we have quite a serious discussion about whether it would help or hinder the UK if National Service came back. When I say a serious discussion, Hamil presumes I know all about National Service and I don't exactly tell him otherwise, as I feel that maybe I should. So, I just nod and make lots of umms and aahs. I don't know anyone that did their National Service back home, my father wasn't quite old enough when it finished.

Soon, the conversation is over and we're back to the fondling and kissing, which starts to get even more amorous than before and I start to feel the beginnings of apprehension creep up on me, but quickly force them to the back of my mind. I'm sexy and sultry, I tell myself, and I refuse to be a wuss.

Hamil has sidled over to my sun bed and squeezed himself on, pressed up beside me. He runs his finger along my face and then kisses me really passionately. His hands cup my breasts and his thumb rubs over my now hard nipple and I let out a small groan. His hips are moving slightly rhythmically against mine and I start to almost consider the offer of a room tour. But, I suddenly become aware of whispering behind us and open my eyes to see that some of the waiters are watching us. Hamil follows my eyes, smiles at them, then at me and asks, 'Is Libby at home?'

'No,' I reply, 'She's working until tonight. Why?'

He winks at me and says, 'Let's go to your place, it's more private than here.' I agree. It's a bit disconcerting having the waiters watching us, although they're being quite discreet about it considering it's virtually a live sex show. Well, ok, perhaps not that explicit but I'm just getting used to this new sexy and sultry persona and I'm not finding it particularly easy. The apprehension is back again, cowering just below the surface and I try to shake it off, but it's not as quick to go this time. Despite my show of bravado, I'm having second thoughts about moving forward with Hamil. Is it really what I want, or have I just talked myself into it to get back at Seth or to prove something with Libby? I know I've told myself that I'm a modern, empowered woman and all that stuff, but

I actually think I've conned myself. I've never been like that, and I'm not sure I ever can be.

I get dressed into my shorts and top and pack the few things into my bag before walking over to Hamil who is saying goodbye to the waiters. There's a bit of whispering and sniggering going on and I feel like I'm back in the playground at school. I see Hamil whisper to one of the waiters who looks at me approaching, smiles and then pats Hamil on the back, and they all laugh. If I had doubts before, I feel really uncomfortable now. The problem is, Hamil has no idea how I feel. In fact, I've done nothing but flirt and respond all day and I realise, with slight panic, that I've got from here to the flat to try and work out what I want to do, and then deal with it.

We walk back, hand in hand, and Hamil kisses me several times on the hand and cheek. His eyes roam hungrily over my tight t-shirt each time I catch him watching me and I regret not putting my bikini top back on underneath. I try to cross my arms over my chest but, when I catch a glimpse of myself in a car window, I realise I just look weird. And, all that happens, is that Hamil starts to walk slightly behind me instead and eyes up my backside in my slightly too small shorts. I can't remember a time when a man looked at me in this way and I picture Seth, and how he greeted me that night we went to the restaurant, how he looked me up and down. His glance was one of approval and attraction. Hamil is literally salivating.

We reach the apartment and although I'm no nearer a get-out plan, I have made a decision. This isn't what I want at all and I need to stop it before it goes any further. We go inside and, for once, it feels unusually cool in here. The shutters have been closed up and I go to open them but Hamil takes my hand, shakes his head and kisses me again.

He pulls my body up against his and grabs at my hair, pushing his mouth harder against mine, and my head is whizzing around confused and unsure. His lips go to my neck and I tilt my head back, gasping, liking the feel of his hands now roaming over my body but it's not so pleasurable that I forget how I need this to stop. I open my eyes and look around the flat to try and pull myself out of my aroused state and notice that, behind Hamil's head, there's a note pinned to the fridge door. I squint to try and read it, but it's just a bit too far away. Although I'm aware of Hamil's hand now inside my T-shirt, I push him backwards a little so I can get nearer to the door and try and read the note again and can just make out the name at the bottom, Seth. I pull away from Hamil, which isn't easy as he's a bit like a leech glued to me, and go to read the note.

It simply reads '*Lou, forgive me. I need to explain things to you. Let me know when you're back. Seth xxx.*' I feel my heart thud as all of the hormones that had been whizzing round my body just a few minutes ago grind to a halt, somewhere in my stomach.

Hamil has followed me across the kitchen and turns me to face him, pushing me up against the worktop and then lifting me to sit on it, pushing himself between my legs before kissing me again, but I put my hands against his chest and push him back. He mistakes my apologetic smile for a playful one as he just presses up against me again and pulls my legs to wrap around his waist. Before I know it his hand is inside my shorts and I feel his warm palm against my skin. His breathing is becoming harder and his other hand is back in my T shirt, cupping my breast, with his thumb rubbing over my nipple. I almost start to weaken again, it feels so good, but the note from Seth has changed everything and all I can do is picture him. I can't do this with Hamil.

As I push Hamil away again I say, 'No, I don't want this,' and he first looks confused, but then a bit angry. There's a long silence and I feel uncomfortable but also ashamed for leading him along like this. It's not as though I'm a teenager, trying it for the first time and then changing my mind half way into it. I'm a grown woman and have given him the signs all day yet have now decided to stop. It's not fair.

'What do you mean?' he asks. 'You were not complaining at the pool, you've let me kiss you and touch you all day. Am I a joke to you?'

'No!' I say, shaking my head. 'Absolutely not. You've done nothing wrong. It's not...'

He laughs and cuts me off. 'Not you, it's me. Yes, I've heard that one before.' Hamil's expression is a mixture of anger and humiliation, and I feel really sorry for him. I go to touch his arm but he pulls it angrily away.

'Look Hamil, it's complicated. I didn't mean to do this, any of it. Well, I did want to... but...I just can't... I don't want...' I can't explain to him what this is all about, as I don't understand it myself.

Hamil shakes his head. 'You're crazy,' he sneers at me and turns to go, and I don't even argue as I think he's right. I'm a single woman, he's gorgeous and I could now be enjoying passionate, wanton sex with him when, instead, I've turned him away all because of a note from a guy who's confused me and upset me since I got here.

As he walks out the door, I go to stop him, to try and explain but we both bump into Seth coming through. Hamil pushes past him and Seth stops him with his hand.

'Hey, what's the problem?' Seth asks him, and looks at me.

'That crazy bitch,' Hamil shouts, pointing at me before going down the stairs and Seth is looking at me confused.

'You ok?' he asks.

'I'm fine,' I say, but my eyes are welling up. He comes over and puts his arms around me.

'Has he hurt you?' he asks.

'No, not at all,' I say. 'I treated him really badly.'

'What did you do?' Seth asks.

'I kissed him, rubbed myself up against him, let him put his hands in places that no one has fondled for a long time.'

'Wow,' Seth replies, 'I hope you treat me badly too.' That makes me smile a little and I rest my head on his shoulder. I have to admit I'm quite grateful that Seth turned up when he did. I'm not sure if Hamil would have left quite when he did, or whether it would have turned into a massive row, or worse. I pull away and go to sit on the sofa, my legs a bit wobbly, and Seth follows. Hours in the sun, passion and frolics, and then the drama of the last few minutes. I'm definitely not cut out for this. I really shouldn't be let out on my own within fifty metres of a man.

'Although it's none of my business, what made you stop him?'

'Your note,' I say. Seth looks at me surprised. 'Well, I'd sort of changed my mind before that. I thought I'd have a bit of fun but it's really not me. And then I saw your note and it got even more confusing.'

'My note? Look, I really do want to apologise, I haven't treated you well and there's so much going on that you don't know about. But I'm sorry if my note caused you even more problems.'

'Then tell me what it is that's going on,' I say.

Seth shakes his head. 'I can't right now.'

I tut and get up and walk around the room. 'But your note sort of gave the impression you want to tell me everything.'

He nods. 'I do, and soon it's going to be sorted and then

you'll know everything. But the time's got to be right. This isn't just about me, there's others involved.'

'I'll be back in the UK in a couple of weeks. Any plans to tell me before then?' I ask sarcastically.

'I hope so,' he replies. 'Lou, please stay. You know how much Libby wants you to, and so do I.'

'Really?' I say, starting to smile. Wow, Seth wants me to stay. 'But what about her, your *friend*?'

He shakes his head. 'That's exactly what she is, a friend.'

'Are you sure about that?'

'Absolutely,' he says and looks straight into my eyes. And, I see no lies there, or mocking or anything else. Just the truth.

Then he kisses me. Not hard, like Hamil, but gently and carefully and with lots of affection. I kiss him back too and hug him. Then, with a smile, he turns and walks away and is gone. I sit back on the couch and let out a long sigh. This has well and truly been the weirdest of days with a bit too much kissing, if you ask me. How can I have got my self into such a confused mess? What was I exactly looking for with Hamil? And why do I trust Seth so much after everything that's happened? Well, according to him, I should find out all of his secrets soon and I'll hopefully be able to accept them all because, to be honest, I'm falling in love with him.

CHAPTER TWENTY-ONE

Not content with travelling to one country, I'm now in another. We're in Rhodes. And by 'we,' I mean the four of us; Libby, me, Seth and Jude. It seems that the boys made friends a couple of days ago and Jude came up with the idea of us all going to Rhodes for the day, as he didn't feel he'd got to know me very well yet, and it's going pretty well considering the mega row the other night. Nothing has been said about it, and I'm almost wondering if it really happened the way I remember it.

Libby announced our trip last night when she got in from work. It was before I recalled my day, which to be honest, left her speechless for quite a few minutes. In fact, more than that. I had to pour her another glass of wine to get her speaking again. But, we eventually talked it through. At first, she was cross about Hamil, almost accusing him of being a pervert until I told her how I'd reciprocated every single sexual gesture through the whole day, brought him back to our place, got him excited and then stopped him dead in his tracks. And she now feels sorry for him and cross with me instead. I feel a complete bitch about it and can't believe I've messed up so much since coming here. Nothing

I think, or say, or do makes any sense whatsoever. I've no idea why Seth has got into my head having known him for just 2 weeks and, for the majority of that time, have been angry with him. And, then there's Grant too who isn't totally out of the picture until he accepts it's over. I have to keep reminding myself how old I am, and that I'm not exactly a love-sick teenager but a mature woman.

I hadn't noticed the voicemail from Grant come in until I was getting ready for bed last night. And, upon hearing it, I rushed into Libby's bedroom to let her listen too, hoping I was getting the wrong end of the stick. But no, Grant was very clearly saying, 'I'm going to try and get a flight and I'm coming to find you.' I freaked out, literally, starting to run around grabbing my stuff, ready to pack my bags and go into hiding somewhere. I even asked Libby if the British Embassy might take me in for safekeeping, to which she replied 'unlikely.' But, like Libby said, he doesn't have her address and Marmaris is a pretty big place. And, he was probably drunk or something and will feel different when he wakes up. But, I'm not that sure. And so I rang him this morning, really early UK time, and we had a big row and it ended with him saying he wouldn't waste his money on a flight and all of that type of stuff. So, I think I'm safe. For now.

I was a bit nervous about seeing Seth this morning, as he may have totally changed his mind about how he feels, seeing as he's done this several times before, but everything so far has been fine and he's been a total gentleman. We're back to being friends, there's been no kissing (I think I had enough of that yesterday and my lips are grateful for the day off), we've made small talk and, once or twice, he's held my hand. But, that's been it. Jude also seems in a good mood and very demonstrative with Libby, which I haven't really seen much of since I arrived. I presumed he's one of those guys that doesn't like to show his feelings when others are around, only in private, but he's hugged her, kissed her and walked with his arm around her. It's been nice to see. We've all chatted a lot and I feel like I'm finally getting to know Jude a little, and he's much funnier than I thought, quite the comedian. He's definitely showing a different side to his personality today and I finally get what Libby sees in him. Although, I'm cautious as I don't totally trust him.

We left Marmaris port fairly early this morning on one of the first boats to Rhodes, which was reasonably quiet, and we arrived to moor up alongside a line of yachts and one cruise ship, which I cooed over as we walked to the small border control. When I say border control, well, it was a gate with a very official looking lady asking to see our passports. After looking us up and down a few times, we were in.

After a morning of looking around, we're now sat outside a restaurant in a square which is surrounded on all sides by bars and shops. There are no high rise buildings, only a couple of tavernas on the rooftops, and the square is lined with tables and white parasols, full of customers all eating, drinking and enjoying the sun. It's quite different to Marmaris, quiet in comparison, and we've eaten a light lunch and are now enjoying ice cream. This restaurant doesn't actually stock it as, when we ordered it, the waiter called over a small boy, gave him some money and sent him in the direction of an ice cream parlour type shop on the opposite side of the square. And, five minutes later, the boy ran back holding the ice-creams out for us which we quickly grabbed before they melted.

It is, Jude tells me, a rare day off for him and he seems really chilled out. He's sitting in cream linen shorts, matching short-sleeved shirt, flip flops and dark shades. He's holding the ice cream in one hand and stroking Libby's knee with the other. Despite Jude's attention, Libby has grown quiet as the day has gone on and I'm becoming concerned for her. She looks drained and hasn't removed her dark shades the whole day and I feel bad for keeping her up so late last night, particularly after Grant's voicemail, as I know how hard she's been working plus trying to look after me too. It's good to see her spending some time with Jude and I feel almost guilty for being here too, they need some time alone and they've sacrificed one of his rare days off to spend it with Seth and me.

I look at Seth and, although he's nodding and smiling along with the conversation, he looks distant on occasion and I wish I knew what was going on inside that head of his. He's wearing a really cute panama hat today, which goes well with his curls and clothes, and my heart flutters a little every now and then as I remember the kiss last night, and the relationship that's developing between us.

We're going to be making our way back soon, as Jude has something he needs to tend to when we get back, but it looks like he's planning for us all to spend the evening together too back in Marmaris. Despite Jude saying it's a day off, he's taken quite a few work calls, Seth too, but it's a small price to pay I guess when you're so busy with work and want some free time. I wonder how much Libby has told Jude about the last couple of day's events. If he does know anything, he definitely doesn't give any indication of it. Until now.

'So, how's Hamil,' he suddenly asks me and I look up from what's left of my ice cream to find him looking at me with his head on one side, smiling. I glance at Libby nervously and then Seth, but both are looking at their mobile phones, thankfully oblivious to Jude's question.

'He's fine, I think,' I reply.

'Looked like he was fine when I saw you both snogging the other day in the street, nearly ran you over, you were unaware of anything going on around you.' Jude laughs and I realise that the other two are now looking up at us. I can't help but feel he's stirring up trouble.

'They're just friends, Jude, that's all. Stop causing mischief,' Libby says and smiles at me. But, her smile looks strained.

Jude laughs. 'I'm not causing mischief, I'm purely saying that they didn't look just friends, and it's confusing. One day, it's Hamil, then it's my brother. I want to make sure I'm keeping up, Lou.'

I blush and squirm in my seat. Libby sighs. 'Ignore him, he's obviously getting bored,' she says. I laugh nervously and dab at my face with a serviette, but Jude hasn't finished yet.

'And Libby, it's no good you saying 'they're just friends.' That's what you said you and my brother were when you first came to Marmaris, remember, despite the fact you were dating each other.'

Dating? Firstly, who uses that phrase unless you're born in the 1800's, and...dating? I look up just in time to see Libby look a little shocked. She looks at me and her face softens. 'It was just a couple of dates, nothing serious, as you well know Jude.' I then look to Seth, but he hasn't heard a word of it, he's back looking at his phone.

I nod and stare down to my drink and swirl the glass around a little too vigorously as some of the cocktail spills onto the table. I see that Jude has noticed and he's smugly grinning. Why have neither Libby or Seth told me they dated? In fact, both have both made a real point of saying they've only ever been friends. But I now find out this isn't the case. Why would she have kept this from me?

Once I've calmed myself, I look back up, confident that my face won't betray the way I'm feeling, and see Libby glaring at Jude, and Jude glaring back at her. And Seth is still oblivious. Then, he stands and starts to walk away.

'Where are you off to, brother?' Jude asks. 'The conversation's just getting interesting.'

Seth looks back and says, 'Phone call to make, won't be a minute,' then carries on wandering off.

'Why don't you make the call from the table?' Jude shouts, 'or is it something you'd rather someone not hear?' Jude looks back to me and I look at Seth who appears to have either not heard Jude, or, is choosing to ignore him as he's now stood by the fountain deep in conversation. With whom, I don't know, but I've got a pretty good idea.

Jude shouts, 'say hi to her from me,' then turns and looks back at me and winks. I know that he thinks Seth is speaking to the same person that I do. I look to Libby who is rubbing her head then stops, looks at her watch and says, 'It's getting near the time for the boat to go, let's start making our way there.'

I must admit that sounds like a good idea. Until ten minutes ago I'd have stayed here for hours but it's now all changed. I've discovered more lies and secrets, involving one of the people I trust more than anyone in the world. It's not the fact that I think there was anything serious between Libby and Seth, it's the fact that both of them have always denied anything had ever happened at all, other than a friendship, but I now find out that there has been some type of romantic involvement. Just two dates or not, it's a lie from both of them and I'm left wondering why.

We pay the bill and go to leave, then Libby says she's going to use the bathroom and, before I can go off with her, Jude links his arm through mine and tells her we'll wait in the square. We stand silently in the sun and I watch Seth wandering around in a small circle, still on the phone having what looks like an intense conversation. I look at my own phone, seeing that I've missed five calls and several text messages from Grant. They can wait until later, I'm really not in the mood to deal with those right now.

'Sorry, it looks like I've surprised you with that little bit of news,' Jude suddenly says.

I look up at him and refuse to give him any satisfaction. 'What news?' I ask.

'About Seth and Libby, I thought you knew they'd gone out for a bit, before Libby got with me.'

'Oh that,' I say, 'she probably did mention it but I'd forgotten. It's no big deal, a couple of dates.' I look back to my phone.

'Don't you mind the fact that she always test drives your boyfriends before you take ownership of them?' he asks.

I look up at him, not quite sure what he's getting at. I wait then frown and shrug my shoulders. 'Well, she had a fling with Hamil once, and you've now been with him. Plus Seth. Was just wondering if she had a thing with that boyfriend of yours back home before you and he became an item. Grant, isn't it?'

I start to feel defensive. 'She's never dated Grant,' I say.

'You sure?' he asks.

I nod. 'Absolutely,' and I look back to my phone. My heart is beating so fast and loud, I'm amazed he can't hear it. She dated Hamil? That's news to me too.

'Well,' he says, 'just to say, if she gets fed up with me, I'll date you,' and he laughs.

I make a pathetic attempt at a laugh too. 'I think I'll pass,' I say and this makes him laugh louder. Libby is now back from the rest room and we start to walk, Seth following us closely behind. Although off the phone, he's deep in thought, and Libby's not much different. I'm angry with both of them, for not telling me the truth, and could quite happily not speak to them for the rest of the day. But, that would give Jude what he wants.

What was he trying to get at, about ex boyfriends and passing them on to me? I'm surprised he even knows Grant's name, and it can only be from conversations he's had with Libby. But, I'm pretty sure that she has never had anything to do with Grant. I met him first. Well, she sort of knew him through a mutual friend, but I don't think they had ever met as such, other than maybe to be introduced in a group. In fact, it wasn't until a few weeks after Grant had asked me out that we found they knew each other from somewhere, and it took them ages to work out how. And, anyway, there's only ever been animosity between them.

Unless... my heart feels like it's about to stop. Is it possible there's some sort of history between them that neither has admitted to? I shake my head, this is getting ridiculous. Jude has stirred up a load of nonsense and mischief and I'm going to totally forget about it. Libby would have told me if anything had happened between them, she'd have said. She wouldn't lie to me. Ok, she hadn't told me about Seth, or Hamil, but probably because it was nothing.

I suddenly notice that Seth has caught up with me. 'Have I missed something?' he asks, putting the phone away in his pocket and his arm around my shoulders.

'Nope,' I say, not wanting to go into it. I shrug his arm off, but then feel guilty and so link my arm through his instead. I don't want to give Jude the satisfaction of seeing he's caused any atmosphere between us, or any trouble. 'I didn't know you and Libby had ever been romantically involved,' I say.

241

Seth laughs quite innocently. 'Romantically involved?' he says. 'Hardly. We met on one of her first nights here, I took her out for a drink and we had a couple of dates. Nothing more than a peck on the cheek, because we just didn't really click. Not in that way. I was just one of the first people she met here and then, after a few other dates here and there with other guys, she met my brother and, well, as you know, the rest is history.'

I feel a little better hearing him say this and smile feebly.

'Jude said she dated Hamil too.'

'Did she?' Seth asks. 'That's possible. As I say, she dated a few other guys before meeting Jude but nothing serious. I don't think she'd have gone as far as you did with him yesterday.'

I look at him and see he's grinning mischievously. I have to laugh.

'Has Libby ever mentioned anything about Grant to you?' I ask.

'Other than saying he's an arse, and that you're too good for him, and that he treats you terribly?'

I look at him with raised eyebrows. 'She said that?'

He grimaces. 'I shouldn't have told you that. Ignore me. She never said anything at all.' I smile and put my head on his shoulder as we walk. 'Look,' he says, 'What I do know is that she's absolutely over the moon you're breaking up with him. As am I.'

He kisses me gently, tilting my chin up with his finger, and I cradle his face in my hands for a moment.

'I've a bit of a surprise for you.' I look at him, my mood lightened again, all apprehension and worries virtually gone. Until I look ahead of us and see Libby and Jude walking and having a bit of a row. I can see Jude keep trying to hold her hand and she flicks it way and says something out of the corner of her mouth. He looks like he's enjoying it, but she looks near the point of tears.

'What's the surprise?' I ask, coming back to the matter in question.

'If you're agreeable,' he asks, which I smile at as, who says 'if you're agreeable' in this day and age. These brothers have some strange sayings. 'I'd like to take you away for a couple of days.'

I stop walking and look at him, and then to Libby who has now walked ahead of Jude, him following behind calling out her name. 'Don't worry, Libby knows, and she's fine with it,' he says. 'In fact, it's going to work out well as Jude needs her to help him with work over the next couple of days and she was worried about not spending time with you. In fact, this surprise is more Jude's doing than my own. It was his idea.'

Was it, indeed, I think to myself. It's a shame that Jude didn't suggest us going away so he can spend quality time with Libby, rather than working her a little harder. Somehow, I can't think of anything Jude would do that would be for anyone else's benefit other than his own and I'm wondering if Libby really does know about this at all. But, Seth is looking very pleased with himself and my heart softens a little.

'Where are we going?' I ask.

'Ephesus,' he replies. Ephesus, I've heard of that. I think back to the research I did on the Internet and know that it's a very old city, near to the resort of Kuşadasi. I'd hoped we could visit it during my stay but Libby had said it was too far, unless we booked a trip. Won't she mind not coming with me, I wonder? I'll talk to her tonight, but for the moment I'll let myself get a little excited. Not just because I'm going to Ephesus, but because it's with Seth, just the two of us, and we'll be staying overnight.

CHAPTER TWENTY-TWO

We've been on the road now for about 3 and a half hours, having stopped for a quick coffee and pastry, and it's been a more enjoyable journey than the last one I spent with Seth after he'd collected me from the airport on my first day here. I think of everything that's happened since I arrived, including the experiences I'd rather not remember, such as Hamil, and I can't bear to think of my trip back home to the UK which is now under two weeks away. It's gone way too quick.

It's more comfortable in this car without a huge holdall on my lap. Our overnight bags are in the boot and we've got the roof down, plenty of water and sweets to eat, and life is good. Libby seemed almost relieved that I'm going to be away for a couple of days which, if I'm honest, hurt a bit. She could have looked at least a bit disappointed. Have I been such a bad houseguest? I do obviously want her to have a break from juggling me and her workload, as well as her new business, but...well, I'll make sure she cries bucketfuls when I leave in a couple of weeks, that'll teach her.

It sounds like Jude has quite a bit of work planned for her

so she's not exactly going to get much rest. His chief bar maid has gone AWOL, no idea where but they think it involves a customer that visited a few months back but has returned and swept her off her feet. Good luck to her, let's hope she's found romance and happiness and enjoys being away from her tyrant boss. Which is exactly how I see Jude. I started off by not liking him, warmed to him during the day trip to Rhodes yesterday and then ended up disliking him big style.

Well, I don't have to think about him, or Libby, or Grant or anyone else for a while as I've two whole days with Seth and a night too. OK, maybe we won't be spending the night together as in being in the same bedroom, it is in separate rooms but they're next to each other I've been informed. I wonder if the rooms will have adjoining doors. Ooh, exciting, I've never had a room in a hotel with one of those before. Will we need the door at all? So far, Seth and I have had a peck on the cheek and he's stroked my hand a couple of times. I'm wondering if he's purposefully taking things slowly due to my incident with Hamil, or whether he's just a gentleman. And, to be honest, this suits me. It's nice to have his companionship, and I do have strong feelings for him, but I'm still not 100% convinced that he's honest or trustworthy, and I'm also quite sensitive about the revelation of his past with Libby. Then, of course, there's the small matter of his mystery woman who he still hasn't explained. I'm not going to force him to tell me about her, like he hasn't forced me to talk about Grant. I think it's best we just pretend both of those people don't exist for the time being.

It'll be nice to stay in a hotel tonight. Libby's apartment is great, but I'll enjoy the privacy and quiet of my own room and bathroom, a comfy bed and air conditioning. And Seth in the room next to me. I feel a flutter in my stomach and force my mind back to other things, such as Ephesus which we'll reach very shortly.

The drive up from Marmaris, on the south west side of Turkey, has been mainly motorway but Seth says he'll go a different way back tomorrow, to take in some sights. That sounds good, the more I see of this beautiful country, the better. I see the signs to say we're in Selçuk County in the province of Izmir, and Seth tells me we're close now. I'm not quite sure what to expect, and he doesn't want to tell me too much, he wants me to witness it first hand, but assures me I won't be disappointed.

We eventually arrive in the southern car park, at the upper end of Ephesus, which is pretty busy already and I wonder if we should have gone with Seth's suggestion for us to leave Marmaris much earlier as it's supposed to be half empty at about 9am. But, that would have meant leaving at 6am or earlier, which neither of us particularly fancied. I could count on one hand the amount of times I've got up before six in the morning, and I didn't fancy starting it on this holiday. The four of us had a late night last night, going out for food at about 10pm as Jude got caught up longer than he'd hoped with a work problem. I did suggest a few times we could go out just the three of us, but unfortunately no one took up the offer. Jude behaved himself at the meal, at least, and all mischief making ceased. Until next time, no doubt.

Seth manages to find a parking space, squeezed between two minibuses, and we grab our hats and water. I've brought a light long sleeved shirt with me, as advised by Libby, as the temperatures combined with the open space will be pretty high and I don't want to risk burning after taking care of myself for the last fortnight. I'm covered in lotion from head to toe which has probably given me a slight clown appearance. But, I'm not fussed.

From where we're parked, we'll come out of a completely different spot when we leave the site, having walked downhill through it. It's quite a walk back although Seth says we can get a taxi from the other end to here. I'm happy to see how I feel when we've finished. Although I enjoy walking, I've struggled with it here due to the blistering heat, and have no idea how the locals do it. I was hoping I'd have acclimatised by now, Libby seems to have done, and I wonder if I'll be still sweating like a pig when I get back to Abingdon. Great… no home *and* smelly.

When we pay and go through the entrance, we decide to buy the map and audio tour, so we can get as much from the visit as possible. Although there are signs dotted around which explain a bit about the place, Seth says that the tour will tell us so much more, and that he hardly found out anything about the history on his other visits here. I'm secretly pleased about this, as I'd been watching people walking around with headphones, and it means I'll get to look like a spy, tracking a baddie whilst being directed by a hovering helicopter using thermal imaging equipment. Not that I have any idea what that is. Ah, and with the tour map in my hand, I can pretend I'm a guide. Within a minute, I'm holding the map in the air and telling Seth to follow me. He's smiling now, but I can guarantee he'll be fed up with me within a few minutes.

Although I knew a little about Ephesus I still wasn't prepared for the sight that's now in front of me. I actually stop dead in my tracks, only to have a couple of tourists run into the back of me as they were studying their own map and trying to get the audio on to the right language. I apologise and wave them around me, guiding them with my map. There in front of us are the Great Baths and, while the audio guide begins to explain how they have been excavated, and the method used to heat the water through them, I'm picturing how it would have looked all those years ago. The first human settlement here was in 6000 BC and I can't quite get my head around that. It's hard to imagine life that long ago. I wish I'd taken more interest in history when I was at school, as my knowledge seems to have jumped from dinosaurs to the Ice Age and then to Queen Victoria, missing out some pretty important stuff.

Apparently, business and politics were discussed in these baths. Imagine that? Trying to bathe whilst talking about all serious stuff with your peers. I try to visualise me and the accounting team back in Abingdon, having our Monday morning meeting in a huge bath, blowing bubbles at each other and strategically positioning the flannel so as not to offend anyone. Hey, this was where networking actually began. See, who needs social media, we should all just go and bathe together. Seth doesn't seem to agree with this suggestion, and I suppose he is an *actual* businessman and knows more about networking than I.

A young man approaches me and offers some old coins to buy. I go to look at them, held out in his hand, but Seth ushers the man away saying something that I don't understand as it's in Turkish, but I guess it wasn't very nice as the guy looks frustrated. Apparently, they're not that old, the coins. In fact, Seth informs me they were probably made last night and I give the back of the man's head one of my looks as he walks off. We watch him go to the next naïve tourist, who gets out their money to buy some within seconds, and I'm pleased to have Seth with me or else I'd have parted with my cash too.

As we continue to walk, we find it grows more difficult to keep together in the growing crowd. It isn't just because of the volume of tourists, but also the heat and the fact that many of the locals are carrying quite large brollies to keep the sun off their heads. I'm pleased we brought our water with us and take a few sips. Let's hope it lasts, I think to myself, or else I may feel like I did that day when I arrived at the airport and had to sit there, slowly dehydrating. I still feel grateful that I survived that day, although no one else seems to take my brush with death seriously at all.

Apparently, despite the hordes of people, today isn't that busy. It's all down to the number of cruise ships docking, and Seth checked last night and saw that there's not that many today. On some days, several dock at the same time, all running excursions to Ephesus for their thousands of passengers, and you can hardly move. This is definitely not the place to be if afraid of crowds.

The view ahead of me gets better and better, if that's possible. I think of my cousins in the States, who tell me how the Americans always talk of coming to the UK because of our history we have in the country, but we truly have nothing compared to this. We reach the Odeon, a structure that the audio tour guide calls the City Council Hall, where members gathered and discussed the city's future, but also used the place for listening to musical concerts. I try to picture myself, sat on the stone steps along with the other 1500 people that it could accommodate. The audience would have been protected from the sun and rain by a fixed roof, and I wish in a way it was still here today. I touch the top of my hat and it's boiling, almost burning my hand.

A couple of times I stumble slightly on the uneven ground and Seth quickly grabs my arm. Soon, though, he takes my hand and I'm grateful as it means I won't lose him in the crowds. What if I did lose him? There's no way I could find him here, not until nightfall, when the place would be fairly deserted. We stop for a while at the Prytaneion, listen to the commentary and then find a space to sit on the ground and take a rest. A sacred fire was kept alight here at all times, to symbolize the city's continued existence, and we joke how it wouldn't be allowed now with all the Health and Safety laws. Each time Seth looks as though he's going to cuddle up to me, he's asked to take photos of couples passing us and, after several requests, he asks if they'll return the favour, gives them his own camera, pulls me up to stand beside him, and wraps his arm around me before we both smile for the shot. When the camera is handed back, he keeps his arm around my waist and kisses me gently. My hat bangs into his eyes and we giggle, and his hand gently strokes my back. We sit down in my little space I found, me leaning against him, and drink some more water and watch the crowds go past. I really can't begin to imagine what it looks like when it's even busier than this. How can more people fit onto these streets?

We soon continue our tour, seeing more monuments and temples such as the Government Agora, and we stop at the Gate of Hercules to allow a tour group to pass. I love the eccentricity of the tour guides, holding up all manner of items to keep the group with them; umbrellas, walking sticks, flags. We follow behind them soon finding ourselves in Kuretes Street which is largely paved in marble but with some parts in stone, and there's a deep drainpipe running underneath our feet. This would have been very much like our own High Streets now, with shops, restaurants and workshops along the edges.

'Enjoying it?' Seth asks. I realise this is the first time we've actually spoken since arriving here. I've been too busy listening to the audio tour, and am a little overwhelmed so I nod enthusiastically.

'Are you?' I ask Seth. I'm worried, as I know he's been

here before and could be bored.

'Loving it,' he says and kisses my nose. This makes me laugh and I stroke his face. Just as I do so, my phone vibrates in my bag which is against my hip and it makes me jump. I take it out and see it's just Grant, so I turn the phone off and put it back into my bag. I'm sure that if Libby needs me urgently, she'll ring Seth. Everyone else can wait.

'Grant?' Seth asks and I nod. I grab hold of his arm and pull him along, and he follows, squeezing my hand tight. We pass more and more wonderful relics and monuments and stop for a moment at the Latrina, the Public Lavatory which was built facing the baths of Varius. I sort of wish these were still usable, there's been a definite lack of toilets since arriving and I've drunk a lot of water. But, there's no way I'd use them due to the complete lack of privacy. Well, I know that we all go to the toilet, and it's a natural bodily function and all that stuff, but it's still hard to believe people sat next to each other, lifted up their togas and all 'went' at the same time. I find it hard enough if there's someone in the next cubicle to me, so there'd be no hope if they could actually see me. I'd have had to wrap a blanket around myself!

As we move forward, I suddenly see the most wonderful sight I've come across so far. There, in front of me, is the Library of Celsus, on the corner of Kuretes Street and the Agora. It's a huge building in light coloured stone, with four vertical magnificent and tall structures which each have an elegant statue set in an alcove. There's another layer above, and the whole building is entered by a set of stone steps. I find out it wasn't actually discovered until the excavations in 1905 and restored about 70 years later. And, what a wonderful job they've done. The Audio tour guide, who I've decided to name Bernard, no idea why, tells me that at one time there were probably 12,000 books in this library. Imagine that? We go up the steps to stand alongside the extremely tall pillars and I look up at the floors above. Seth takes a couple of photos of me, learning against them, and I do the same. Then, he's accosted by more couples to take their photo and I have a little wander before I'm accosted too. We should start charging, we'd make a fortune here. In fact, I'd make a good photographer. I'll add that to my list as soon as I get back to Libby's.

After the library, nothing else can really compare, not even the Grand Theatre, one of our last stops with Bernard. Although impressive, it doesn't take my breath away like the Library did, although I still think it's fantastic. I sit on the steps and listen to Bernard's last few words. I'll miss him, I decide. I ask Seth if he'll miss Bernard too and he looks a bit confused, not really getting it even when I explain. I'll tell Libby when I call her later, she would like Bernard. We sip our water and sit quietly for some time, Seth's arm loosely round me, and I close my eyes, enjoying the sun on my face. Seth does the same, although I think it's so he avoids eye contact with any tourists looking for a photo to be taken.

'Ready to go?' he asks a while later and I nod, stand up and brush my self down. When Seth turns to walk in front of me, I notice the dust on the back of his shorts and brush it off with my hand before I realise what I'm doing. He looks round at me, deadly serious, and I blush. Then he laughs and tells me to carry on as he thinks I've missed a bit. I smile and we walk to the exit, firstly returning Bernard to his collection point where I say goodbye. We decide to have a slow and leisurely walk back to the car we'd left at the other entrance and resist the offer of free rides, mainly because you have to agree to go to a carpet shop on the way, not that there are any around on the way back to the car, but still. I can only imagine they take you on a bit of a mystery tour. It's a nice walk and we're silent, but it's not uncomfortable. I'm trying to digest everything I've seen and I know I'll remember this forever, with or without photographs, as I know the memories will stay in my head as vivid and clear as they are right now. To try and explain it to anyone who hasn't been here would be impossible, I'd never do it justice. I'd just do what Libby, Seth and anyone else that had visited here did when they spoke to me, I'd just say 'Go and see Ephesus, you won't regret it!' We arrive back at the car and I'm grateful to sit on a comfortable seat after only having the odd rock to perch on for the last few hours. We put the roof down for some shade from the blistering heat and sip the last of the water we have. We're only half an hour from Kusadasi and so I know it's not long until I can get a nice, new cold bottle, and freshen up in the hotel. I think again of an adjoining door between our bedrooms but dismiss it quickly from my mind as I want to take this slowly and not have a repeat performance of what happened with Hamil. I can't trust my emotions at the moment, one minute I want Seth to kiss me but then the next minute I don't. I've no idea what's going on with my head and so it's best I do nothing at all about it.

And, on the slow journey back, I feel my eyes grow heavy and know I'll be asleep within minutes, probably snoring just like I was on my first day in this country when driving along with Seth. I'm not exactly the best travelling companion one could wish for.

CHAPTER TWENTY-THREE

Seth woke me gently when we arrived at our five star hotel which is, may I add, fabulous and we went to our respective rooms, showered, freshened up and met in the bar downstairs. There is no adjoining door between our rooms, not that it matters, obviously. My bedroom is lush, minimalist and swish, with a gorgeous shower and separate bath, which I'm going to try out later. I've missed my baths, I haven't had one for a very long time as Grant's apartment doesn't have one, and neither does Libby's. Grant's just has the hugest shower I've ever seen which is the full width of the bathroom. When we were first together, it was fun being in it at the same time but I can't remember the last time we did that.

As soon as we met in the bar, we decided not to have a drink here but to get out into Kuşadasi and make the most of the evening. So, we walk out into the cool evening air, and the hustle and bustle of the town, which is similar to Marmaris, but I personally find slightly more sophisticated. I could imagine Grant tolerating it here, compared to hating the touristy feel of Marmaris and its fun and craziness.

Kuşadasi is situated in a lovely gulf within the Aegean

region and, I find out from Seth, its name means Bird Island. It's in easy distance of so many wonderful sights and, although not sure yet, we may call at the House of the Virgin Mary before heading home tomorrow, and the Temple of Artemis, one of the seven wonders of the ancient world. I'm really keen to see both, as I don't know when I'll get the chance again. I definitely won't before I go home in a couple of weeks and I really can't say for sure when I'll be back here to Turkey. I hope that it will be soon, but it depends on a lot of factors, primarily money. I'm going to need every penny I can get to find my own place in order to save me from the doom otherwise known as 'mother's craft room.'

We're heading to a fish restaurant, which Seth assures me is one of the best he's ever been to, although it was some time ago and I'm not to blame him if it doesn't quite work out. To be honest, I'd be happy eating fish fingers, I'm having such a great time. I'm not going to ask who it was he came here with, even though I'd love to know. There's so much I don't know about him, and I'd love to ask but I've known him for what, under three weeks? Not quite even that. And, there's no obligation for him to share his past with me. Even if he knows everything about me. After all, I've washed my dirty washing in public several times since being here, particularly in terms of Hamil and Grant.

There's a part of me that worries that Seth is a rebound thing, trying to replace my partner of eighteen months with someone else I've known for as many days. I've no idea why I have this pull towards Seth, but I do, and the feeling seems mutual. I know I'm over-thinking everything and should just stop and try to enjoy the moment, and make the most of this opportunity here in this bustling town.

It's hard to believe that it was once a small village but now it's jam packed with carpet and leather shops, bars and restaurants, and doubles in population during the summer months purely because of tourists. Where Marmaris has ferries going over to Rhodes, Kuşadasi has links to nearby Greek islands like Samos and Mykonos, and I really wish we could have longer here so we could spend a day on one of those. I'm not sure why I want to, I think it's something to do with watching too much '*Mama Mia*' and '*Shirley Valentine.*' Maybe I'll get to go there another time, if and when I come back.

We walk down a narrow street lined with Irish bars and everyone we pass is smiling, and I soon find myself smiling too. The music changes from one bar to the next and it's a young person's paradise down here. That's what I love about the places I've visited so far in this beautiful country, there's something for absolutely everyone, whether historical sites is your thing, or cultural and religious places of interest, or just plain fun and sun.

We head towards the harbour and soon come across the restaurant, going up a few steps to a table on the terrace. Seth chats casually to the waiters in Turkish and asks for the menus, and I read mine and choose a dish quickly, as I soon realise I'm absolutely starving. I look back over to the port where I can see a few cruise ships slowly leaving the harbour. I feel for those that are on the ships as they won't get to spend the evening here like me. They generally only stay for a few hours in the daytime so tourists can go to Ephesus and other surrounding sights and then they're off again, to someone new. But, they're missing so much as the place really comes alive at night.

I've ordered sea bass and I watch the waiter place the plate in front of me and I immediately dive into it as soon as he's moved away to the next table. Seth ordered white wine, to go with the fish, and it's a good choice.   Cold and refreshing.

'What do you think of Kuşadasi?' Seth asks me.

I smile. 'Quite simply, I love it, just as I love Marmaris. In fact, I love all of turkey.'

Seth laughs. 'You've hardly seen any of it yet. '

I nod in agreement. 'But what I've seen so far, I love,' I say. 'Where else would you recommend I visit over here?'

Seth frowns, then puts his knife and fork down, sits back and studies me whilst contemplating my question.   He eventually answers, 'If I had to choose one place, I'd say Istanbul.'

I'd been thinking of this myself. It's one place I've always wanted to visit, mainly because my parents went there years ago and loved it. And, because I saw it once on a TV reality show and, well, it looked amazing. I don't tell Seth this bit, as I think he probably already has doubts about my cultural and geographical knowledge, and him finding out my main source of reference is via a TV show may push him further away from me.

Seth gets a napkin and takes a pen out of his blazer pocket and proceeds to draw a map of Turkey. He points out where Marmaris is, Kuşadasi and then Istanbul. Although on his small napkin it looks a tiny distance between everything, I quickly realise how vast this country is as Seth explains travelling times between each place. Istanbul will need to stay on my wish list for the moment, there's no way I can fit it in whilst here this time. But, I'm determined to go one day.

'Where is it in your wish list?' he asks. 'A higher priority than your USA road trip or lower?'

I give this some thought before replying. 'Depends on who I go with.'

'Ah yes,' he replies, 'the road trip is with the love of your life. Whereas Istanbul doesn't need to be, or does it?'

'Nope, it can be on my own,' I reply. Seth smiles.

We share the flat bread that the waiter brought out with the meals and dip it into the cemen, a lovely tomato based dish that I've had a few times now. I must get the recipe for this so I can cook it when home, wherever home may be. If it's at my mothers then I'll attempt to get her to try some but she thinks a Viennese Whirl is 'fancy foreign food' and avoids anything that she either can't pronounce, spell or that sounds slightly exotic. I start to tell Seth about my mother, as I'm thinking of her, and how I've spoken to her a few times since coming here, and that she's said she might come out with me one day if I return to visit. I'm really pleased about this, as I would never have expected her to travel again, she seems to have given all of that up.

'What did your mother think of Grant?' Seth asks, tucking into his main course, a huge seafood pizza.

'She likes him, I think,' I reply, 'but she doesn't really know him. She just sees him as a rich guy who's fallen for her daughter and that could promise me a life of luxury and happiness. Plus, I just think she's happy that I found someone. She'd given up.'

Seth laughs. 'I think I might marry him myself,' he says, 'sounds a catch. Remind me why you're splitting up again?'

'Why we've split up, not splitting up. He's already in my past. Well, he will be once I've seen him face to face and got all my stuff back.' I smile. 'We just really didn't match up well. We had absolutely nothing in common and I was just his project. He wanted to 'fix' me.'

'You don't look like you need fixing to me,' Seth says and I watch him eat and could continue staring for the whole evening but this sea bass is so delicious I dive straight back into it. Loving looks between Seth and I will have to wait.

'Grant isn't all bad,' I continue. 'It hasn't just been arguments and upsets. We've had fun too and he's been very generous. But, it hasn't been the real me that he's loved, and I can't act the part any longer. This holiday has made me realise that, although I think I've always known.'

We continue to eat in silence for a few minutes, and every now and then I look up to see the beautiful view of the dark sky now meeting the water with its ships and boats bobbing around. There are private yachts pretty close by and Seth and I start to chat about who might own them, and we make up a whole life for the people we can see milling about. I haven't tried a boat trip yet, although Libby has said we're going to go on one hopefully the day after tomorrow. It won't be on one of these yachts though, it will be on a gulet, a wooden type boat that goes around the coastline and is supposed to be the most relaxing day. I can't wait.

'What about if Grant changed?' Seth asks.

I frown. 'What do you mean?' I ask.

'Well, if he loves you so much, he might offer to change and be more like you, rather than making you be like him.'

I shake my head. 'That's what he's told my mother, in his many phone calls to her this last fortnight, apparently. But, like I said to her, he'd end up feeling like I do now. You know, missing the old him and wanting his life back. No, he needs to find someone he's suited to, who he can be himself with and who loves him for who he is and vice versa.'

'I like you as you are,' Seth suddenly says and rubs my arm. I put my knife and fork down, hold his hand and smile at him.

'And I like you how you are too,' I smile. Seth leans over and kisses me gently on the cheek and I stroke his face. Then, he kisses me on the lips and I respond. We don't kiss for too long, as I'm really conscious of the candle very close to my blouse and can picture an awkward moment involving a waiter throwing a jug of water over me, but I enjoy the few seconds that the kiss lasts.

I slow down my eating a little now, realising that I look like a pig with most of my food gone whilst Seth still has half of his, and I take the time to savour the tastes, conversation and atmosphere, not wanting tonight to end. For Seth, it must be great to have a night off work, although he does talk about his job and Jude, and how those two things don't always go together. And, the only thing I find a bit uncomfortable is when we talk about Libby as I still have that small doubt about her relationship with him. I know it's in the past, and it's none of my business, but it's the fact that neither of them declared it to me. Seth, I can forgive. Who am I to question him and why should he tell me? But Libby? We've always told each other everything and I just don't get it. She's laughed it off, as has Seth, in that it was nothing, just a quick date or two upon her arrival here, but there's a bond between them I don't get. And, although I shouldn't have let Jude get to me, the comments about her relationship with Grant has really bothered me too. I can't help but question why there's such animosity between them, when they're both supposed to love the same person, me.

After we've eaten, we enjoy the liqueur we're given by the waiter. I try to drink it daintily but end up gasping for air as though I've just drunk white spirit. Wow, that was strong. We bid our farewell to the waiter and take a slow walk back to the hotel, neither of us fancying a nightclub, or a bar. We're both shattered, and a noisy place full of holidaymakers would ruin our relaxed mood. Well, when I say relaxed, that's not entirely true as this thing about Libby is starting to niggle away at me. It's how I am, I get something in my head and just can't let go. And, even though I know we're really getting on and that I could ruin it all by bringing up a subject that would cause Seth to prickle, it's eating away at me and will burst out soon. So, rather than ask him about his relationship with her, I ask him about Grant instead. I try my hardest to be diplomatic and cool, but it comes out as 'Why does Libby hate Grant so much, what's gone on between them?' This stops Seth dead in his tracks and he looks at me confused.

After a few seconds he says, 'The reason I think she dislikes him is because she's your friend, and she cares about you. And, he's treated you really badly. Is that not easy to understand?' I hesitate before answering, part of me cross that, as usual, he's so on her side. It's not that I've said anything bad about her, is it?

'Look, I think something has happened between them that I don't know about. Grant won't even allow her name to be mentioned at home, Libby isn't much different about him, and I don't get it.'

Seth shrugs and starts walking again. 'Maybe he's jealous of her, because you miss her so much and have such a great relationship with her, better than the one you have with him. And he just can't handle it.' I study his face as we move along, trying to see a sign of any secrecy, but there's nothing. What he's said sounds plausible, and I should believe it, but I still don't feel happy. The feeling is still niggling away. 'Just stop now,' I tell myself, 'you'll ruin everything.'

'Has she ever said she went out with him once? Or that anything happened between them?'

'No,' he says, and shakes his head. 'Firstly, why would she tell me. And secondly, why would you even think she'd do something like that? From what I know, she can't stand the guy, so anything happening between them is a ridiculous suggestion. Anyway, you're really close, she wouldn't keep a secret from you.'

I laugh a little sarcastically which, in my case, means very sarcastically. 'She didn't tell me about you two.' Oh, I had to say it, didn't I.

Seth stops again and rolls his eyes. 'Lou, there was no 'us two.' We've both explained it to you but you're just not listening. Libby arrived from the UK, we met in a bar on one of the first nights, I bought her a drink and asked her out for a meal. We went out a couple of times, but it just didn't go anywhere, and then she met Jude. End of. You've got to let this go and stop being paranoid.'

OK, the niggle is going to now kick off. If it's one thing I hate, it's being called paranoid. Even if I am a bit, but it's the principle. 'Well,' I start to say, brewing for a fight, but before I can, Seth grabs me and kisses me and all thoughts of a row ebb away. The niggle has been calmed.

'Now,' he says, 'that's something that Libby and I never did, and never will. Does that make you happy?' His face is so cute as he says it, I can't help but smile. I wrap my arms around his neck and kiss him back, for several minutes, oblivious to the crowds of people that are surging around us, on their way to a club or bar, or to a hotel. We just completely hog the street and neither of us cares. The kiss has worked, he's right. I really do need to let this go.

Within minutes, we're back at the hotel and I must say that both of us upped our walking pace to get here as quickly as we can. Seth has his arm around me and, each time I look at him, he smiles and I smile back. We quickly ask for our keys at the hotel foyer, bid the receptionist goodnight, and go quickly into the lift where we kiss all the way to our floor. When we step out, we go to our neighbouring rooms and just hold hands and look at each other.

'Well...' I say

'Well indeed,' he answers and pulls me a little closer.

'Is this where I'm supposed to invite you in for a coffee?' I ask. 'Because, if so, I don't have any, I drank two cups before we left.'

'In that case,' he says, 'maybe you should come to mine for a cup. Can't have you going to bed without a cup of coffee.' The smiles from us both grow broader as we giggle on our way into his room.

Inside, it's pretty cool due to the air conditioning that's been left on and, for this, I am so grateful. What I'd do for air conditioning back at Libby's. I go to sit on the bed and watch Seth as he takes off his blazer and then he sits next to me.

'What happened to the coffee?' I ask as he puts his arms around me.

'Gone off the idea,' he says. 'Have you?'

I nod. 'Yes, it seems I have,' and then let out a low moan as his lips find my neck and ears. I wait for the feeling I had when I was with Hamil, the wish for Seth to stop or to slow down, but it doesn't come. Instead, I just don't want it to end. Seth pushes me gently onto the bed and I wrap my legs around him, pulling my fingers through his hair and return the kisses to his neck, which he seems to enjoy as much as I did. He suddenly cups my face with his hands and stares into my eyes. I think he's going to speak and so I kiss him again, not wanting to let him say anything in case it's 'we shouldn't' or 'let's not,' and he kisses me back but then pulls away.

'I need to tell you things, let you know what's really going on,' he says. 'I don't want any secrets between us.'

I shake my head and put my finger against his lips.

'There's no need,' I say and try to pull him back towards me but he doesn't move.

'You need to know about her.'

I shake my head. 'No, I don't,' I say. 'You've told me there's nothing between you but friendship and I believe that. I trust you. And, right now, I really want you.'

And I really do. And so, with that, we hungrily kiss and feel each other, and I moan again as I feel him undo my blouse and kiss my throat, my chest, then my stomach as he pushes down my skirt and I frantically pull at his clothes to undress him. And, within moments, we're making love, gently and passionately and I know that there's no other man I would rather be with. Not now, and not ever.

CHAPTER TWENTY-FOUR

Libby and I are lying on the top of a gulet, a beautiful wooden boat which is gently bobbing up and down in a gorgeous, turquoise bay just off the Aegean coastline around a small island not far from Marmaris. My eyes are slightly open and I'm looking at the pine-clad mountains. We're on the top deck, along with many other sunbathers, and the lower deck has tables and chairs for those that would rather relish the views without the sun beating down on them. I am totally relaxed, probably for the first time since I arrived. We'd talked about doing one of these day trips since I got here and I am so grateful we finally fitted it in as it is heaven and I could happily do this every day until I leave. That's if I leave, as I've done nothing but think of ways to stay whilst I've been laying here. What a difference a few days make.

The boat set sail at about 10:30 this morning and is almost full, with tourists of various nationalities although most are either from the UK or Germany. I've gathered that some are returning customers, having been on the trip two or three times already during their two week stay, and I can see why. So far, we have sailed along the coastline of unspoiled bays, jumped off the boat into the gorgeous blue sea for a cool down and a swim and have eaten a beautifully prepared lunch of BBQ'd chicken, rice and salad. The staff on board have been nothing short of fantastic, looking after every single passenger and supplying us all with refreshments whenever requested.

We're now back on our sunbeds whilst moored up in another bay where you can dive into the sea and/or snorkel, or just lay like couch potatoes exactly like we're both doing.

'Does this remind you of your saucy night away,' Libby asks casually.

'What?' I ask

'The gentle bobbing up and down...,' Libby laughs and I hit her with my magazine that I've tried to read a few times but given up. I'm so tired.

'It was romantic,' I say, 'not sordid.' I laugh too and I know that I've had a grin on my face for virtually the whole day. Libby has quizzed me on the intimate details of my night away with Seth since breakfast this morning, and I've shared some information, but not everything. It was just too special and I wouldn't be able to make it sound as romantic as it was. What I've said has reassured her that I had a good time, and so did Seth. That's all she needs to know.

Although Seth and I had planned to spend the morning in Kuşadasi and then drive to see the House of the Virgin Mary, after our night of passion we'd stayed in bed until almost the check out time, making love, cuddling, chatting and making the most of the time together. I hadn't told Seth this, but I was also making the most of the air conditioning and talked him into having a romantic bath with me seeing as I'd missed baths so much. It wasn't the relaxing bath I'd perhaps dreamt of, but I enjoyed it very much indeed.

Once we'd checked out, we decided to have a slow drive back, leaving the tourist spots for another time, going a different way to pass Lake Bafa, a beautiful lake and nature reserve, which was absolutely stunning. We chatted a lot, easy going stuff, nothing about secrets or our past. I trust him and he'll tell me what he needs to in good time, I know in my heart that it's nothing that will hurt me, he just wouldn't do that, not after the night we had together. It's changed everything between us.

I hadn't wanted the journey home to end and wish we could have stayed away for more days together, but there was a small part of me that wanted to get back to Libby as our time together is running out. If I go home as planned I have a week and a half left here, that's all, and I need to make the most of every minute with her and somehow juggle my remaining time between both her and Seth.

When Seth and I had pulled up outside the apartment upon our return, I'd sort of expected that we'd see each other that evening, once he'd gone to the bar and sorted out any work stuff, but Seth picked up a voicemail whilst we sat in the car and then said he'd need to go to work with Jude that night, which was fine. It would give me time to chill out and recover from a really tiring couple of days, tiring in more ways that one. In fact, the night had been more tiring than the days. I don't think we'd had more than an hour or two of sleep. Just the thought of that makes me go warm and fuzzy inside.

I had burst into the flat, ready to tell Libby all about my trip away, but she wasn't there and had just left a note to say she'd be out for the night and would see me in the morning, stating the time I'd need to be up for the gulet trip. I worried about her, knowing she must be doing the night-flight airport run, and hoped she'd be able to rest whilst on the boat for the day which, of course, she has. So, I had a quiet night in, watching the TV with a relatively early bedtime and the best night's sleep I've had for weeks. I ignored the texts and voicemails from Grant, knowing they'd be hostile or traumatic or very sad. In fact, I just deleted them without reading them, the first time I've actually done this, and I felt much better for it. Maybe that's the way to go.

Grant is still convinced we can be together and has gone on and on about how he's the only guy I can trust, and that I'll regret leaving him. He can't see how any man will ever treat me as well as he has, and that anyone I surround myself with will just lie to me and betray me, predominantly Libby. I'm tired of this continuous dissing of my friend. I know that Libby isn't Grant's biggest fan either, but she never goes on about it. In fact, it's the opposite, as she now refuses to talk about him at all.

With my front boiling hot, I roll over onto my stomach, to even out my tan which has come on quite nicely during the time I've been here. I'm covered in sun tan lotion and lay there smiling. I can't remember the last time I made love so many times in 24 hours and it's left me with a pleasant ache, which is is far more noticeable when laying on my front. Whilst there's a definite sexual attraction to Seth, I also have some very real feelings for him and I think this stands a good chance of turning into something. Should I be jumping straight in with someone so soon after Grant? I really don't know, although it would be sensible to take it slowly but I just can't help this depth of feelings I have for the guy. It's as though we were meant to be together.

I turn my head on the side and look at Libby, who is laying on her back, sunglasses on, but I can see her eyes are slightly open. 'What are you thinking about?' I ask, 'Jude?'

She turns to look at me, and I notice that she is a bit tearful. I put it down to tiredness before, but I can see now it's more than that. 'Yes,' she answers simply, faintly smiles and turns her face back up to the sun.

'Is everything ok with you guys?' I ask.

'Of course,' she says, we're always ok. He's just got a lot on his mind, that's all.'

'Like what?' I ask. I decide to prop myself up on my elbows, grabbing my bikini top to me seeing as we're laying right in front of the captain's window. Is he called a captain on a boat like this? He doesn't exactly look like one, in his vest top and shorts, and with a cigarette hanging from his mouth, but he's steered the boat pretty well when it's been moving and he sits looking at the female sunbathers when we're moored up. I use my other hand to dab my face with the towel I'm partly laying on. Sweat is literally running down it and I don't even want to imagine how I look.

'Just work,' she replies, 'there's something going on, not sure what, and I don't ask him. He'll tell me if he wants to.'

'Is it something to do with Seth?' I ask.

'I think it could be, although he hasn't said anything specific. I'm pretty sure it's also about me and the jeep business. He keeps going on about how I should have put the business through him as, if we had, we might have actually earned some money. He says he's 'lost face' in his circle of associates because I've failed.' She sees my face and adds, 'yes, he's a bit of a jerk. But, he's my jerk.'

'What's it got to do with him?'

'Everyone knows everyone over here. Even though it's not his business, the fact that I'm involved is as good as. And, he says that all his business contacts are laughing at him, and that I need to take this more seriously and do a proper job of it. I don't really think he agrees with women working, to be honest, he's a bit 'old fashioned.' You wouldn't think it, would you, to look at him?'

'Old fashioned?' I laugh. 'Umm, no.' More like a male

chauvinist pig who I'd quite like to slap, I think to myself.

'Apparently, Seth feels the same way,' Libby adds.

'Has Seth said that?' I ask. This surprises me, he doesn't seem the male chauvinist sort, and he definitely hasn't said anything to me to give that impression.

'Not to me, but apparently to Jude. Has he said anything to you?' Libby asks.

I shake my head. 'No, nothing like that. Not exactly.' Libby sits up and looks at me. 'Well, I think he feels it might have been better with a Turkish business partner, or someone that knows the ropes over here, but he hasn't said anything about you not doing a good job.'

'Wish they'd keep their noses out,' Libby says. 'It's nothing to do with either of them. Arses.'

'Knobs,' I reply and we laugh then lay back down flat. 'I'm pleased you and Seth get on now,' Libby says, 'at least it's shut you up going on and on about those bloody jeep keys. Did you not find any other stolen goods in Seth's pockets when you gave him a strip search?'

'Nope, I didn't find anything untoward,' I say, grinning.

'Thank goodness for that,' Libby smiles.

I'm worried about Libby and Jude. I didn't think there was a hint of a problem between them when I first arrived here but, lately, I've noticed a few cracks. Well, more than cracks, some big old chasms. No surprise, when they work as hard as they do, and they're like ships in the night, barely spending time together. Is it because things are becoming more serious between them, and that it was just a bit of fun before?

'Maybe you and Jude need some time alone, an evening where you're both not working and can sit and relax and talk about things.'

'Nah, we did that last night but Jude was still away with

the fairies thinking about more important stuff.'

It takes me a second to realise what she's just said, and I prop myself back up. 'You were working last night, weren't you? That's why you were out?'

'No,' she replies, sitting up again, and reaching for the sun tan lotion. 'Can you put some on my shoulders?' she asks. I nod and sit up, swinging my legs around to face her back. 'I was due to work but Jude rang and said let's go out. So we did. Had a good meal, a drink, a walk along the promenade. Other than the constant waves and hellos shouted to him by passing females he's entertained in his bar, I generally had him all to myself. But he barely spoke the whole time.'

'But I thought Seth and Jude were working last night together,' I say, rubbing the lotion in, much to the enjoyment of the guy observing us from the window. I give him one of my looks but he just waves at me and carries on watching.

'No,' she replies. 'They were supposed to but Seth left a message for Jude the morning you went off to Kuşadasi to say he had something to sort out last night and wouldn't be back until gone midnight. We presumed he was hoping things would go well between the two of you and you'd be spending another night together. That's the reason I came home so late, to be honest, I didn't want to disturb the two of you in case you were, well...'

I shake my head. 'He definitely wasn't with me. He dropped me off at about seven and said he was off to work with Jude.'

Neither of us speak for the moment and Libby turns round to face me and says, 'Oh no, I recognise that look. What do you suspect he's up to now?'

I'm too upset to even think about it. Just when I start to believe him, and trust him, he lies to me again. I've just spent over 24 hours with him, slept with him, been intimate with the guy, several times actually, and still he lies. The question now in my mind is, if he wasn't with Jude, who the hell was he with? And why did he lie to me about it?

CHAPTER TWENTY-FIVE

Being woken early this morning by the alarm clock was not appreciated seeing as I hardly slept. On top of being an incredibly hot night, even more than normal, I tossed and turned getting myself all worked up about Seth after the latest revelation that was divulged on the gulet trip a few days back. I've avoided him since, despite him coming round and ringing me. I just don't want to see him, I really don't. How can I, when he lies all the time. I know what would happen, he'd look at me with those blue eyes, toss his gorgeous blonde locks around and, before I can even quiz him, I'd be in bed with him with my legs wrapped round his waist only to be sulking a couple of days later. I don't trust myself, let alone him. No, there's no way I'm setting myself up for yet another fall. In fact, I don't even want to have it out with him and find out what he's hiding and what's going on. I'm going to avoid him and try not to speak with him again during my last week and a bit here.

'Is he actually hiding anything though?' asks Libby as we sit on the small boat at a ridiculous early hour waiting for our trip to Turunç, a small resort next to Içmeler. 'He did offer to tell you everything, the other night, but you said no.

So, you can't really blame him.'

I haven't even got the energy to roll my eyes at Libby or to answer. Yes, he did offer to tell me, but I didn't want the magic to end the other night, and I didn't think it would be anything that could jeopardise our relationship. Not that we have one. All we are is obviously two people who know each other a bit and had a 24-hour sexathon. That's it.

'He was with someone the other night, and it wasn't Jude, despite him saying that's where he'd be. So, whoever it was, he lied to me about it. And that's all that matters,' I answer. I feel a little nauseous as the boat rocks gently. I couldn't face breakfast again, due to the time and the heat and my mood, and I now feel sick. The boat is due to leave in a couple of minutes and is quickly filling up. Every time someone else gets on, it rocks a bit more. As soon as we get to Turunç I'm going to force some food down, if I can.

'I feel ill,' I say to Libby. 'Not enough sleep and it's too hot.'

'Nothing to do with the bottle and a half of red wine you threw down your neck last night then?' Libby asks.

Did I really drink that much? Wow, no wonder I feel ill. I shrug my shoulders and she laughs. 'Lou, you came here to try and relax and have a good time and all you seem to have done is meet guys who have stressed you out, and argued by text and voicemails with your soon to be ex. Come on, chill out a bit. Your holiday will be over soon and you'll soon be wishing you'd made more of it.'

'It hasn't all been bad,' I say. 'For example, being mistaken as an escort was a delight.'

We both laugh at that. Actually, it hasn't all been bad at all and, if I'm honest, all problems I've encountered I've brought upon myself.

I'm desperately sad every time I think about leaving. I

can't believe how quickly the first part of the trip here went and, in 10 days I'll be back in the UK. I feel stupid as tears begin to brew.

As if reading my mind, Libby says, 'Don't go.'

I look at her and hold her hand. 'I don't want to.'

'I miss you and want you here with me,' she replies, and this forces a tear to roll down my cheek. I brush it away quickly, but it's too late and she's seen it. 'What's there to go back for?' Libby asks. 'You hate your job, and you're going to have to find another home anyway. Why not here with me? Come on Lou, it's always been me and you, ever since school days.'

'I can't just leave my job,' I reply. 'I'm an important cog.'

'So you keep telling me,' she replies, and I see the hint of a smile on her lips. No one seems to take this 'cog' thing very seriously.

'Well, I'd have to give in my notice.' I think of Mr Simpson, sat at his desk, shouting out some inane order to anyone that will listen in the office. Would he notice if I went, other than getting thirsty due to a reduction in the amount of coffee being offered to him? 'And there's my mum,' I say. 'She needs me there.'

'She's got your Dad,' replies Lou, 'and her craft room. And, they can visit. They've been to Turkey before.'

'Yes, about 80 years ago,' I reply, which we both know is an exaggeration.

'Its not as though you see them every day,' Libby continues, 'they'll hardly notice you're missing.' I have to admit this is true. I phone, and visit maybe once a month, and Christmas and birthdays, but that's all. Which is pretty bad seeing as they live only a few miles away. My stomach flips again at the thought of moving in with them. I love my parents dearly, but...

The thought of staying here is so tempting, despite the Seth situation, and I've been thinking about it a lot over the last week or so. My main worry is what if I get lonely? Who would I have here? Sure, it's great with Libby now. But what about Jude? What about when things get more serious and they want to live together, and I'll have to find my own place? Who would I have then? Three's a crowd. I then picture Libby and Jude being with Seth and his mystery woman, in a foursome, just like we were in Rhodes the other day. I would just be in the way, their single friend who just doesn't *fit*, that they'd feel compelled to invite to a BBQ every now and then, and try to fix up with single Brits that are holidaying alone. No, I can't do it, I just can't.

I look at Libby's expression so desperate for me to say yes, that I'll stay, and I smile. 'I'll think about it,' I say. She has enough on her mind already without a discussion over my impending departure.

The reason for our trip into Turunç so early is that Libby has a meeting with a hotel owner there to discuss a business opportunity, and she's taking me for moral support. Not that I've any idea what to say or do, other than to try to look professional and reasonably sensible, neither of which I have any history of doing well. The difference with this meeting is that Libby has set it up all by herself with no others involved. This guy in Turunç has contacted her directly, after hearing about her from a tourist staying at his hotel, so there's no chance of this meeting being sabotaged in some way, or of us being mistaken for hookers. And, Seth has had no involvement, which is a plus point. I do try to point this out to Libby but she dismisses it. She still doesn't think he's had anything to do with any of the other disasters. She just can't see any bad in the guy.

I'd seen Turunç on the boat taxi placards, and the gulet

cruise passed the place the other day so, once this hangover passes, it will be a great day out as, once the meeting's finished, we can spend some time looking around. It's only about 20km from Marmaris and accessible from either road or boat taxi and, like the town where I'm staying, was once a small fishing village. Although the tourist trade has slowly started to develop the village into something bigger, it's small enough to avoid the large amount of visitors who visit Marmaris and Içmeler and so has a more relaxed atmosphere. It sounds like more my kind of thing. To be honest, Marmaris has exhausted me a bit with its hustle and bustle. I'm ready to slow down the pace a little.

Finally, the boat sets sail, off we go and thankfully the rocking stops immediately. Following the line of the Marmaris coastal path, I can recognise, in the distance, hotels and bars that I've visited or walked past. I take a few photos knowing that I'll be looking at them in just over a week, probably sat at my mother's, surrounded by decoupage and her card making stash. I'm worried that I won't be able to picture the sights in my mind and the photos will be all I have to show of my trip, and I can't bear the thought of forgetting the places I've seen. The coastline makes Marmaris look so different, and I notice again how quiet it is at this time of day. Many of the tourists don't tend to wake up and walk around until near midday and I can just make out the odd figure moving about, probably waiters who get up early to make the restaurants and surrounding pathways look fantastic. I admire how hard they work.

I can't quite place where the apartment is in comparison to the coastline and eventually give up and ask Libby, who points to a gap between two large hotels, and I can just make out the street which would lead up to our road. I compare this to when I'm in Abingdon, coming home on the bus, which I rarely ever do, and I can see the paths I followed so many years before when Libby and I used to walk home from school. She would always be walking slightly ahead of me, urging me to keep up whilst I trailed behind. Her legs were so much longer than mine, and I could never keep up.

It's nice to sit in silence, the only noise being the whirring of the boat motor, my mind calmed by the sunshine, turquoise sea and beautiful landscape. I have an urge to dangle my hand over the side into the sparkling water with glimmers of sunshine bouncing off, but I can't quite reach. I've purposefully put my phone on silent, having relented over the last few days by reading Grant's texts again and then replying. Why, I've no idea, but at least I've disabled my voicemail so I can't listen to any stressful messages and get wound up. It just leaves the texts for me to read. His last one said 'We'll speak very soon.' Yes, I know, you don't have to rub it in Grant. I'll be home very soon and I'm sure you will speak *at* me, in a very loud tone and angry manner, and you'll probably throw things around the apartment. Even my cushions which, may I remind you, are not called pillows!

Last night, after drinking the bottle and a half of wine that I'd forgotten about, I actually tried to ring Grant. I'm not quite sure why, it was almost as though I wanted to hear his voice to see if it changed how I feel. Luckily, he didn't answer. I'd have been regretting it this morning, even more than I'm regretting drinking the large amount of wine. It's just that, every time Seth has let me down, it's made me question whether Grant really has been that bad after all and if there is a chance we could work things out. As far as I know, he hasn't ever lied to me, or been unfaithful, and truth is the most important thing in a relationship, well to me it is. I sigh as I silently admonish myself for even considering being with Grant again. This, I remind Libby, is what Seth has driven me to.

We soon arrive at the boat's initial stop in Içmeler, to drop off the first passengers, which turn out to be most of those on board. Some are waiters and staff and a couple of them kiss the guy steering the boat on the cheek before jumping off. Only two more people get on to continue to Turunç; an elderly couple who speak to each other in German, but say good morning to Libby and I in English. It always amazes me how so obviously English we are that people instantly know where we're from just by looking at us. I may as well be wearing a Union Jack dress, like a *Spice Girl*. I could have so been a *Spice Girl*. I'd add that to my job list but I think I've missed the opportunity…

We're soon on our way again and shortly see our destination, tucked into the edge of horseshoe shaped bay of beautiful, clear blue water. As the boat pulls in I admire the sheltered beaches of sand and shingle. They're virtually empty at the moment although I presume they'll fill up quickly by late morning if it's anything like Marmaris.

As we go to get off the boat I stretch and yawn, nearly falling over as I'm caught off guard by the rocking of the boat. Libby laughs at me. 'Is it a long walk from here?' I ask, ignoring her blatant mocking.

'Massive,' she replies, 'but you'll love it.'

I groan and follow her, shuffling along in an act of protest, which she ignores, and stepping off the boat aided by a young guy who I thank. He could probably spot the signs that I was a likely candidate to fall in and it would delay the boat turn-around. The last time we went on one of her *walks*, it was several kilometres to Içmeler. I really don't think I can do something like that again. It's the equivalent of me running the London Marathon, which is something that will never happen. I sling my bag over my shoulder, push my sunglasses on more firmly and start on our pilgrimage, only to stop ten seconds later as Libby sits down at a table outside a bar just barely 20 yards from the shoreline. 'Here,' she says, 'we made it!'

I slap the brim of her hat with my hand. She's bought a big floppy one like mine since I've been here and it really suits her. I've left mine at home today, no idea why, as it's supposedly going to be the hottest day so far this season, and, my head is already pounding. My relief that the bar is close by is obvious as I slump into my seat as if I haven't sat down for hours.

'I thought we were going to a hotel?' I ask.

'This *is* part of the hotel,' Libby replies, 'it's beautiful, isn't it?' I nod. I watch as the boat we just came in on is already turning round with passengers to head back to Içmeler and Marmaris.

'What if there's no spaces on a boat later for us to go back?' I ask. 'Will we be stranded here?' I picture me being like Tom Hanks in *Castaway*.'

'We can get the dolmuş back. It's a little quicker but the journey can be scary on the mountains.'

Oh, I quite fancied the notion of being stranded. I forgot we could travel by road from here, and I don't fancy a scary journey that could involve me having a goat bleating at me on my lap.

'How often do the boats come and go?'

'Every half hour or so,' Libby replies.

'It looks nice here,' I say, looking around. I don't know why, but I already feel at home in this place.

'It is,' she replies. 'Quite a few of my customers have stayed here and they love it. I wouldn't mind working in this resort instead of Marmaris, but I'm not sure if I'd find it too quiet. I've kind of got used to the madness of Marmaris.' I have to agree, I really can't see Libby working here.

'Ladies.' Libby stands and turns to greet a middle aged guy dressed in a suit and holding a briefcase. It amazes me how anyone can wear so many clothes in this heat, and not have a bead of perspiration on their forehead. I stand too and put out my hand, which he shakes. He doesn't kiss me on the cheeks, like he did Libby, and I'm grateful as it's highly likely he'll smell the red wine oozing out of my sweaty pores. I'm quickly introduced to Ali, the hotel owner. He's very smiley and seems totally approachable, and his English is perfect, just like almost every single Turkish person that I've met on this trip. I feel embarrassed at my lack of any bilingual skills, other than a tiny bit of French which I've practised just a couple of times when on a shopping trip to Calais. This holiday has made me determined to learn a new language as soon as I can, but which it will be I have no idea. Maybe I'll have a go at Turkish, who knows. Within a minute of Ali sitting down, a bottle of water has appeared with three glasses and the conversation shortly turns to business.

I sit back slightly in my seat, not too comfy as I'm worried I might fall asleep, and let Libby lead, joining in every now and again to enthusiastically confirm something she says. I watch her, smiling at her confidence and passion that she exudes regarding her jeep safari business, and I think how she used to be back home in Abingdon. She's changed so much and I start to daydream about whether I can turn my life around like she has. The more I sit and think, the more disappointed I start to feel about my life and how I haven't done any of the things I once wanted to do. Why have I given up on all my hopes and dreams? In fact, what were they? Did I ever have any? If I did, they are way gone, along with my old favourite comfy clothes, car, cat... my life before

Grant. When I get back to the apartment, I'm going to start making a list of all the things I want to do in life. Like my USA road trip. Wow, I just haven't thought about it for so long, about all the places I want to see on the way, the Vegas chapels, the diners, the love of my life I'll be sat next to on the open roads. That quickly puts a stop to my day dreaming, by the time I find my perfect guy, I'll be driving around the US in a fully computerised hover car wearing some science fiction type outfit, and aged about 80.

Libby and Ali are going through a document and talking over various paragraphs of what seems to me very boring terms and conditions. It doesn't make much sense, what they're saying, although I've never been too good with professional type talk. It's probably why I haven't progressed much in a career, it all just seems so serious and people talk in riddles. I go to top up Libby's water but a young waiter appears literally from nowhere and grabs the bottle from me, topping up instead. I smile and he smiles back and disappears, so I sit back again, and look out at the shore. I realise that half an hour has gone by so quickly, as a boat taxi heads in. It's more full than ours was, a mix of tourists and locals, young and old, and I realise it's a different boat with a different driver. Some of the passengers stand ready to disembark even before it's come to a halt, and I realise that most of these are obviously used to disembarkment etiquette as it rocks gently from side to side. I watch the guy waiting on the shoreline grab at the rope that's thrown to him and then hold out his arm to steady each person getting off the boat. At first, I don't see the man at the back, patiently waiting for the others to get off first before moving forward. But then I feel a jolt as I recognise the hat, shades, linen shirt. It's Seth.

He shakes the boat driver's hand, obviously acquainted

with him, and jumps from the boat. He walks slowly, pausing for a moment to look at his watch and then reaches for his phone. He grins as he looks at it, obviously reading a text or an email, then walks forward again and, for a moment, I think he's heading literally straight for us, and I slip down slightly in my seat, somehow feeling this will make me invisible. If only I had my floppy hat to pull over my face. But he turns suddenly to the right, and walks quickly in the opposite direction of the beach and past a huge palm tree set in the centre of the road next to us.

I crane my neck to watch him go and then stand up to get a better look. Libby and Ali stop their conversation to look at me.

'You ok?' asks Libby, frowning.

I nod. 'Cramp,' I say, and straighten and bend my leg dramatically a couple of times, making ridiculous oohs and ahs as I do so. She frowns. 'Do you mind if I go for a little walk to, well, get rid of it?' I ask.

She puts her head on one side and looks me up and down, suspecting something but not knowing quite what I'm up to. There's little she can say other than 'No problem', and they both smile then get straight back to the paperwork Libby is holding.

I hurriedly walk around the table and the corner of the bar, then the palm tree, and can just see Seth in the distance. And, despite my tiny piece of 'sensible' brain yelling at me to not do this, I start to follow him. I'm not sure what it is I think I'm going to gain from it, but I just have this feeling that I need to, to see what he's up to as it's the only way I'm going to ever find out the truth.

CHAPTER TWENTY-SIX

Seth's walking reasonably fast and so I have to quicken my pace a bit, whilst conscious of the fact that I look like I'm very obviously trying to follow someone. I try to focus and imagine myself as a spy in one of those TV thriller type shows, all gorgeous, strong and, well, spy-like, rather than hot, sweaty, tired and clumsy. It doesn't work and I find myself bumping into a middle aged lady in a bright, white vest and very bright green shorts, and we do one of those ridiculous dance movements where we both go to move in the same direction and, after a couple of failed attempts, I put my arms on her shoulders to keep her still whilst I move around her. She just stares at me and utters something in a language that I don't recognise, and I smile politely and leg it. She can join the queue of people who think I'm mad. It's growing every day.

I go past two or three shops that all have inflatable lilos and swimming aids hanging from metal bars stretching across the top of the entrances and smile as I see two children pointing excitedly at them and asking their mother to buy one. She's busy on her phone, probably texting someone, and the shop owner sees his chance, untying the inflatable and passing it to one of the children. I wish in a way I could stay and watch her reaction when she sees what he's done, but I've got to go after Seth and so I hurry on. I have no idea what I'll say to him when I catch him up, or what I'll do. If it wasn't for the adrenalin shooting round my body, I wouldn't be hurrying around in this sun at all, as my head is now throbbing and I feel a bit sick. I wonder what the shop keepers would think if I suddenly turned and threw up in the gutter.

I stay close to the shop fronts in case I suddenly have to dive out of his view if he turns round. Luckily, Seth is staring straight ahead as he walks, checking his phone every now and then. He has such a self-assured gait which, even though I'm angry with him, I still find incredibly sexy.

The paths are now growing more crowded, full of tourists, and I can move slightly away from the shop fronts, hopefully blending in enough with the other pedestrians if Seth was to suddenly turn around. In the distance at the end of the road I can see the mountains, such a mixture of colours, green, brown and sand, and I admire the wonderful backdrop. What a beautiful place this is to be on a spy mission.

Eventually, we come to a junction that branches off to a car park on the left and a collection of bars to the right. Seth stops for a second, looking each way and then suddenly looks round. I dive behind a car that has one of those covers on the windscreen to keep it cool and I wait a couple of seconds thinking that, if I pop my head up to take a look, my eyes will meet his gorgeous blue ones and my cover will be blown, which will mean I won't find out what he's up to. But, when I finally pick up the courage to peek around the car, he's walking again and has chosen the right turn towards the bars. A man with his dog has stopped beside me, eyeing me suspiciously as I'm crouched on the ground, so I pretend to tie my laces which is ridiculous seeing as I'm wearing flip-flops, and he shakes his head at me and walks on. I jump up and follow Seth again, keeping my head down as much as possible, and I see a Chinese restaurant in front of us which Seth appears to be walking towards. It stretches over an expanse of water which I can't work out if it's a river or a brook, or just an inlet from the sea, and the restaurant has tables surrounding it with large white parasols above each. It's set in front of a brown and white building, with matching white drapes at the windows, which could either be someone's home or business premises. It's hard to tell. Bobbing about on the water is a small red and white boat, with a large parasol over the top, and I can see an elderly man laying in it, snoring away. What a life, I think to myself. I wish I could swap places with him right now. Would he mind if I got in and had a nap alongside him?

Seth hovers around the tables at the restaurant and I step in to stand just inside a shop from where I can peek at him. Is he going in to eat Chinese, at this time of day? It's not long past breakfast although, when I check my watch, I see that it's actually half past midday already. How long have I been chasing him?

I watch as he turns slowly round in a circle, clearly looking for someone, then pulls his phone back out of his pocket. Just as he goes to dial, he stops and looks up. He's heard something, and I heard it too, the sound of a child's voice calling out, and we both watch a small boy, just 4 years or so, run towards him. The small lad, in a red t-shirt and cute denim shorts, jumps up into Seth's arms, smiling and laughing, and they hug each other tightly. Seth laughs as the lad yells the same words over and over again to him. I don't recognise what he's saying but I'm pretty sure it's Turkish as Seth seems to understand him and continues to hug the lad affectionately, kissing the top of his head. They're obviously close and I get the impression they may not have seen each other for a while. I wonder who he is. Seth hasn't mentioned any children at all and, just as I start to question why a child so young would be out on their own, a woman appears. She's come from the same direction as the boy and walks slowly towards Seth who has his back facing her, and she calls his name. Seth turns round, lowers the boy to the ground, and then walks slowly towards her, arms outstretched. She reaches up to him, put his face in her hands, then kisses him on the cheeks, then they hug and the child watches them, smiling, before then dancing around them in a circle. Seth pulls away from the woman and they both watch the child and laugh. Then, they both each grab one of the lad's hands and walk towards the seats of the restaurant.

The woman is absolutely stunning, with beautiful tanned dark skin, long wavy dark hair and wearing an ankle-length floaty dress. She has beautiful necklaces and bracelets on and I recognise her face immediately from the photo that came up on Seth's phone that night in the restaurant when she'd sent the text. So, this is his mystery woman, the relationship he describes as complicated, and as I look at the boy I can now see why. The hair. Although a different colour, the curls of the boy's dark hair matches Seth's blonde and I feel sick as I realise the eyes are the same shape too. So large and round. He's a mini version of Seth.

I watch as Seth reaches inside his pocket and pulls out what looks like an envelope, and passes it to her. She pushes it away at first, but he insists and she takes it from him, then opens it and takes out what's clearly a wad of money. Wow, there's a lot there and she looks incredulous and surprised. She shakes her head and tries to get him to take it back from her but he puts his hands around hers and pushes her hands back towards her, and she smiles and throws her arms around him, then kisses him and ruffles his hair.

They're giggling and laughing and I haven't actually realised that I've walked away from the protection of the wall and am actually heading towards them, right to where they're sitting. My emotions have taken over, I feel outraged, confused and humiliated, all at the same time. Is this really the man that I was with two days ago, and slept with? That I kissed and talked to and told him so much about myself, and considered possibly staying here and having a relationship with? I should have gone with my gut feeling about him, right from the start. I was so right to not trust him, he's full of lies and betrayal.

I'm almost at their table when Seth looks up and straight at me, along with the woman and child. They're all staring at me, this strange woman walking right towards them, shaking with anger and crying. I stop dead and Seth's eyes and mine literally lock and I see Seth's expression, that clenched jaw and frown, a look of disapproval, that he can't believe I've the nerve to walk up and ruin his moment like this, when he's with her and this child, cocooned in his family bubble and... and... I just can't think, my head is pounding and I want to shout at him. I want to ask 'why?' and let him know how I feel, let her know that he's lied about her, let his son know that his Dad hasn't even told me about him. But, what would Seth care? I'm nothing to him. This is his life. I'm just a woman who's come to visit a friend for a few weeks and obviously looked needy and vulnerable. And, he took advantage of it.

Just as he goes to stand, I turn and run, past the waiter who has walked towards the table with a menu, past the man still sleeping in his boat, and back along the street I came down before diverting off to the side. I pass underneath a canopy between two shops and head towards the beach which I can just see at the end. I might be further up the town than I need to be but I know the beach will take me back to Libby and the boats. I only look behind me once, but he isn't following me, and why would he? Why would he leave her to chase after me, someone that's just ruined his family get together. I would doubt he'll ever speak to me again, and that's fine, because I don't think I can ever bear to even look at him, let alone speak, ever.

I run across a small wooden arched bridge that crosses where the sea comes into the town, quickly passing a young couple who are trying to walk holding hands and seem disgruntled that they have to stop to let me go past them. I'm crying, tears streaming down my face, and people are staring at me as I scurry past. I'm soon on the promenade that lines the beach, one side an expanse of grass belonging to a hotel, and on the other is a line of small boats bobbing happily in the water. I wonder if this hotel is the one that the bar is joined to where Libby and I sat. A boat trip guy tries to stop me going past and holds out a leaflet and, when I don't take it, he chases me smiling, thinking it's a game with me running, and I end up snatching it from him, which is useful as I use it to flack my face to try to dry the tears that are running down rather than rubbing with my hand and smudging my mascara, although I think it's a bit late for that. I'm close now to the bar and I sit on a small brick wall, just for a minute, to try and calm down, and after fanning my eyes I pull my sunglasses back over to disguise the redness and walk to the corner where I find Libby still sitting where I left her, now on her own.

'Where have you been?' she asks, jumping up and grabbing her bag.

I smile, the best one I can muster. 'Cramp was worse than I thought,' I say then, 'how did it go? Where's Ali?' I try to sound as normal as possible and glance over my shoulder just to check that Seth isn't there, which of course he isn't, and then back to Libby who I now realise is looking very excited indeed.

'It went really well. Brilliant, in fact,' she exclaims, putting her arms round my shoulders and hugging me. 'Ali's gone back to the hotel, we're all sorted. The deal's been done, we're in business!' She grabs hold of my hand and pulls me along with her, heading over towards the boats to stand with a group of other passengers.

'Are we going straight back?' I say. If we are, I'm relieved, I don't want to risk seeing him with her, his girlfriend, or wife, or whatever she is.

'Afraid so,' she replies. 'I know I promised you we'd look around, but I need to get straight to the bank to sort out this paperwork. Sorry, we'll come another day though. Ali wants to go ahead, so, lots of work for us both. I think we've done it!'

Libby is obviously happy, but the word 'we' is not one I want to hear anymore. I can't think of anything worse than staying in Marmaris, that close to Seth, not after what I've just seen. I can't tell her now though, I can't ruin this moment for her.

'There's only one small fly in the ointment,' she says, looking casually at the paperwork.

'What's that?' I ask

'Seth,' she replies.

I spin around, in case he's here and she's seen him, but he's not. 'What's he done this time?' I ask, hearing my own voice wobble a little and so I cough to try and pretend I've a frog in my throat.

'Well, it appears that Ali didn't just hear about me from a customer. It was Seth who rang him, a couple of days ago, and suggested that Ali get in touch with me.'

'So he's behind this deal?' I ask. Libby nods. 'Then don't do it! Every single thing he's been involved in hasn't worked out. He's going to ruin it for you.' I realise I'm shouting and a couple of passengers look around.

'Calm down,' Libby says. 'I'm not that happy about it either. I thought I'd done this all by myself built on reputation. But it could be a lot worse.'

'No, it's wrong,' I say, pulling on her arm. 'You've got to believe me, Libby, he's up to something if he's put you in touch with this guy. He's trying to ruin your business, and it's all going to go wrong. You won't make it work.'

Libby looks annoyed and pushes my hand away from her arm. 'Thanks for having so much faith in me,' she snaps, 'I *can* make this work, with or without Seth or anyone else, so nothing is going to go wrong. If Seth called him because I'm good at what I do, what's it matter? Let this go, Lou, for once can you let something be about someone else other than yourself.'

We stand awkwardly for quite a while not speaking as I don't know what to say, and I long for the boat to come in, but there are none heading towards us. My headache is worse, I feel as though I'm about to throw up, and I just want to get home. I go to sit on the small wall near to where we're waiting, and hold my head in my hands. Just the thought of being on the rocking boat makes me retch. 'How long till the boat?' I eventually call to Libby.

She looks at her watch. 'We'd just missed the last one, so about 20 minutes. Do you want to catch a dolmuş instead?'

I nod and she leads the way just up the road and round the corner where there's one parked up, half full and almost ready to leave. She gestures to the driver so that he knows we're on our way to board and he acknowledges her with a flick of his hand. It will take about 40 minutes at the most, but it's better than standing for ages waiting in the sun, barely talking. Plus, it's quite a walk from the boat stop when we get to the other end but the dolmuş drops us not far from the apartment road and I'll be able to just get straight in, lie down and go to sleep and pretend this day never happened. I know that none of this is Libby's fault and I put my hand on hers in the dolmuş and say sorry, which she acknowledges with a weak smile before looking back to her paperwork. This was supposed to be such a special day for her and I've ruined it.

Why didn't Seth tell me about that woman and his child? Something so significant and huge, why couldn't he have just said and be done with it. I'd have accepted it. Well, maybe. But now, I can't ever forgive him. All of a sudden, Grant seems like an angel compared to Seth, Hamil and every other man I've met here. Maybe Grant's not as bad as I thought. At least he's honest. Did I make a mistake giving him up like that? Have I let something special slip away? I find myself actually longing to be back in the life I had before coming here. However bad it was, it wasn't as bad as this.

I spend the dolmuş ride back listening to Libby who starts to talk slowly at first but then is soon bubbling with enthusiasm about the deal. It looks like Ali wants to book two days a week for the first two weeks to see how it goes and, if all is well, will extend to six days a week. It will mean a guaranteed payment, a good rate too. Plus, Libby will be able to keep all the tips, which are likely to equal the daily rate. She's achieved her dream, and I'm really happy for her.

When we arrive in Marmaris, Libby asks if I want to go to

the bank with her but I decline saying I don't feel a hundred percent and need to lie down. Seeing her concerned face, I reassure her I'm absolutely fine and that I don't want her to come back with me. I've ruined enough of this day for her already. I promise I'll drink lots of water and will be right as rain by the time she gets back. She frowns and strokes my cheek before walking away, turning once to wave and I turn around and make my way back up the road. Each day until now, I've thought of it as going home when I've walked this route, but not anymore. This isn't home, I need to start preparing myself for the fact that I'm going back to the UK and the fairy-tale is over. Seth has seen to that. Although, I blame myself as much as I'm the one stupid enough to fall for everything he said.

What a difference a day makes, I think to myself as I make my way back. Mystery woman I could have accepted. After all, I have my own 'ex' to sort out. But a son? Well, in some ways it's made things easier. This is just a life that I'm not destined to lead. And, the sooner I accept that, the better.

CHAPTER TWENTY-SEVEN

I walk limply into the apartment, having nearly passed out from the walk up the stairs, and kick off my shoes, not caring that one flies across the hall and into the kitchen. I'll put it properly on the mat later. The mood I'm in, it's lucky it didn't go through a window. I pour a huge glass of water and walk through to fall on the bed. It's like an oven in here, and the ceiling fan seems to just waft the warm air around when I switch it on. Lying down, I close my eyes and let myself cry, huge sobs erupting from my over-heated, fragile body. For the first time since I arrived, I pine for home and then it hits me again that I don't even have a home now, so the sobs get louder and stronger. I lay for quite a few minutes like this, knowing that I need to get a grip, but just not being able to. I've reached an emotional point of no return.

The fact that I've only known Seth for a few weeks doesn't ease any of the pain, it just makes it worse as I feel so stupid getting involved so quickly. I should just shake this off, put it down to a quick fling that went wrong and laugh about it. After all, I'm a grown-up, aren't I? But, that didn't stop me stupidly trusting him and allowing Seth into my heart. I've only myself to blame. How stupid was I to have got involved with anyone, so soon after Grant, a guy that still expects me to come home to him, I remind myself. My future, at this moment in time, is just a big, scary, black hole of... nothing. Maybe I could accidentally board the wrong plane and go on a mystery tour around the world, landing in an exotic country very far away where I can start a new life with a new me, and all of this won't matter anymore. Or, I could do my road-trip to the States. It doesn't have to involve a Mr Right, does it? I'll ditch my mobile so no one can get hold of me and, back home, anyone that cares may wonder where I've gone but will soon move on and I'll just be the '*one that vanished and never came back.*' I sob again as I realise that the only people who may notice that I haven't been in touch are my parents. Possibly Libby, but absolutely no one else. Not even Grant once I've left his life for good.

I look at my mobile and see there's no missed calls or texts from him this morning. This makes things even worse. Not even Grant cares anymore! I've spent the last three weeks dreading the phone buzzing or ringing and, now there's nothing, I'm wishing there was. Just like earlier, I'm still not sure I made the right decision about him. I mean, compared to Seth, at least Grant wanted to be with me, he proposed, didn't he? It was me that didn't want *him*. With Seth, it's the other way round. I want him, but he wants someone else and has his little family and has had his cake and eaten it too. He's just one big, key stealing, cake eating liar! What a mess I've got myself into.

Somewhere in my self-obsessed misery, I suddenly think of Libby. My poor, dear friend that I've given virtually no support to, and have only whined and moaned in her ear for the three weeks I've been here whilst slagging off Seth who is, after all, her friend. I've been utterly selfish. I know that, if someone were slating me to her, she would stick up for me and tell the other person where to go. I really shouldn't have behaved the way I have, and I can't believe she actually wants me to stay here. If I disappeared off on a mystery tour, would she miss me, or would she be grateful my miserable face had gone? She's got her business off the ground and she has Jude. No, she's better off without me here, dragging her down. And, once I'm settled somewhere, I'll get in touch and let her know I'm ok. And maybe she'll visit one day and we'll be best friends again. Maybe.

I jump as I hear a knock at the door. Who is this, disturbing my 'oh woe is me' mammoth pity session I'm having? There's no way I'm going to answer it, no matter who it is, not looking like this with my tired, puffy, red eyes and with tears oozing everywhere. They'll go in a minute. It's probably the very sweet lady downstairs, bringing us borek. She'll set me off, as she always looks at me as though I need support and medical care, patting my arm and sighing whenever she meets me on the stairs. Hey, maybe I could move into her flat secretly for the next week and then refuse to leave. I'd still get to see Libby, through the window on the balcony. Actually, I *could* do that. It would solve the problem of where I'm going to live, will free Libby from this depressing burden and Seth could never find me either, or Grant, or anyone. Sorted.

They knock at the door again, this time much louder and I know it's not the lady as I don't think she has the strength to knock that hard. She's barely bigger than a budgie. I suddenly get a sense of dread as I realise it might be Seth. Maybe he's come to try and explain everything, and beg forgiveness, plead me with me to love him and marry him and run away with him somewhere. Bah, who am I kidding? He has his woman and son, and they're welcome to the liar.

I nod my head defiantly at my reflection in the mirror and fold my arms.

There's more door banging again and I realise that whoever it is isn't going away and I'll need to answer it or else it will upset the neighbours. I tut dramatically, for whose benefit I have no idea as I'm the only one here and my reflection doesn't seem to care, and I stand up and make my way to the door. Whoever it is, I hope they're ready for the hideousness they're about to be confronted with. This is really not a good look. I open the door and freeze.

'Hi, sweetheart'

I just stare and say nothing, although I actually feel like I'm going to throw up and for a moment I consider running to the bathroom and locking myself in, but my feet don't move. Standing in front of me is Grant, grinning, eyes bright and excited, moving awkwardly from one foot to the other. Realising that I haven't moved or made a sound, he's puts down a backpack and holds his arms out to me, but I still can't do anything at all. I'm frozen to the spot. I suddenly think to myself that maybe I did fall asleep on the bed after all and am dreaming, so I slap myself round the face, quite hard, to wake myself from this nightmare. But, when I open my eyes, he's still there, arms still outstretched but the smile slowly drooping. He's looking a bit scared.

'Lou?' he says, concerned. I still stare at him, and he waves his hand in front of my face, fearing I've gone into some sort of shock or have lost the plot. Both are actually true.

Grant frowns. 'You're still angry with me,' he finally says and sighs, closes his eyes as though in pain and puts his arms back out towards me. I still don't move, and he awkwardly puts his arms down again. He walks closer towards me, hesitates, then steps forward and kisses me on the cheek.

Although I feel his breath, his touch, I don't move. I don't actually know what to do.   Yes, I admit that only minutes ago I was having second thoughts about whether I'd done the right thing to say no to his proposal, and to run away. But now he's in front of me, I don't actually feel anything at all. Every part of me is shocked to the core.

I finally find my voice. 'Grant, what are you doing here?'

He looks a bit embarrassed, shrugs then picks up his backpack and gently moves around me into the apartment. I continue to stand there and look at where he was standing a few moments ago, taking a few seconds to realise he's actually now moved inside. I close the door and spin round, suddenly finding my limbs work after all, and follow him. He's now standing, still glancing around the apartment with a look of obvious distaste but, when he sees I'm watching him, he changes his expression to one of fake approval. It's so obviously false that I laugh.

'Look, I had to see you, so, here I am. I couldn't wait any longer for you to come home.' He makes sad eyes and his face reminds me of one of those puppy pictures that people circulate within social media apps, asking for a *like* if you think they're cute. 'I've missed you.'

He comes towards me and wraps his arms around my resistant body. For a few seconds, it almost feels ok, comfortable and familiar, and I come close to relaxing into him.   Even though it must have been hours since he's showered and dressed, I can smell his familiar aftershave, and shampoo, and fabric conditioner. Our fabric conditioner, from our apartment, our home.   I pull away quickly, not wanting it to feel like this and Grant looks disappointed, his eyes quickly dropping to the floor. I realise he's wearing trainers and I hurriedly tell him to take them off and put them by the door, which he starts to challenge but then realises it means I'm at least not throwing him out straight away.

When he is finished, he comes back over to me and looks me up and down. 'You look amazing,' he says. Now, this I know is not true, seeing as I've been crying buckets and am still suffering from a hangover. I shake my head and he smiles. 'You do,' he says, 'you're so tanned and slim and...gorgeous.' I can't blame the guy for trying, and *trying* he most definitely is. Grant walks away, slowly drifting towards the kitchen, and he takes a look inside, even opening a couple of cupboard doors, before moving to look around the other rooms. I don't accompany him but wait for his return which comes pretty quickly due to the size of the apartment.

'Is this it?' he asks.

I sigh. 'What do you mean,' I ask 'is this it?'' I walk to the kitchen and fill the kettle, not really knowing why. Don't they always say that tea makes everything right? If so, we're going to need a big urn-full here. I decide to make him an apple tea, as I know he'll hate it.

'It's just not very big,' answers Grant. 'And it's so hot. Has the air- con broken?'

I snort and give him a look, even though it was exactly what I thought when I first arrived here. I prepare the apple tea, which he wrinkles up his nose at, and pass him the glass.

'Thanks,' he says with a grimace.

I lean against the worktop, hands cupping my drink, and stare at him.

'I thought she'd live somewhere a bit more... well... I'm not really sure.' he says.

I continue to stare, forcing him to squirm a bit.

He then adds, 'I just had an image of what her place would look like and this wasn't it.'

'How would you have the first idea of what type of apartment Libby would have? You don't know her.'

'I know enough about her,' he mutters under his breath, but loud enough for me to hear it and I bang my glass down making him jump. I refuse to get into an argument with him about Libby, it's a waste of time and energy, but at least I can show him I'm not amused.

'I think your mother's right,' he says after a while.

'What's my mother got to do with anything?' I raise my eyebrows at him. 'What's she been saying?'

He looks like he's already regretted saying anything.

'Grant?' I ask loudly and he jumps, spilling a little of the hot beverage down his t-shirt.

'Well,' he says, brushing at the liquid, 'she thinks this is all a bit of a... well... sort of midlife crisis. You know, you coming over here and being so confused.'

'Midlife crisis?' I say. 'Grant, I'm only in my thirties. And there's no confusion, believe me. I've never been more sure of anything.' Actually, I'm totally unsure about everything, but there's no way I'll admit my mother's right.

'Look, she thinks you've panicked about getting older, and got yourself all upset that you haven't settled and had babies and all of that sort of stuff. And that you don't really have a career or your own home and...'

'Is there anything else you and my mother want to point out that I've failed at?' I interrupt. Wow, my family can frustrate me. Why has she never raised this with me, choosing to speak to Grant about it instead? She's been as sweet as anything when I've chatted to her on the phone since being here, but now I find out they've been plotting together, relishing in all my inadequacies.

I take a deep breath and calm myself as much as I can. 'Grant, I'm not having any type of crisis, I just don't want the life I've been living for the last eighteen months. I want something different.'

'Different?' he asks. 'In what way?'

'I don't really know, I just know I want something different to what I have.'

He nods and smiles. 'Exactly,' he says. Then, all of a sudden, he dramatically falls onto one knee and for one moment I think he's fainting or keeling over. No such luck.

'Lou,' he begins.

'Stop right there,' I say, putting the palm of my hand up at him, realising what he's doing.

He ignores me. 'Lou, I don't have a ring with me, but...'

'You asked me a few weeks ago and I said no. I haven't changed my mind,' I interrupt.

He completely ignores me. 'Will you marry me?'

And, for that one moment, everything stops. The pounding in my head, the nausea, the sound of the clock in Libby's kitchen. I stand and look at him, hardly breathing, studying his face, which is a pathetic expression of hope, and memories of our first weeks together appear in my head, those good times, with the laughs and newness of our relationship, and how he supported me when Libby left and he treated me like a princess. And I compare it to the hurt Seth has caused me in just these few weeks, and I think of how I don't have a home to call my own, and how my life is so totally messed up right now. I could become Mrs Harrison and have a privileged life of holidays and trips and clothes. I could be swanning up the aisle in a matter of weeks and Seth would just be a distant memory, one of life's lessons, a lucky escape. And I very nearly say yes. Just for that one moment.

CHAPTER TWENTY-EIGHT

But that one moment doesn't last long. I'm not sure what exactly pulls me back to reality, but something does. Something from deep within me that starts as a mild rumble but builds up and up until I suddenly hear a voice shout 'NO', and it takes a few moments for me to realise that the voice came from me.

'No,' I say again, less loudly.

It's as though he hasn't even heard and he continues talking. 'And, have babies with me. Lots of babies.'

'Absolutely not!' I shout again.

'A cat then? I know how much you want a cat. We could get one, and I'll learn to love it and everything will be great. Everything you've always wanted.'

I put my hands to my head and scream a little. When I look up, he's still there on his knee, gazing at me expectantly. 'Grant,' I begin, 'the answer is most definitely no.'

'To which bit,' he asks, again with such hope.

'All of it,' I reply, 'no to getting married, to babies and to a cat.'

'But you love cats,' he states, before standing up, rubbing his knees and brushing his jeans down as though the floor is the dirtiest he's ever knelt on in his life.

'Yes, I do. But I don't want one, not with you anyway,' I reply, 'I used to have one, remember? And you made me get rid of it.'

'Exactly, that's why we could get one. So you can see how much I've changed.' I shake my head and turn my back to him, but he walks towards me and spins me round to face him, grabbing my hands. 'Look Lou, I get it, you want to be like the old you, to be yourself and all of that stuff. And that's fine, you can be, and we'll be happy for always.'

'No, we won't. You'll still want me being the girl you've tried to mould for months, into what you think is right, and perfect and how a woman should be. But, I don't want to be that person, Grant. I've gone back to the old me over here and I miss myself, and I want it all back, my old life.'

I pull my hands away and go back over to my tea. I stir my glass rather aggressively then walk to the sofa and sit down, placing it on the coffee table, and he follows me with his own cup, sitting beside me. He goes to put his mug on a coaster and sees there isn't one, and this sends him into confusion before he sees me watching him and begrudgingly puts it directly on the table. I know he'll be thinking of ring stains for at least the next minute or so.

'How long are you going to keep this up, Lou? You'll soon be bored of slumming it again, you know that. Let's just grab your things, go to a nice hotel and talk things through. You'll see what you've been missing and we can get the first flight home tomorrow. I've totally forgiven you.'

'Forgiven me?' I scream in frustration and turn to face him. 'Forgiven me for what? I don't want to go anywhere with you Grant, don't you get that? This, to me, is not slumming it. This is real and how I want to be. I don't want to live in a house where I'm like a fake, reality TV star, playing up for the cameras and being something I'm not.'

He studies me for a few seconds before asking, 'Do you want to go on a reality TV show, is this what it's about? Because that's fine'

I slap my head in frustration. 'No, I don't want to go on a TV reality show, you are not listening to me!'

Grant pats my leg. 'OK, we'll stay here and talk then. Forget the hotel.'

I sigh and put my head in my hands. 'I don't want any of it, Grant, I don't want us.' Even though I've told him this in our texts and brief chats on the mobile, I realise by the very shocked and sad expression on his face when I look at him that he really hadn't believed I actually felt that way. He just wouldn't believe I could possibly not want him and I can actually see it start to sink in, as it moves though his face down his body, making his shoulders slump and his torso curl in on itself. I look away so that I don't start feeling too sorry for him. Not only does he now have that puppy face, he's like an unwanted pet you see on those train posters and charity TV adverts.

I feel a small glimmer of hope as it looks like he's giving in, but he suddenly sits back and grabs at my hands to hold them again. 'Lou, whatever it takes, I'll change for you,' he pleads. 'You name it, I'll do it. We'll move.'

'Move? Where and why?' I ask, frowning.

'We'll go anywhere. Somewhere that's more... you,' he replies.

'More me?' I ask. 'What exactly does that mean?'

Grant looks scared to answer as he realises my question is loaded, and he has to think of the correct thing to say, and quickly too. I put him out of his misery. 'Look, you don't know me at all. You know what you'd *like* me to be, but not who I am. Relocating somewhere new for us is not an answer, it won't solve anything. We'll still be the same, a couple that shouldn't be together, that have nothing in common. I'll still be a huge disappointment to you, Grant.' I can feel myself getting angry, my voice becoming more high pitched. Months and months of pent up feelings, all fighting for prime position to explode and spew out.

I carry on, on a roll. 'I like to be lazy sometimes, I like to eat normal things at home, take-aways, food I've cooked and burned.' I can see the memories of some of my meals register on his face. 'Restaurants are ok, sometimes, but meals at your friends' mansions are boring as hell and I leave there starving, craving a kebab, chicken wings and any carbs I can cram into my mouth.' This clearly makes him feel nauseous. 'Yes, chicken wings, Grant. I love them, the picking them up with my fingers, and letting the juices drip on my chin.' He's turning green... 'And, onto the carpet in the flat which, I'm sorry to have to tell you, has happened a few times when you've been in bed and I've sneaked out to get them after one of your friend's revolting dinner parties. And talking about the carpet, my favourite thing is walking around bare-foot when you're not there, not in slippers but hot and sweaty bare feet!' I stare at him, waiting for some sort of response or answer, but he actually looks very queasy.

'Do you think you can put up with that?' I ask him. 'Could you change enough?'

After a few seconds he says, 'I can eat chicken wings.' He sees my face. 'Or not. Whatever you want, babe, I'll give it a go. And, the carpet can always be cleaned.' He raises his eyebrows optimistically.

I scream. I actually scream out loud, stand up, and I jump up and down, then scream again. Grant cowers slightly in his seat.

'Its not about the chicken wings,' I yell, 'or the bloody

305

carpet. It's about me, the opposite of you!'

I watch his smile start to wane. 'Grant, I really need you to go. I can't do this anymore. Please.'

Grant stands up and paces the floor and I can tell this is going to take a while. He turns to me, with pleading eyes. 'I shouldn't have come, I should have let you have the last week, the space, to get it all out of your system before you come back and then we could have sorted it. We still can. Look, I'll go now and not contact you till you get back to our flat. Let's pretend this never happened.'

This has *so* happened! 'I'm not coming back to the flat, Grant, other than to collect my stuff. Can't you get that into your head?'

He looks around the living area and I see his face change, and the old Grant is back. He gestures with his hands round the room. 'Are you seriously telling me that you enjoy staying here?' he asks. I nod. 'With her? In this... shack?'

'*Her* is called Libby, my best friend, and this *shack* has given me a safe home for the last few weeks, where I can be me and actually enjoy myself for a change,' I answer. 'So yes, I love it here.' Inside, I don't actually know if I do love it here, seeing as only an hour ago I wanted to leave to secretly move in with the neighbour, but I'm not having him put my friend or her home down.

He hesitates before saying, 'I knew she'd be behind this. She's always been the one to put these crazy ideas in your head. And, you're so gullible, you've believed every little bit of poison she's thrown at you.' He turns his back towards me.

'Poison? What the hell are you talking about? This is not about Libby and she's guilty of nothing.'

Grant spins back round to face me, his face hard. 'Really? I think you'll find she's guilty of stuff you have no idea about.'

'Like what?' I demand.

'You are making the biggest mistake of your life if you refuse to see her for what she is.'

I'm fuming, way past that point of caring what I say to him anymore. 'Grant, you've been my mistake for the last 18 months. It was never meant to be, we forced it and it hasn't worked out. This is nothing about Libby, so stop slagging her off and just leave.'

'Are you ready for the truth about that slut of a friend of yours?' he sneers.

Slut? Who the hell does he think he is?

'That last night, when she stayed at ours before leaving for her shag fest over here. Do you remember it?' Grant asks.

I nod. 'Of course I do, I hated it and didn't want her to go.'

'And she didn't even stay and say goodbye. She legged it whilst you were still sleeping. Why do you think that was?'

I sigh. 'Because it was too difficult for her. You wouldn't understand, Grant, what it's like to lose a friend like that. We'd been together for years, since school. It was just easier for her to leave and for there to be no sad goodbyes.'

Grant shakes his head. 'Do you want to know the real reason?' he asks me, eyes now wide and demonic.

I roll my eyes. 'Grant, this isn't getting us anywhere. Why bring up the past like this? Just go.'

Grant laughs. 'I threw her out that night,' he says.

'Why would you do that?' I ask and feel the fury build back up in me. He goes quiet and so I walk towards him, searching his face for clues. 'You knew how much I wanted to say goodbye, how painful it was for me. Why would you do that if you cared anything about me at all?'

Grant laughs again. 'You instantly think that it's me in the wrong, perfect Libby can't have had anything to do with it. Lou, get this into your head and understand it, I threw her out for you!'

I gasp. 'How could it have been for me? You're crazy, I want you to go.' I go to walk past him, to open the door, but he grabs my arm and stops me.

'Not until you hear me out. I threw her out because she made a pass at me. Whilst you were in the flat, sleeping in our bed,' he shouts.

I laugh. I actually laugh at the absurdity of his statement. 'You're lying.'

'Remember how drunk you both got?'

'Not drunk,' I argue. 'Merry, yes, but not drunk.' Actually, we were both pretty drunk, it was easier that way, all too painful to go through it sober.

'You were both pissed and emotional, and went to bed, remember?'

I nod. If I agree with him, it might make him leave quicker.

'You fell asleep straight away so I switched the light off. Then, she walked in twenty minutes later, still crying and making a fuss. So,' he continues, 'I switched the light back on and guess what? Libby was standing there half naked.'

Now, this doesn't actually bother me. Grant is quite conservative about what women wear. She was probably in short pyjamas or a nightie, not half naked at all.

'I'm not listening to this,' I say and fold my arms, glaring at him.

'I took her back to her room and gave her a hug to comfort her. And she started kissing me.' Grant walks to me and grabs my arms, a little too forcefully for my liking. I go to pull away but he has me held tightly. 'Lou, believe me, I tried to push her away, I really did. But, I admit, I did kiss her back, just a bit. I'm sorry. I'm only human.'

There's no way she would do this, drunk or not. 'This is crap.' I say. 'Libby would never do that to me.'

Grant shakes his head. 'She didn't just want me to kiss her, she was all over me, telling me it would be ok, you'd never know and all that stuff. She was lifting her top up, and pressing herself against me. I'd have had to have been a monk to not get a bit excited. But, I stopped before it went too far, I swear. '

I shake my head and glare at him. 'You're lying,' I say, and jut out my chin. I'm not taking any more of this. If he doesn't get out, then I will.

'I threw her out!' he spits. 'That's why she'd gone when you got up. I told her to get out and never come back. That's why I hate you being here with her. She's a slut, she betrayed you and she'll do it again.'

I finally pull my arms away from him. 'Grant, you need to go now, or I'm going to. And, I never want to see you again. Do you understand me?' And, I turn to leave but Grant's blocking my way.

I'm starting to feel sick again, and very, very warm. I need more water, or else I'm going to keel over. What ever possessed me to make a hot cup of apple tea? I see his face show a flicker of concern and realise how bad I must look, and he goes to put his arm round me but I flinch and shrug him off.

'Don't touch me, Grant,' I say and give him a warning look.

'You're angry with me, because I kissed her back and had a bit of a feel for those few seconds. But, you can't just blame *me* for that.'

I shake my head but it makes it woozier than it was. Whether he kissed her or she kissed him makes no difference to me. It's the fact there's a chance something happened between them. I want to believe he's lying, but it does explain the animosity and atmosphere whenever I mention one of their names to the other. What if it's true?

'Lou,' he says, almost sneering at me, 'believe me, I should have taken her up on the offer, instead of turning her away and coming back to bed. Like an idiot I tried to do the right thing yet, here you are choosing her over me, a woman who tried to shag me after a couple of drinks too many. This is how you re-pay me.' He slams his hand against the wall and I jump. 'Have you any idea how much I've done for you?' he asks, 'I gave you a home, I paid for clothes so you didn't look a state like you did when we first met, I took you out and showed you a life full of things you'd never get the chance to experience in your sorry little lifetime.'

Sorry little lifetime? How dare he. Yes, I'll admit I was on an all time low. I hadn't got a career, I wasn't really living it up or travelling or experiencing any new things. But, it wasn't a sorry little life, and I was happier before we met than I have been with Grant in it.

I need him to leave, and the thing I haven't yet tried is to be nice to him. 'Look, I'm grateful for what you've given me...'

'Given you? I'm not a charity. I shared my life with you because I wanted to. Have you any idea how my friends laughed at me, and how I stuck up for you? Your accent, your clothes. Why did I bother, they were right all along.'

'So why did you do it?' I ask. 'If I was that much of an embarrassment and a lost cause, why did you bother with me?'

Grant sighs and starts to calm. Then, he puts his hand out and strokes my face. 'I just wanted to make you better,' he says.

'Better?' I say. 'I was fine how I was, thank you.'

He looks sad and beaten, puts his head in his hands and breathes deeply before saying, 'I've got you a ticket on the same plane as me. It leaves in the morning. Come with me.'

For a moment, I pause and consider, but only because I'm struggling to find any other options for me. What if it's true about Libby, that she came onto him that night? She covered up her fling with Seth and Hamil, so she's capable of keeping secrets from me. I've never considered a point in my life where I can't trust her, and I don't know how to fix this.

But, even in the state I'm in, I see sense. 'No, its over,' I say 'I don't want to be with you, and I'm staying here until my holiday is over, and then I'll go back home and start a new life. But, it won't be with you, or with Libby. It will be on my own.'

Grant bites his lip and backs away from me. 'Ok,' he says, holding his arms out, 'I admit defeat.' He sits down on the sofa and I silently urge him to get out of the apartment but really can't face another argument. So, I grab my bag and walk towards the door. I hesitate for a moment, as I really don't want to leave him in here, but I can just about trust him to not trash the place or steal anything. There's nothing in here he'd want anyway. I need to get away and talk to Libby.

'I want you out of here within ten minutes of me leaving,' I say.

He nods. 'Any chance I can grab a shower first?' I go to argue but I really couldn't care less.

'There'll be no hot water I wouldn't think,' I say and he rolls his eyes. 'But grab one if you want. There's a towel on my bed' I gesture to which bedroom is mine. 'Just leave it there when you're done and leave. Pull the door up, it doesn't need locking.'

He nods. 'Thanks,' he says feebly.

As I walk through the door he calls out, 'I really did love you, you know.'

I turn and look at him, then say, 'I know you did. But it wasn't the real me you loved, it was who you wanted me to be.'

I leave the apartment, slamming the door shut and my mind goes back to the last time I said goodbye to him, just a few weeks before, when he'd thrown a vase against the door when I left. I'm grateful I don't hear anything being thrown against it this time. I wish he'd gone, so that I could collapse on the bed and cry and sleep and float away to somewhere far away from here, to a time before Grant's revelation. If I could turn the clocks back a day, none of this need to have happened and I wouldn't have seen Seth with his family. But, Seth's no longer my main concern. It's Libby and, if it's true what Grant said, I don't know if I'll ever be able to forgive her.

CHAPTER TWENTY-NINE

I run around all the bars and hotels at top speed. Well, my top speed, which isn't particularly fast especially when I feel like I'm going to collapse. I can see tourists staring curiously at me as I pass them, wondering what the emergency is, my face red and sweaty, my make up probably all over my face, if there's any left from all the crying I've done. Maybe they think I'm an undercover police officer, on a drugs bust or something. Actually, I'd be quite good at that, but not sure whether to add it to my list of jobs or not. I'll have a think.

Despite me checking all the normal haunts, Libby's nowhere. It's likely she's still at the bank but I've been hoping she might have finished up by now and stopped somewhere to refuel. After all, she hasn't eaten since breakfast. None of the waiters and staff we know have seen her and I start to feel quite desperate. I end up going to the one bar I really don't want to face today, where Hamil works, and my heart sinks when I see him in there. But, to my surprise, he walks up to me, smiling as usual and gives me a brisk peck on each cheek. I stand and wait for a comment, a sneer or put-down, but there's nothing. It seems the awkwardness of a week or so ago has passed and we're on good terms again. I wish I was as forgiving as him, I'd be holding a grudge for months, even years.

As soon as I begin to ask about Libby I find myself crying, huge tears streaming down my face and I put my hand on his shoulder to steady myself as the giddiness returns. He carefully guides me to one of the padded benches in the corner of the bar and sits me down, then goes and gets a glass of water from the bar and hurries back with it. He stays with me whilst I sip it, glancing nervously around at the other staff, probably hoping one of the females will come over and tend to the mad woman he's been lumbered with but they unsurprisingly stay well away. With this temperature, the lack of water, the hangover, no food and all the upset, well, it was bound to floor me sooner or later. Saying that, I've cried more in these three weeks than I think I have in the last five years. Hamil eventually gives me an awkward hug and I thank him. I'm lucky he'll even talk to me after how I treated him a week ago.

'Maybe she is still at the bank,' Hamil suggests, 'have you not tried there?'

I shake my head. She probably is, but I don't know which one it is and there are quite a few in the town. It's probably not a good idea for me to fly around all of them trying to find her. I'd probably get arrested with the state I'm in. As if by magic, a plate of melon and banana appear on the table, delivered by a new waitress that I haven't seen before, and Hamil winks at her and she smiles shyly back at him. Ah, this is why he's not coming across as awkward with me, he's moved on to better things quite obviously. Well, I'm pleased for the guy. At least someone is being lucky in love.

'She's nice,' I say. Hamil nods. I look at him for a few seconds and then say, 'I'm really sorry, you know, about what happened between us. I should have stopped you before, shouldn't have led you on, I just ...'

He puts his finger against my lips and says, 'Ssh, I deserved it. I get a bit carried away some times, with such a beautiful woman.' I smile and am pleased he's back to his charming and cheeky self. 'I'm just pleased we can be friends.' He leaves me to eat the fruit and I instantly start to feel better although, as soon as I think of Libby and Grant together, my stomach churns and I close my eyes and groan.

Hamil comes back after a while and asks, 'Any news?'

I wave my phone at him and shake my head. 'Why doesn't she have her phone on? It goes straight to voicemail.'

'If she's in a meeting at the bank, she won't want to be disturbed. Or, maybe she just wants some time out. Not necessarily from you, it could be from anyone.'

I look at him and notice he's become uncomfortable, as though he's said too much. 'Like who?' I ask. He hesitates and shrugs. 'Hamil,' I say a little more loudly and assertively, 'like who?'

He fidgets and then looks around to make sure no one is listening, and says 'I don't think things are going well with Jude.'

I frown and urge him to continue. 'My friend at his bar said they've been arguing and he really shouted at her the other day, in front of the staff and some female customers, and she walked out. He was making fun of the jeep business, in front of everyone. He's not a kind man.'

Umm, he's right there. Why hasn't Libby talked to me about it? She hasn't said a thing. But then, I guess she hasn't had much of a chance as I've done nothing but whine and moan about Seth and Grant and how crap my life is. I haven't asked her how hers is going lately. I'm so selfish.

Jude should be proud of what she's doing with the jeep

business, I just don't get it. That's probably why Seth stole the keys and set us up as hookers, he's sticking with his brother, the two of them in cahoots. I want to find them both, right now, and give them a piece of my mind, shout and scream, tell everyone how they really are. But, would anyone either care or believe me?

Just as I'm feeling sorry for Libby, I remember the conversation I had with Grant just a short while ago and feel instantly confused by my feelings for her. If she's betrayed me, she can sort this one out on her own. I'm not getting involved in her battles, I've enough of my own.

Hamil goes to speak to a table of customers who've just arrived, laden with bags from the market, and I put my head in my hands and breathe deeply. I need to get a grip and calm down, or I'll collapse spectacularly in the middle of the bar and have to be medically attended to, possibly by Hamil who I don't particularly trust to give me an examination that doesn't include a grope and fondle, even if his new love interest *is* working here.

'Come to visit your boyfriend for a quickie?' I look up and see Jude, grinning smugly, standing by my side.

It takes me a second to realise he means Hamil and I shake my head defensively. 'No,' I quickly say. 'He's with her,' and I point at the waitress who is chatting with customers at the entrance. I've no idea why I felt the need to tell him this, I don't have to justify anything I do.

'Can't keep up with your love life,' Jude says, loud enough for Hamil to hear and look around. He gives Jude a filthy look and turns back to his customers.

'What are you doing here?' I ask. 'I didn't think you liked this bar.'

'Just popped in to see the owner Eric, to drop some paperwork off he needs.' Jude removes his sunglasses and looks at me. 'You look terrible,' he says and puts his glasses back on as though to protect his eyes from the hideous sight.

'Thank you,' I say quietly back and get up to leave. 'Hamil,' I call out, 'thank you for the fruit and drink, can I pay you later? I need to go and find Libby.'

'No problem,' Hamil says, smiling and blowing me a kiss before throwing another look at Jude. I wearily sip the last of my water and go to walk away.

'I'll walk with you,' Jude says.

'I'll slow you down,' I argue back, hopefully putting him off. "I'm on a go slow today and really do need to find Libby.' I don't want him to walk anywhere with me, I just can't stand the bloke.

'She's at my bar,' he replies.

'What?' I say with obvious exasperation. 'But I've looked for her there and I couldn't see her. I speed up my pace to go through the doors.

'Keep your hair on,' he says. 'She's only just got there after some *incident* at your flat.'

'What?' I stop still, turning to face him, and frown. What is he talking about?

'Well,' he smiles smugly again, 'I'm not sure which man you have now, but she found a naked one getting out of the shower.' I groan and close my eyes. Grant. What was he still doing there? 'You're a busy woman.' He waves his finger at me and laughs, but I don't. Why the hell did Grant not have a quick shower, and get out of the place before she got there, like I asked. They probably threw themselves at each other again, Libby unable to resist him wrapped up in a towel. My headache starts to come back, probably from the speed my blood has started to pump around my body, and I ignore Jude's comment, walking off as quick as I can. I don't even want to explain to him who it was in the flat. Let him

317

think what he wants although he doesn't look as though he's particularly interested anyway.

He follows me from the bar and we walk uncomfortably together in the sun.

'How come you lost each other?' he asks. 'I thought you went to Turunç on the business mission.'

I pretend I haven't noticed the sarcasm in his voice. 'Yes, but we came back quite a while ago. She was heading to the bank.' I say.

'The bank?' he asks. 'Oh, don't tell me she's really going forward with this business idea?' He shakes his head.

I stop and look at him for a few seconds and then ask, 'Why not?'

Jude puts his head on one side and looks at me as though he pities my lack of understanding. 'Look, she knows nothing about business. She's just playing at it,' he says, 'take it from someone that knows. I've been in business here for years and it's tough, you've got to know the ins and outs and all the tricks. And, Libby just hasn't got a clue. She should stay in her safe rep job, and leave it all as a pipe dream, because that's exactly what it is.'

I want to argue with him, but I stop myself. Why should I stick up for her if what Grant has said is right? I need to leave this to Libby and Jude to sort, even if I am riled by his attitude. But I can't help saying, 'Libby's more than capable of running a business.' I continue to walk, upping my pace. The quicker we get to the bar, the quicker I get rid of this jerk and can have it out with Libby. Then, who knows? I might be on a plane by nightfall because that's exactly what I feel like doing right now.

Jude hurries along beside me again and I look out the side of my sunglasses at him. His eyes are so like Seth's and, as he tucks his curly dark hair behind his ears, I feel a pang of disappointment that things haven't worked out between Seth and I, because I really did like him and thought he was so different to this guy.

'Look, I know you're fond of her, and I am too. But, Libby is a typical tour rep. She's come over here for a few months, got to like the place and wants to stay. But, she's no idea what it's really like. It's just temporary.' Jude is trying to give me a friendly expression but it comes across as a smug grin that I could quite happily beat off his face with my flip-flop. But I haven't the energy to do so and there are more important things to sort.

Thinking of flip-flops, I look down at my feet, noticing how swollen they've become again, and wish I was lying on my bed. But, I won't go back to the flat until I know the coast is clear. The mood I'm in, I could easily push Grant off the balcony if he's still there.

'Have you seen my dear brother today?' Jude suddenly asks.

I shake my head and say nothing. I don't want to talk about Seth.

'So you don't know about our argument last night?' he asks.

'Why would I,' I ask. 'I haven't seen him for days and it's no business of mine.'

'Lover's quarrel?' I grunt at Jude's sarcastic tone and pretend to try and find something in my bag as we walk, anything to avoid me having to communicate with him.

'Do you know,' continues Jude, not caring that I'm clearly not interested in joining in with this conversation, 'it would not surprise me if, wherever Libby's been these last few hours, it would have been with Seth. They're very close, but then you probably know that. I'm sure she tells you everything.' I can feel him watching me, searching for any

319

sign that he's getting to me, but I stay calm.   Well, not exactly.   I look reasonably calm but inside I feel the pressure is building up and I'm not quite sure if I'm going to blow or not.   'The problem is, whatever I have, my brother wants. And, those two have wanted each other for a long time, they should have stayed together from the start.'

OK, so my plan to stay calm and not get into a discussion with him fails. I stop dead, stare at him and feel my face start to go redder and redder.   'That's ridiculous, and you know it,' I spit at him, instantly regretting it as I can see how much my response has pleased him.

'You don't like to hear the truth, I see.' Jude pats my arm in a condescending manner.   'Look, you're best off without either of them.'

'That's your girlfriend you're talking about!' I snap.   'And anyway, I don't have to be with either of them and I'll be out of here on a plane really soon. But you? You'll still be with both of them.   One's your brother and the other is your girlfriend. So, it sounds like you have more problems to sort than I do.'

Jude looks me up and down and nods.   'I think you're right,' he says.   'Maybe me and you should get together instead, that will show them.'

I shake my head in disbelief at this comment and almost retaliate but stop myself.   Instead, I calmly say, 'When you see Libby, will you tell her I'm looking for her? I'm going to go and sit for a while, near Ataturk's statue. I'll wait for her there.'   And with that, I rush off, relieved that he's not following me. I'm not sure that Libby will come as firstly, it's unlikely that Jude will pass on my message, and secondly, she probably won't want to. So, if she doesn't, I'll grab a cab back to the apartment, where hopefully there'll be no ex-boyfriends draped in bath towels, and I might just pack my stuff and get out whilst I can.

CHAPTER THIRTY

I reach the statue and go straight into the chemist opposite, on the corner, as I need painkillers and fast. Chemists are called *eczane* here which, as Libby has told me many times, you pronounce as egg sarnie. I had found this amusing, but today it's annoying. In fact, everything about Libby and this place she calls home annoys me now, it's all changed. The girl behind the desk is very helpful and, in perfect English, tells me I look 'shit,' am clearly dehydrated and must drink lots of cold water which she gives me from the water cooler in the corner. I thank her for her kind words and say I'll take care, swallow two of the tablets then pay and leave.

I expected to see my normal gaggle of boat trip touts by the statue and am disappointed when I find it empty as they could have cheered me up. I'm become quite fond of them all but, for them, today is a good day as it means that all the boats are out earning an income.

I flop down on the bench and pull my knees up to my chest, balancing my feet on the edge of the seat, head on my knees. There are a lot of tourists around, and I look up to people watch, fascinated by how many different foreign languages I hear as they pass. I wonder if they're talking about similar problems to mine, how they have a best friend who appears to have tried to get it on with their boyfriend. I doubt it, as they all look happy as they go by, whereas I look thoroughly miserable. Maybe they just haven't found out yet. A few hours ago, I was oblivious to it all, and I wish I could feel like I did then.

I'm determined to act cool when Libby arrives, I won't suddenly burst into tears, fly at her like a screaming banshee then accuse her of trying to have it off with Grant. No, I'm going to be dignified and cool because, I've decided, that's the new me. I'm going to toughen up and let things go over my head. Oh yes, this worm has well and truly turned.

I've only been sitting for a few minutes when I feel arms grab me from behind and then a light kiss on the cheek.

'Where have you been?' Libby demands, 'I've been trying to find you everywhere.'

'What the hell have you been doing?' I scream at her. Ok, the 'new me' hasn't quite arrived yet.

Libby laughs, thinking I'm joking and sits beside me. 'Well, other than the bank visit, I've been getting over the shock of what I found in our apartment.'

'*Your* apartment,' I snap. The apartment is nothing to do with me, I huff to myself.

'Ok, my apartment,' she says, giving me a strange look before smiling again to continue. 'I opened the door, heard the shower running and thought it was you, and poked my head round to tell you I was home and, who did I find? A naked Grant!' I don't reply and she stares at me. 'Well? Any comment to make?' she asks.

'Not really,' I reply, not knowing what else to say.

'Well, how did he find the place? Did you give him the address?'

I shake my head. Actually, how did he find me there? I

hadn't even thought about that. Had I left the address written down somewhere at the flat and forgot all about it? I did a full sweep of the place, FBI style, it wasn't anywhere. I suddenly start to feel myself growing calmer and, for a moment, am very proud of myself until I realise it's the headache tablets. The chemist did say they might make me drowsy and 'chilled out.' I rub my eyes and put my head back onto my knees.

'I can't believe he's here,' Libby continues. I still don't reply and Libby frowns and pulls my head back up. 'Are you ok? You look terrible.'

'Yes, so the Egg Sarnie lady told me, and everyone else I've seen, except for Grant who told me I look fabulous.' I put my head back on my knees and just wish she'd go and leave me alone. I could happily fall asleep here and sort all of this out another day. The boat trip guys will be back soon and they'll look after me. I could sleep on one of the boats over night and pretend I'm a pirate. Actually, I'd make a good pirate…

'I've looked for you everywhere. Seth's been looking for you too,' she's saying, and I drift back out of my pirate dream. Trust her to mention Seth. I mentally make a note of any boyfriends I've had, even dating back to primary school days, and wonder how many of them she's snogged or worse.

I sigh and lift my head up. 'Don't tell me, you and Seth have been together, chatting and searching and... and... being all *couple-ly*.'

'No,' replies Libby, ignoring my 'couple-ly' dig. Typical. 'He just came into the bar when I was there and asked after you. He seemed really worried about you, actually. So much so, I didn't have the heart to challenge him about referring me to Ali for that jeep contract. It can wait.'

'He's not worried about me, it's a guilty conscience,' I snap. 'The same as the one you have, probably!' There, I've said something that's actually made her sit up and notice that I'm not happy. Finally.

Libby looks genuinely confused. 'About what? Lou, what's going on.'

I look away, feeling my eyes start to fill, these damn tablets having ripped any clout out of me.

Libby fumbles in her bag and then hands me a tissue and offers me a bottle of sun tan lotion 'You need this,' she says, 'your face is really red and it's the hottest day for weeks.' I grab the tissue but go to push the bottle away, but she pushes it back towards me and I begrudgingly take it.

After applying it haphazardly, I can't hold it in any longer. 'Grant told me,' I say so quietly, she must have struggled to hear. 'About your last night in the UK, and why you didn't stay.'

'He did?' asks Libby. 'Oh.'

'Yes, oh,' I reply, staring at her. She looks uncomfortable. I really hadn't expected an 'oh.' It's virtually admitting to something. I'd have preferred a 'like what?' or 'don't be ridiculous.'

After a few seconds she asks, 'Did he tell you all of it?'

All of it? As if I want to know all the intimate details. I feel crushed, and want to shout and scream and slap her, but all I can do is ask, in a rather pathetic voice, 'Libby, how could you?'

'I did it for you!' she shouts, attracting attention from the passing tourists. A couple stand still, possibly wondering if we're a street entertainment act.

'How the hell can you justify that it was for me?'

'Lou, how could I have stayed after what happened? It would have made things even worse for you.' We both now look as confused as each other. I realise she thinks I'm referring to the way she left the apartment without saying goodbye.

'Libby, it's not the fact you left, it's what you did before you scarpered. You tried it on with my boyfriend, behind my back, whilst I slept in the other room. Virtually naked with your bits on display and pushing up against him. You're disgusting!' She looks aghast. 'Vile!' I yell in her face, huff and then spin around so my back is towards her.

I'm aware of a couple of guys standing near us pretending to read a map, but are very clearly just earwigging. I shout out to them, 'Are you lost?' and they look at each other then scurry away. Maybe these tablets are starting to wear off.

Libby looks mortified. 'I swear to you, I did no such thing,' she says. She tries to turn me round to look at her, but I freeze so she can't move me, so she gets up instead and sits the opposite side, grabbing my hands. I try to pull them away, but she won't let go. 'You have to believe me, Lou. I'd never do anything to hurt you. Ever'

She looks anxious, the colour drained from her tanned face and her eyes slowly becoming watery. She looks genuinely shocked.

'But why would Grant lie about it?' I ask.

'Oh Lou, think about it. This is a guy that's proposed to you, you turned down, then run away to another country to be with your friend that you've missed madly since she's been gone, rather than wanting to stay with him.'

'Haven't missed you that much!' I interrupt.

She ignores me and continues 'and he thinks that, if he turns you against me, you'll go back home with him and his life will be back to the way it was before. Look, I never tried it on with him, and I never would. And it's not just because it's Grant and I don't like him, it's because I'd never betray you, ever.'

'Not even with Seth?' I demand.

'What?' she asks, eyebrows literally flying up to her hairline. 'When the hell have I betrayed you with Seth?'

'You were an item, and never told me.'

Libby holds her head in her hands. 'Lou, I can't keep going over and over this. We were never an item, we went out a couple of times when I first came here, it was nothing!'

'Then why didn't you tell me?' I ask. I'm wound up, I'm hot, I've a headache again, and I feel sick. I just want answers now as quickly as possible so that I can go and lie down and scream into my pillow.

'Because I knew you'd be like this,' she says. She stands, puts her hands on her hips and leans towards me. 'Sorry, this might be hard to hear Lou, but to hell with it. I didn't tell you because I knew you'd over react and think the worse thing possible, like you *always* do. And, I didn't want to have a fight and have to tread on eggshells. Look at you, you've got yourself into this state over something that didn't even happen. I was absolutely right.'

I go to argue back but stop myself. She is actually right. I've flipped out, and it's not just because she didn't tell me, and that I had to find out through Jude. I flipped out because I'm insecure, and precious and jealous and I couldn't stand the fact that she'd been an item with a guy who I have fallen in love with, and that he'd been with her first. Libby has always been the one to have men falling over themselves for her, chasing her and asking her out. And only then, when she's either said no or got bored, have they come to me, the second choice.

'If you didn't try it on with Grant, why did you leave that night, without saying goodbye?'

She sits back down and I watch her twist her hands

around in her lap, and I can tell that she's wondering if she should say something, her lips keep going to open, then closing again. She eventually takes a deep breath, turns to me and says, 'It didn't seem right to tell you, not when I was about to leave you for my new life. I couldn't see what it would achieve. I'm sorry, it wasn't me that tried it on,' she says, 'it was Grant.'

'Oh come on Libby, you can do better than that!' I snap. She's just saying this to cover herself.

She sighs, puts her head on one side and rolls her eyes. 'You'd gone to bed, really upset, and I stayed in the lounge to calm down and sober up a bit with a coffee. But, Grant decided he wanted to stay with me, which was very annoying as I wanted time to be alone. Plus, I can't stand the guy. But anyway, he got a little too close on the sofa and I started to feel uncomfortable so l excused myself and went to bed. He wanted me to stay, but I just kept walking and closed the bedroom door.'

She stops, watches me for a few seconds, takes another deep breath and carries on. 'I'd just taken my top off and thrown it in my suitcase, turned around, and he was there, leaning against the door, watching. I had nothing near to me to cover myself up, my pyjama top was on the bed next to him, and so I had to move near him to grab it. But, he held onto it, refusing to let it go, just staring at me. I was freaked out and my reactions were slower, everything was slower, because we'd been drinking, and I was upset, and....'

Libby starts to cry and then she carries on talking, becoming animated, waving her hands around like she always does when upset and, I realise she's telling the truth. I've seen her like this before, I know her, I've watched her for so many years and I know she's being honest with me. 'He finally let go of my top but carried on staring at me whilst I put it on, saying all this stuff, about how he'd always liked me, and asking why he hadn't asked me out first, rather than you. I told him to get out, and it started to get a bit heavy, because he wouldn't go and started to get nasty, saying I was common and had no class, and that you'd be so much better off without me as I'd been holding you back for years and years. It became a massive row, I'm surprised you didn't hear us.'

I shake my head. I hadn't heard a thing but, to be honest, I was so out of it I wouldn't have heard anything anyway.

'As soon as I got him out of the room, I sat on my bed for a while and wondered what to do. I panicked about him coming back in, and he'd said that, if I told you, he'd deny everything and tell you it was all me and that I'd be ruining your life. I didn't want us to end like that, I didn't want you having those doubts and hating me. So, I packed my bags and went. I just couldn't watch him with you the next morning, knowing how he'd betrayed you. You'd have sensed something, I know you would, it just wouldn't have been fair.'

I watch Libby and then I close my eyes and rub my head. If my head doesn't combust in the next five minutes, I'll be amazed. I desperately need to get out of this sun. 'Libby, I really need you to be telling the truth. Are you? Because, if not...'

'I promise you,' she interrupts, 'I swear on my life, yours, everyone's.' I stand and pace around for a few minutes, Libby anxiously watching me like a crowd in a court public gallery waiting for a verdict, and I turn, fling my arms round her, squeezing her tight.

'I'm so sorry,' I say, 'I should never have believed him but, well, with everything else that's been happening.' We continue hugging and I look over her shoulder and see that the taxi boats are coming back in, one after the other, causing a scurry of local men who have appeared from nowhere and are hastily preparing to tether them all up. I wonder if the boat guys have had as much of an eventful day as I've had. Somehow, I doubt it very much.

CHAPTER THIRTY-ONE

We both sit and watch the boats for a bit whilst we try to calm down. 'Why's Seth been looking for me?' I suddenly ask.

'Well, he was understandably very upset about what had just happened.'

I shrug. I don't really care if he's upset or not, it's his own doing. That's what comes from keeping your offspring secret. 'Well, he's only himself to blame. He should have thought twice before hurting me like that.'

'Hurting you? I think it's the other way round,' replies Libby. I frown at her. 'Grant. Naked in our apartment?' I groan and she rolls her eyes at me. 'It must have been a bit of a shock.'

'Why was Seth even at the apartment?'

'To find you, and Grant answered the door.'

I sigh. Why didn't Grant just go to his hotel and sit there in a dark room until the flight tomorrow, keeping away from people especially those I know. Mind you, I'm not sure I actually care that Seth's upset about seeing Grant in the flat. In fact, I'm quite pleased.

'Well, I think he was probably surprised when Grant

answered the door only wearing a towel and a smile.' Not exactly naked then, I think to myself. 'And Grant told Seth you couldn't come to the door because you were '*asleep*', and he did those quotation-finger-things as if to say that sleep actually meant you were tired from all the shagging.' Ah, I can see why Seth was a bit upset then. I can picture Grant doing the quote marks in the air, it used to drive me crazy and I want to find him, slap him and stop him ever doing the quote mark symbol again.

I guess I can't blame him for taking an opportunity to wind Seth up. I mean, a handsome guy comes to the door looking for me, Grant's ex girlfriend/almost fiancée, after I've told him how we'll never be together again and that I hate his company. He took a final opportunity to make trouble for me and it sounds like it worked.

'I wasn't in bed,' I say. 'I wasn't even there. I let him use the shower before he made his way to the hotel, as long as he was quick. I wanted to come to find you, but I should have stayed and checked he actually left.'

'I know,' she replies. 'I'd only been there a few minutes earlier than Seth, remember?'

'I can't believe this!' I say. Then, I start to giggle. The giggle gets louder and deeper and, before I know it, I'm laughing, Libby too. And then we're belly laughing and a couple of my boat friends have come over and they're laughing too, even though they have no idea why. And this makes us laugh even more. They slowly get bored and wander off, and will probably talk about us for several minutes and make those 'mad' signs to each other, twirling their fingers round and round the sides of their heads. And that's fine because, at the moment, I do actually feel a bit crazy.

After a few minutes we've stopped and I regain my

composure. 'Well, I'm not happy about Grant saying that to Seth. But, after what Seth's done? Grant's done me a favour and Seth deserves whatever he gets.'

Libby groans. 'Oh come on, you can't keep blaming him for everything. You're a big girl and you went away with him, had a good time, and yes, he then spent the evening with someone, somewhere. But, he has tried to contact you since, and it's you that's refusing to speak to him.'

I laugh sarcastically. 'Believe me, if that's all he'd done, I'd be getting over it by now. After what I found out today, he really doesn't deserve your pity. I know you don't like to think anything bad about him, and he can do no wrong in your eyes, but that guy has a secret that you just won't believe.'

'Is this about the jeep keys again?' she asks, rolling her eyes.

'No,' I snap, 'Forget the jeep keys, I don't care about them anymore, it's nothing in comparison to what I saw today.'

'But you've been with me today, and then the apartment with that ex-boyfriend of yours. What could you possibly have found out?'

I don't even know where to start. Should I actually tell her at all? What will it gain, other than maybe proving to her how he's not the man she thinks he is? I try and put it into some logical order in my head so it doesn't come out all garbled and will be in words that are objective rather than subjective, which is what Libby has encouraged me to do in the past. But, I fail miserably and just say 'he's got a whole secret life Libby, with people in it, and a love child, and a whole load of lies and secrets and... and...mysteries.'

'Mysteries?'

'Ok, not exactly mysteries, but he's a liar and a cheat.'

'Did you say love child?' she asks, and I nod. 'And the

secret woman, have you found out who she is?'

I nod again. 'I've seen her, and watched him with her, and he wasn't even hiding the fact that he's got a child. A son, Libby, a little boy who was holding his hand and kissing him and laughing.'

Libby's eyes grow wide. 'No, no way, you must be wrong. He's never said anything about being a Dad, or mentioned a child, and I'm sure he would have done. And so would Jude.'

'He never said anything about a woman either,' I say, 'but he has one. I saw them, both of them.'

'Where?' Libby asks, looking confused.

'In Turunç, today. He got off the boat whilst we sat outside the bar and he went off to meet them. I followed him.'

'I knew you didn't have cramp!' she exclaims. 'You were so faking it.' She looks at my expression then says, 'sorry, go on.'

'I followed them, and they were kissing, and hugging, and the boy had Seth's eyes and hair, just a different colour. And they were a perfect little family'

'Are you sure?' asks Libby. 'I know he's been a bit secretive. But a family? I can't believe it, it's just so not like Seth.'

'Well, it's what I saw. And now he feels all guilty and wants to talk to me about it.'

'Did he see you?' she asks.

'Yep, he looked straight at me but didn't even try to explain. He just stayed with her and the boy, and glared at me, all cross because I'd caught him out.'

Libby shakes her head in disbelief. 'But Jude would know, surely?'

I think for a few minutes and then gasp. 'That's why he's

been so down on Seth, why they've argued so much, it's about her! Ooh, ooh,' I say, frantically bobbing up and down as I remember, 'Seth gave her money, in an envelope. I saw her take it out and thank him, the boy too. Maybe Jude knows about the cash and is angry because Seth's giving away his money.'

Libby shakes her head. 'No, that doesn't make sense. What's it to do with Jude if Seth has a woman and child and gives them money. It's his cash, after all. He can do what he wants with it. Jude wouldn't care.'

'Unless,' I say, now totally going into my detective mode, 'he gives her money from the business, out of their joint profits. Jude wouldn't like that.' I nod, stand up and pace around on the spot, dramatically tapping my chin. I wish I had a notepad and pen, I could jot down all the clues and then ponder like they do in films.

Libby shakes her head again. 'Why would he do that? He's got money, he's not short of a penny or two, so he wouldn't touch the business funds. No, there's got to be something else about it that's making Jude mad, that's if he *is* mad about the woman and kid, and not something else.'

'Hey,' I say, 'maybe Jude doesn't like the fact that Seth is interested in me whilst he should be looking after his dependants.' Even I find this a little dubious, Jude having morals. But, it's possible.

I wonder how Seth is actually feeling right now. His partner and son have probably gone back to their home, wherever that is, and he's come back to Marmaris, feeling guilty and thinks he can just find me and explain and it will all be ok. The fact he's bumped into Grant has just made the whole thing more complicated than it already was.

I think back to the conversation with Jude just before I came to the statue to wait for Libby. 'Jude does seem really

335

mad with everyone today.' I say. 'I saw him earlier and he was going on about all sorts of stuff.'

'Like what?' Libby asks.

'Well...' I hesitate, maybe I shouldn't mention this, it could open up a whole can of worms. But, then again, I've had enough secrets for a lifetime, so I decide to get everything out in the open. 'Jude was obviously rattled about something, and was going on about Seth and was suggesting that, well, you and his brother having a very close relationship and that I might find you together today.'

'Together?'

I nod.

'What's he mean, together?'

I go to explain but she guesses before I get a chance. 'Together in that sort of way? Why would I be with Seth? I've never done anything to make Jude suspect me of being with anyone, let alone his brother. Yes, I like Seth, and I've never pretended I don't. But, not in that sort of way, and Jude knows it.'

'Sounds like it's his brother he doesn't trust,' I reply. 'And, he has good reason now we know what's been going on. Maybe Jude's right to be so suspicious.'

Libby slowly shakes her head and says, 'Seth's a Dad...no, that just doesn't sound right. Are you sure the boy is his?'

I nod. 'You should have seen him Libby. It was a mini-Seth, the eyes and floppy hair. They were really close, all three of them.'

'They can't be that close if Seth has to keep them a secret,' Libby says. Umm, I hadn't thought about that. Why does he keep them a secret?

'You said he and the woman kissed?' she asks, and I nod. 'On the lips?'

I shake my head. 'No, but there was lots of it, on cheeks.'

'Cheeks? What, all the time?' Libby asks.

'No, when he met up with them.'

'So, as in a greeting,' she replies, 'like we do with the waiters and people we know.'

I think about it for a moment and have to say yes. 'But, it was different,' I say in my defence.

'If she was his secret woman, wouldn't he have kissed her on the lips?'

'I guess so, but maybe he was being discreet, in case someone was watching. Which, I was.' Libby looks at me doubtfully. 'Look, I can't explain this very well, but it was definitely something between them. And the boy loves him. He called out to him as soon as he saw him, shouting 'Dad, Dad.'

'He said Dad in English?' Libby asks. I shake my head. 'What, he called him Baba?'

I shake my head again. 'What's baba?' I ask.

Libby looks at me. 'Dad' she replies. 'You said he called him Baba.'

I shake my head. 'No, I said he called out to him. I presumed it was Turkish for Dad. Maybe it wasn't in Turkish then. Maybe they're from somewhere else.'

Libby sighs. 'Lou, it could have been anything he called out. You might have got yourself upset over nothing.'

I feel such an idiot and wrack my brains to remember what it was the boy shouted when he saw Seth. Maybe it was a pet name, or a TV character or children's superhero or something. I suddenly hear it so clearly in my head. 'It was Amca' I say. Yes, that was definitely it, I can hear the little boy shout it out just before he ran into Seth's arms. I do an impression, me running around on the spot as though I'm running to Seth, as a little boy going 'Amca, Amca.' I stop and look at Libby but she doesn't look impressed with my impression. In fact, I suddenly realise that she's staring into space, tears running down her cheeks.

'What's the matter?' I ask, moving towards her and putting my arm around her shoulders.

Her face has drained of colour and she stands up, a little wobbly and puts her hand on my shoulder to steady herself. 'That's not Dad' she says. And then she runs, literally sprints away, back in the direction of Jude's bar.

'Who's Amca?' I shout after her, 'and what's it got to do with Seth?' But, she's gone, already in the distance. So, despite the headache and my non-athletic body, which is screaming to be allowed to rest on a comfy bed, I chase her and just hope that I make it to the bar without the need of a paramedic.

CHAPTER THIRTY-TWO

We're almost at the bar before I catch up with her, and it reminds me of when we used to run cross-country at school, and the two of us would hide in the hedges just outside of the school gates and wait for the class to come back before joining on the end of the line of runners to jog back in. We were hopeless. A running friend of mine recently told me you should only run at a pace where you can comfortably say four words at a time. I don't think I'd be able to say one right now, I can barely breathe. Just as we get to the bar entrance, Seth strolls out and I stop dead in my tracks. I try to avoid eye contact and move around him but Libby yells at me, 'Speak to Seth, I need to see Jude alone', and she's gone inside, leaving me hanging, standing uncomfortably, moving from foot to foot. When I finally meet Seth's gaze I realise that he's carrying some bags.

'Off somewhere,' I manage to say, although the words are interrupted by a desperate panting for breath. Wow, I need to exercise more.

'Yep,' he replies and goes to move around me. There's a moment of awkwardness as we both go to move in the same direction, and bimble around. The expression on his face remains as hard as slate. I look towards the bar to see if I can see Libby, but I can't and I just hope that she's ok. What was that all about?

'Seth,' I finally say, 'can we talk?'

As he goes to answer, the waitress comes outside with drinks for one of the tables and glances back at the bar. 'Doesn't sound good in there,' she says and we realise she's gesturing to the office out the back.

Seth looks into the bar and then back to me. 'What's going on?' he asks.

'Long story,' I say. 'Have you time to hear it?'

'I've a flight to catch,' he says.

'A flight?' I should be happy he's flying away somewhere but I feel disappointed. Where's he going? I suddenly realise it's probably somewhere with his girlfriend and their son. Where else would he be going?

'I'll probably bump into you at the airport,' he says.

'Me?' He doesn't reply so I ask him, 'Why am I going to the airport? My flights not for another week.'

'Thought you'd be packing and going home with your fiancé,' he says and stares me out.

'Oh, that,' I say.

'Yes, that,' he replies and goes to walk past me again, but I stop him with my hands against his chest.

'Don't Seth, just give me a few minutes. There's things we need to talk about.'

He hesitates and, for a moment, I fear he's going to storm past me and that will be that. But, he eventually sighs, goes back in with his bags and then comes back out again empty handed. 'Let's walk,' he says, 'but it needs to be quick, I don't want to miss my flight.'

We walk the opposite way to the marina, towards Içmeler, and I'm sort of grateful he doesn't have much time or he might make me do that really long walk that I did with Libby, and my legs would give way and I'd need medical aid which I'm sure Seth would be reluctant to give.

'He's not my fiancé,' I say to break the silence.

Seth laughs sarcastically. 'Back to that one,' he says. 'Sorry, boyfriend. Whatever.'

'He's not a boyfriend, fiancé, even friend,' I say again. Seth's face clearly shows he doesn't believe me. 'Seth, please listen,' I say and I stop and grab at his sleeve. He looks at my hand, which makes me slowly remove it, and I pat at his arm as though to remove a crease. He's clearly not in the mood to be grabbed.

We start walking again. 'So, if there's nothing between you, what was he doing naked in your apartment whilst you were sleeping it off on the bed?' Seth asks.

'I wasn't even there,' I exclaim very loudly and a couple walking past stare at me. I have really got to stop this shouting in public. I don't think I'd ever shouted until I came here. It must be something in the apple tea.

Seth stops walking and turns to look straight at me. I can see by his eyes that all trust is lost between us, and I suddenly feel annoyed that he has the nerve to doubt me, and question things I say. He's the one with the secrets.

'Look,' I say. 'Grant turned up today, out of the blue, on our doorstep and begged me to go home with him, and to marry him and all sorts of mad stuff. And I said no, that I don't love him and that there'll never be us. Ever.'

'And he celebrated your announcement by stripping off and giving you a good seeing to?' he replies.

'No!' I shout, not caring who is listening. 'There was no being seen to at all. I left the apartment to find Libby and he stayed there, and I said he could use the shower quick and get out. That's all. I promise you.'

Seth starts walking again and shakes his head.

'How dare you judge *me*,' I suddenly say angrily. 'You, who hasn't told me the truth once since I've been here. I saw you today, at Turunç, remember?'

'What?' he says, stopping again and spinning round. 'I haven't lied. I just kept things quiet, for a reason. I haven't betrayed you in any way.'

'And I haven't betrayed you either'

'Apart from spying on me?' He glares at me so hard, I blush.

'I wasn't spying,' I reply, defending myself. 'Yes, I admit I was watching you, but it's different to spying. And, it was a good job I did too, or I wouldn't have found out about your secret woman, and child. *Your* child.'

He raises his eyebrows. '*My* child?' I nod and look down at my feet. I'm too scared to even look at him as I suspect he won't care less that I know and will probably be smirking. 'Lou, I offered to tell you everything the other night,' he replies, 'but you said I didn't need to. And, so I didn't. I really respected you for not pushing it as you're right, it is a secret, but it's not mine to tell. It would destroy her if she found out like that.'

'Who, your secret woman?' I ask, not really getting what he means.

'No, of course not. I mean Libby.'

Ok, I'm now really confused. What's this to do with Libby? I should have guessed that it would be some woman he's worried about other than me, that's how it's been from the start.

'What's your child got to do with Libby?' I ask.

'He's not my child,' he almost screeches at me.

'But I heard him, he called out to you. He called you Amca.'

Seth throws his head back and then shouts at me, 'Amca's not Dad, it's Uncle.'

'Uncle?' I ask and then stop walking and take in what he's just said. Uncle, that means...

'Oh no,' Seth says. He walks to me and pushes my chin up so I'm looking directly at him. 'You didn't tell Libby, did you?'

I nod slowly. We both look back towards the bar and Seth closes his eyes, holds his head and walks around groaning.

'This is not how she should find out,' he says. 'Lou, this wasn't your secret to tell, it wasn't anything to do with you. Don't tell me, you were pouring all your problems out because, that's what you do, just blurt everything out without a care for anyone else. You're unbelievable.'

This really stings and I feel like he may as well have slapped me round the face or beaten me with a stick. 'That's unfair, I had no idea,' I begin to say. But, he's right. Today I've told her something that will absolutely break her heart, without even stopping to think.

'I thought he was your child,' I say, 'I didn't stop and think he could be Jude's.'

'No, that's the problem Lou, you never do stop and think,' he says. 'You do your detective thing, looking for clues that aren't there, and forming suspicions and imaginary problems, and then you reach a conclusion that has no impact on *your* life but devastates someone else's. Well done, Lou.'

'You have just as much to feel guilty about,' I say.

'Please tell me what I've done to feel guilty about,' he asks and looks so smarmy I could honestly slap his face.

'He might not be your child, but you've got her, and you kept that relationship a secret.'

He shakes his head. 'What makes you think I've a

343

relationship with her?' he asks.

'The kissing, and smiling, and... and...' he's looking at me expectantly, 'the giving of money, ha!' Yes, the money, I'd almost forgotten that bit.

He's just stood there staring at me now. That's shut him up, he's going to have to try and talk his way out of that one.

'Any ideas what the money was for, Officer Granger?'

I narrow my eyes and ignore the jibe. 'Well, I don't know, but there's clearly something going on between you. '

'I'm not involved with her, neither have I ever been,' he says. 'I'm helping her out, because Jude doesn't even acknowledge either her, or the fact he has a son. So, I give them money whenever I can, to try and support them. So do my parents.' Seth watches me for a moment, waiting for a response. 'Cat got your tongue?' he asks, and I actually start to feel really bad about it.

'You and your parents help them?' I ask.

Seth nods. 'Yes, and Jude doesn't like it.'

I wince. This is awful. I didn't even stop and think there could be an explanation like this.

'How can Jude not acknowledge him?' I ask, 'he's gorgeous.'

Seth smiles, his genuine one rather than the smirk, accompanied by the crinkly eyes. It's obvious he's fond of the child, his nephew.

'Anything else you want to accuse me of?' he suddenly asks, and the smile has gone again, 'apart from my womanising and fathering a child?'

'Well, you can't blame me for thinking it. He has your eyes, and that really silly, floppy hair.'

He tilts his head on one side and I have a word with myself about saying things out loud without applying a filter. Silly, floppy hair, oops.

Seth turns and starts to walk slowly back the way he came. 'Why didn't Jude stay with her?' I ask, walking quickly to keep alongside him 'when he found out about their son.'

'Because it's Jude,' Seth replies. 'They were together a year. She fell in love with him, then fell pregnant, and he was off. It was just a bit of fun for him.'

'Do you think that's what Libby is?' I ask, 'just fun?'

'I don't know for sure, but it's possible.' I feel gutted for her, she's been so keen on him. 'Anyway,' he says, 'we haven't discussed the other crazy allegations yet. You seem to have left the subject of the jeep keys and my sabotaging of the business. Have you made peace with that now?'

'Look,' I say, 'in my defence, it wasn't just the keys. It was the hookers and...'

'And?' he interrupts.

'...Ooh, the jacket, that day we tried to find the keys to go to that first client, and we found them in your jacket pocket. They didn't just jump in there, did they?'

Seth shakes his head. 'I hadn't worn that jacket for ages. I'd lent it to Jude that day you arrived. Then, he left it in my car for me later that evening and I was going to wear it. But, I gave it you to wear. Do you remember?'

'Yes,' I admit, 'and that was a very gentlemanly thing to do. But, I didn't put those keys in there. I didn't even know about them.'

'I know you didn't,' he replies.

'Then why did you put them in?' I ask, getting a little angry again.

'I didn't,' he replies.

I'm confused. If I didn't put them in, and he didn't put them in, who put them in there. Seth is watching me and I see him smile as he realises I've worked it out.

'Jude?' I ask. 'He hid the keys in there?'

'I guess so,' he replies.

'And Libby and me being hookers? Was that him too? Was it him that told the guys that's what we would do for them?'

He nods and looks embarrassed and I suddenly feel for him. I'd be heartbroken if my brother Robert behaved like that.

Why?' I ask. Seth doesn't reply but just shakes his head again and looks away. None of this makes sense. Why would Jude treat Libby like this? Does he really not care about her at all?

'What really gets me though,' says Seth, 'is that you just presumed it was me.' I feel quite guilty and look down at my feet. 'I mean, I never gave you any reason to. But you just presumed it. I guess Grant really messed you up.'

I can't even argue about this, as it's true.

'Oooh,' I suddenly announce. 'I've got something that is definitely you, all you!' Seth stops and folds his arms, waiting for the impending announcement. 'Libby thought the appointment today at Turunç was all based on recommendation, but Ali told us it was you that tipped him off about her and said to give her a chance. Why?'

He winces. 'Now, that's regretful he told her.'

I gasp. 'You're not even denying it?'

'Ali did have Libby recommended to him, but someone else was about to make a move and try to get the business. So, I made a call, and asked him to speak with her first. She deserved the contract more than anyone else. .'

'Who's the other person?' I ask. A thought hits me out of the blue. 'Is it the one who pinched our first booking?' But Seth says nothing. 'Seth,' I almost shout at him, 'who else is involved here.'

'Jude,' he replies. 'He's been trying to set up a jeep

business for ages, ever since Libby first mentioned it, and he was trying to get in there first.'

I can't believe that guy. Why would he try to out-do his own girlfriend? I suddenly can see everything so clearly. 'That's why he hid the keys, and set us up as hookers. He was trying to sabotage everything so he could have the business.'

Seth doesn't say anything but he doesn't need to. After a moment of silence I say, 'That's why he wanted her to go into business with someone, probably him or someone acting on his behalf, and he'd take all the credit and she'd have been no better off than when she was a rep.' This is terrible, all the time it was the man Libby trusted the most that was behind everything that was going wrong. And it was his brother Seth that was watching her back, and protecting her.

'Oh Seth,' I say, 'I owe you such an apology. Everything has been about you protecting Libby. That's why you kept the woman a secret because you didn't want her to find out about Jude and be hurt.' Rather than betray her, he's let me think it was him behind it all.

We're now back at the bar and Seth walks in and straight back out again, with his bags.

'Where are you flying to?' I ask solemnly.

'To visit my folks, I need to update them about Ayse and her son. Plus, I really need a break from here, from everything.'

I nod, it's all I can do. I'm not surprised he wants to go.

'Maybe we can talk when you're back', I say, 'that's if you ever want to talk to me again.'

I smile at Seth and wait for his smile back, but there isn't one.

'You are coming back, right?' I ask.

He hesitates and then nods, and I feel relieved. 'But not

until after you've gone,' he says. My heart sinks. 'You've only a week left and I need to get a lot done, so I won't be back in time to see you before you leave.'

I feel desperately sad and want to plead with him to come back sooner, but there's no point. I've done enough damage as it is.

'So this is goodbye?' I finally manage to say.

Seth nods. This is it, our goodbye. It's not what I had hoped it would be. I thought we could make things right again and maybe pick up from where we left off. It's not supposed to be like this.

But, it is. And, as Seth leans forward, and kisses me on the cheek, I know he's made his mind up and we're never going to be together. We lock eyes for a moment and then he turns and walks away, and I stand watching him, willing him to turn round, but knowing that he won't.

I don't know how long I stand there, but I suddenly come back to Earth and see that Libby is standing in front of me. Her face is tear stained and she looks overwhelmed by everything. I know that what's happened between Seth and me is nothing compared to what she's going through right now. I feel selfish for letting myself be so heartbroken that Seth's gone. After all, we didn't really have anything, did we? We'd fallen out more times than we'd been good together and, yes, I'd had a great night away with him, and I guess I'd fallen for him. It sounds ridiculous when I say it in my head, the fact I've fallen for a guy I've only just met. But, the truth is, I think I fell for him when I first saw him at the airport three weeks ago, even though at the time I refused to accept it. And now I've messed it all up and it's just never going to be. But, Libby? None of this is her fault, none of it. She's done nothing wrong yet her life has just taken a really big battering.

So, I do the only thing I can do. I go to her, wrap my arms around her and hug her. And, we stand there a while, without saying a word, and then we start walking back to the apartment to see what we can do about this whole sorry mess even though my head is screaming at me to go into the bar and really lay into Jude. But that can wait. Libby is now my priority and I'm going to help patch her up. Because, that's what best friends do.

CHAPTER THIRTY-THREE

It's freezing. Not just chilly, but bloody freezing. I've gone from roasting hot to shivering cold in just a few hours, and this just adds to my pure misery at returning home. Home. I could cry at hearing the word and quickly remind myself of Libby's 'positive thinking' mantras that she tried to drum into me when she waved me off at Dalaman. 'I'm not going home, I'm visiting the UK just to sort things before coming *home* to Marmaris.' I try saying it a few times but it doesn't help and I just want to stand here at the baggage reclaim and cry. If I cry enough, they might put me on the next available plane to Dalaman so they don't have to deal with me. Somehow, I don't think any one will care less here.

I guess that it may actually be warmer outside. After all, this is just the air con in here and air con is always chilly. But, the view from the plane window when we landed didn't look too hopeful. Chilly with drizzly rain. Wonderful.

I watch the conveyor belt, willing it to start moving so I can get out of here, but nothing happens. I'm just one of many people standing, wishing we were back in Turkey, rather than waiting for our dirty washing to appear in our battered bags and then trudge back to normality. For many people here, in a couple of days they'll feel they've never been away. They'll be back at work, long hours, no lunch break and a crap day. Routine and ordinariness.

For me, I'll never forget I've been away and I've got to try and somehow fit back into some form of a routine whilst I work everything out so that I can get back to Marmaris as soon as I can. First thing I need to do is try to get my belongings from the apartment. Grant hasn't answered any of my texts and I'm hoping he hasn't thrown my stuff out or I'll have to go and buy some emergency jumpers. I look around me and can't understand why no one else seems to notice how cold it is. There are groups of people, all in their T-shirts and shorts, flip-flops and sandals, and not a shiver or a shake amongst any of them. Maybe they're just trying to make their holiday last just a little bit longer.

The final week or so of my time with Libby went in a flash, there was so much to sort and do. Libby's coped really well considering the bombshell dropped on her. Jude is well and truly in her past, just someone she occasionally has to acknowledge if she sees him when she's working. But, other than that, she doesn't give him a second of her time. He's tried to win her back, tried to defend his actions, but she's having none of it.

Apparently, as far as the business sabotage goes, he did it *all for her.* He knew she wouldn't voluntarily go into business with him, and so he was trying to show her how 'cut-throat' it all is, and prove how vulnerable she would be. That's laughable, vulnerable is not a word I'd use to describe Libby. Ever.

She wasn't actually that bothered by the business interference, she knows she'll make it work with or without anyone's help. But, it was the secret child and ex-girlfriend that she just couldn't accept. Jude's attitude towards the two

351

of them is unbelievable. He refuses to accept they even exist and continues to mock Seth and the support he gives them. According to Jude, she was a one-night stand and purposefully got herself pregnant, falling madly in love with him when he hadn't reciprocated in any way other than sleeping with her. Unbelievably, he already has a new girlfriend, a waitress in the bar who joined only a couple of weeks back. She's from Wales and has fallen for his charms. Poor girl.

The conveyor belt suddenly bursts into life, and a small cheer erupts from a group of young men who are obviously coming back from a lad's holiday. I wonder if they were in Marmaris, if I passed them walking to and from the bar, or saw them on the beach. Did they find it as magical as me, or is their memory tainted by the large amount of fishbowls consumed?

I wonder how Grant's trip home went, whether he had one last bit of hope I'd turn up at the airport, begging for forgiveness, or if he'd accepted it was definitely over. At the time, neither Libby or me seriously questioned how Grant found me that day, it sort of got lost in all the more important stuff. But, we found out later that it was Jude that contacted him and gave him the address. He wanted me out of the way, less of an influence on Libby, so it would make things easier for him.

Everyone now stands anxiously, waiting for the suitcases to start coming through. I have an urge to get onto the conveyor belt and go for a ride around, and I wonder how far I'd get before being escorted out by security. I'd have to ring my mother and ask her to come and vouch for my sanity and release from custody. Actually, would a cell here in the airport be a better option than the craft room?

I feel awful even thinking it, staying with mum is going to

be fine and I've really missed her whilst I've been away and will stay at her house until everything is sorted which could take a month or more. I doubt she said all the things to Grant that he claims, it was probably just one more lie he was making up to try and make me get back with him. She's really happy about me staying, as Dad is on one of his walkabouts right now, so I'll be good company for her. According to mum, when I spoke last night, Grant has delivered some of my stuff to her house but it's just a couple of boxes, and she doesn't think it will be clothes. I pray for a heat wave as the only clothes I'll have are the holiday ones in the suitcase I'm waiting for right now. Mother said she'd been and picked up a couple of bits from the market, which I know means comfy slacks and long, baggy tops which will shrink in the first wash. But, it will be better than nothing.

I wonder how many of these passengers will be off to work tomorrow and if there are any like me, who will be going into the office to tell their boss they're leaving for a new life in a foreign country. Mr Simpson is going to fall off his chair when I announce the news, and he'll ask if I've thought it all through, and if I'm allowed to travel back to Turkey, or if there's a chance I'll be imprisoned for crimes against some visa restriction or other. And that's when I'll explain that I have an appointment in a couple of weeks time with the Embassy to get everything sorted and to make sure it's all above board and that I won't need any legal representative sent over to get me out of jail. Just having to work the few weeks back in the office will be hard, but at least I know it won't be for long. I think of how I'll need to listen to my colleagues moaning about what they did or didn't do at the weekend, how I'll fetch Mr Simpson biscuits from the hidden tin behind the reception desk so that no one ever tells his wife, and I'll just have to try and stay positive by thinking of my return to Dalaman.

It was hard leaving the airport this morning, and I clung onto Libby's arms in protest, begging her to keep me there and not let me go. But, I had to leave as I owe it to Mr Simpson to hand in my notice properly, and I couldn't swap the dates on my flight ticket. Libby and I hugged, she said 'see you soon' and walked away from me without looking back. That was our agreement, that neither of us would make a fuss, and that we'd just keep our eyes ahead and not look round. Despite knowing I'll see her really soon, I was still heartbroken at leaving, particularly as Libby has so much to sort with the business and could have done with an extra pair of hands. All the hard work will have been done by the time I get back, and she'll be shattered.

There's a whoop as suitcases start to appear and I hope that mine is quick to come out as I just want to get moving and head towards mum's and start the four weeks of mundaneness as quick as I can.

I watch a couple, standing just to my side and feel such sadness watching them together, as it makes me think of Seth, and what we had for that short while. I wonder if he's going through the arrivals at Dalaman right now, just as I'm doing the same in the UK, knowing it's safe for him to return as I'm gone and safely out of the way. I'd hoped for some contact from him, some form of communication where we could have at least said hello and cleared the air, and become friends. But, there's been nothing. Libby hasn't said if she has spoken with him or not, but I suspect she has. She was desperate to thank him for protecting her in the way he did, and knew he was probably thinking that he'd offended her, or she'd feel angry he wasn't honest with her and covered things up, but she completely gets Seth and has championed him from the start. It's been me that's been the doubter and

I should have trusted him too.

I've thought so often of that night together, the days too, in Kuşadasi and, when I close my eyes and really think hard, I can feel his lips on my neck, his hands on my waist and his floppy hair brushing against my face. I'm hoping that, when I get back over there, he'll be prepared to speak to me and we can be friends again. I'd love to have more than that, but I can't imagine him ever forgiving me, not after the way I've treated him. I can't blame him. After all, I accused him of stealing jeep keys, setting Libby and I up as hookers, trying to sabotage her business and then, of course, having a secret girlfriend and son. I haven't exactly shown him much trust or respect.

I suddenly see my case and get ready to grab it as it comes past and it seems to take an age to reach where I'm standing. I pull it towards me, nearly breaking my back as I do so as I've gone a bit mad with present buying during the last few days. There are gifts for mum and dad, the girls at work, Mr Simpson and his wife and a couple of bits of designer-wear for me. Plus some new handbags. Oh, and new shoes. In fact, most of the presents are for me.

I'm soon through customs, doing that expression that everyone does as they pass through 'nothing to declare.' You know, where you're totally innocent yet try not to look suspicious and then look incredibly suspicious even though you've got nothing to look suspicious about. But, there's no one there and we all file through unchallenged. I wonder how many of my fellow passengers are breathing sighs of relief due to things concealed in their cases or on their person. I've seen it happen, on those documentaries about airports, and some of these people look very dodgy.

I come through arrivals and see a wave of people waiting for travellers they're come to collect, some holding up pieces of paper with names of strangers, some waiting for loved ones, waving madly and bobbing up and down with joy. I wish in a way I'd told my mother what flight I was getting or to which airport, as I know she'd have been here, bobbing up and down with them. It would have been nice to have someone here, someone pleased to see me come home. Someone I love.

I walk with the others at a slow pace, slowed down by a family with at least six children, all of whom are creating a great deal of stress and major exhaustion for their parents by running and stopping in front of the trolley, causing several near-collapses of a suitcase mountain. As there's no hope of moving any quicker, I decide to look at the names on the papers being held up by those waiting along the row, as strange names amuse me and may bring me out of my doom and gloom mood. Smith, Reynolds, Patel... even the names are so normal today. Granger... Granger? That's me. I look a little closer and see it says 'Lou Granger' and for that moment wonder if someone else has the same name as me, and what a coincidence that would be, that we'd arrive at the same time. Then, it dawns on me it could actually be me that someone is waiting for. I look up at the person holding it and catch my breath as I see the floppy hair and the blue eyes and the most gorgeous smile I've seen for, well, at least a week or so.

'Seth!' I call out and lean over the barrier, flinging my arms around him and kissing him on the cheek.

'I'm here to collect a Lou Granger,' he says, very officiously. 'And I'm hoping that she's going to be a bit happier than the one I last picked up at an airport.'

I laugh. 'I am happier, I'm the happiest I've been for ages.'

I run round with my case to come out the other side

where he's now there to hug me properly.

'Why?' I ask. 'Why have you come to collect me. And how did you know I'd... Libby!' I yell, answering my own question. So, she has been in touch with him. She's told him about my flight and arrival time.

'I'm here to fly off somewhere,' he says, and my heart drops.

'Oh, of course, you're on the way back.'

'No,' he says and holds out a ticket to me.

'New York?' I'm confused and tilt my head, frowning at him.

'Don't tell me you've other plans for the next two weeks,' he says, 'as I thought you might fancy a USA road trip. The flight goes in three hours.'

What about Mr Simpson, and my mother and my belongings? Can I do this? I've the offer of a road trip, what I've always wanted.

'I'll only come if it's really identical to my dream,' I say. 'Where it's with the love of my life, my soul mate, someone that I want to be with forever and that wants to be with me.'

'Then I guess we need to go to check in as soon as we can,' Seth says. Then, he puts his arms round me, grabs my case and we're off on a new adventure.

Acknowledgements

To Wendy, for her feedback, patience and wonderful book cover. To my readers of the first three chapters, and for their feedback & encouragement to continue: Roger, Wendy, Nikki, Suzan, Jackie and Jacky (Mum). To Zeynep, for all her advice and help about 'all things Turkey'! To Suzan and Carole, two authors who have given me continued support, advice and encouragement along the way. To Ruth, my 'radio script' co-writer, who has taught me to be organised and to have a 'structure', despite my continuous rebellious moans and groans. And to Roger and Ayesha for being so understanding and supportive throughout this process.

Message from the Author

Thank you for choosing to read 'Friendship, Love and Apple Tea', my first novel. I really appreciate your support and I hope you enjoy it. I'd love to know what you think, so please do get in touch. You'll find me at:

www.pennycanvin.com

pennycanvin.wordpress.com

Twitter: pennycanvin

Lightning Source UK Ltd.
Milton Keynes UK
UKOW02f0304201014

240308UK00001B/3/P